Dee He...

Ted Dekker & Bill Bright

Craig Parshall

Mel Odom

Travis Thrasher

Penelope Stokes

Penny Culliford

Blackston

Robin Jones Gunn

Chris Walley

Sheila Jacobs

Bill Myers

Steve Dixon

Tricia Goyer

Michael Phillips

Linda Chaikin

Lori Wick

C. S. Lewis

Adrian Plass

Randy Alcorn

Francine Rivers

Angela Hunt

Terri Blackstock

sam books

British Library Cataloguing in Publication Data
A catalogue record for this book is available from the British Library
ISBN 1 9008 3640 8

Cover Design by Peter Barnsley, Carlisle
Typeset by PCS Typesetting, Shepton Mallet. 01749 344479
Printed by Carwin Ltd

Contents

Foreword

The first book I wrote as a born-again Christian was Redeeming Love, based on Hosea which had a profound impact on my life. I poured my heart into the story, and made it my statement of faith to readers who had followed my career in the general market. I hoped an allegory about Jesus would serve to break down the walls of others as Hosea had broken down mine. From the many letters I have received from prison inmates, battered wives and survivors of unbelievable abuse, I know the Lord is using Redeeming Love to reach others with His incredible, healing and boundless love.

Every book I have written since becoming a Christian has started with a question for which I had no answer, or an issue with which I was struggling. My writing has become a way to worship Jesus, a means of going before the Lord to seek His perspective. He is all-wisdom, all-truth, all-love, a patient Teacher through the Holy Spirit.

My experience as a Christian writer is not unique. Writers have become bolder over the last ten years, speaking from pain and confusion, and trusting in the Lord as they write. I know many others who use writing as a way of worshipping Jesus and sharing their experience and hope through story. In today's Christian market, there is something for everyone's interest, be it historical, contemporary, mystery, thriller, comedy and tragedy.

Jesus used stories to teach the masses. Most listened and left un-enlightened, but for those who hungered and thirsted and stayed to ask for more, Jesus revealed Himself. Jesus used stories to draw His disciples closer, to speak Truth in a way they could understand, to make them ponder. He whetted their appetite through story so that they would seek Him for deeper spiritual meaning, and become His people, living for and through Him. That is what the Christian writers of today are accomplishing.

There is power in a story. General lists are full of brilliantly written books that offer no answers to the meaning of life, no hope. Christian fiction can bring the Gospel to people who have no interest in reading the Bible, or who are so hostile toward God that the mere mention of the Bible sends them into tirade or flight. A novel can be a non-threatening gift to a soul hungering and thirsting for Truth, a person struggling with all manner of life's great trials, a Christian who needs encouragement. A story can open a rebellious heart to repentance and make the reader yearn for a relationship with Jesus Christ. A novel can illustrate how scripture is applicable to our lives today, that God's Word holds the answers to our struggles, and reveals the Lord Himself.

We encourage you to consider the tremendous value fiction can have as a witnessing tool in a world desperate for the Good News of Jesus Christ our Lord.

May you be blessed by this small sampling of what is now available to readers.

                                                            Francine Rivers

The Negotiator

Dee Henderson

FBI agent Dave Richman is about to meet Kate O'Malley, a hostage negotiator in Chicago. Kate is a legend on the force, willing to walk into any situation, but unlike Dave she's not a believer. It's clear to Dave why Kate's so tough — her family were abandoned as children and they struggled to stay together. But an airline bombing, tragic news and the appearance of a brother Kate didn't know she had will soon change her life.

The Negotiator is a suspense-packed mystery novel for fans of crime fiction.

ISBN 1 5767 3819 1
PB

Price: £9.99
£6.99 Special Offer
Special offer ends 31/08/03

Chapter One

Kate O'Malley had been in the dungeon since dawn.

The members of the emergency response group comprising the SWAT and hostage-rescue teams had been relegated to the basement of the county building during the last department reorganization. The metal desks were crammed together; the concrete walls needed repainting; the old case files made the room smell musty; and the hot and cold water pipes coming from the boiler room rumbled overhead.

The team was proud of its little hovel even if the plants did die within days. The location allowed for relaxed rules. The only evidence of bureaucracy was a time clock by the steel door so those not on salary could get paid for all their overtime.

Despite the dirt on her tennis shoes, Kate had her feet propped up on the corner of her desk, her fingers steepled, her eyes half closed, as she listened to the sound of her own voice over the headphones, careful not to let the turmoil of her thoughts reflect in her expression. She was reviewing the last of four negotiation tapes. Case 2214 from last week haunted her. A domestic violence call with shots fired. It had taken six hours to negotiate a peaceful conclusion. Six agonizing hours for the mother and two children held in the house. Had there been any way to end it earlier?

As Kate listened to the husband's drunken threats and her own calm replies, she automatically slowed her breathing to suppress her rising emotions. She hated domestic violence cases. They revived unwanted memories… memories Kate had buried away from the light of day.

The cassette tape reversed sides. She sipped her hot coffee and grimaced. Graham must have made this pot. She didn't mind strong coffee, but this was Navy coffee. Kate tugged open her middle desk drawer and pushed aside chocolate bars and two heavy silver medals for bravery to find sugar packets.

She found it odd to be considered something of a legend on the force at the age of thirty-six, but she understood it. She was a negotiator known for one thing – being willing to walk into any situation. Domestic violence, botched robberies, kidnappings, even airline hijackings – she had worked them all.

Kate let people see what she wanted them to see. She could sit in the middle of a crisis for hours or days if that's what it took to negotiate a peace. She could do it with a relaxed demeanor. Detached. Most often, apparently bored.

It worked. Her apparent boredom in a crisis kept people alive. She dealt with the emotions later, after the situation was over – and far away from work. She played a lot of basketball, using the game to cultivate her focus, let go of the tension.

This was her fourth review of the tapes. Her case notes appeared complete. Kate didn't hear anything she could have done differently. She stopped the tape playback, relieved to have the review done. She pushed back the headphones and ran her hand through her ruffled hair.

"O'Malley."

She turned to see Graham holding up his phone.

"Line three. Your brother." "Which one?"

"The paramedic."

She punched the blinking light. "Hi, Stephen."

"Let me guess; you're screening your calls."

She was, but it was an amusing first observation. "I'm ducking the media for a few days. Are you off duty?"

"Just wrapping up. Had breakfast yet?"

Kate picked up the tension in his voice. "I could go for some good coffee and a stack of pancakes."

"I'll meet you across the street at Quinn's."

"Deal."

Kate glanced at her pager, confirming she was on group call. She slid her cellular phone into her shirt pocket as she stood. "I'm heading to breakfast. Anyone want a Danish brought back?" Quinn's was a popular stopping point for all of them.

Requests came in from all over the room. Her tally ended with three raspberry, four cherry, and two apple Danishes. "Page me if you need me."

The stairs out of the dungeon were concrete and hand railed so they could be traversed with speed. Security doors were located at both ends. The stairway opened into the secure access portion of the parking garage. The team's specially equipped communications vans gleamed. They'd just been polished yesterday.

Kate slid on her sunglasses. June had begun as a month of glaring sun and little rain. It parched even the downtown Chicago concrete, coating the ground with crumbling dust. Traffic was heavy in this tight narrow corridor. She crossed against the traffic light.

Quinn's was a mix of new interior and old building, the restaurant able to comfortably seat seventy. Kate waved to the owner, took two menus, and headed to her usual table at the back of the restaurant, choosing the chair that put her back to the wall. It was always an amusing dance when there were two or more cops coming to Quinn's. No cop liked to sit with his back to an open room.

She accepted a cup of coffee, skimming the menu though she knew it by heart. Blueberry pancakes. She was a lady of habit. That decision made, she relaxed back in her seat to enjoy the coffee and tune into the conversations going on around her. The ladies by the window were talking about a baby shower. The businessmen to her left were discussing a fishing trip. Two teenagers were debating where to begin their shopping excursion.

Kate stirred two sugar packets into her coffee. Normal life. After ten years as a negotiator, there wasn't much normalcy left in her own life. The mundane details that most people cared about had ceased to cause the slightest blip on her radar screen. Normal people cared about clothes, vacations, holidays. Kate cared about staying alive. If it weren't such a stark dichotomy, it would be amusing.

Stephen arrived as she was nursing her second cup of coffee. Kate smiled when she saw the interest he attracted as he came to join her. She couldn't blame the ladies. His sports jacket and blue jeans didn't hide his muscles. He could walk off the cover of nearly any men's fashion magazine. Not bad for someone who spent his days dealing with car accidents, fire victims, gang shootings, and drug overdoses.

He wouldn't stay in this city forever – he talked occasionally about moving northwest to some small town with a lake, good fishing, and a job where he would finally get to treat more heart attacks than gunshot victims – but for now he stayed. Kate knew it was primarily because of her. Stephen had designated himself her watchdog. He had never asked; he'd just taken the role. She loved him for it, even if she did tease him on occasion about it.

He pulled out the chair across from her. "Thanks for making time, Kate."

"Mention food and you've got my attention." She pushed over the second cup of coffee the waitress had filled, not commenting on the strain in his eyes despite his smile. That look hadn't been there yesterday when he'd joined her for a one-on-one basketball game. She hoped it was only the after effects of a hard shift. He would tell her if he needed to. Within the O'Malley family, secrets were rare.

At the orphanage – Trevor House – where family was nonexistent, the seven of them had chosen to become their own family, had chosen the last name O'Malley. Stephen was one of the three special ones in the family: a true orphan, not one of the abandoned or abused.

They might not share a blood connection, but that didn't matter; what they did share was far stronger. They were loyal, faithful, and committed to each other. Some twenty-two years after their decision, the group was as unified and strong as ever.

They had, in a sense, adopted each other.

"Did you see the news?" Stephen asked once the waitress had taken their orders.

Kate shook her head. She had left early for the gym and then gone straight to the office.

"There was a five-car pileup on the tollway. A three-year-old was in the front seat of a sedan. He died en route to County General Hospital."

Kids. The toughest victims for any O'Malley to deal with. "I'm sorry, Stephen." He decompressed like she did. Slowly. After he left work.

"So am I." He set aside his coffee cup. "But that's not why I called you. Jennifer's coming to town."

Jennifer O'Malley was the youngest in the family, everyone's favourite. She was a paediatrician in Dallas. "Oh?"

"I got a call from her this morning. She's got a Sunday flight into O'Hare."

Kate frowned. It wasn't easy for any doctor to leave her practice on such short notice. "Did she say what it was about?"

"No. Just asked which day I was off. She was trying to set up a family gathering. There's probably a message on your answering machine."

Kate didn't wait to find out. She picked up her cellular phone and called her home number, listening to the ring; then the answering machine kicked on. She punched a button to override, added her code, and listened as the messages began to play.

Their breakfasts arrived.

Jennifer had left a message. It didn't say much. Dinner Sunday evening at Lisa's. Kate closed her phone. "I don't like this."

"It gets worse. Marcus is flying back from Washington for the gathering."

Kate let that information sink in as she started on her hot

blueberry pancakes. Their oldest brother, a U.S. Marshal, was interrupting his schedule to fly back to Chicago. "Jennifer is one step away from saying it's a family emergency." Let any member of the family say those words and the others dropped everything and came.

Stephen reached for his orange juice. "That's how I would read it."

"Any ideas?"

"None. I talked to Jennifer last Friday. She didn't say anything."

"Did she sound tense?"

"Tired maybe; unusual for her, but given the schedule she keeps, not unexpected."

Kate's pager went off. She glanced at the return number and grimaced. One of these days she was actually going to get to finish a meal. She set down her linen napkin as she got to her feet. "Work is calling. Can you join me for dinner? I'm off at six. I was planning to grill steaks."

"Glad to. Stay safe, Kate."

She grinned. "Always, Stephen. Put breakfast on my tab."

"I've got it covered."

She didn't have time to protest. It was an old debate. She smiled and let him win this round. "See you at six."

FBI special agent Dave Richman dealt with crises every day of his life. However, being a customer when a bank hold up went down was not one he would recommend.

His heart pounding, he rested his back against the reception desk and prayed the gunman stayed on the other side of the room.

The man had come in through the front door, shot four holes in the ceiling with a handgun, and ordered some of the customers and staff to leave, specific others to stay.

Dave had nearly shot him in the first few seconds of the assault, but the dynamite around the man's chest had halted that idea. The FBI playbook was simple: When facing dynamite, a loaded gun, and a lot of frightened people – don't get anyone killed.

In the initial commotion, Dave had managed to drop to the floor and get out of sight. He had about six feet of customer counter space that ended in an L that made up the reception desk he was hiding behind. So far, it was sufficient. The gunman had the hostages clustered together on the other side of the open room. He hadn't bothered to search the offices or the rest of the room. That most likely meant he was proceeding on emotion – and that, Dave knew, made him more dangerous than ever.

Dave would give anything to have his FBI team on-site. When the local cops surrounding the building ran the license plates for the cars in the parking lot, the trace on his own blue sedan would raise a flag at the FBI office. His team would be deployed because he was present. He had trusted his life to their actions in the past; it looked like he would be doing so again. The sound of sirens and the commotion outside had died down; by now he was sure they had the perimeter formed.

He leaned his head back. This was not exactly how he had planned to spend his birthday. His sister, Sara, was expecting him for lunch. When he didn't show up, she was going to start to worry.

There would be no simple solution to this crisis.

He was grateful God was sovereign. From the tirade going on behind him, it was obvious this man had not come to rob the bank.

They had a bank robber that had not bothered to get any money. Kate was already assuming the worst.

The security camera video feeds had just been tapped and routed to the communications van. Four different camera angles. Two were static pictures of empty areas, the front glass doors, and the teller area for the drive up. One was focused high, covering the front windows, but it did show the hostages: five men and four women seated against the wall.

The fourth camera held Kate's attention. The man paced the centre of the room. He was big and burly, his stride impatient.

The dynamite trigger held in his right hand worried her. It looked like a compression switch. Let go, and the bomb went off. There was no audio, but he was clearly in a tirade about something. His focus seemed to be on one of the nine hostages in particular, the third man from the end.

This man had come with a purpose. Since it apparently wasn't to rob the bank, that left more ugly possibilities.

He wasn't answering the phone.

Kate looked over at her boss, Jim Walker. She had worked for him for eight years. He trusted her judgment; she trusted him to keep her alive if things went south. "Jim, we've got to calm this situation down quickly. If he won't answer the phone, then we'll have to talk the old-fashioned way."

He studied the monitors. "Agreed." Kate looked at the building blueprints. The entrance was a double set of glass doors with about six feet in between them. They were designed to be energy efficient in both winter and summer. Kate wished the architects had thought about security first. She had already marked those double doors and those six feet of open space as her worst headache. A no-man's-land. Six feet without cover.

"Graham, if I stay here —" she pointed — "just inside the double glass doors, can you keep me in line of sight?" He was one of the few people she would trust to take a shot over her shoulder if it were required.

He studied the blueprint. "Yes."

"Have Olsen and Franklin set up to cover here and here." She marked two sweeps of the interior. It would be enough. If they had to take the gunman down, there would be limited ways to do it without blowing up a city block in the process.

Kate turned up the sleeves of her flannel shirt. Her working wardrobe at a scene was casual. She did not wear a bullet proof vest; she didn't even carry a gun. The last thing she wanted was to look or sound like a cop. Her gender, size, and clothing were designed to keep her from being perceived as one more threat. In reality, she was the worst threat the gunman had. The snipers were under her control. To save lives, she would take one if necessary.

Kate glanced again at the security monitors. There was a lot of the bank floor plan not covered by the cameras. There might be another gunman, more hostages – both were slim but potential realities. The risks were inevitable.

"Ian, try the phones one more time."

Kate watched the gunman's reaction. He turned to glare at the ringing phone, paced toward it, but didn't answer. Okay. It wouldn't get him to answer, but it did capture his attention. That might be useful.

It was time to go.

"Stay safe, Kate."

She smiled. "Always, Jim."

The parking lot had been paved recently; spots on the asphalt were sticky under her tennis shoes. Kate assessed the cops in the perimeter as she walked around the squad cars toward the bank entrance. Some of the rookies looked nervous. A few veterans she recognized had been through this with her before.

Her focus turned to the glass doors. The bank name was done in a bold white stencil on the clear glass; a smaller sign below listed the lobby and drive-up teller hours. Kate put her hand on the glass door and smoothly pulled it open, prepared sometime in the next six feet to get shot.

Dave saw the woman as she reached the front doors of the bank and couldn't believe what he was seeing. She came in, no bullet proof vest, apparently no gun, not even a radio. She just walked in.

God, have mercy. He had never prayed so intently for someone in his life, not counting his sister. Absolutely nothing was preventing that gunman from shooting her.

He pulled back from the end of the desk, knowing that if she saw him, her surprise would give away his presence. He moved rapidly toward the other end of the counter, his hand tight around his gun, knowing he was likely going to have to intervene. "Stay there!" The gunman's voice had just jumped an octave.

She had certainly gotten the gunman's attention.

If she had followed protocol and worn a vest, Dave could have taken the gunman down while his attention was diverted. Instead, she had walked in without following the basic rules of safety, and his opportunity filtered away in the process. He silently chewed out the local scene commander. The city cops should have waited for the professional negotiators to arrive instead of overreacting and sending in a plainclothes cop, creating more of a problem than they solved.

Lady, don't you dare make things worse! Listen, say little, and at the first opportunity: Get out of here!

"You didn't answer the phone. Jim Walker would like to know what it is you want."

She had a calm, unhurried, Southern voice. Not what Dave was expecting. His initial assessment had certainly not fit his image of a hostage negotiator, but that calmness didn't sound forced. His attention sharpened. The negotiators he had worked with in the past had been focused, intense, purposeful men. This lady looked like everything about her was fluid. Tall. Slender. A nice tan. Long, auburn hair. Casual clothes. Too exotically beautiful to ever make it in undercover work, she wasn't someone you would forget meeting. She even stood relaxed. That convinced him. She had to be a negotiator; either that or a fool. Since his life was in her hands, he preferred to be optimistic.

"I've got exactly what I want. You can turn around and go back the way you came."

"Of course. But would you mind if I just sat right here for a few minutes first? If I come right back out, my boss will get ticked off." It was how she said it. She actually made the guy laugh. "Sit down but shut up."

"Glad to."

Dave breathed a silent sigh of relief and eased his finger off the trigger. They wouldn't send a rookie into a situation like this, after all; but who was she? Not FBI, that much was certain.

Kate sat down where she stood in one graceful move and rested her head against the glass doors. Her heart rate slowly decelerated. She hadn't gotten herself shot in the first minute. That was always a good sign.

She scanned the faces of the hostages. They were all nervous, three of the women crying. The gunman was probably not enjoying that. The man the gunman was focused on looked about ready to have a coronary.

At least there were no heroics going on here. These nine folks were scared, nervous, ordinary people. Seeing it on the monitor had been one thing, confirming it directly was a relief. No athletes. No military types. She had lost hostages before who acted on their own.

She wished she could tell them to stay put, but the only communication she could make with them was in her actions. The more bored she appeared with the situation, the better. The goal was to get the gunman to relax a little. His barked humor had been a minor, very good sign. She would take it and every other one she could get.

Kate studied the bomb as the gunman paced. It was everything she had feared. Manning, her counterpart on the bomb squad, was going to have a challenge.

It was a pity God didn't exist. Someone, God if no one else, should have solved this man's problems before he decided to walk into this bank with dynamite and a gun. The gunman wouldn't agree with her, but options now were limited – he would end up in jail or dead. Not exactly happy alternatives. She had to make sure he didn't take nine innocent lives along with him.

Ten, counting hers.

She couldn't have the guy shot; his hand would come off the bomb trigger. She couldn't rush the guy; she would get herself shot. If she got shot, her family would descend on her like a ton of bricks for being so stupid. As she knew from firsthand experience, it was difficult enough recovering from an injury without having the entire O'Malley clan breathing down her neck as she did so.

Negotiating to get the hostages released was going to be a

challenge. He didn't appear to want anything beyond control of the bank manager's fate – and he had that. Releasing hostages took something to exchange. She could go for sympathy for the crying women, but that would probably get her tossed out as well.

As time wore on, bargaining chips would appear she could use – food, water, the practical reality of how he would handle controlling this many people when faced with the need for restroom visits.

She could wait the situation out indefinitely, and slowly it would turn in her favor. But would he let that much time pass? Or would he escalate before then?

Dave had a difficult decision to make. Did he alert the cop of his presence and risk her giving away his position with her expression, or did he stay silent and watch the situation develop? He finally accepted that he had no choice. It would take more than one person to end this standoff. That was the reality. He eased his badge out of his pocket and flipped it open.

He moved forward, leaning around the end of the desk.

There was not even a twitch to indicate her surprise. No emotion across her face, no movement of her head, no quick glance in his direction. She flicked her index finger at him, just like she would strike an agate in a game of marbles.

An irritated flick at that, ordering him back.

Dave sat back on his heels. He would have been amused at her reaction had the situation been different. That total control of her emotions, her facial expression, her demeanor was a two-edged sword – it would keep his location safe, but it also meant it would be very hard to judge what she was thinking.

Her response told him a lot about her though. That silent flick of her finger had conveyed a definite order – one she expected to be obeyed without question. She knew how to get her point across. He felt sorry for anyone who would ever question her in a court of law. She must give defense attorneys fits.

He had to find some way to talk to her.

He opened the receptionist's desk drawer a fraction at a time and peered inside. He found what he hoped for – paper. He silently slid out several sheets and took out his pen. He had to make the message simple and the letters large and dark enough so she could read them with a mere glance. What did he say first?

4 SHOTS. 2 LEFT.

She adjusted her sunglasses.

Okay, message received.

The best way to take this gunman down was from behind, by surprise. But the gunman would need to be close so that Dave could put his hand around that bomb trigger.

MOVE HIM TO ME.

She read the message. Several moments passed. When the gunman paced away from her, she shook her head ever so slightly.

Why not? His frustration was acute. There was no way for her to answer that.

RELEASE HOSTAGES.

She gave no response.

Dave grimaced. This was the equivalent of passing notes in high school, and he had done all of that he would ever like to do when he was a teen. Why had she not even tried to start a dialogue with the man?

TALK TO HIM!

Her fingers curled into a fist.

Dave backed off. Whatever she was considering, at the moment she didn't want to take suggestions. Frustration and annoyance competed for dominance within him. She had better have a great plan in mind. His life was in her hands.

He had no choice but to settle back and wait.

Kate flexed her fingers, forced to bury all her emotions into that one gesture. She would give her next pay check to be able to go outside for about ten minutes and pound something. She not only had a cop in her midst, she had a would-be hero who wanted to give her backseat advice!

Someone had a federal badge; he thought he understood how to deal with any crisis he faced. That suggestion she move the gunman toward him had been truly stupid: Before any negotiations had been tried, he wanted to force a tactical conclusion. There was one word that defined her job: patience. This cop didn't have any, and he was going to get them all killed.

She had two people to keep calm: the gunman and the Fed. Right now it looked like the FBI agent was going to be the bigger problem. If he got it in his head to act, some innocent person was going to get killed, and she was the one sitting in the direct line of fire.

She never should have gotten up this morning.

Deal with it. Do the job.

Kate drew a quiet breath and turned her full attention to the man pacing away from her.

Dave shifted to ease a leg cramp as he listened to the conversation between the negotiator and the gunman. He knew her name now. Kate O'Malley. A nice Irish name for someone who didn't sound Irish.

The conversation had begun slowly, but over the last hour it had become a running dialogue. So far the topics had touched on nothing of significance to the situation. It was all small talk, and she had that down to an art form. It was too well controlled for it to be an accident. Dave wondered how long she could talk about nothing before she drove herself crazy. He knew very few cops who could tolerate such small talk. They were too factual, cut to the bottom line, take-charge people.

The gunman was still pacing, but his stride had slowed. Her constant soft cadence was beginning to work. Dave knew what she was doing, but he could still feel himself responding to that calm, quiet voice as well, his own tension easing. The stress of the situation was giving way to the fatigue that came from an overload of adrenaline fading from his system. He could only imagine how she was managing that energy drain. The last hour and a half felt like the longest day of his life.

He no longer wondered if she was the right person for this task; she had convinced him. She had a voice that could mesmerize a man. Soft, Southern, smooth. Dave enjoyed the sound. It conjured up images of candlelight dinners and intimate conversations.

This lady was controlling events with just her voice; it was something impressive to observe. Part of her plan was obvious. Wear the other side down; remove the sense of threat; build some equity that could be used later when it would matter.

He was learning a lot of minor information about her. She loved the Cubs. Disliked sitcoms. Thought the potholes in the neighborhood were atrocious. When she went for takeout, her first choice was spicy Chinese.

The topic shifted to which local restaurant made the best pizza. Dave knew what she was doing, trying to convince the gunman to request food be sent in. It would probably be laced with something designed to calm the man down. He had to admire how she was working toward even that minor objective with patience. He reached for his pen again. She was making him hungry, if not the gunman. He had been trying to figure out what he could do to help her out. This kind of negotiation was tiring work. He might as well make this a three-way conversation.

YOU FORGOT THE MUSHROOMS.

She never dropped the conversational ball as she smoothly mentioned what exactly was inside a mushroom cap, if anyone wanted to know.

Dave smiled.

Since her plan was to sit there and talk, he could think of a few more questions for her. She had to be running out of topics. He was more than a little curious to learn about Kate O'Malley. She had him fascinated. She was sitting in the midst of a stressful situation, accomplishing a nearly impossible task, and yet looking and sounding like she didn't have a care in the world. Her conversation was casual, her smile quick to appear. If this was what she was like on the job, what was she like off duty?

FAVORITE MOVIE.

His query was met with the glimmer of a smile. Minutes later, she smoothly changed the subject of the conversation to movies.

He had to stifle a laugh when she said her favorite movie was Bugs Bunny's Great Adventure. It didn't matter if she actually meant it or was simply showing an exquisitely refined sense of humor. It was the perfect answer.

IS THIS OUR GREAT ADVENTURE?

High Noon. Dave leaned his head back, not sure how to top that one. Kate O'Malley was apparently a movie buff. It was nice to know they had something in common. If she could get them out of this safely, he would buy the tickets and popcorn to whatever movie she wanted to see. He was certainly going to owe her. The idea was enough to bring a smile. It was one debt he would enjoy paying.

Blink

Ted Dekker

Miriam al-Asamm is fleeing an arranged marriage and a whole regime. An Arab princess, she is engaged to evil Omar bin Khalid who, she fears, intends to overthrow the government and return the state to fundamentalist Islam.

Meanwhile, in the US, a genius graduate student Seth Borders is discovering he has a unique and mysterious gift to see multiple possible futures. Meeting Miriam unawares at a party, Seth uses his gift to help Miriam escape from Khalid's henchmen.

Blink is a novel of the moment, dealing with the threat of fundamentalist Islam in an adrenaline-pumping thriller.

ISBN 0 8499 4371 X

PB

Price: £11.99
£8.99 Special Offer
Special offer ends 31/08/03

8

SAMIR DROVE MIRIAM FROM THE MARKET WHERE they'd left Sultana. Miriam watched suburban Riyadh drift by like a dream made of mud and brick, her stomach tied in knots. Her voice came tight and strained, that much she couldn't control, but she managed to pass it off on Sita's death.

Of course, she couldn't let Samir know the truth: She was actually considering – no, planning. She was actually *planning* to flee the country, Allah forgive her. She didn't dare tell him. Not only because he had a direct line to her father, the sheik, and so by default to Omar, but because telling Samir would put *him* in terrible danger. When Omar discovered her missing, he would naturally suspect Samir's involvement and question him thoroughly. The less he knew the better.

The knowledge that in the morning she would betray him made her ill. She repeatedly swallowed the lumps that choked her throat. She couldn't even tell him good-bye! She did slip a hand over to him and squeeze his hand. He simply blushed and drove on. One way or another, she knew they would end up together-they'd been born for each other. She would leave a letter for him with Sultana, telling him of her undying love and begging him to come for her. A tear slipped from her eye. *Get ahold of yourself, Miriam!*

Miriam explained Sultana's insistence that she must accompany her on a private shopping trip to Jiddah the following day. It was a private getaway, only for part of the day, she explained, so please don't tell any of the others. Samir agreed with a knowing smile and a wink.

If only he *did* know!

She left Samir in the garage, hurried into the house, and walked straight for her room without removing her veil. Nothing must appear out of the ordinary. The last thing she needed was for Haya or Faisal to see her with a tear-stained face. Fortunately, neither of them was around. Miriam locked the door to her room, walked to the bed, and sank to it slowly. Alone for the first time, she lowered her head into her hands and wept.

An hour slipped by before she wiped her eyes for the last time and stood up. A full-length mirror showed her standing, still dressed in her black abaaya. The princess. She walked up to the mirror and studied her face. Her eyes were red and swollen, but the dark tones of her skin hid most of her crying well. She sniffed and ran her hands back through her shiny black hair. A very small black freckle spotted her right cheek. When she was thirteen, she'd wanted it removed. But then she'd looked through a copy of Cosmopolitan magazine that Sultana had smuggled into the country, and she'd seen a stunning model with a similar mark on her cheek. She agreed with Sultana that men must be attracted to it, or the makers of the magazine would have covered it up.

That had been six years ago, and, other than family, the only man who'd seen her face was Samir. Her life had been divided between heaven and hell, she thought. A princess in a prison. And under Omar ...

She turned from the mirror, set her jaw, and pulled off her abaaya. Then it was time to get on with it!

Salman owned a large oak desk he'd flown in from Spain. Actually, he owned four identical desks, one for each of his villas. Miriam assumed they all had fire safes under them, like the one in his study. It had taken her nearly a month to find the combination two years earlier – part of the escape they'd planned. Haya knew the combination, of course. Someone besides Salman had to know how to access the valuables. He had entrusted his young bride with the code, knowing the young girl would never dream of abusing his trust. And in her youth, Haya certainly did not suspect that she was violating that trust by bragging about the combination to Miriam late one night. Coaxing the numbers from Haya had not been an easy task, but when Miriam slipped into the office later that same night and opened the safe, she knew it had been worth it.

After washing her face and applying some color around her eyes, Miriam. went out to find Haya. She was in the piano room, plunking away some awful tune that had no business being played beyond sealed doors. She stopped and stood as Miriam walked in.

"Have you seen Faisal?" Miriam asked.

Haya stared unblinking and for a moment Miriam imagined she knew of her plans. Haya turned sad eyes toward the French doors that led to the gardens. "No."

"Sita was a very good friend," Miriam said.

"Her father is a barbarian."

"And so is Salman."

Haya hesitated. "Yes. He is."

I hope he doesn't take my insubordination out on you."

"Salman will get over it," Haya said, turning. "Did you buy anything?"

"No."

"Hmm. What were you shopping for?"

Miriam took a breath. She walked over to the piano and traced the polished black wood with her finger. I won't be single forever, Haya. You know that."

Haya faced her. "Of course. Although you are becoming an old maid. What man would want an old maid?" A teasing glint shone in her eyes.

"If I'm lucky, no man will want an old maid." The corner of her mouth lifted in a half-smile, then fell again. "But I don't think I'll be so lucky. I turn twenty-one in three months."

Haya nodded. She knew about the age restriction, but no more.

"I've decided to start a new wardrobe," Miriam said. I won't have long to spend Salman's money, so I should make the most of these last few months."

Haya nodded.

"I've also decided, after today, that the shops in Riyadh are too conservative for my tastes. Sultana is taking me to Jiddah in the morning. just for the day. And if Jiddah doesn't have what I want, I'll just have to go to Spain, won't I?"

Haya smiled. "Maybe I should come with you."

"Wonderful idea. Although I'm not sure Salman would approve." Haya would not be allowed to leave town after this morning's outburst. Not until Salman had flushed the anger from his blood. A shadow crossed the younger girl's eyes.

Miriam pushed, encouraged by her progress. "But you won't tell him that I've gone, will you? We're flying in one of Sultana's husband's jets in the morning and will be back in the afternoon."

Haya's eyes went blank. She walked to the piano and sat. "Don't worry, your secret is safe with me," she said. "Maybe I'll join you for the trip to Spain, but you're right about Salman."

Miriam walked over and kissed Haya on the cheek. "Thank you, Haya." She turned and left the room. It was a good-bye kiss a er this evening she might never see Haya again. The thought held some sadness.

Miriam went carefully through her possessions, deciding what she could take that would fit in a single carry – on suitcase and a vanity. In the end, she settled for what Sultana and she had agreed on in their initial planning: two changes of Western clothes-jeans and blouses that would allow her to blend into California; basic toiletries; the Qur'an; one jewelry box filled with her most expensive jewels-well over a million dollars' worth; and a CD Walkman. The rest of the space would go for the money. With money she could buy whatever she needed in the United States.

She had talked scandalously with Sita and Sultana about embracing

Western ways one day, and now that day was here. Jeans might not be acceptable in Saudi Arabia, but Miriam could hardly wait to don them at the earliest possible opportunity. She felt desperate to distance herself from the abaaya and smother herself in the symbols of freedom. In the United States she would be anything but Saudi. She would eat and walk and talk like an American. She'd done it before for a summer in California, and she would do it again–this time permanently. Her accent might be English, but her heart would be American.

The evening crept by like a slug making its way across a pincushion. Faisal came home, his normal obnoxious self, wearing an air of superiority. He wouldn't tell them what Salman intended to do about the morning's events, but the glint in his eyes said that some form of punishment was forthcoming. Haya's dread was enough to turn the house into a mausoleum for the night.

It was 1 A.M. before Miriam slipped through the darkened villa and entered Salman's office carrying her small suitcase. Except for her own breathing, the house was dead silent. She walked lightly on the thick carpet across to his desk, trying in vain to still her heart. She had to kneel to reach the safe under the desk. Using a flashlight she dialed the numbers in the order she'd burned in her mind. But her fingers trembled and she overshot on the first try. The second produced a soft click and she pulled the door open.

She played the flashlight's beam over the contents, positioned exactly as they had been two years earlier: the passports and traveling certificates on a small shelf and wads of cash on the safe floor. Like most Saudi men in his position, Salman kept a healthy stash of money in the event that a political emergency might force him on the run. There were several stacks – euros, francs, and American dollars. Miriam. was interested only in the dollars.

She paused long enough to satisfy herself that the house was still asleep. Working quickly, she shuffled through the documents and withdrew her own passport and a blank traveling document. She would have time to execute the document giving her permission to travel to the United States and sign it with Salman's signature tomorrow. They had all practiced the appropriate forgeries – Miriam only hoped hers would stand up to scrutiny.

She pulled out twenty bundles of hundred-dollar bills, each an inch thick, and placed them in the suitcase. they'd guessed it was roughly $500,000. A small amount of cash in royal Saudi terms, but enough for a start in America, surely. If not she could always fall back on the jewels.

Miriam dosed the safe, spun the dial, and left the room with a new tremor in her bones. She had just committed an unforgivable crime and had no doubt Salman would insist on amputation if she were caught. The traditional punishment for stealing was one he would be only too glad to enforce, especially on a daughter he resented.

It took her an hour to pack and repack the case, hiding the money beneath the clothes. The airport authorities rarely checked the bags of royalty, but there was always the possibility. Unless they rummaged through her clothes, they would find nothing. Of course, if they did open the suitcase, they would rummage, wouldn't they?

She finally locked the case and forced herself to bed again.

The morning came slowly and without a wink of sleep. The two hours of light leading up to her departure with Samir went even more slowly. Miriam walked downstairs at eight-thirty and saw with no small relief that the house was still quiet. She donned her veil one last time and walked to the garage, carrying the suitcase in one hand and her vanity case in the other.

Samir helped her with the bags. If he noticed the weight, he didn't show it. Once again she was thankful for the abaaya that hid her skin – the adrenaline racing through her blood had surely flushed it red. Or drained it white. She only hoped he wouldn't notice the tremble that had set into her limbs.

What if Salman came to withdraw something from his safe before Miriam got to the airport? What if Samir dropped the suitcase, spilling its contents on the ground? What if… There were too many what ifs! *This is a mistake, Miriam! You should run back to the house. You could tell Samir that your cycle came early.*

They pulled away from the villa. Traffic bustled with expatriates headed to work and Saudis headed to oversee them.

"What do you suppose the weather in Jiddah will be like today?" Miriam asked.

"Beautiful," Samir said. He cast her a side glance. "As beautiful as you.

She forced a smile under the veil. "And how do you know that I haven't grown warts under this sheet?"

"Warts or no warts, I would love you, as Allah is my witness."

"Before you saw me unveiled, I was just a walking sheet. And then you saw me and I am your undying love. What if I'd been ugly?" They teased each other often in the car's privacy, but now the talk felt distant. Fleeting.

"Okay. I admit that I'm a man. And like most men, the beauty of a woman does strange things to my mind." He gave her a coy smile. "Your beauty nearly stops my heart. I honestly Don't know what I would do, seeing you walk around the house unveiled. It might kill me."

They passed Riyadh's water tower, a structure that made Miriam think of a champagne glass every time she saw it.

"You would have to marry me first." She turned to him. "We can't pretend forever, Samir. You know as well as I that I will be married within the royal family. I have to produce a son of royal blood, remember? That's the whole point of this agreement my father made."

Samir cleared his throat and stared ahead.

"As long as we're in this country, we'll never be allowed to marry," she said.

"Then we'll have to leave this country," he said.

It was the first time he'd said it. Miriam's heart skipped a beat. But no, she couldn't say anything now.

"We will?"

He looked at her and then returned his gaze forward. "You think

I don't realize how impossible our situation is? I've thought of
nothing else for the last year. We have only two options. Either we
accept the fact that we can never love each other as a man and
woman are meant to love, or we leave the country. Leaving would be
… dangerous. But I think … I really think I would die without you."
He paused and took a breath. I am a good Muslim, and I will always
be a good Muslim. I love this country. But if it makes no difference
to Allah, I think I will take you as my wife."

Miriam felt her heart swell. Everything in her wanted to tell him
why she was really going to Jiddah.

She reached a hand over and rested it on his arm. "Samir … I
would leave Saudi Arabia to be with you even if all the king's guards
were after me." A tear broke from her eye and she fought to control
her emotions. I want you to make me a promise."

I would promise you my life," he said.

"Then promise me that you will marry me. No matter what
happens, you will marry me."

"As there is no God but Allah, I swear it," he said.

She wanted to lift her veil and lean over and kiss him. She glanced
around, saw that the closest car was nearly fifty meters back, and did
just that. She kissed him quickly on the cheek and her lips felt on fire
at the touch.

He blushed and glanced in the rearview mirror. His eyes suddenly
grew misty and he swallowed. If I had been born a prince," he said,
"then I wouldn't bring any danger-"

"You are a prince! You will always be a prince. The only real
danger I face is being separated from you," she said.

They drove toward the airport in a heavy silence of mutual admiration and desire, and Miriam thought her heart would burst with
love.

The Resurrection File

Craig Parshall

Will Chambers' life is a mess. An alcoholic lawyer, his only client is his last hope. And it's not an easy case: he's a defendant in a defamation case, having published an article attacking an archaeological discovery that, if true, would render Christianity a sham. Will must save his client's reputation and defend the truth of the resurrection. But this might be even more difficult than it sounds – Will is an agnostic.

The Resurrection File is suspense-laden lawyer fiction in the mould of John Grisham.

ISBN 0 7369 0847 1
PB

Price: £8.99
£6.99 Special Offer
Special offer ends 31/08/03

Published by Harvest House
Eugene, Oregon 97402

6

FOR WILL CHAMBERS, WINNING IN court had always been the first thing and the last thing. But now-and in fact for a long time-it was not enough. Now it merely provided him with a handy excuse for celebration, usually alone, usually drinking himself into the regions of full-blown selfpity, of which he was already hovering at the borders on a daily basis.

Driving back on Interstate 95 after winning Tiny Heftland's case, Will entertained the idea of going straight back to the office. Working through lunch. Getting things under control at the office. As he cruised along in his Corvette convertible with the music blasting he decided to turn his cell phone of. He started to sour on the idea of skipping lunch. He needed to celebrate.

Will pulled off the freeway and into Monroeville. He decided he would go over to the Red Rooster tavern and grab a sandwich and a few drinks.

At the tavern, he ordered a steak sandwich but only took a few bites. He downed several vodkas while he pretended to watch the Orioles game on the overhead television.

Will lost track of time. But he got to thinking that maybe he had had too much to drink. He figured that he would 90 to the office, put in an hour or so, and then go home early and sleep it off.

When he pulled up in front of the law firm building he noticed a truck parked in front with men loading it on his way up the stain he noticed the moving men were carrying furniture that looked familiar. Then he realized they were walking down with the lobby chairs from his office. He began to run up the stain but missed a step and almost fell facedown.

Jacki Johnson was waiting for him in the empty lobby area of the office.

"What is going on?" Will yelled out.

"We've been tying to call you on your cell phone."

"I turned it off"

"Well, what can I say?" Jacki said, visibly upset. "Things are real bad. The partners voted you out, Will. They're taking you out of the firm. They pulled the plug on you. The partnership property – the furniture and everything – is being taken down to the Richmond office. They're dosing the office here in Monroeville."

Jacki could see that Will was thunderstruck.

"I'm really sorry to hit you with this," she continued. "They're sending you a check for your share of your partnership interest – less the amounts they say are due to the firm from you. We got the message by email and then by fax just a few minutes before the moving men arrived. They've taken all the files, and they say they have contacted all the clients. You're closed out for good, Will – I'm so sorry."

"This is not the partners, I'm telling you that right now. This is all because of that twisted 'managing partner' Hadley Bates – he's behind this, that little scumbucket." Will ran toward the telephone in his office.

Jacki grabbed him and looked him in the eye.

"You've been drinking," she said in an irritated voice.

"I'm going to kill that…"

"No. You're not going to pick up the phone, not right now. If you do, you'll end up saying something to Hadley that you'll regret."

"He can't do this."

"He can. And he did. You have to move on. I think I'd better drive you home in your car. Betty can follow us in mine."

Will was shaking with rage, but he was too humiliated to look at Jacki, so he kept his back to her.

"Come on," Jacki said sympathetically, putting her hand on his back. "I'm going to drive you home to that big old mansion of yours. I just wish you had someone to be with you tonight."

"I'll be fine," Will muttered, but his voice was barely audible.

Jacki drove Will's Corvette away from the office with Will sitting in the passenger seat.

"This is ridiculous," Will snapped, "I had two drinks."

"Oh? Just two?"

"Maybe three."

"That's all you'd need now. To get arrested for DUI. You know, you don't need an assistant lawyer. What you need is a full-time nanny, a drill sergeant, and a priest, all rolled into one. And frankly, Will, that person is not me."

"Give me a break."

"No. You give *me* a break. I tell people you're one of my heroes. Which is really a remarkable thing considering the fact you're white, and you're a guy. But I'm tired of handling your screwups, like that client conference this morning."

"What client conference?"

Jacki sighed heavily and shook her head.

"There is other stuff going on out there in the world, Will besides your pain. You are going to have to get around to doing whatever you have to do – forgiving yourself for Audra – getting on with your life. Check yourself into rehab. I don't know."

"I'm no alcoholic."

"Maybe not. But I'm seeing you heading for a cliff. And I'd rather not go along for the ride.

Then Jacki took her left hand off the steering wheel and, reaching over across to Will, waved her hand in front of his face.

"Look at this, Will, what do you see?" Jacki asked.

"Nice manicure."

"The ring, Will, the ring. Howard proposed to me two weeks ago.

I've been wearing this diamond on my finger for two weeks. I wanted to see how long it took you to climb out of that cave you live in and notice it."

"I noticed it."

"Then why didn't you say anything. 'Congratulations.' 'Jacki, I'm happy for you.' Anything."

Will looked at her, then he laid his head back against the headrest, and looked out the window.

"Congratulations."

They drove in silence for a few minutes. Then Jacki said, "We need to talk business, Will. You and me. My life is taking a different turn now. Howard and I are going to be married. I have to have my career settled. I can't afford to work in an office where I don't know what my future is."

"Come on, you know what your future is with me."

"Do I? Hadley said in his e-mail that the firm has secured written consents from every one of your clients in the last forty-eight hours – to dump you, now that you are out of the firm, and to continue with the firm instead"

"Every client? He's a liar."

"Let me amend that," Jacki said. "Every client except two. One is that big loser Tiny Heffland. Bates said that you can have him, and any money due to the firm from him – as if you will ever recover it – you can keep. And then there's just one other client."

Will gave Jacki a strange, puzzled look. It was the kind of look you would expect from someone at a Chinese restaurant who had just opened a fortune cookie and then read his own name inside.

Jacki continued talking, not noticing Will's expression. She was looking for the cross street to start leaving the city – to leave the historic district with the two-hundred-and-fifty-year-old churches and the little shops and houses that were cloistered together, shoulder to shoulder – with their wood-planked front doors and black-iron door knockers – tucked up dose to the cobblestone sidewalks of Monroeville.

"So this MacCameron definitely has a one-of-a-kind case. He wants to be defended in a defamation and libel case. You've really got to read the Complaint to believe it. Angus MacCameron and his magazine, *Digging for Truth*, are both defendants. He's alleged to have written an article that libeled this big-wig professor about an archaeology discovery," Jacki explained. "Some kind of ardent writing found over in Israel. The plaintiff – Dr. Reichstad – has published some scholarly journal still about the writing – it's apparently a two-thousand-year-old piece of papyrus. Reichstad has been saying that the fragment proves that Jesus was never resurrected. MacCameron really flipped out over that and then wrote some nasty stuff about Reichstad in his little magazine."

"Angus MacCameron. Why is this sounding familiar?" Will was musing.

"I don't know," Jacki replied. "You sounded like you didn't know about the appointment."

"I don't remember this meeting being scheduled," Will commented. "But Tiny was telling me about referring some new case to me. Oh man, this must be the case." Will gave out a low groan. "You know, I don't think Tiny has sent a decent case over to me in all the years I've known him."

"No, that's not true. Remember that case involving the police chief – I think that one was a referral from Tiny. Remember? The city wanted to terminate him for drinking on the job."

"Yeah. I guess you're right," Will said, sounding distracted and distant

"What was the deal on that case?"

'They said he showed up drunk at a bank robbery in progress."

"Yeah, that's it He was the chief of police of some small town in southern Virginia, wasn't he?" Jacki asked.

"Yep."

"Yeah," Jacki said, "I remember that. They had the bank surrounded. A single gunman was holding some hostages. And somebody died, right?"

"An officer died in a shoot-out," Will responded quietly. "The board of inquiry blamed him for giving the order to go in shooting rather than waiting for the hostage negotiators. They said his drinking was a contributing factor."

"So how did the case end?" Jacki continued.

"I got him his job back There was a technical mistake in the way they fired him. We won on a procedural argument."

"Whatever happened to him – the police chief?"

Will was silent.

"What ever happened to that guy?" Jacki asked again..

"He died."

"Oh, yeah?"

"Yeah."

"How?"

Will was silent again, but Jacki probed a little more. "So what was the deal with that guy? Did he stay on with the police department awhile, before he died?"

Will didn't respond at first But when he did, his voice was almost inaudible.

"After we won the case I tried to contact him. I called him at his house. He hadn't showed up at the police station for a couple of days. He didn't answer the phone. So I took a drive over to his house. His car was parked outside. The shades were drawn, so I couln't see in. I knocked on the door. No answer. I called the police." Will paused for a few seconds. Then he concluded. "They broke down the door. They found him sitting in a chair with a glass of booze in his hand. Eyes wide open. His liver disintegrated – or he had a heart attack – something like that."

They were in the Virginia countryside now, and Jacki pulled the Corvette into the long driveway that led, through the arch of trees, up to General's Hill.

Jacki pulled the car to a stop near the front pillars of the old mansion, and then turned it off. She eased back in the seat for a moment. There was only the sound of the breeze rustling in the leaves, and a few birds up in the trees.

"Can he pay? This MacCameron guy?" Will asked.

"He's got funding from the magazine, so he may be able to pay a fairly substantial retainer. I really didn't talk money with him. I figured you ought to do that. His daughter, Fiona, was with him. She's some kind of Christian singer. A very classy-looking woman. I did notice she didn't have a wedding ring, which is interesting Especially with a face that looks like it belongs on a fashion magazine. I got the feeling she's sort of looking after dear old Dad. But Dad says he won't take a penny of his daughter's money – he insists on funding his defense himself. This guy MacCameron, he's really a hoot. You know, a real 'praise the Lord' type, except I think he's Scottish or something. And I read the article he wrote against this Dr. Reichstad; it's something else. He brought the article with him. He really goes after Reichstad."

"Oh. Like how?" Will asked, trying to act uninterested.

"Like accusing him of fraudulent scholarship in interpreting this piece of ancient writing he found. And MacCameron even implicated Reichstad in the murder of an archaeologist friend of his in Jerusalem."

"Boy, that's a bad start to the case. Accusations of professional incompetence, coupled with the imputation of the commission of a crime. Classic examples of defamation per se," Will noted. "Tiny told me J-Fox is representing the plaintiff. Arguing a case against Sherman is like getting your teeth drilled."

"Yeah. This Professor Reichstad must be really well-connected to snag the Sherman firm, "Jacki said, her voice trailing off. And then she added, with some genuine empathy, "Will, even if the money for your fees is there, maybe you need to let this case go. Sherman is going to try to bury you," Jacki continued. "Once he finds out that you are on your own, and that you're out of the firm, he's going to smell blood – it's going to be like a great white shark in a feeding frenzy. Not that you couldn't handle it. But is it worth the hassle? Maybe you ought to cash in your 401(k) and just take some time off."

But Jacki could already see that Will was thinking about the case.

"Anyway," Jacki continued, "the way MacCameron describes it, this Reichstad is a media hound, and he's clearly a public figure. So that means that your only real defense is to prove a lack of actual malice on MacCameron's part. I mean, that's basically what your defense would be, right?"

Jacki's question hung in the air as the leaves rustled around them in the treetops.

"Maybe not."

"Oh?" Jacki gave Will a strange little smile. "So what's the defense? I mean, assuming you even want to get involved in this dogfight. What would the defense be?"

"Truth," Will said as he reached over for the car keys and pulled them out of the ignition.

And then added as he climbed out of the car, "Truth is always a defense to a lawsuit for libel and defamation."

Down at the bottom of the long, winding driveway Betty pulled up with Jacki's car.

"You going to be okay?" Jacki asked.

"Sure. Me and Clarence. A man and his dog."

Jacki then told him, with strained optimism, "I checked on our office space. The rent is paid up through the month. The firm gave notice they were vacating. I called the landlord. I hope that was okay. I told him that you would be personally renting the space from then on. He said you can keep working out of the same office, as long as you can come up with the rent."

"Fine. Say hello to Howard for me," Will said. "Tell him he is a very lucky man."

"Look, it will take me a couple days to clear out. So you'll be seeing some more of me. I do think you will have to talk to Betty. She wants to know if you can afford to keep her on," Jacki added.

"Tell her I'll talk to her tomorrow."

"I'll do that," Jacki called out as she made her way down the driveway. "Oh, don't forget, you've got this Reverend MacCameron coming back in again tomorrow. He wants to meet you personally."

Will Chambers waved goodbye and trudged in the front door. Clarence, his golden retriever, came loping across the living room, his big pink tongue flapping. Will gave his does head a quick pat as he headed for the liquor cabinet

7

AFTER POURING HIMSELF A GLASSFUL of Jack Daniels, Will settled into the oversized chair in front of his big-screen television. He flipped through the channels and began downing the glass of whiskey in generous gulps. After losing interest in a made-for-TV movie, Will switched back to the news.

But he found himself thinking back to the police chief in Hadleysburg. He couldn't forget the day that he entered the house with some of the officers from the police department. He remembered the stench, and he recalled the bizarre and terrible sight of his client sitting, in full uniform, in his chair in front of the television set. There was a full glass still in his hand. His eyes were empty, fixed straight ahead. The chief's skin was yellowish and artificial looking, with black discoloration around his lips and eyes and in the folds of his skin.

Will got up and poured the glass out in the kitchen sink. He went to the refrigerator, found some orange juice, and poured it into another glass. And then he sat down at the table that overlooked the rolling green hills and the white-flowered mountain laurels that spotted the acres of what he used to think of as "*our* property."

No, he thought to himself, it is not "*our property*." There was no "ours" anymore. It was only *his*. The whole world had been divided into that which was *his* and everything else that belonged to everyone else in the world. But *us*, and *we*, and *ours*, no longer existed. Audra was gone. She was no longer part of this huge house. Her perfume didn't precede her into a room anymore. Her laugh didn't make him smile anymore despite himself. She was not there to keep him from taking himself, or his work, too seriously. He thought about the feel of her hair when it brushed against his face. He felt the aching loss of her touches and caresses.

He had met Audra at Georgetown during his law-school years. She was in the art department. She was an earthy blonde with a quirky sense of humor and an easy, winning smile. When he moved from his first job at the, ACLU in New York to rural Tennessee for the Law Project of the South, she supported him. Audra sold her paintings at galleries in the tourist towns and taught art in the community colleges.

But when Will was fired from that office and then finally got the job with what was then Bates, Burke, Meadows & Bates, Audra, had hoped it would last. And it did, for a while. But after five years, the rest of the partners suggested that Will move up to central Virginia to open a branch office. They said it was to get him closer to D.C., where they wanted to open their third branch, but Will felt the real reason was to get him out of the Richmond office, where he had become a constant irritation to the others.

Yet after the move to Monroeville, both Will and Audra felt an immediate sense of belonging. It was a city with a lot of charm – and history. Monroeville was connected with several of the Founding Fathers. General Robert E. Lee had once marched down the street, right past the very building where Will's office was now located. The buildings and shops had carried their age quietly and well among the pear trees that lined the streets, trees whose blossoms would draw tourists in the spring through the fall.

But it was Generals' Hill, situated prominently in the rolling

Virginia countryside just outside of Monroeville, that most symbolized the couple's sense of belonging.

They had bought the dilapidated pre-Civil War mansion with the idea of restoring it. Audra poured herself into the loving reconstruction of the great house. It was small as Southern mansions go, but to them it was a thing of beauty: It had tall white columns in the front, and a huge fanshaped window just below the peak of the roof. Inside there was a curving staircase that led to the second floor.

Audra taught a few art classes at the local college. She split the rest of her time between the restoration of the house and painting in watercolors and acrylics in the studio that they had created in one of the extra rooms. She loved the house, but with her pacifist's heart had tried to get Will to agree to change the name of the mansion from "Generals' Hill" to something less warlike. But Will was too wedded to historical truth for that. The mansion had switched hands between the South and the North several times during the course of the Civil War. The name of the place was enshrined in local history. Besides, Will liked the idea of living in a house that had been near the focal point of great battles. After all, he thought, unconfirmed reports within the State Department have suggested that it may have been carrying some type of device of mass destruction – possibly a thermonuclear weapon.

"The driver, Mr. Ajadi, is in custody in New York City at an undisclosed location. We have been told at this time only that he does not possess a valid passport. We know of no criminal charges as of yet But we will certainly keep you apprised of any further details as we receive them.

"But one final interesting note. Jim Williams, our reporter in New York City, has already commented that this is a story of 'strange twists.' Well, here is yet another one.

"In a twist of remarkable irony, the truck was stopped by a New Jersey State Patrolman, Ezer Nabib, an Arab and apparently a devout follower of Islam. He had been put on the alert for the make and model of the truck. Apparently the United States government had also received an anonymous tip that the truck might be carrying a very dangerous weapon, and federal authorities and the military all converged on the scene.

"By the time the FBI and the Pentagon and all the other high-powered agencies had arrived, Officer Nabib already had the driver under arrest and the truck secured. Clearly, if there is one hero that is emerging in this story, it is State Patrolman Ezer Nabib, who just may have single-handedly averted one of the worst terrorist attacks in the history of our nation.

"Lastly, there is of course much speculation that this incident may also be tied to Abdul el Alibahd, one of the world's most-hunted international terrorists and a suspect in the Wall Street bombing of last year. Folks up in Manhattan who have had to recover from the horrendous World Trade Towers tragedy, then had to deal with the truck bombing may nearly have had to face yet another terrorist attack-but this one much worse. It is too early to tell – yet – how close we may have come to the brink of nuclear destruction within our own borders if it had not been for the courageous work of New Jersey State Trooper Ezer Nabib."

Will kept the television on into the night, catching every detail of the news story While there were a variety of opinions given by military and law-enforcement experts, authors on terrorism, and cultural and religious commentators – who noted the irony of an Arab Muslim foiling the apparent suicide mission of an Arab terrorist-no new information was forthcoming.

Will wanted to pick up the telephone and call someone – anyone – to talk about the news. But he realized he had no one to call. When his eyes were too heavy to stay open, he plodded up the curving staircase to go to bed. His faithful dog, Clarence, followed him close behind.

Apocalypse Dawn

Mel Odom, Tim LaHaye and Jerry B Jenkins

This new thriller runs alongside the phenomenally successful Left Behind series, which has sold more than 50 million copies worldwide.

With action taking place on the decks of U.S. Navy carriers patrolling the Mediterranean to Georgia, and amid the sands of the Turkish-Syrian border, new characters and situations are added to those from the explosive series, raising the temperature even further.

Boasting the high drama and technical accuracy of a bestselling military thriller, *Apocalypse Dawn* is sure to satisfy the fans of the original Left Behind series and attract many new converts.

ISBN 0 8423 8418 9
PB

Price: £9.99
£4.99 Special Offer
Special offer ends 31/08/03

Published by Tyndale House Publishers, Inc.
351 Executive Drive
Carol Stream IL 60188

Chapter Thirty-One

United States 75th Rangers 3rd Battalion Field Command Post 35 Klicks South of Sanliurfa, Turkey Local Time 1542 Hours

The world hung suspended from a single strand as thin as a gossamer spider web above the gleaming jaws of death.

Cal Remington sat in his ready room in the command post and reflected on that thought. The prose was too purple to put in a field report, but the summation would stand out in a biography or an episode of the History Channel.

The Ranger captain had no doubt that history was being made and that he would probably figure large in that history. A third of the world's population had disappeared with no apparent catalyst – except for a sudden border skirmish that had flared up in the Middle East. The Middle East had been a hotbed of terrorism and world threat for decades-centuries, even. But never before had the fighting been liked to anything like this. Some weapon of imaginable power had been unleashed, and Remington had been at Ground Zero.

Rosenzweig's magic formula had changed the balance of power within the Middle East. If there were any fingerpointing later, Rosenzweig would surely bear the brunt of the blame for beginning the change. Perhaps the Israeli scientist had come up with the miracle growth serum, but someone else – surely the Russians or the Chinese – had come up with the weapon that had eradicated all the missing people.

But why give it to the Syrians to use?

That was the question.

Sitting behind the desk, Remington rested his elbows on the chair arms and rested his hands together, fingertip pressed to fingertip. He felt tired. He was coming up on almost forty-eight hours without sleep. But he'd never needed that much sleep, and he'd always been able to get from his body what he demanded of it. He wouldn't accept any less now.

He scanned the notebook computer in front of him. The LCD screen filled the small lightless room with soft blue illumination that grayed out all the color of his BDUs and the blue steel of his Colt .45 lying in the modular holster on the metal desk. An earbud connected him to the computer so that he could listen to the files he wanted to without being overheard.

Now that the Crays were up and running at peak performance, Remington had the files archived off-site where he had access to them for reviewing through the notebook computer. He scanned the FOX and CNN feeds coming through, as well as the OneWorld NewsNet footage.

FOX and CNN covered most of the domestic scene in the United States, including the disaster areas that had been declared in all the major cities. Chicago had been hard hit, and Los Angeles had experienced looting, fires, and riots the like of which had never been seen even in the city's colorful history. DC, New York, Atlanta all had their own share of troubles. The list went on.

The footage rolled, showing wrecked cars, burning buildings, downed planes shattered across airfields and cities. One catastrophe followed another. Martial law had been declared in several metropolitan areas, but the understaffing of the police, fire, and National Guard units that had experienced even larger percentages of disappearances than the population at large had made it almost impossible to enforce.

A knock sounded at the door.

"Come," Remington said.

"Sir," Corporal Waller, one of the computer techs, said. "There's something on OneWorld NewsNet that you might want to see."

"What is it, corporal?" Remington let the irritation he felt at being interrupted sound in his voice.

Waller hesitated.

"You're burning daylight, mister," Remington warned.

"Yes, sir. Sorry, sir. It's just kind of hard to explain. The OneWorld reporter, she's with the 75th, Captain."

That wasn't news. The presence of the news teams in the area, with the acknowledgement that they couldn't fault the military in any way, had been one of the concessions Remington had granted to Nicolae Carpathia's liaison. Evidently Carpathia was planning to address the United Nations when he made an upcoming trip to the United States. The new Romanian president wanted to use some of the footage of the military engagement along the Turkish-Syrian border to make whatever case he was going to present.

"I knew those people were in the area," Remington said. "As you might recall, I authorized their presence."

"Yes, sir. I know that, sir. But the story they're covering. That's what I thought you might be interested in."

"What is it?" Remington prepared himself to royally chew out his intelligence teams. If he had to learn of an enemy incursion into the protected territories through a news service, heads were going to roll.

"It's the 75th, sir. They're—" The corporal paused.

"Spit it out, soldier." Uncertainty, one of the feelings that Remington most hated in the world, nibbled at the edges of his confidence. The planned retreat from the border was scheduled on a precarious timetable. He wouldn't allow anything to circumvent that schedule.

"Well, Captain, there's a man baptizing soldiers out there."

At first, Remington was certain he hadn't heard right. He couldn't possibly have heard right. "What man?"

"I don't know, sir. One of ours."

"Dismissed, corporal."

"Yes, sir." The corporal left with alacrity.

Remington closed the windows and opened a live streaming feed from OneWorld. The screen cleared, showing a beautiful brunette standing in front of a slow-moving stream. He recognized her from earlier transmissions that had basically introduced her to the viewing audience and re-capped the situation along the border.

"This is Danielle Vinchenzo of OneWorld NewsNet," the young woman said. "We're only a few miles – or klicks, as the soldiers of the United States Army Rangers would say – from the border s-eparating Turkey from Syria. Nearly nine hours have passed since the devastating launch of the SCUD missiles that piled up casualties here at ground zero along the border and several targets deeper into Turkey. The soldiers here – the Rangers, the United Nations peace-keeping effort, and the Turkish army – know they are in for the battle of their lives."

Glancing past the woman, using the zoom function on the video program, Remington focused on the stream in the background. The cameraman almost had the shot in the frame. He couldn't recognize the man doing the baptisms, but his actions were plain enough. Remington saw one line that was on the east side of the stream, judging by the sunts position, made up of soldiers from all three units stationed along the border as well as civilians. They stood quietly and patiently. And they appeared to be singing.

"Events have gone rather badly for the 75th Rangers," Danielle said, "as they have for every soldier stationed along the contested border. The death count from this morning's attack is still not finalized. Nor have the lists been compiled of those who had simply ... vanished as has happened around so much of the planet."

Remington clicked the touchpad, bringing the image back to normal.

"But here in the heart of the darkness that has swelled and burst over these two ancient enemies," the reporter went on, "a man seems driven to snatch hope from the jaws of despair."

The video suddenly cut away and brought up stock footage.

Remington immediately recognized the replay of Goose carrying the wounded Marine from one of the downed Sea Knight helicopters.

"So many of you are familiar with the horrible accident that knocked Marine reinforcements from the air only two hours after the blistering attack launched by the Syrian military. Many of you first came in contact with this man then."

The image zoomed in tight on Goose's face, showing the blood and the sand-encrusted kerchief over his lower face, and the haunted blue eyes. The scar along his right cheekbone stood out blood red against sunburned flesh.

Remington had seen the footage several times. Goose was clearly being molded into a hero by the media. But not Goose's captain. The OneWorld reporter hadn't sought him out for an interview. The fact chafed him. Goose hated media attention, yet here he was becoming a poster child for the Syrian engagement.

"This is First Sergeant Samuel Adams 'Goose' Gander," Danielle said, "of the United States Army, 75th Rangers. He helped organize the rescue of Glitter City, the television and media center north of the border, after the initial SCUD launch, then arrived back at the border encampment to bring in reinforcements from the 26th Marine Expeditionary Unit/Special Operations Capable from the Amphibious Readiness Group in the Mediterranean sea headed by USS Wasp."

The video changed again, showing a quick snippet of Wasp cutting across the ocean under a full head of steam with helicopters flaring around her.

"In minutes, Sergeant Gander was forced to go from bringing a reinforcement team into the area to help his flagging troops recover from the devastating attack to rescuing the survivors of that attempt."

Video footage rolled, showing Marine helicopters exploding.

Then the image changed and showed Danielle standing on the stream bank again. "With the reinforcements they'd been promised lying under tents in the primitive triage area they've been able to put together or as casualties still lying across this battleground, with no hope of other reinforcements for some time to come, and knowing that they've been left in charge of defending this country, most soldiers would be daunted to say the least. Others might even give up."

The camera swung past the woman reporter and focused on the two lines of men that met in the center of the stream. Several of the soldiers carried gurneys with wounded aboard.

"But the men of the 75th Rangers are not ordinary men," Danielle said in a voice-over. "They are the best of the best. The cream of the crop. Even now, facing tremendous odds with the Syrian army standing down–at least for the moment–on the other side of the border, these soldiers have found a renewed faith."

The camera focused on the huge man standing in the middle of the stream. Remington didn't know the man – yet. But he would, and there would be an accounting two seconds later. The big man placed his hand over the face of a UN soldier, then lowered him into the water and raised him.

"I'm told this man, Corporal Joseph Baker, one of Sergeant Gander's handpicked crew, was an ordained minister who had given up his church after losing his wife and child to tragedy." Danielle's voice quieted. "Some said his faith was broken. But Baker has found that faith again, here on one of the bloodiest battlefields that has happened in recent years."

The footage continued to roll. The mountain of a man dealing with the tide of men coming at him from both sides worked like a machine. He talked briefly to each man in turn, covered the man's face with a big hand, and dunked each man.

"Most of the soldiers have to hurry back to their posts," Danielle said. "In the beginning, I'm told Corporal Baker simply came here on a water detail assigned by Sergeant Gander. When one of his crew asked to be baptized, Baker granted that request. Other crews from the UN peacekeeping forces and the Turkish army were on hand getting water as well."

The camera view pulled back and shifted to show a broader view of the stream. Hundreds of men lined the hillsides.

Remington swore in disbelief. What had Goose been thinking by leaving Baker in place instead of taking the man into custody?

The camera view tightened on Danielle Vinchenzo again.

"Some of the men consented to talk to us," Danielle said. "Although most preferred their experience here today to be kept private." She turned to look off-camera and gestured to someone.

A soldier wearing the familiar baby blue headgear that identified the United Nations peacekeeping teams stepped on-camera with Danielle. He was big and young and nervous and soaking wet. Deep scratches showed on the left side of his face.

"This is Corporal Flannery O'Doyle of the Irish contingent of the United Nations peacekeeping," Danielle said, turning to the man. "Corporal, I'll only take a few minutes of your time. I know you've got to get back to your unit."

"Yes, miss. Me an' the boyos, we've been powerful busy." O'Doyle looked slightly embarrassed. When he smiled, he showed a gap between his two front teeth.

"This assignment hasn't turned out as you had expected."

Sadness touched the young corporal's face. "No, miss. I lost three of me mates this mornin', I did. Good men. All of 'em."

"I'm sorry to hear that, corporal."

"Yes, miss. Thank you, miss." O'Doyle put his hands behind his back at parade rest.

"What brought you here?"

O'Doyle looked over his shoulder, squinting slightly against the sun to the west. The deep scratches on his face showed more. "I heard about a man baptizin' in the stream, miss. An' I had to come."

"Why?"

The big Irishman shrugged. "I was raised Presbyterian, miss. I already been baptized once. When I was just a wee lad. Me ma, she saw to that. She was a right stubborn old lady when she put her mind to it, she was. An' she puts her mind to it often." He pursed his lips. "But I never saw to gettin' baptized on me own. A decision like that, why it seems like it ought to be left betwixt a man an' his Maker, you know?"

The camera tightened on O'Doyle's face. He stuck his chin out, obviously having trouble speaking.

"This mornin', after that ferocious battle, all them men dyin' an' them bombs droppin' from the air, why it was like–" O'Doyle pursed his lips and sucked in a quick breath. Tears glittered in his green eyes. "I held one of me mates when he died this mornin', miss. That's just somethin' you don't forget. But as I sat there holdin' him, feelin' him goin' away from me, I felt like God Hisself put it in me heart to get right with Him. To come to Him on me own two feet." His voice broke.

"And you heard about Corporal Baker," Danielle prompted gently.

"Yes, miss. I did. An' I asked me sergeant if I couldn't come out here an' get right with the Lord. He sent me on, he did. An' I got here an' Corporal Baker, why he rightly baptized me." O'Doyle looked at Danielle. "I tell you, miss, I haven't felt like this in me whole life. I feel like I done been reborn. I come up outta that water, an' I knew everythin' was gonna be okay."

"You mean with the coming battle?"

O'Doyle shook his head. "No, miss. We got a powerful lot of fightin' ahead of this. Our commandin' officers, they all tell us that. I don't know if I'll make it back home or not, but whatever happens, I know it's gonna be all right." He touched his wet uniform. "I'm not alone any more, miss." He nodded back out at the stream. "Me an' these men what's here, them what has had God Hisself speakin' into our hearts, why we'll never be alone on this battlefield again." He shifted his assault rifle over his shoulder and touched his blue beret. "Now, if you'll excuse me, miss, I gotta get back to me unit."

"Of course, corporal," Danielle said. "Thank you for sharing that with us."

"Miss," O'Doyle said with deadly earnestness, "if you go through somethin' like that back there, bein' saved in the Lord, I mean, you'll find you just gotta tell somebody. It's too big to just keep all to yourself. I'll pray for you, miss, that God will keep you safe in His sight, an' that you'll make your own peace with him." Without another word, he turned and trotted away.

Danielle Vinchenzo appeared to have been caught off-guard. She fumbled the smooth transition back to the camera. "This is Danielle Vinchenzo, on special assignment for OneWorld NewsNet, where a miracle is taking shape on a battlefield."

The news channel switched back to the anchor and the stories moved on to the disappearances that had taken place around the world again.

Remington tapped the touchpad and broke the television feed. He leaned back in his chair and stripped the earbud from his ear. Anger swirled through him. He swore.

The mission had fallen apart. He'd been used by the CIA and didn't know the full extent in his culpability in precipitating the attack, had been in command of the rescue mission that had ended up scattered across the hardpan. His First Sergeant was allowing a crazed corporal to baptize the men of three armies while the event was filmed in front of an international audience.

Remington didn't want to hear about it when the Joint Chiefs learned of the baptisms. He rubbed his face. More than anything, he needed a win. And to get that win he knew he needed to start putting his foot down and take command of the unit that Goose had let slip through his fingers.

And Remington was going to start by putting an end to the nonsense taking place in that stream.

The Second Thief

Travis Thrasher

Tom Ledger is still at the office in the middle of the night. He's not working though – he's stealing his employer's most inflammatory secrets which he plans to sell to the highest bidder. But after a terrifying plane crash and an encounter with the criminal underworld, things start getting out of hand. Tom soon realises he needs to find a way out.

The Second Thief is a rollercoaster thriller that will keep you glued right to the last page.

ISBN 0 8024 1707 8
PB

Price: £8.99
£6.99 Special Offer
Special offer ends 31/08/03

Published by Tyndale House
Wheaton, Illinois 60189

If you knew you were about to die and could call me, what would your final words be?"

Tom looks across the room at the lanky blonde who asked the question. Her short hair is wet from the shower. She's watching some sort of TV newscast.

He grins and goes back to reading the paper, standing at the island of the condo's kitchen.

"What was that look for?" she asks, no longer focusing on the television.

"That's a big assumption."

"What? That you'd die?"

"That I'd call you."

She makes a face at him but he just smiles, rubs his freshly shaven face, then finishes the glass of grapefruit juice and places it in the kitchen sink.

Janine turns back to the story about a man in California who called his wife from the scene of a bank robbery moments before he was shot to death.

"Isn't that awful?" she asks.

"Quite."

"So you wouldn't call me? "

"I don't think I'd want to draw attention to myself during a bank robbery."

"But what would you say if you could?"

Tom Ledger looks at the morning beauty in the white terry-cloth robe, shakes his head, and crosses the room to give her a good-bye kiss on the neck. She is used to his not answering questions such as this.

"Will you call?" she asks.

"Of course." He knows this is a lie.

"By the way ... where'd you go last night?"

A suitcase and matching briefcase rest by the door to Janine's one-bedroom condo.

"Just went out to get some air," he says. Another lie.

"Air? At like two in the morning?"

"Sure. Couldn't sleep, so I went out."

"I heard the garage door open around three. Is everything okay?"

He nods. Everything's perfect.

"You've been kinda on the moody side the last couple days. Even last night–"

"The limo's here."

She pauses, and he knows that she knows better than to push it.

"Have a great trip."

He picks up his bags and walks out the door. He has known Janine for over two months. She's six years younger than his thirty-four years and around a dozen younger in terms of maturity. Some might question what he is doing with her in the first place and exactly how much maturity that shows, but Tom doesn't care.

He won't be seeing her again anyway.

He leans back in the leather seat of the Town Car as it heads for O'Hare International Airport. He thinks of Janine's question.

"What would your final words be?"

If he could call anyone, who would he call anyway? Not Janine. The obvious answer occurs to him. But he knows Allegra wouldn't accept a call from him or allow him to get out five words. And no one else comes to mind.

Vacations 1, 2, 3, and 4 echo in his head. He thinks of making the California trip a quick one, then maybe going down to Florida and finally getting to see the Keys and losing himself down there for a while. A month. A year. He's not entirely sure.

The landscape of suburbia blurs by him. Street upon street upon store upon subdivision. He passes the time by comparing this northern suburb of Chicago with what he knows of Key West. He knows the Keys are probably not that different from Wood Grove or any other location. It probably has its share of secrets, its ugly little realities. And it also has its share of people trying to ease the pain of living with their mistakes.

The difference is that, in a place like Key West, you have ocean sunsets to make it all a little easier.

Tom waits in an airport bar drinking a club soda with lime. Around him sit passengers who are either about to board or just getting off a plane, most of them laughing and drinking and having a good time. He finds locales such as this comforting. He can sit alone, and as long as he appears to be drinking something heavy and continues to tip the bartender enough, he can remain unbothered.

The phone at his side vibrates.

"Yeah."

"It's me."

"Yeah," Tom says again, recognizing the male voice.

"That easy, huh?"

"Told you. Been there long enough to know what it's like."

"Are you sure no one knows?"

"Very few people would even have a clue as to what is really valuable inside. And how to get it."

"So you got everything?"

"You'll see it tonight."

"We'll have to celebrate. Dinner's on me."

"That won't be the only thing."

The man on the other end laughs, and Tom hangs up. He sips his drink and stares to his right at the passengers shuffling between gates. A family of four meanders past, and he studies them. A man about his age with light-brown hair and a well-worn sports coat. A pretty but tired-looking wife in a conservative, flowing skirt and a jeans vest over a white T-shirt. The woman holds a baby against her shoulder while the man links hands with a little girl, perhaps four or five.

Soon they're out of view, and Tom resumes being invisible. His thoughts shift to pondering the type of yacht he'll be purchasing in the next few weeks. He has narrowed it down to three. The choice will be an important one.

Two aisles cut through the 767. Tom heads down the one on his right after stepping onto the plane and takes the aisle seat numbered 17B. He shoves his briefcase into the overhead bin along with his sports coat. The memory stick remains in his wallet. Looking through the oval window, he sees the long, sleek wing shining in the morning sunlight.

Normally Tom travels first class, but he normally travels on business and books well ahead of time. This was the only seat left on the 10:30 A.M. flight to San Francisco when he called a few days ago. He finds himself wishing for the space and privacy of the first-class seats ahead of him. As strangers pass, he wonders who will occupy the lone seat between him and the window.

A man laboring with a large suitcase stops next to Tom's row. He struggles with his piece of luggage as he tries to fit it in the overhead bin.

"Sorry," he says to the people behind him as he tries to jam it in.

Tom gets a clear look at his face and recognizes the family man he saw with the wife and two kids. The stranger carries a cordial grin even though he knows he's holding up the line.

A carrying case slips off the man's shoulder and lands in Tom's lap.

"Oh, sorry. Excuse me."

Tom says nothing but takes the black canvas bag, the sort they hand out free at conventions, and puts it in the aisle. He notices an inscription on the front of the bag: "Riverside Bible Church."

"Sir, we'll need to store that in the back," a flight attendant tells the man. The row of travelers behind him has grown, and irritated stares pierce his back.

"Sorry, I thought it'd fit," he says with an apologetic smile.

The attendant takes the suitcase with her to the back of the plane.

She says she will store it there and he will have to wait until all the passengers are off before retrieving it.

"Thank you. I'm really sorry."

The brown-haired man picks up his shoulder bag looks at his ticket stub. He appears confused as Tom stands to let him in, but he slides into the window seat, apologizing again while Tom says nothing.

The man wiggles in his seat, looking out the window and then staring at the row. He clears his throat.

"Um, excuse me?" he says to Tom.

Tom looks at him but says nothing. The last thing he wants is to have a conversation with this man, especially this early into the flight. He knows better than to give passengers next to him an invitation to talk.

"You know, the travel agent told me this was going to be an aisle seat. I guess I should've checked, huh? I don't fly much."

Tom continues to stare at him, saying nothing.

"Would it be a big deal to switch?"

Tom shakes his head, waving his hand and making it clear that's impossible. He looks ahead again.

"Look, I know that might be a lot, but I've been battling a bad stomach thing — I mean, it's not contagious or anything. I just worry — I might need to take a quick trip to the bathroom."

"I can let you out," Tom says.

The man next to him, probably in his early or midthirties, wipes the sweat off his temple and smiles a nervous grin.

"I just — I know it's a lot. Maybe just this one time. To be honest, it's been years since I've flown. I'm not the best flyer. And being next to a window kinda freaks me out."

Tom stares at him without making an expression. "You can shut the window cover."

He stares at the seat in front of him while the man next to him continues staring at him, probably surprised at his comment. He slowly stares ahead, and Tom can see him strapping in his belt buckle in silence.

The passengers file by, and the full 767 bustles in the early summer morning. Tom thinks of the last time he flew, and a chill unexpectedly rushes through him.

Business travel became a way of life, and making a trip every week became the norm. While working in sales with several different companies, Tom grew used to flying. With Hammett-Korning, he flew less often but stillmade at least a couple of trips each month. The last flight he took, a red-eye from Dallas to Chicago, ended up being the most turbulent flight he ever rode in.

It's one thing to have turbulence on a normal trip in the daytime. But at night, with darkness blanketing the cabin and only a handful of reading lights on, with the window blinds shut and half the craft empty, massive turbulence is quite another thing. Tom couldn't sleep, and when the turbulence started, it started with a bang. The plane took a hard nosedive and Tom's stomach lurched, just as it would on a roller-coaster ride. It wasn't a quick, two-second drop either, but a lengthy doubledigit-second drop. That's what caused the full wave of panic to seep in afterward. He kept imagining the turbulence getting so bad that they would do another nosedive and never come out of it again.

Tom remembers the sick feeling in his stomach, not nausea but a tight, visceral fear. He hadn't felt that way for a long time, and being alone only made things worse. He remembers sitting there in the sanctuary of first class, his palms and the lower part of his back sweating, afraid of dying. And hating the fear, the worthless feeling it gave him. But after half an hour of the worst turbulence Tom ever experienced, the flight became stable again, and Tom ridiculed himself for being so petrified.

"Everyone dies," he reminded himself. His father used to say that a lot. That's why you're not supposed to fear death. And Tom used to believe he didn't fear it. Until that flight.

Now, a couple months later, he scolds himself again for ever giving in to that fear. It's not that he wants to die. There is so much he still wants to do. But dying is nothing to be afraid of. If it's your time to go, so be it.

So be it, Tom hears in his mind as the plane begins to back up. That's what his father always said. He wonders if his father said that the moment his heart seized up many years ago, the seconds before the blood finally stopped flowing and the instant before he died alone on the kitchen floor of their ranch-style home.

When fourteen-year-old Tom discovered the body later that afternoon, he didn't instantly think *So be it.* He wishes he had. And since then he's tried to tell it to himself many times. But deep down, he still feels the same way he felt years ago when shaking his lifeless father's body to try and wake him up.

It's too soon.

He doesn't wish for another father, and he doesn't hold Benjamin Ledger responsible for leaving him. He doesn't long for the kind of backslapping, fishing-buddy kind of father-son love that he's seen in books and movies. He appreciates his Uncle Dale and Aunt Lily, who raised him and his brother. He simply wishes that his father had had more time.

Everyone deserves more time than that.

The plane, hurtles up into the sky, and Tom realizes he's fine with flying. No fear, just weariness from a long week's worth of work and raw nerves. He hopes to get some rest during this five-hour flight. Perhaps take in the movie they show – enjoy the novelty of being entertained instead of slaving away at a laptop. Perhaps read from the paperback he bought moments earlier in the airport.

Tom ventures a glance at the open window. The man next to him begins to chew on his lips with nervous energy.

"Fly much?" he asks.

Tom nods and stares back ahead.

"I hate leaving the family behind. I'm glad I don't have to do this on a regular basis."

Again, Tom ignores the man next to him.

Moments later, already ten minutes up in the sky, the man next to him reaches into his case and takes out a folder. He begins to read from a stack of papers. Tom is curious but doesn't dare even glance at them. He wants to be left alone.

The Amber Photograph

Penelope J Stokes

Shortly before her mother dies, Dierdre McAlister is handed an old sepia-tinted photograph and given a cryptic message to discover the secrets which will explain who she is and where she came from. Dierdre must now follow the clues and try and find the answers to her deepest questions, even though it might cost her her innocence and expose the unseen dark side of her family's past.

The Amber Photograph is a tense thriller dealing with serious issues in a sensitive way, which will have the reader trying to put the pieces together throughout.

ISBN 0 8499 4283 7

PB

Price: £7.99
£5.99 Special Offer
Special offer ends 31/08/03

Published by W Publishing Group
A division of Thomas Nelson
PO Box 141000, Nashville, Tennessee

Part 1

The Spinning Dream

Dreams, like faith,
arise from deep within and far beyond us.
We hold to them
no firmer than we grasp the dawn
or anchor ourselves to wind.
Dreams, like faith, escape us,
and yet the gift,
hidden where only the heart can find it,
still remains.

1

The Intruder

HEARTSPRING, WORTH CAROLINA
APRIL 1995

Cecilia McAlister held her breath against the agonizing stab that shot through her. She shifted in the velvet chaise and tried to sit upright. When the pain subsided, she straightened the afghan and lay back on the pillows, breathing heavily. The slightest movement was a monumental effort now; just getting from the bed to the chaise could sap her energy for half a day.

Still, she was determined not to give in. The hospital bed-that hideous metal monster with its electronic controls, brought into this room eight months ago and installed in the corner – was her coffin. If she stayed there, she would die; she was certain of it. As long as she could get up and move to the chaise, have Vesta fix her hair and put on a little makeup, wear a nice bed jacket, hold a book on her lap, she might fend off the Intruder for a little while longer. It was a futile deception, but at least for the time being she might fool Death into believing he still had a fight on his hands.

Her breath came a little easier, and Cecilia looked around what once had been the music room of the massive house. What echoes this room held, with its grand piano and big bay windows looking over the garden. Memories of singing and laughter and voices calling her name. When she sat like this, with her back to the hospital bed, she could almost believe things were now as they once had been. She could see flowers blooming beyond the patio and watch spring storms building over the mountain vistas beyond. From the very beginning, this one room had been her refuge, her sanctuary, the single corner of the world where she felt alive and whole and–

She could barely think the word: *normal*. Nothing had been normal for years. And now, facing the inevitable repossession of her soul, Cecilia was forced to consider what might have been, if only she had claimed the power, years ago, to say "no" to her husband. No to his grandiose dreams, his ambition. No to his vision of what their life should be. No to – well, to a lot of things.

But no one – not even a wife-said "no" to Duncan McAlister. When he had built this house thirty years ago, he had claimed he was doing it for *her* – a doting husband giving the wife he loved a grand home.

But she knew the truth then as she knew it now-this house had never been built for *her*. It was Duncan McAlister's giant billboard, a huge, hulking "I-told-you-so" to all the people in his past who had called him a nobody, the good-for-nothing son of an alcoholic and abusive father.

Well, he had done it. He was rich. He was Somebody. A real estate mogul. Mayor of one of the Top Ten Small Towns in America. An icon. An idol. There was even talk of erecting a statue in his honor on the neatly trimmed town square.

Her husband had proved himself, Cecilia mused. But what had become of the man she had married, the gentle, wounded, compassionate boy who haunted her memories? Had he ever really existed, or had he only been a product of fantasy and imagination and wishful thinking?

She willed the question away. She didn't have enough years left – or enough energy – to answer all of life's dilemmas. You couldn't pull every loose thread, or the whole thing would unravel.

Death had a way of bringing life into focus, of distilling out peripheral concerns and leaving you with pure, undiluted, pristine truth. A truth that had to be spoken-now, quickly, while there was still time.

A line from Keats wandered through her drug-fogged mind: *Truth is beauty; beauty, truth* ...

Cecilia shook her head. It sounded high and noble, such poetry, but until you had everything stripped away and were left with nothing but your last gasping breaths and a world centered in pain, you couldn't begin to imagine how infernally ugly reality could be.

The truth might set you free, but first it would drag you through hell and back.

2

The Dreamer

A narrow shaft of sunlight pierced the slit between the closed curtains and invaded Diedre McAlister's left eye. Groaning, she threw one arm over her face, but there was no escaping it. The shaft of light pierced through until she could see the road map of blood-red vessels silhouetted against the thin flesh of her eyelids.

She rolled toward the wall and pulled the covers up higher. It was no use. Sleep might offer a few blessed hours of respite, of welcome oblivion, but morning always came again, bringing with it pain. Duty. Worry. Responsibility. A mother dying by inches from the ravages of cancer. Ubiquitous reminders of the fact that Diedre was losing, one tortured breath at a time, the person she loved most in the universe.

It was too much for a twenty-four-year-old to bear.

Then she remembered. Today was her birthday. She was twenty-five. Twenty-five going on seventy, if the weariness in her body were any indication.

She heard the creak of hinges as the bedroom door opened, the scrabbling of toenails against the hardwood floor. A leap, a thump, and then a series of joyous canine grunts. Diedre caught a whiff of dog breath and felt a warm tongue licking her cheek and ear.

She groaned again, opened her eyes, and struggled to a sitting position. "All right, Sugarbear; take it easy, girl. I'm getting up."

The dog pawed playfully at the covers and thrust her muzzle under Diedre's hand, and Diedre felt a rush of warmth well up in her. A shelter pup, primarily a mix of cocker and Lhasa, Sugarbear was the original dumb blonde – not the brightest bulb in the chandelier, but intensely loving and loyal. And despite the abuse and neglect heaped upon her by her previous owners, the beast was blessed with a disposition that made Pollyanna look like a curmudgeon. She had been with them for ten years, and no matter what Diedre's emotional state, she could always count on Sugarbear to make her smile. Prozac with paws.

The bedroom door opened a little farther, and a seamed and wrinkled brown face peered around the doorjamb. "You awake, honey?"

"I am now." Diedre propped the pillows against the headboard, moved Sugarbear to one side, and motioned Vesta Shelby to enter the room. Vesta had been with the McAlisters for ages, and Diedre adored her. To a little girl who had grown up as an only child, Vesta represented an eternal, apparently inexhaustible source of unconditional love and uncritical acceptance.

The stooped old woman pushed her way into the room bearing a tray loaded with scrambled eggs, bacon, and — Diedre's favorite — French toast made from cinnamon challah bread.

"What's all this?"

"It's your birthday breakfast, of course." Vesta set the tray on Diedre's lap and eased into a small chair that sat next to the bed. "Surely you didn't think your old Vesta would forget your birthday."

"To tell the truth, I wish people *would* forget. I don't exactly feel like celebrating."

"You don't mean that, honey. Just 'cause your mama's sick don't mean you stop livin'."

"How is Mama this morning?"

"'Bout the same, I reckon. Eat your breakfast, now, before it gets cold."

"Maybe I should—" Diedre pushed back the quilt and started to get up.

"You can't make her well by worryin'," Vesta said firmly. "I took her medicine to her an hour ago. She'll sleep for a while yet. Now, eat."

Diedre relented, transferring half the eggs onto the French toast plate and rearranging the breakfast to accommodate two. "You are going to help me eat all this, aren't you?"

Vesta pulled the chair in closer and accepted the plate Diedre held out in her direction. "I can't hardly believe my baby is twenty-five years old."

"I haven't been a baby for some time, Vesta."

The old woman smiled and winked at her. "You'll always be my baby. You should know that by now." She raised a warning finger toward the dog. "Get off the bed, Sugarbear," she commanded in her sternest voice. "You can't have people food."

In response, Sugarbear edged closer and held very still, gazing up at Diedre with soulful eyes. "Just one little piece," Diedre said, breaking a slice of bacon in half. The dog wagged all over.

"It ain't good for her."

"It's not good for me, either, if you want to get technical. But I'm going to eat it anyway."

Vesta laughed, and Sugarbear, aware that she had won this round of the ongoing begging controversy, gulped down the bacon before Vesta had a chance to protest again.

When the meal was finished, Diedre laid the tray aside and let Sugarbear lap up the remains from the china plates.

"You know your Daddy don't like her doing that."

Diedre shrugged. "What Daddy doesn't know won't kill him. Besides, it saves you time. Now you won't have to rinse everything before it goes in the dishwasher." She took a sip of coffee, leaned back, and sighed. Sugarbear settled on top of the blanket, as close to her human as she could possibly get. Absently Diedre stroked the dog's head. "You need a grooming, girl," she murmured. "Just look at that mustache, poking out in all directions."

"She's going to Dapper Dogs for a bath and trim tomorrow morning," Vesta answered. "And if you ask me, you could do with a little sprucing up, too."

"I haven't had time."

"You haven't *taken* time, you mean." Vesta reached out a shaky hand and fondled a wayward curl behind Diedre's ear. "You ain't been out of this house in who knows how long. Miss Celia won't mind you takin' a little time to yourself."

In exactly the same way Sugarbear nuzzled in to be petted, Diedre found herself leaning in to Vestals touch on her neck. For a moment, just a heartbeat, she became a little girl again, recalling what it felt like to be safe and comforted, free of the anxieties of adult life. Then she sat up and ran a hand through her unruly hair. "You don't like my hairdo?"

Vesta chuckled and tugged on the curl. "I think you could use a new cut." Her smile faded, and her dark eyes went sad. "I can take care of your mama, honey. You don't have to be here twenty-four hours a day. Why don't you go down to Asheville, buy a birthday present for yourself, maybe have lunch with your little friend Carlene?"

Diedre smiled inwardly at Vestals description of Carlene as "her little friend." Nothing about Carlene Donovan could justifiably be described as "little." A large, exuberant woman given to wearing purple and red and fuchsia, Carlene was the flamboyant, extroverted yang to Diedre's subdued yin. She had been Diedre's best friend since undergraduate school, and they had remained close even while Diedre was at Duke pursuing her master's. For the past five years Carlene had taken it as her personal mission in life to teach Diedre how to dream big. She had almost succeeded.

Carlene's most recent dream – and, by extension, Diedre's–was to open a shop in Biltinore Village. A boutique called Mountain Arts, dedicated to featuring the work of local painters and sculptors. Now that Diedre had completed her education, she and Carlene were ready to begin the process of opening the shop. Their plan was to be equal partners in the venture – Carlene would run the shop and do most of the buying, while Diedre, who had put up most of the money for the place, would pursue freelance photography and display and sell her prints. It would be an instant success, Diedre was certain – if for no other reason than the compelling force of Carlene's personality.

They had gone as far as making an offer to purchase a storefront a block down from Holy Trinity Cathedral, and during her last semester of grad school, Diedre had begun to do Internet searches for a house of her own. But when Mama's cancer had returned, Diedre had put the dream on hold and come home to Heartspring, leaving Carlene to do the legwork in Asheville.

For a minute or two Diedre let herself revel in the idea of spending the day in Asheville. It was a beautiful spring morning, and she desperately longed to get away – to sit with Carlene on the terrace at La Paz, their favorite Mexican restaurant, soaking in the sunshine and the ambiance of Biltmore Village. But she couldn't. Given her mother's condition, it was out of the question.

"Why don't you call Carlene and make a day of it?" Vesta prompted.

"You know I hate shopping," Diedre hedged. It was the truth, but only part of the truth. How could she say to Vesta what she could barely admit to herself? Mama was still sick. Diedre's life was still in limbo. The burden of responsibility still circled over her like a vulture waiting, for its prey to drop. A shopping spree, a new haircut, or a lunch with Carlene wasn't going to change anything.

Coming home had been the right thing to do, Diedre was certain of that. But after four years of college and two years of grad school, living under her parents' roof again had engendered a kind of schizophrenic division in her, a languishing of soul she could neither overcome nor control. She could no longer be who she perceived herself to be – an independent woman of twenty-five, with two university degrees and a bright future ahead of her. Instead, she had by sheer force of will taken on the roles of both parent and child. Her mother now depended upon her, and once again her father's overbearing protectiveness threatened to smother her.

She was trapped – locked in a gilded cage, perhaps, but imprisoned nevertheless. And even though love had compelled Diedre to volunteer for the duty, she still felt shell-shocked, captive to a war that seemed to have no end.

She changed the subject. "Is Daddy home?"

"Mr. Mayor? He hightailed it outta here about seven-thirty this morning. Said something about a breakfast meeting with a bunch of those real estate investors." Vesta frowned. "He needs to be here, with his wife, where he belongs."

Her eyes widened suddenly, as if she had shocked herself with this outburst. Diedre, however, was not surprised. This might be the first time she had ever heard Vesta speak an unguarded word about her employer, but with Vesta, words weren't always necessary to convey her innermost thoughts.

"Give him a break, Vesta," Diedre said softly. "He's hurting, too; he just doesn't know how to show it. It's hard for him, watching her like – like this."

Still, Diedre had to admit that she felt the same way about Daddy sometimes. He was loving and concerned, even to the point of smothering her. She had spent years trying to convince him that she was an adult, capable of taking care of herself. But occasionally, she caught a glimpse of something in him that held back. Something hidden, as if he nursed some secret wound that rendered him incapable of giving himself fully. He had been this way with Mama of late. Apparently watching her waste away was simply too much for him to bear, and so his only choice was to withdraw, to take his pain to work and bury it there.

"You look tired, honey," Vesta said, interrupting Diedre's thoughts.

"I didn't get much sleep."

"Worrying about your Mama?"

"Yes." Diedre paused. "And the dream."

"You been having that dream a lot since you came back home."

Diedre nodded. It made sense, she supposed, that returning to the house of her childhood would resurrect what she had always called the Spinning Dream. In the vision, she was young, maybe three or four years old. The other girl, she was pretty sure, was the older sister she had never known.

For years the dream had haunted her. But no one ever wanted to talk about it. It made Mama cry and made Daddy sullen and silent. At last she had given up with everybody except Vesta.

"Tell me about Sissy."

Vesta shook her head. "It don't do no good, resurrecting the dead." Although the words were harsh, the tone was kind, compassionate. Almost wistful.

"But I need to know, Vesta. She was my *sister*."

Vesta gathered up the breakfast tray and got to her feet. "Why don't you get cleaned up and go see your Mama? She'll be awake by now."

She paused at the door and turned back toward Diedre, her ancient eyes watering. "You need to let it go, child," she declared. "It don't have to mean nothing. Sometimes a dream is just a dream."

Theodora's Diary

Penny Culliford

Anybody attempting a funny diary of the life as a Christian today is bound to attract comparisons with Adrian Plass's perennially successful Sacred Diaries. Theodora's Diary, though, brings a whole new perspective to the genre: a female one!

Summing up the challenges of being a modern Christian woman, Penny Culliford's diarist will instantly endear herself to her readers. *Theodora's Diary* is a light and funny novel, perfect for the holiday suitcase. It reminds you of the most important things in life – faith, hope and chocolate.

ISBN 0 0071 1001 4
PB

Price: £6.99
£4.99 Special Offer
Special offer ends 31/08/03

June

Monday 29 June

Chickenpox! How can a grown woman, who spends her whole life avoiding children, have contracted chickenpox? It must have been one of that hideous brood of Hubbles. They always look as if they're harbouring some disease or other. Anyway, the doctor says it will mean at least four weeks off work, two of them in isolation, so it does have its benefits.

Tuesday 30 June

This chickenpox is a blessing in disguise. I am determined to use the time to grow spiritually by reading all the latest Christian books, listening to proper Christian music (not just Cliff Richard) and by keeping a journal. It will be a record of events at St Norbert's and will document my journey through the year. I know it's a bit unusual to start a diary at the end of June, but I've never been one to pander to convention. I'll try it for a couple of weeks – I don't think I've ever stuck to anything for longer than that. Then I can look back at how I've rocketed spiritually upwards in this time of enforced solitude.

St Norbert's is a funny sort of church. Perched on top of the hill, squinting down at the village like a benign, geriatric vulture, its solid grey bulk veers more towards cuddly than sinister. It's not quite Norman (more Nigel, really), not quite Victorian, and definitely not quite modern. I've been going there for as long as I can remember. I sometimes think it's easier than finding anything else to do on a Sunday morning. Practically everyone else I know goes there too. I suppose our outlook is basically evangelical, as long as it doesn't involve actually talking to anyone. Our major concessions to the twenty-first century are the overhead projector and the tea urn.

St Norbert's itself would probably be all right, but for the fact that it seems to attract the strangest people – an assorted assemblage of 70 or so, as diverse in age and temperament as it is possible to get. Kevin, who hardly ever sets foot in the place, says that it's no stranger than any other collection of deranged cranks, psychopaths and simpletons. That's rich, coming from a man who thinks nothing of spending the entire weekend at a draughty football ground watching 22 grown men kick a ball up and down a field. Sometimes I wonder why I go out with him. I think he must be spiritually degenerate!

Ariadne persuaded me to keep this diary. She said it would stop me sitting here feeling sorry for myself and worrying about things like why there's only one Monopolies Commission, how the person who wrote the first dictionary knew how to spell the words, and who owns the copyright to the copyright symbol. 'That, and scratching your spots, then phoning up to whinge at me,' she said.

Honestly – sisters! Does she think I'm completely neurotic? No, this journal is going to be a record of dynamic living and a fascinating insight into the mind of a modern Christian woman. I would fist as my major influences the Acts of the Apostles, the diaries of Samuel Pepys and Adrian Plass's *Sacred Diary,* probably in reverse order.

July

Wednesday I July

Kevin was rather short with me last night, when I rang him in the middle of the televised match to ask him to call into the Christian bookshop for some spiritually uplifting material for me. I must still have been in bed when he called round this morning, because I found a package on the doormat with a scribbled note:

> Theo,
> Sorry I didn't have time to call into the bookshop.
> Hope these will do.
>
> Love Kev.

Inside the package were a *1982-1983 Goal of the Month* video and a book entitled *Astro-Turf – A Guide to Players and their Star Signs.* The latter lists the zodiac signs of all the premier league footballers. I really think he is spiritually degenerate. Still, his heart's in the right place.

Friday 3 July

I read two famous and very elderly books today – *The Screwtape Letters* and *The Cross and the Switchblade.* Some would describe them as classics, but I think it just goes to show that it's been a very long time since I last bought a Christian book.

Out of desperation, I also listened to a cassette I found right at the back of a drawer. I must have bought it at the Greenbelt Festival over 10 years ago, when I first met Kevin. It was by a Christian heavy-metal band called The Ungrateful Lepers. Kevin and I had gone to hear them in a damp field after a veggie burger and two cans of Albatross cider. It was during the song 'Send Down the Plague' that we had our first kiss. Now I remember why I haven't played it for 10 years.

My spots itch. Mustn't scratch.

Saturday 4 July

Kevin came to visit today. It was all rather unsatisfactory, as he was petrified of catching chickenpox and wasn't in full command of his faculties because he's still coping with his grief over his team's relegation at the end of last season. He insisted that I should prop open the letterbox and sit on the opposite side of the hall before he would talk to me.

'How are you feeling?' he bellowed across my flat from a distance of about 30 feet.

'Terrible!' I yelled back.

'Me too!' he screamed.

'Why? You haven't caught it, have you?' I shouted.

'No, haven't you heard the news? We're selling the goalkeeper … and he was our best scoring player!'

Sunday 5 July

I couldn't go to church today, but someone dropped a copy of St Norbert's newsletter, *The Church Organ,* through my door. My eye was drawn to one of the notices:

> *The first notice is an apology relating to an item which appeared in last week's newsletter The item announced simply as 'Reverend Graves – slides in hall' was in fact referring to the vicar's photographic slides. The PCC apologizes sincerely to those disappointed members of the congregation who turned up hoping to see the shoeless vicar run very fast and slither from one end of the hall to the other*

Monday 6 July

Well, that's it. I've read every Christian book and nearly every other book I own – except, of course, *The Complete Works of Shakespeare,* which everyone has on their bookshelf but no one has ever read.

Ariadne suggested I tried reading the Bible for once. I think she was being facetious. I've watched Kevin's football video forwards and backwards (backwards was vastly more entertaining) and am currently reading a women's magazine from 1972 that I found in the airing cupboard. Aesthetically challenged as I am, I find it hard to believe that people *ever* really made crocheted toilet-roll covers 'in co-ordinated shades of lilac, tangerine and lime'.

A 'get well soon' card arrived through the letterbox at lunchtime. It was from Jeremiah Wedgwood, whose purpose in life seems to be boring or frightening sick people better. It read:

To comfort you in your time of infirmity and affliction

How nice, I thought, until I read the Bible verse he'd included:

My body is clothed with worms and scabs, my skin is broken and festering.

(Job 7:5)

Please God, don't let him visit me.

Things are getting so bad, I may have to resort to watching one of those daytime DIY shows which tell you how to 'update' a perfectly acceptable wardrobe using zebra-striped paint effects with a 'fashionably kitsch' neon pink silk lining.

Tuesday 7 July

Much to my disappointment, there were no daytime DIY shows on. My wardrobe remains untransformed. Instead, I watched with horrified fascination the American interview show where people with deep-seated emotional and relationship problems come to a television studio to hurl abuse (and occasionally chairs) at each other in front of millions of viewers.

I wonder why they do it?

After several hours of 'entertainment', including repeats of

American detective shows from the 1970s and cookery programmes for incompetent or unwilling chefs, I have come to the conclusion that daytime television is a government conspiracy to deter malingerers. If you can endure daytime television, you must be *really* ill.

Wednesday 8 July

Every inch of my skin itches, I look like the one who got turned down for a part in *101 Dalmatians* for being too spotty, I want to strangle Cliff Richard, and if I spend another day alone I shall start talking to the fridge.

Thursday 9 July

Just as I was asking the fridge what it thought I should have for lunch, the buzzer on my entry phone sounded.

'What do you consider to be the purpose of life?' enquired an earnest-sounding voice. I pressed the entry button and soon two smartly dressed young men carrying briefcases and magazines appeared at the door of my flat. They eyed my spots apprehensively.

Three hours later, after giving them the benefit of my opinion on the purpose of life, heaven and who would get there, blood transfusions and the meaning of the Book of Revelation, the two young Jehovah's Witnesses finally persuaded me to let them leave.

Friday 10 July

I got a phone call this morning from Charity Hubble, the chintz-upholstered curate's wife. I was so desperate to communicate with another member of the human race that even Charity seemed bearable. She reminds me of a well-manured cottage garden – covered in flowers and extremely fertile.

'Hello, Theodora. How are you feeling?'

Even though I couldn't see her, I just knew she was smiling in that seraphic, 'I'm just brimming over with joy' way I find so utterly nauseating.

'Oh, I'm just fine thank you, Charity,' I lied.

'How are the spots?' she enquired.

'A bit itchy, but they're getting better,' I fibbed.

'Look, Theodora, I hope you don't mind, but I wonder if we could come and visit you. I've had chickenpox already, but none of the children have. If we came round today and they caught it from you, they would all get it over and done with in the school holidays.'

My stomach lurched. All eight Hubble children in my flat! Like a priest in a department store who has accidentally wandered into the ladies' lingerie department, I frantically searched for a way out. I found none.

'Yes, that would be fine,' I said through gritted teeth. 'About four o'clock?"

The visit of the Hubble tribe, though lasting less than an hour, was simply too hideous to record. Suffice it to say that I lost my temper with six-year-old Bathsheba, who spent half an hour following me around with a felt-tip pen in her hand, eyeing me in anticipation. I tried to dodge into the bedroom, but she followed me in there. I nipped smartly into the bathroom and whipped the door shut, but when I turned round, there she was, standing by the washbasin. I started to wonder if she was some sort of apparition.

'Why are you following me?'

Two blue eyes stared out from a puffy gerbil face. She said nothing, but studied my face and bare legs. The felt-tip pen in her hand twitched slightly. I unlocked the door and flung it open.

'Go away,' I snapped. 'Leave me alone.'

'But I only wanted to play join-the-dots!' she wailed, and ran to find her mother.

Saturday 11 July

The visitor I was looking forward to about as much as a turkey looks forward to Christmas arrived this afternoon. Jeremiah Wedgwood strode into my flat wearing an expression which made me think of a vulture watching a creature about to take its last breath. 'Greetings in the name of the Lord! When I noticed you hadn't been to church, I feared you had backslidden. Then, to my great relief and joy, I heard you were ill. How is your poor, tortured body today?' he enquired in a voice that sounded like a very bad impersonation of a Conservative politician.

'Oh, er … not too bad, thank you, Jeremiah. Still a bit … spotty.'

'Visiting the sick is my "ministry", you know.'

I nodded vigorously, trying to humour him.

'Bringing succour to the afflicted and relief to those in tribulation! You look very pale. Are you sure it's only chickenpox?' He peered at me with watery, blue eyes.

'Yes, yes, that's what the doctor said.' My mouth started to feel dry.

'Doctor? You've had the doctor in?' He shook his head and tutted. 'You want to be careful of doctors, you know. It was a doctor who told my Uncle Sid it was only chickenpox. She prescribed him calamine lotion, but –' and he glanced behind him, lowering his voice to a chilling whisper, '– dead within a week'.

'Really!' I ran a finger around the inside of my collar, which had suddenly become two sizes too small.

'Yes, he was on his way to the chemist to collect his prescription when he got run over by a bus.'

I could feel the perspiration beginning to break out on my forehead. How long was I going to be able to endure Jeremiah's 'ministry'?

'I don't feel too good. Perhaps I'd better not keep you.' I tried to sound as if I was suffering bravely, which of course I was.

'Nonsense, I've got all afternoon. I always allocate the whole of Wednesday and Saturday afternoons for my ministry of visitation.' Jeremiah's immediate departure was clearly not going to be that easy to secure. 'Anyway,' he continued, 'I haven't given you your present yet.'

'Present! Oh, that's extremely kind of you. You really shouldn't have bothered.'

He rummaged around in his holdall and, to my astonishment, pulled out a five-pound bag of King Edward potatoes. My mind searched frantically for a suitable response.

'M-m-most people would have brought grapes,' I stammered eventually.

'No, no, no. Potatoes are *much* better for you. Vitamin C and loads of roughage. You look as if you need more roughage. How are your –'

I leapt in before he could quiz me on the workings of my digestive system and thanked him profusely for his generous gift. It was clear by now that he was here for the duration and little short of an atomic bomb would deflect him from his intention to 'minister' to me. Desperately, I tried to engage him in conversation. If I kept him talking, he couldn't lay hands on me.

'So how did you come to this ministry, Jeremiah?'

That was the wrong question. Apart from intestines, his ministry was his favourite subject. His already watery eyes welled up, threatening to burst their banks.

I made mental arrangements for my funeral.

I was sure I wasn't going to make it through this visit alive. Even if I survived the boredom, I feared I might drown in his tears.

'Oh yes! I've been doing it ever since I had The Dream.'

I didn't ask.

'You'd be amazed how many people can barely stagger from their bed of pain when I arrive, but by the time I leave, they're changed and restored. I've witnessed people who start off looking pale and drawn, becoming flushed with health and positively leaping across the room to see me out by the end of my visit, sometimes after only three or four hours. It's little short of miraculous, truly it is. It's so precious to be able to bless people in this way.'

He withdrew a handkerchief from his pocket and mopped at the deluge.

'D'you know, there was one poor soul I used to visit – a Mr Barrymore, who drove a really splendid little red sports car. He lived right at the top of the steep hill in the village. Anyway, he became unwell and I used to walk up that hill to visit him every Wednesday. I would pray for him, then we would talk about his garden and his car. He really loved that car. He used to polish it every day until it shone, even when he got really poorly and couldn't drive it any more. One day something truly wondrous happened. God worked mightily in that situation. It was nothing short of a miracle.'

I was stunned. Maybe I had misjudged him. 'You mean he was healed and got better?'

'No! He died and left *me* the car. Lovely condition, beautiful bodywork. As I said, a miracle!'

I felt a sensation of overwhelming weariness. I would have to grasp the nettle and ask him to leave. 'I'm suddenly feeling rather tired. I think you'd better go so I can get some rest.'

'But I haven't prayed for you yet!'

That was the final straw. He *had* to go. Pray for me, like he did for Mr Barrymore? No thank you! When most people ask God to undertake in a difficult situation, they don't mean it literally.

'By the way, that's a lovely china figurine you've got on your table,' Jeremiah said. 'I've always wanted one of those. Do you have any plans for it when ... well, you know ... Have you made a will?'

I couldn't believe my ears. He was supposed to be making me feel better. Instead he was practically measuring me for my coffin!

'I'm perfectly all right,' I hissed through clenched teeth. 'It's only chickenpox, you know.'

'Are you absolutely sure about that? It could be some deeply concealed, unconfessed sin – greed, perhaps, some demonic attack upon your psyche, some heinous iniquity festering away in your sub-conscious, manifesting itself in physical affliction.'

'No it isn't! It's chickenpox!' I snapped.

'You look a little tense. It could be a stress-related anxiety disorder.'

I had a desperate urge to say, 'Look, you will be suffering from a boot-related backside disorder if you don't leave pronto. I'm supposed to be ill. You come in here with your potatoes, scare me half to death with stories about dead uncles, try to worm your way into my will, then accuse me of being demon-possessed and mentally unstable!'

Instead, I summoned the dregs of my energy, hoisted myself to my feet and opened the door. 'Please, Jeremiah, you really can go now. I'm suddenly feeling much better.'

To my utter amazement, Jeremiah seemed delighted to be evicted. His moist eyes shone and he rubbed his hands together with glee. He was beaming, as I stood pleadingly by the open door.

'You see,' he chuckled with delight, 'a miraculous recovery! Works every time. What a gift!'

Sunday 12 July

Kevin popped round to bellow at me again through the letterbox and drop in some supplies. One of the items he deposited through the letterbox was the latest copy of *The Church Organ*. I've always been sure that church magazines only exist to stop people nodding off during the boring bits of the service, and it looks as if that's right. Among the notices about the Ladies' Guild and the Sunday School outing was a note in very small print, right at the bottom of the last page. It read:

If you are reading this, the sermon must be <u>really</u> dull.

Monday 13 July

I have the feeling that my period of solitary confinement is nearly at an end. Today I sat and thought about all the things I could have done, even *should* have done while I had the time and still didn't do. I thought of the painting-by-numbers set, still in its box under my bed. I thought of the copy of Stephen Hawking's *A Brief History of Time* that Ariadne made me borrow. I haven't even opened it. I guess now I'll never understand how to synthesize the theory of general relativity with quantum physics. Oh well!

There have been benefits. My time hasn't been entirely wasted. I now have beautifully manicured hands and nails, my eyebrows no longer look like Eric Cantona's, and I have a bikini line smooth enough to skate on.

Tuesday 14 July

Hooray! I saw the doctor this morning, and I'm no longer contagious. Theodora Llewellyn is now able to receive visitors.

2 P.M.

No visitors yet.

8 P.M.

Still no visitors. Where are they all?

11 P.M.

Fed up. Spent all day hoping someone would visit me after what seems like years in solitary confinement.
    No one.
    Not one single person.
    Not even Kevin.
    Nobody loves me. I'm going to bed.

Wednesday 15 July

It occurred to me this morning that perhaps I should phone people to tell them I can now have visitors. That might do the trick.

11 A.M.

Kevin popped in on his way back from a plumbing job nearby. He was positively bubbling over with excitement. I thought it was the joy of being allowed near me again, but then he let slip that the reason for his effervescence was that his new football season ticket had arrived in this morning's post. Who said romance is dead?

Flabbergasted

Ray Blackston

Stockbroker Jay Jarvis isn't happy: he's just been transferred to Greenville, South Carolina, while simultaneously being dumped by his girlfriend.

In an attempt to meet girls, Jay finds himself in church and, before long, on the notorious singles group weekend away. There, he meets a hilarious collection of off-beat characters and has his perceptions of church, God, and what it means to follow him, turned on their heads.

Flabbergasted, Jay soon realises his life is never going to be the same again.

ISDN 0 8007 1837 2

HB

Price: £11.99
£9.99 Special Offer
Special offer ends 31/08/03

1

At a quarter past midnight I set my paint roller in the pan, the pan in the tub, my bathroom the latest victim in a week of odd-hour renovations.

Hands scrubbed, teeth brushed, I walked down the hall, cut off the lights, and fell prostrate across a mattress in my spare bedroom. A whiff of khaki latex seeped into the darkness, drifted past my pillow, and reminded me to be up at 8:00 A.M.

In the fuzzy state between sleep and awake, I reached to set the alarm on my digital clock. But I held the button too long and had to wait for the eight to come around as I dozed and saw the numbers, saw the numbers then dozed, and around again went the numbers.

The rumbling of a car engine woke me. It was Sunday morning. I sniffed the air, and above the fresh paint I detected the scent of females four miles away at North Hills Presbyterian Church.

The wind strained to cool my Blazer when I ran the yellow lights, and I ran three. Greenville was an unfamiliar city, and it bloomed green across my new geography, the upstate of South Carolina. Sprawled between two office buildings on the uppity side of downtown, North Hills appeared manicured and popular. A tiny steeple rose from the red brick sanctuary.

The lot was filling fast. I parked in the back row, pausing there to watch well-dressed couples with immaculate children hurry toward

the building. I checked my hair in the mirror and wondered who
might be inside.

Understand that I did not resort to such tactics without good
cause – and the cause was not that unusual.

Modern communication was the cause.

Kimberly Hargrove had communicated to me, by e-mail, that she
was now interested in a surgical resident at West Dallas Hospital and
would no longer be requiring my attention. This humbling piece of
news arrived just six days after I had moved halfway across the
country. Her contribution to this story ends here. Just know that
what had looked promising had totally unraveled with two Thursday
afternoon e-mails.

Relational rope burn.

Maybe you can relate.

Now, I'm aware that being dumped was poor motivation for what
I was about to do. But what I was about to do would not have
happened had it not been for a second piece of communication.

From an older woman.

No, not a romantic interest.

The real-estate lady.

Having just been transferred, I knew not a soul in Greenville, S.C. –
until she had agreed to meet me at a mistreated three-bedroom in the
middle of a suburban cul-de-sac. I had signed the contract on the hood
of her Saab as she stood beside me in her gold jacket and black heels,
looking over my shoulder and drooling for commission. Seconds later
she had tromped through the yard, proudly slapped a SOLD sticker
across her FOR SALE sign, and nearly turned her ankle in the process.

"So where do the single people hang out in this town?" I inquired,
noting that the sellers had even uprooted the mailbox.

"Well, Jay," she said, leaning over to brush grass clippings from her
black heels, "there's the occasional outdoor concert, and in the fall
there'll be plenty of football, but your best bet is in the same places
where I find clients. I usually rotate between Baptist and Methodist."

"Churches?" I asked, not sure of her meaning.

She pulled off her left shoe and shook out the grassy contents. "You know . . . the networking thing. Although sometimes it looks good to tote along a Bible, just to fit in."

"You use churches to network for clients?"

"Almost exclusively."

"Is that, um, legal?" I had a finance degree, and this sounded like the spiritual equivalent of insider trading.

"Who knows. But half the city does it." She paused to empty her other shoe. "You don't have a girlfriend? You look like the type who would have a girlfriend."

"I used to. She sorta dumped me."

"Well, is it 'sorta,' or is it permanent?" She was quite aggressive, the real-estate lady.

I walked over to peer into the mailbox hole. "Feels permanent."

"And she did this recently?"

"By e-mail."

"Sounds like an airhead to me."

After this brief exchange, she leaned against her Saab to check over the contract. She thanked me, tore off my copy, and got into her car. I was inspecting a bent drain spout as she backed out of the driveway. She honked twice, then stopped and stuck her head out the window. "Ya know, Jay, if you really want to meet people, try the Pentecostals. They're very outgoing."

"How so?"

"Quite loud . . . and they stand up a lot."

"I'd prefer to sit."

"Then pick another one. Our churches outnumber the bars by a twenty-to-one margin. You'll figure it out."

So there I sat in my Chevy Blazer on a Sunday morning in May, in the last row of the parking lot of North Hills Presbyterian Church, trying to figure it out, trying to remember the last time I'd set foot inside a church. Four, five years, perhaps?

In retrospect, I suppose it was not the best-laid plan. And one much more common to men than mice.

I checked my hair again. Then my slacks, my jacket, and the buttons on my light blue oxford. *Just blend in, scope the field, and try not to volunteer for anything.*

I stepped out of my truck.

Did I mention I was not wearing a tie?

Bells rang out in two-second intervals as I crossed the parking lot and reached the front steps. Beyond the top step loomed a wooden double door, nine feet high and richly detailed. I pulled it open, and there was a middle-aged man in a midpriced suit standing in the middle of the foyer.

He gave the customary nod and handed me a bulletin.

Down the burgundy carpet sat pews of dark wood, detailed along the sides in the same pattern as the door. I searched for an empty slot. No one looked up. Just five hundred heads staring into bulletins, fascinated, as if Shakespeare himself had penned the announcements.

I took a seat in row twenty-something, next to an old man whose Bible lay open beside him, the pages psychedelic from his marks. Two children scribbled in the next pew, their hands stained by magic markers. Their mother shushed them as a hymn began. The choir sounded rich and reverent, and several sopranos made an impression, although the long green robes prevented me from checking for wedding bands.

Hymn over, the congregation stood to recite a creed, their voices a low monotone, my lips moving in mock conformity. We sat again. The old guy pulled out his checkbook.

Six men in suits worked the aisles, passing and receiving brass plates in the quiet manner of servants. A plate reached me containing a pile of envelopes and a twenty; it left with the contents unaffected.

The two kids turned and smiled. I made a face, and they whirred back around, giggling as their mother gave a firmer shush.

The pastor spoke of being in the world but not of the world, of having eternal thoughts in the midst of the temporary. His sermon was lengthy, definitely not monotone, but left me the same way I'd left the brass plate.

Blessed and dismissed, I shook strange hands, then looked around for a deacon to point me toward the singles class. Kids pulled parents through the pews, parents grabbed markers from the floor, and the elderly – the teeming mass of elderly – paused and dawdled on the burgundy carpet.

Leaving the twenty-fourth pew (I had counted the rows during the sermon), I heard the organist playing a lullaby and wondered if I should've tried the Pentecostals.

I caught the bulletin man midway up the aisle.

"The college class meets in the Sunday school wing," he directed, "just past the junior highs."

"What if I'm a bit older?" I asked. "College was five years ago."

"Ah, the singles," he said. "They meet in the little brick building across the parking lot."

The crowd forced me forward. "Thanks, I'll find it."

My first glance into the building revealed three rows of chairs arranged in semicircles. A thick wooden podium faced the center. A gray-suited man rested one arm on the podium, his back to the chairs, his attention in a book.

I strolled past the empty rows. Muted conversations made their way from around a corner. Morning sunlight angled in through sheer white curtains, and I turned to see a kitchen full of singles. They were having coffee, orange juice, and those white powdered donuts.

The first person to make eye contact with me was a heavyset girl with short red hair, her round face beaming hospitality. She wiped a crumb from her flower-print dress, smiled briefly, and extended a hand. "No ring? Then you're in the right place."

Disarmed by the humor, I returned the greeting. "Jay Jarvis. No hidden rings."

"I'm Lydia," she said, letting go of my hand. "Your first time?"

"Just moved to South Carolina last month."

She gave me a Styrofoam coffee cup and left to greet more visitors. I was filling the cup with decaf when someone tapped my shoulder. And I turned to meet one Stanley Rhone, complete with navy blue suit, sculpted black hair, and a handshake three degrees too firm.

"From where did you move?" he asked. He looked at me cautiously, warily, in the same way toddlers view asparagus. A white hankie sprouted from his coat pocket.

"Dallas," I replied. "My firm transferred me just this – "

The gray-suited podium leaner had called us to attention. Fifty singles began taking their seats in the familiar social pattern of women in front and middle, with males occupying the perimeter. I took a seat at the end of the second row, behind Stanley, and tried to look alert.

A latecomer hurried in and took her seat. "Mr. Rhone will open us," said Gray-suit.

In the act of bowing my head, I deduced that I was a half second behind. I glanced left to check my timing and, across the heads and the silence, our eyes met.

She was likewise in mid-drop, glancing to her right from the far end of the second semicircle. The glare through the curtain backlit the brunette hair resting at her shoulders, but that same glare prevented me from confirming the hint of a smile.

I went with my preferred answer and shut my eyes.

Audible grunts rose from the row behind me. The grunts seemed well coordinated with Stanley's voice inflection, a rising tone producing a louder grunt. I considered turning quietly for a one-eyed peek, but to the best of my knowledge, peekage wasn't allowed.

Stanley finished the prayer, the grunting stopped, and Gray-suit began our lesson from Galatians. Fortunately, there were hardcover Bibles under each chair, and I unstuck some pages to reveal Psalm 139. I figured Galatians was to the east of Psalms, and by the time he finished reading the five verses, I was there.

The word *idolatry* floated through the air, up and around behind the semicircles and past the donuts, bypassed everyone else and landed smartly in my conscience. It stirred around for a moment, clanged between my skull, then disappeared, like the sermon, to that place where all conversation fades.

I glanced again across the room, but she quickly looked away – out the window, at the empty chair in front of her, then down at her sandals, well worn below her yellow sundress. She was one shade darker than the fifty other reverent Caucasians. Definitely American, but without the American condiments. No makeup. No jewelry.

I figured that she, too, might be a visitor. But who knew. Regardless, I wanted to meet her.

More Galatian words hovered over me, dropping now, searching for sin. Gray-suit spoke of fruit, of faith, of goodness and self-control. Heads nodded their agreement, the grunter gave an affirmation, and strictly from peer pressure, I reached in my jacket for a pen.

"Fruit, not *fruits*," said our teacher. "We cannot pick and choose among the attributes of God like the dinner line at a Baptist buffet."

Everyone laughed, but she refused to look my direction. *Please look my direction.*

Closing announcements followed, mentioning a food drive, a visit to see a sick person, and something about a trip to the beach over the long Memorial Day weekend.

I had no plans for the long Memorial Day weekend; maybe she'd be going. Anxious for an introduction, I left my coffee cup on my chair and hurried toward the door.

Too late. The dark-haired girl was already in the parking lot. After a quick and insincere nice-to-meet-ya to Stanley, I peeled off my jacket, flung it over one shoulder, and strolled toward my Blazer.

One row over, her faded red Beetle puttered away.

Tuesday evening while grilling chicken on my deck, I was thinking of brass plates and women, of women and brass plates, and wondered if contributing to that plate would hurry God up as far as meeting the right one. I flipped the chicken over, sprinkled it with lemon pepper, and thought maybe dropping two twenties in the plate would help me meet her this year, or a hundred bucks and we'd meet within a month, or five hundred and the person would arrive in warp speed, like Spock to Captain Kirk.

Smoke was pouring from the grill, my dinner only two minutes from perfection, when the cordless phone rang. The voice on the other end thanked me for visiting North Hills and asked if I had any questions. I was tempted to ask about the girl in the Beetle but stopped myself and muttered something about planning to visit again soon.

"You're in the singles class, then?" asked Mr. Kyle, who mentioned he was both an elder and the membership chairman.

I swatted at a fly with my spatula and said, "Yessir, but I haven't been in one for a while."

"Perhaps you met my daughter, Allie?"

"I don't think so, sir."

"She attends that class," he said. "Whenever she's in town, that is."

I was certain he had some homely daughter with whom he'd try to set me up. I was not interested. "Sir, I'm sure your daughter is a nice girl, but my dinner is on the grill and . . ."

"I understand, Jay. We'll talk more later. But when you do visit us again, please say hello to my Allie. She's easy to recognize — she has dark hair and a year-round tan."

I dropped the spatula on my picnic table. "You say she has dark hair and a nice tan?"

"Yes. She's been working near the equator." My chicken began to blacken. "Elder Kyle, what kind of car does your daughter drive?"

Sisterchicks on the Loose

Robin Jones Gunn

What happens when two unlikely best friends take off on a midlife lark to Finland? A zany adventure, of course! This is a story of Penny and Sharon, two middle-aged women who take the chance of a lifetime to escape from their lives back home for a holiday in Europe.

Sisterchicks on the Loose is loosely based on Robin Jones Gunn's own journey to Finland with a close friend: 'We laughed long, prayed hard and came home changed,' said Robin. 'We also discovered some of the world's best chocolate!'

ISBN 1 5905 2198 6
PB

Price: £9.99
£6.99 Special Offer
Special offer ends 31/08/03

The plane had taken off while Penny and I were in the midst of our discussion. Penny opened her mouth wide and rubbed behind her left ear. I felt compelled to do the same, even though my ears weren't popping.

Penny continued to talk about the love notes she had worked on all night. She described how surprised she felt over her last-minute reluctance to leave her family. "I didn't expect to feel this way. And you know what, Sharon? I have to apologize for a couple of things. First, I want to apologize for being so cold when you were going through the trauma with Ben. I didn't understand. I think I do now. Sorry I wasn't more sympathetic."

"It's okay. I needed to hear what you said. You were right. I'm glad I didn't back out of the trip."

"Really?" Penny's left eyebrow went up.

"Yes, really. Why do you ask? What's the surprise?"

"Is my eyebrow up?"

"Yes."

"Rats! I'm going to have to work on that. I do have another little surprise, and I think you're going to need to read all my facial quirks when I tell you this."

I looked hard at her. I'd forgotten how intense Penny's gaze could be. She had a way of seeing into people as if she were shining a light so the person could search for something lost along the way. I don't know why I let her do that to me. I could turn away and listen sufficiently without looking. But I didn't. I allowed her dark eyes to shine their amber-flecked light on me because Penny knew things. She saw things way before I did. Right now she was looking for something. Apparently I had it.

"This is the other thing I was going to apologize to you about. We don't exactly have everything lined up in Finland. Which I think is fine because all our options are open. But I didn't want you to feel…," Penny searched for the right word, "…uncomfortable."

"That's okay. What needs to be worked on? I have the tour book. We could do some planning now."

"Yes," Penny said slowly.

"What about your aunt? Did she give you any specifics in her letter about things to do?"

Penny's finger went up to her lips. "No. You see, I never heard back from my aunt. And before you say anything, Sharon, it's not that big a deal. We have plenty of money. We can stay at any hotel we want the whole time, if we need to. I wasn't necessarily planning to stay at my aunt's house. I just wanted to meet her. But I don't even know if she's still alive. It's not that important, though. We can try to track her down once we arrive. But if we don't find her, we'll just have fun exploring."

I didn't say anything right away. I'm certain both my eyebrows were down. Penny was watching me carefully.

"So, you're telling me that we got on this plane and we're flying halfway across the world, but when we arrive, we don't have any idea what we'll do."

"Yes and no. We'll take a taxi and find a hotel. Or rent a car. And we'll find a restaurant and have some dinner. Or lunch, or whatever mealtime it will be then. And," she added on an upbeat note, "we'll pray and see what God puts in our path."

I wanted to scold her. I wanted to say, "Penny, people like us don't just show up in big foreign cities in the middle of winter and start looking up names of reputable hotels in a phone book!"

Before I could speak, Penny said, "I know I should have said something earlier, but I kept thinking I'd hear from my aunt at the last minute. I brought all the information I have about her with me. We'll take each step, each day as it comes. Like I said, we've got plenty of money." Penny's eyes were ablaze with dancing sprinkles of hope.

"Whatever happens, I know it will be an adventure."

I reminded myself that "adventure" had been Penny's objective all along, even in the church nursery so long ago. And I had told Jeff I didn't want old age to be the only risky trip I ever took. This was it.

Risky. Adventuresome. Ridiculous.

At this moment, the appropriate adjective didn't matter because when a person is thirty thousand feet in the air, seat belted in business class, she is, for all practical purposes, committed. Two months ago I never would have dreamed up any of this. Two days ago I was still trying to work up the courage to board that plane in Portland by myself. Two minutes ago, however, Penny's left eyebrow went up, and secretly I wanted it to. I wanted Penny to surprise me and make me uncomfortable.

"What do you say, Sharon?" Penny looked at me hard. "Are you okay with this? I know you like life to be organized, but the thing is, now we'll be completely at God's mercy, and nothing is more adventuresome than that!"

With a deep breath, I gave my dearest friend the gift she had always so freely given me, the gift she was looking for when she looked so deeply into my eyes. I gave her grace. "Sure. I'm fine with this. We'll figure it out as we go along."

"Perfect! I was hoping you wouldn't be mad. This is going to be great; you'll see. We're going to have the kind of trip they never write about in the tour books."

My better sense told me I should mention people had good reasons for not abandoning themselves haphazardly to God's mercy, and such erratic trips weren't written about in the tour books for good reasons. But I pressed my lips together and enjoyed the sensation of once again being in the wake of the fabulous, fearless, flying Penny.

****

Penny and I went through the tour book, circling potential hotels and finding a phone number for a taxi company. Until we arrived, we couldn't do much more.

I bent down to put away the tour book, and something extraordinary happened. The clouds, which had cushioned our flight for the past few hours, cleared, and a burst of sunshine spilled in through the window. I turned to lower the window shade and found myself staring *down* on snow-covered mountains. They looked like a row of little girls dressed for their first Holy Communion. They seemed to be waiting for their cue to begin the processional march. I'd never seen anything so pure and majestic.

"Penny, look."

She leaned over. "I wonder if those are the Canadian Rockies. Or would we be past them by now? We're traveling north, aren't we? Into the sun. Our winter day will be short. Canada is so beautiful."

Penny flitted through a recounting of a story I'd heard many times. I guessed it to be one of her favorite memories since she told it often. Two summers before we met, Penny and Dave rode his Harley from California to Banff, Canada. They lived on moose jerky. She wore the same pair of jeans every day for seven weeks and only had two pairs of undies.

One night, when Penny and Dave were sleeping under the stars, a bear ambled within twenty feet of them. The bear licked the gas tank on their motorcycle and then lumbered into the forest.

I listened with my gaze fixed on the magnificent world beneath my window. The world I was watching couldn't possibly contain lumbering bears or hippies on motorcycles. From my viewpoint, the world below was perfect in every way.

The waning sun was already behind us, low in the west. We rapidly headed into the night. Layers of thick, ethereal clouds formed a puffy, pink-tinted comforter beneath us as our 747 rose above it all.

I watched the night come. Or perhaps I was watching us race into the night. Every so often a bundle of clouds would open, and far below I could spot tiny gatherings of light, evidence of life.

Then I saw it. The moon. Round and unblinking, that mysterious silver orb seemed to race toward us, riding an invisible, celestial current. I watched the moon peek in the window at me. I imagined

I could feel its cool, steady light, more fierce and determined than the glow of any night-light. The plane banked slightly to the right. I turned my head to keep an eye on the moon. I watched and watched and then suddenly, in a blink, it was behind us.

I silently recited Ben's favorite nursery rhyme, *Hey, diddle diddle, the cat and the fiddle, the cow jumped over the moon; the little dog laughed to see such sport, and the dish ran away with the spoon.*

I looked out the window again and was certain that the moon now was under us. Turning to Penny with what I'm sure was a look of dumbfounded marvel, I said, "Guess what? We just jumped over the moon!"

Penny laughed. "Like the cow?"

"Yes, like the cow. We jumped over the moon!"

The flight attendant reached to clear my tray, and Penny busted up. "Well, don't look now, but your dish is about to run away with your spoon!"

Our little jokes weren't that funny, but we were so tired they seemed hilarious. We laughed hard, but then I had to excuse myself and stand in line for the rest room. I shifted from right foot to left and looked around at the immense variety of travelers. Did any of them realize we were on the other side of the moon? None of the faces I scanned seemed amazed. I would have to be amazed for all of us. Amazed and delighted and a little bit nervous about being at God's mercy, as Penny called it.

Several hours later...

All my private little dreams scattered when the pilot announced our plane couldn't land in Helsinki due to icy high winds. We circled for almost an hour before an announcement came that we would land at a different airport.

"This can't be good," Penny muttered under her breath.

I reached for the guidebook and found a map. "Do you suppose we're going to Stockholm? It looks pretty far away."

Penny studied the map. "Russia looks closer, doesn't it? They wouldn't fly us into Russia, would they?" It had only been a short year or two since the breakup of the former Soviet Union, and Russia wasn't a travel destination for the average American.

Our landing was rough. The plane came down with a thud on the tires and then bounced up again for three seconds before reconnecting with the runway. Inside our cramped quarters, the passengers responded with a group gasp.

Outside, the sleet came toward us at an angle. As the plane rolled forward, I could barely make out the small terminal's outline.

From all around us came the click of seat belts being unfastened.

The flight attendant spoke over the intercom in three languages. English was the last. By the way people around us were groaning while the message was delivered in the first two languages, we surmised the news wasn't good.

"We ask that you remain in your seats," the voice finally said in English. "We will not be deplaning at this airport. The latest weather reports predict a clearing in the storm. Our pilot has requested clearance to return to Helsinki."

I stared quietly at my hands. The large hook-shaped scar on the back of my right hand looked larger than usual. It had turned a pale, oyster gray color.

I got the scar when I was fifteen and fell against the side of a tractor at my summer job, picking raspberries at Gelson's farm. It took twenty-five minutes to reach the hospital, and I gushed blood all over the front seat of Mrs. Gelson's new powder blue Ford station wagon, even though I was holding the dish towel and pressing hard like she told me to.

Sitting on this icy runway felt a lot like sitting next to Mrs. Gelson in the emergency room. Whatever happened next couldn't possibly be pleasant.

We sat on the runway of the small mystery airport for more than an hour. The flight attendants came by offering coffee.

"Is it okay if we use the rest room?" Penny asked.

"Of course. Please return to your seat, though, as soon as possible.

We expect to receive clearance for takeoff soon."

I decided I better go to the rest room with Penny while I had the chance. The gentleman on the aisle stood silently to let us out. All the stalls were occupied. Penny and I stretched without speaking to each other or making eye contact.

"Penny." I touched her shoulder. "When we return to our seats, why don't you take the window seat? I know you said you don't like the window because it gets so cold, but you're welcome to use my coat as a buffer."

Her expression softened. "Are you sure that's okay?"

"Sure, I wouldn't mind. You need a few more inches of breathing space."

"Thanks, Sharon."

The bathroom stall door opened, and I motioned to Penny. "After you."

"Thanks. I owe you one."

That was a crazy thing for Penny to say. She didn't owe me anything. I was the one who was in debt to her for this whole trip.

I tried to lean against the wall to let a young blond woman with a crying baby join me in the crowded space. "He's not very happy, is he?" I asked.

She answered in a language I didn't understand, but when she slid the knuckle of her first finger into his mouth, I asked, "Teething?"

She gave me a weary look and said, *"Ja,"* before shifting the sobbing baby to her other hip. We were communicating in the universal language of all mothers: baby sympathy. My heart went out to her.

I reached over and gently stroked his damp cheek. "It's okay," I said softly. "It's okay." The tyke turned his round moist eyes toward me and stopped crying.

"That's better. You want me to hold you for a little bit so your mommy can have a break?"

I opening my hands, and the mommy gladly let her chunky bundle climb into my arms.

"How old is he?"

The mother shook her head. She didn't understand my question.

"Is he about nine months old?" I shifted the curious fellow to my left hip and held up my fingers as if I were counting.

"Ah! *Ja, nio.*" She held up nine fingers.

"That's what I thought. My first two boys were solid like this, too." I patted his back, and he released a tiny burp.

Penny stepped out of the stall. She looked surprised. "How did you manage to accumulate a baby in the last three minutes?"

"He likes me," I told Penny. "He stopped crying."

The mom spoke again and motioned toward the available toilet stall.

"You go ahead," I said confidently, as if I understood every word she had said. "I'll hold him for you."

Penny stood next to me, staring for a moment. "I'm going back to our seats."

"I'll be – " My response was cut short by a raging wail from baby boy.

Penny gave me a "he's all yours" look and left quickly.

I jostled the little one, touching his cheek and trying to comfort him by saying, "It's okay. Your mommy will be back in a minute."

He tucked his chin and leaned into my shoulder. I patted his back. "There, there. It's okay."

With a stifled sob, his head came straight up, knocking me hard on the chin and causing me to bite my tongue. Then, without warning, the little prince reared back and spewed partially digested airline pretzels and sour milk all down the front of me.

The stall door opened. I held out the baby and motioned with my head so his mom would see the disaster. With profuse apologies in whatever language she spoke, she took her son into the stall and closed the door, and there I stood, aware that a trail of baby barf had found its way under my shirt and was pooling in my bra.

Somehow, when your child throws up on you, it's never as bad as when it's someone else's child.

The second stall door opened, and I rushed in, locked the door, and thought I might be sick from the overpowering smells in the small space. First I tried paper towels to clean up and flushed them before realizing I might clog the whole system. Oh, what a sorry sight I was, trying the dabbing method on my shirt but only making matters worse. I wet more paper towels and then gave up and stripped to the waist.

I had just wrung out my bra when a bright red light flashed. I stared at the light and then looked at my reflection in the mirror.

"What are you doing here?" I asked the woman who was standing topless in front of me in this suffocating, sour bathroom stall, trapped on the runway of some undisclosed airport, which was possibly inside the border of the former Soviet Union, in the middle of an ice storm.

The absurd looking woman in the mirror didn't answer. However, an invisible flight attendant did. In three languages, no less. "Please return to your seat," the voice said over the intercom.

"I would love to return to my seat," I answered politely. "But Houston, we have a problem here."

No one could hear me, of course, but my banter helped me to stay focused. "My shirt is ruined," I went on. "My bra is soaking wet. Can you smell me? I can smell me. If I can smell me, then Penny…well, Penny is…"

I tried to dry my bra by pressing it between two paper towels.

Someone knocked on the bathroom stall door.

"Yes! I'll be out in just a minute."

"You must return to your seat," the heartless voice said.

"Okay. I'm coming right now."

I still can't believe I did this, but I had no choice. I put on my wet bra and slipped the rancid, damp shirt over my head. Unlocking the door, I made my way back to the center seat with my head down, certain that every eye in that part of the plane was fixed on me. Every nose was probably fixed on me as well.

Poor Penny! The look on her face! She turned away from me, staring out the window as I gave an abbreviated explanation.

I swallowed hard and tried to take tiny breaths. My tongue had swollen from when I bit it right before Junior was sick all over me. I could feel a cold, wet stream zigzagging across my middle and soaking the waistband of my jeans.

The man in the seat directly in front of me stretched to glare at me over the top of his seat.

"I know," I murmured in a tiny voice. "I'm sorry. This isn't exactly pleasant for me either."

Our takeoff was terrifying. The plane seemed to be flapping oversize, weary wings as we rose into the air. We bucked a dozen air pockets, rising and falling like a ship at sea.

Penny grabbed for the bag in her seat pocket and held it up to her mouth and nose. She didn't get sick, but I'm sure she felt she was about to.

We landed in Helsinki at 7:20 P.M. Without a word, Penny and I walked into the terminal and went directly to the rest room.

"Here." Penny wheeled her suitcase into the first open stall before I could grab some wet paper towels. "Anything you want to wear is yours."

I found a new sympathy for my daughter. *So this is how Kaylee felt when I told her she could wear one of my blouses to the school choir performance.*

Penny's underwear was large on me. Not too large. Just loose and funny feeling. The bra and panties were, however, silky black and a far superior quality to anything I ever owned.

The larger size of her clothes didn't matter because I opted for a baggy pair of sweatpants and a yellow sweater that were easy to pull out of the suitcase.

With my soiled clothes in a wad, I exited the stall to see a line of women waiting. Penny stood near the sinks. "You are going to throw those away, aren't you?"

I hadn't planned on it. I was going to ask if she had a plastic bag. Surely they sold good strong laundry detergent in Finland. I could soak these clothes back to life, if I had the right laundry soap.

Penny moved closer when she saw me stalling. "If I'm right," she said in a low voice, "your bra is at least eight years old, and it's about half an inch from self-disintegrating."

Penny knew all too well the areas in my budget where I'd scrimped over the years to keep four growing children clothed.

"And if I'm guessing correctly, that shirt found its way into your life in the mideighties. Its shelf life has expired, Sharon. You need to set the poor thing free."

Part of me was glad that Penny felt well enough to be flippant. That was a good sign. But I wasn't too happy about her painfully accurate comments about my wardrobe.

"I'm not trying to be mean," Penny said quickly. "Look, you said you packed plenty of clothes. And I packed way more than I need. We should be fine with what we have until your luggage arrives. If not, we'll go shopping and buy new clothes. Now wouldn't that be tragic?"

I opened the top of the trash bin, and against all my frugal instincts, I threw away a perfectly usable set of clothes.

"Didn't that feel good?" Penny said.

"No. Nothing feels good at the moment." I pushed up the sleeves of the baggy yellow sweater and went to work washing my hands and forearms. My sticky chest and stomach would have to wait. We had an audience in line, and I wanted to get out of there as soon as possible.

"Thanks for letting me borrow your clothes," I said as Penny and I followed the signs to baggage claim. The directions were in three languages, with English the last listed. I noticed how quiet the airport was.

"Of course, you're welcome to borrow anything you want." Penny's voice seemed unusually loud as she turned toward me. "I hate to tell you this, but I can still smell you."

"I know. I need to wash up some more."

"Why didn't you do it back in the rest room?"

"All those women were watching me," I said, lowering my voice.

Penny laughed. "But just think! You could have started your career as an international underwear model."

"Not in your black silkies," I muttered.

"What?" Penny's voice still seemed loud.

I shook my head and mouthed the words, "Never mind." In a whisper I added, "It's so quiet here."

Penny listened a moment. "It is."

We looked around at the people as we walked past the boarding areas. Some were looking back at us. Some were reading. Some were sipping coffee from white ceramic cups at small round tables. No loud announcements were being made. No elevator music filled the air like audio Novocain. We had landed in a somber place.

"This is spooky," Penny muttered. "I'm so used to background noise."

"I think it's serene," I whispered.

My voice must have been too low for her to understand my comment because Penny replied, "I know. It is a scream, isn't it?" She laughed. The sound echoed in the large terminal. Penny covered her mouth with her free hand, and we proceeded to baggage claim.

We didn't realize that we would have to go through customs again. This time they motioned for the two of us to step up to the window together, probably because we seemed to be traveling together.

The officer opened Penny's passport first. He looked up at her and carefully pronounced, "Penny Lane?"

Penny smiled and said flippantly, "Yes, yes, I know. I'm in your eyes and in your ears and under blue suburban skies and all that. Yes, that's my real name."

He didn't blink.

Penny smiled more broadly at the officer. "Aren't you going to start singing to me?"

Silence.

"The Beatles, you know? Penny Lane? Or did the Beatles never make it over here to Helsinki?"

I cringed.

The officer repeated, "Penny Lane?"

"Yes, that's my name. It's my real name. I am Penny Lane."

"Thank you."

"You're welcome."

"Visit to Finland for business or leisure?"

"Leisure."

"Length of stay?"

"About a week and a half."

Without changing his expression, the man stamped her passport and reached for mine.

"Sharon Andrews?"

"Yes."

Unshaken by Penny's vibrant monologue, the officer asked me the same string of questions.

Blessedly, we both made it through customs and arrived at baggage claim. However, my suitcase didn't fare as well.

My luggage didn't make it to Helsinki.

The Shadow At Evening

Chris Walley

In a universe where peace has reigned for thousands of years, a dark spectre is creeping slowly into view. Although the people can barely believe their eyes, it soon becomes obvious that evil has returned to paradise – and it will have to be fought.

The Shadow At Evening is the first part of an epic fantasy in the tradition of J.R.R. Tolkien. The worlds of science, technology and the supernatural are skilfully woven into a novel that will grip all fans of the fantasy genre.

ISBN 1 8602 4269 3
PB

Price: £6.99
£4.99 Special Offer
Special offer ends 31/08/03

Chapter 6

One morning some three months later, Merral looked up from his work on the map of the proposed northern extension of the Great Northern Forest and gazed out of his office window. The view looked eastwards over the waters of Ynysmere Lake and Merral had positioned his desk so that whenever he glanced up he saw the water and the rolling hills beyond. In winter, it encouraged him to come in early and catch the sunrise. But today the only view he had was one of a buffeting dull grey wetness in which it was hard to distinguish between the spray of the breaking waves, the blowing rain and the cloud above.

Wondering at the weather, Merral shook his head. Winter had dragged on this year and spring was more a fickle, fleeting guest than a permanent resident. Dry sunny weather would come, and for a few days spirits would lift, windows would be opened and jackets be left at home. Then abruptly, out of the

north would come a bitter whistling wind, or cold, soaking rains would blow in from the ocean far away to the east, and winter would be back. He consoled himself with the certainty that spring and summer would come in the end. Besides, he thought with a certain amusement, if the tropics posting – now almost certain – did come through, then he would doubtless miss the long wet winters of north-eastern Menaya.

He bent down to the map again but as he did so, the diary adjunct link on his watch pulsed gently three times. He glanced at his diary lying on the desk and saw that the screen confirmed an urgent and private call. He tabbed an acknowledgement back, got up and closed the door, trying to remember when he had last had such a message. He sat down and rotated the diary so its lens could image him and ordered it to open the link.

The image that flashed onto the tiny screen was that of Barrand and Zennia. They were sitting at the desk in his uncle's cluttered narrow office. The moment he saw them Merral knew something was wrong. Zennia was plainly agitated, her face pale and taut, her eyes constantly flicking towards her husband while she clasped and unclasped her slender hands together. Barrand, by contrast, was sitting still, but his hands were tightly folded together and his stern face had a determined look.

'Greetings, Uncle Barrand, Aunt Zennia.'

'Greetings to you Merral. Thank you for your prompt response.' Merral found a strange stiffness and formality in his uncle's voice. There was a weak, strained, smile from his aunt.

'Ah Merral. Thank you,' Barrand continued. 'I'll come straight to the point. We have a problem here. It's very odd. We need some advice.'

'I'm ready to help all I can. Tell me all about it.'

Barrand looked briefly at his wife, as if for encouragement, and then turned back to the screen.

'It's Elana. The day before yesterday, you remember? It was dry. At least with us. The first such day for a week. What a winter, eh? Anyway, she went out into the woods above Herrandown. Just north-west of us. There she says she saw something.' He paused, clenching his hands tight and glancing

at Zennia. 'Now she describes it as like a small man, only brown and shiny like a beetle. It scared her badly –'

'She's still scared,' Zennia said, cutting across him.

Merral felt his mouth open and snapped it shut, 'Sorry, Uncle, try it again. She saw *what*?'

'Something like "a small man, only brown and shiny like a beetle".'

Zennia nodded. Merral tried to visualise what she had described but failed. 'I mean – an obvious point – this isn't some sort of well . . . *story*?'

Barrand shrugged but Zennia shook her head strongly and turned to the screen. 'Merral, I *know* my daughter. And if she did make up a story, she scared herself silly doing it. And us. She came running in screaming. She won't go outside alone and she is sleeping next to our room.'

They looked at each other. I have, Merral realised, a potentially serious problem up in Herrandown. Maybe it was already past the potential stage. Usually able to say something in any situation, Merral suddenly found himself floundering. 'Look . . . ' he said, 'how big did she say this creature was?'

Zennia spoke, 'She said it was about her height.'

Merral realised he was staring blankly at the screen. 'Baffling, quite baffling,' he responded and realised it sounded banal; but what else could he say?

He paused for a moment. 'Well, you both know the problem, I'm sure. We have an inventory of every species on the planet; we may not know numbers exactly but we know what we have. And all the brown, shiny, beetle-like things we have are small enough that you can hold them in your hand. In fact,

anywhere in the Assembly to our knowledge. At least to mine.'

Barrand shrugged and threw his arms open in bemusement. 'Merral, I know. But she's convinced she saw something.'

Zennia nodded in affirmation. 'And I think she did.'

'Aunt, how is Elana otherwise?'

'Physically fine, the nurse can find nothing wrong. There's no evidence of hallucinatory activity; it's not associated with a fever. Blood tests, neural activity: all read normal.'

Merral found himself admitting defeat. 'Uncle, Aunt, I have to say I'm baffled. Absolutely. She just saw it and she ran away?'

Barrand gestured to his wife to speak.

'No, it was staring at her from behind a bush, she says. It realised it had been observed and ran away.'

Merral was silent. He threw up a quick request to heaven for wisdom and tried to run through the various options. He had to have more time.

'And what do you two think?'

Barrand shifted on his seat. 'I don't know. . . . I suppose it must be nonsense, a dream or something. . . . I went to have a look but I could see no sign of it. I haven't searched the area thoroughly. But –'

Zennia nudged him into silence and she spoke. 'Elana saw *something* Merral. And we think there's more to it than that.'

Technically, Merral told himself, the guidelines were such that in the rare event of a psychological problem with a colony a forester would call in specialist help. In his case, Ghina Macreedy. Of course, if it was something in his forests that had caused it then that was a different matter. But this was a curious affair and they were family. Perhaps too, if it could be dealt with quickly, then a deeper crisis could be avoided.

Barrand was stroking his beard restlessly. 'Yes, I'm afraid Merral there is something odd here. Or there may be. . . . The animals are agitated, especially the dogs. Particularly since we lost Spotback.'

'Spotback! I never knew you'd lost him. He was a good dog. How did that happen?'

'A good question. We saw him one morning about five days ago heading northwards from the farm. Then he just vanished.'

Suddenly, Merral knew that, at least, his aunt and possibly his uncle had worked themselves into a highly concerned state. And recognising that, Merral knew what he had to do.

'The other families?'

His aunt shook her head. 'Elana is the only one that's seen it. The others feel the same as we do. You can call them.'

'Perhaps, I'll see.'

There was one last question he wanted to ask. 'Now, Thomas.

Chris Walley125

What does he think?'

Barrand's face looked pained. 'Our son Thomas is, I'm sorry to say, acting scared. He will only play outside the front of the house. And he comes inside well before dusk.'

So he's affected as well, Merral thought. That settled it.

'Look, I think I'm going to come up and see you. I'll see if I can't get one of our fast Recon vehicles and be with you tomorrow. Just for a day. Talk to Elana; take a look around.'

Zennia's green-brown eyes showed gratitude. 'Oh thank you, Merral! We'd feel better for that. See if you can make sense of it. You think it's a good idea, Barrand?'

There was a pause 'Ho! Why not? Better our Merral than a host of people we don't know. We might be able to solve it.

Yes, come up. As soon as possible.'

Then, with abbreviated family news, they closed the conversation.

After the call Merral did nothing immediately but sat at his chair staring at the rain and waves thinking through what he had heard and seeking guidance. He found himself very disturbed by the Antalfer's state. Forward Colony families were always personally selected for their ability to handle remote small communities and few facilities. For them to be so uneasy was extremely odd. The whole thing defied analysis. Elana couldn't have seen what she claimed to have seen; yet something had shaken her up badly. And not just her: if Zennia was correct the whole community seemed to have slipped into a similar state. To be so close to that sort of irrational fear was extraordinary. Fear was something associated with illness and even then it was rare. But here a whole community was affected.

Merral decided that the mostly likely cause was that Elana, perhaps helped by her active imagination, had had some sort of waking dream or hallucination.

But, whatever its cause, the event had generated some sort of real collective anxiety. And that needed a rapid resolution. Not only were the Antalfers his own family, they were also a

good team with a lot of experience. If they had to be rotated out, they would be hard to replace.

After ten minutes, Merral got up and walked down the corridor to where his director was working and put his head around the door. Henri was in his thinking pose. He was reclining back in his chair, with his lean arms behind his head and his feet up on the desk, staring at the giant map of northeastern

Menaya that occupied most of the opposite wall. At the sight of Merral he swung his legs down and gestured him in with a wave of an arm and a genial smile. 'Merral! Come in, man. Take a seat.' Ten years in Ynysmant hadn't blunted Henri's distinctive Tablelands intonation.

Closing the door behind him, Merral took the proffered seat. 'I hope I'm not disturbing any deep thoughts?'

Henri stroked his carefully trimmed brown beard and stared at him with his close-spaced deep-set dark eyes. 'Thoughts? Yes, I'll say so. We have just lost a hexapod; got washed away at the Grandell Cleft. It's how to recover what's left of it. And the weather this winter. . . . *Ach!*' He frowned. 'When I started here they were worried about polar ice sheets shrinking; now they are expanding too fast. This planet is like an unbroken horse; it runs this way today and tomorrow that. But this winter — it's been so long — means there is the danger of us all being way behind schedule. Summers are short enough in our northernmost zones. I'm thinking of ways of saving time when the weather does improve. My other issue is how to replace you. Assuming you go. You'll be missed, man. Really missed.'

'Sorry. I'll miss here.'

'*Ach,*' he smiled, 'not with this weather. . . . Anyway, what can I do for you?'

'We have a problem at Herrandown.' As Merral paused, trying to work out how to tell the story, Henri clucked sympathetically. 'Man, that's bad news. I've got your quarry team ready to go to the ridge. But tell me about it.'

Very carefully, Merral spelt out the substance of his call that morning while Henri listened attentively and without comment. 'So you see Henri,' Merral ended, 'I'd like to go up and check it out personally. I think that way we can best reduce the strain on the family.'

There was a nod of affirmation. 'I can see that. If you can fix it.' He looked across at the wall-high image of Mount Katafana as if searching its icy slopes for inspiration. 'Yes. Ghina is out south; otherwise I'd suggest you took her. You really ought to go with someone with some psychological background. I mean that's what you think it is I take it? *Psychology*?'

'There doesn't seem much other option does there?'

His director thought briefly. 'No,' he asserted, shaking his head. Then Henri looked at the image again and Merral remembered how he was planning to climb Mount Katafana this year.

'No man, I'm at a loss to think of any other explanation.' He gave his beard a further stroke and stared at Merral. 'You've got much experience in talking to troubled fourteen-year-old girls?'

'Not really. Although I know the girl at the centre of the problem.' Then an idea struck him 'Mind you, I know someone who has experience.'

A look of gentle amusement came onto Henri's face. 'Ah yes. I should have thought of her. Yes see if you can get Isabella Danol to go with you. Get a Recon vehicle booked now. Check they've still got the winter tyres. Normally, by now we'd be starting to grapple with dust, not mud. But not this year. Oh no.'

'Thanks, Henri. Thanks a great deal.'

Merral turned to go. As he did, Henri spoke again in a low voice. 'One last thing, man – if it turns out to be serious then just ask for help. The Antalfers deserve our best efforts.'

★ ★ ★

Back in his office, Merral had an idea. He pulled off his diary and asked it to call 'Anya Salema Lewitz, location unknown'. Moments later the response came from the Planetary Ecology Centre in Isterrane where a man who identified himself as Anya's assistant answered. He apologised that she was in a conference but expressed the confident opinion that she would call him back as soon as she was free.

Merral had better fortune with Isabella, who was in her office. There were the usual pleasantries and then he came down to the reason for his call.

'Isabella, I have had a problem this morning that you may be able to help me with. It's right in your age group. The Antalfers, you remember them?'

She nodded, her thin face thoughtful. 'Of course. Barrand and Zennia out at Herrandown. She is your mother's younger sister.'

'But very different, my mother wouldn't last a week in Herrandown. Zennia's much more placid. Or she was. Anyway, their oldest girl – Elana – has had a disturbing experience. Two days ago she claims to have seen a creature her size in the wood, brown and shiny, hard skinned like an insect.'

Isabella said nothing for what seemed a long time. In fact, Merral thought that if it hadn't been for the slight frown on her face he would have assumed that she hadn't heard. When she did speak, she spoke very softly. 'Poor thing. Is she all right?'

That's Isabella, Merral thought, caution and concern. Everybody else, me included, leaps in and says the thing can't exist. She thinks of the girl first.

'Pretty unhappy apparently.'

'So I should imagine. Hmm. How old is she?'

'Just fourteen. Becoming a young lady.'

'I see. And this thing was *her* size?'

'So she claimed. Of course, as you know, there is nothing like that. What do you think?'

Isabella put her head on one side for a moment and looked back at him for some time before answering. 'Sorry Merral, I can't judge on that. It's odd and there isn't enough data, I'm afraid. I mean, I'd have to be sure that such a thing was ruled out. It has to be an illusion? I mean it's not an escape of something is it?'

'No. There are no such things. In – or out – of captivity.'

She nodded. 'Thought so. Well. . . .' She paused, leaning back as if trying to get the best position to think in. 'You would have to know her up-to-date psychological profile. And a lot of other things.'

'Such as?'

'Physical health, recent diet, allergies, mental state, etc. It's fairly common for temporary and mild psychological perturbations to occur in puberty. But seeing things is a bit odd. I think there would have to be something else. Hmm. . . .' She lapsed into silence.

That is what she would say, Merral thought; she wouldn't be so highly rated if she had made an instant diagnosis in a case like this. But then who could?

'Look Isabella, I'm going early tomorrow for the day to see them and to try and sort out what's happening. Henri has okayed a fast Recon vehicle. Can you come up with me? We'd be back early evening at the latest.'

There was a moment's pause and then the faintest hint of a smile. 'Yes, if I work this evening. I'd like that, Merral. It sounds like you might need some help.'

'All right. Meet me at the end of your street at half six tomorrow.'

★ ★ ★

Anya Lewitz called back just before lunch, her broad, freckled face and sky blue eyes grinning at him from the screen of the diary before he'd even said a word. With her lively manner, flaming red hair and perpetual dynamism, Merral had always thought her pretty in an unsubtle, rather obvious way. The

image he saw offered nothing to change that view.

'*Merral D'Avanos*! Where have you been? Still up to your waist in bogs planting trees, eh? Growing roots? It's been so long since we met up. When was it?' The voice was as bright and cheery as ever.

'The last round of planning for Northern Menaya; you were talking about the problems with the introduction of mammals from different Terran continents into a world with a single supercontinent.' He remembered that she had had her red hair shorter then.

'Ah yes, the old purity versus practicality debate. Do you have either American or Eurasian faunas or do you do what we've done here and just mix them up and see what does best? Yes, I remember it. I'm now on reconstruction work actually.'

'Reconstruction? I sometimes think that I'd like to be involved in that. Restoring species and environments that humanity destroyed in the past. That's valuable.'

'Oh nonsense!' She snorted. 'So is planting trees, Merral. Bringing back the dodo is neat but you can't breathe dodos. In fact, I'm told they are rather ugly and stupid.'

'True, trees play a pretty important role in the great scheme of things. Anyway I enjoy my work so I'm thankful.'

'That's good.'

There was a slight pause.

'Anyway Anya, the reason I'm calling you is that I have an odd situation.' He hesitated again, feeling strangely certain of how his question would be received. 'See, I have a girl here on the edge of the Great Northern Forest who claims to have seen something strange. She says she saw a creature like a small man, brown, with a shiny hard skin like a beetle. Is this a case for zoology or psychiatry?'

'The latter I'm afraid. No question.' The response was immediate and Anya's smile radiated confidence.

'No other possibilities? I mean Farholme was, of course, dead when it was seeded?'

The red hair bobbed as she shook her head emphatically. 'The last bacteria here died out a thousand million years ago; about average for this sort of world. And there is no evidence that anything beyond the usual simple forms developed. And everything was sterile here long before the *Leviathan-D* arrived.'

'As I thought. And our existing beetles?'

'The biggest beetles on Farholme could fit in the palm of your hand. On the tropical islands.' She sighed. 'I'm afraid you are talking psychiatrist. P, S, Y, C, H, and the rest. Sorry.'

'Well, it's what I concluded too. They are my forests. But, as a matter of interest, what would you need to be convinced otherwise?'

She looked surprised. 'I'd need a specimen, dead or alive. You've got a full description; skin or cuticle samples? Still or video images?

Even a drawing?'

'Not at the moment. You have all the data I have. I hope to interview her tomorrow. Oh, the thing ran off when she saw it.'

The blue eyes flashed with amused exasperation. 'Oh you tree experts! Learn to describe movement! Try to improve on that "ran off" line. Did it lope, bound, slink or scuttle? And *please* on how many legs? From the description it could be two, four, six or eight.'

'Okay. Thanks for the tip Anya. I'll remember that. But I suppose it is a hallucination? You've not reconstructed Cretaceous beetles?'

She smiled and tossed her head. 'I'm sorry, especially for the girl. No, the Reconstruction Mandate has strict limits. You know them but I'll remind you. It has to be a species made extinct by man, so we are still arguing over whether or not we reconstruct the mammoth. I'm voting yes, incidentally. But I'm

afraid your guess is right. I can state categorically that it is an illusion. For a start, physics gives a finite size to insects because of their breathing mechanism. If you doubled our oxygen levels you might get them a *bit* larger, but a metre plus high? No hope! And they never look human unless . . . ' She moved closer to the screen as if trying to peer down below Merral's waist. 'Say, how many legs do you have up there in Ynysmant?'

Merral laughed. 'You haven't changed Anya. I have just the usual.'

'Sorry, it sounds like a waking nightmare. Talk to the psychology crowd. But if there is any hard data, and I mean *hard*, Tree Man, let me know and I'll get the lab ready. And I'll lay in a ton of triple-strength cockroach killer. Incidentally, what's this I hear about you and the tropics?'

So it's news in Isterrane too, Merral thought.

'True Anya, it's being worked on. Almost certainly I'm being posted to Faraketha at the end of summer. Do you know it?'

'Hot, hot and hot. And that's the cool season: you'll sweat off a few kilos in days. Actually, I've only flown over it. It's very poor quality at the moment, mostly very low diversity jungle. I'm no expert but I think you ought to use a vortex blaster on it and start over again from scratch.'

'I've heard it's an option. But I need to take a look.'

'Actually in fact I'm going to be working with the Madagascar Project on Terelka. That's only five hundred kilometers south. But milder.'

'You are going to be on that? I'm impressed, that's a grand vision.'

Anya raised her hands in excitement. 'Maybe too big. It's still in the design stage. But here, we think we can risk the ecological purity approach. Specific reconstruction of a whole long-gone subcontinental ecosystem. Lemurs, small mammals, birds, reptiles, vegetation, the lot. It will take a

millennium before we know if we have achieved a viable recreation.' She suddenly became conscious of her enthusiasm and laughed sheepishly. 'Sorry, Merral, I get excited.'

'That's how it should be! Well I'd better get on with my work. I'll hope to catch up with you soon, Anya. But thanks for the opinion. It confirms what I think.'

She shrugged. 'Apologies about that. Giant anthropoid beetles would be interesting but I think we'd know if they existed. Blessings, Merral.'

'Blessings, Anya.' The image faded away.

★ ★ ★

Like Isabella, Merral could only make time for a trip north by working extra hours, so he brought his lunch back to his office and stayed on until the early evening. For most of that time he managed to keep the Antalfer's problems out of his mind. But the idea of a community running from shadows dogged his thinking. Merral felt certain that there was something about the story that was familiar, that it had resonances of something he had heard fairly recently. Who had told him about it? Just as he was just about to leave the deserted building that evening the answer came to him: Vero. It had been Vero who had talked of a Sentinel investigation on a world where there had been a communal problem and his opinion was that, in the end, it had all turned out to be a psychological matter. It would be useful to see that data. But where had it been?

Through the diary he located Vero. He was on Aftarena Island on the other side of Farholme where, with the time difference, he would be asleep for a few more hours yet. Merral left him a message on his diary. Then he ordered the building lights off and walked home across the causeway and up through the wet streets of Ynysmant.

★ ★ ★

Vero returned the call just as Merral was getting ready for bed. He quickly pulled his night-suit on, sat within view of the diary and switched on the screen. Suddenly the dark, lean face of Vero appeared. He was wearing a lightweight, shortsleeved shirt and there was bright, low angle sun streaming behind him.

'Merral! It's been quite a few weeks. I'm sorry I haven't called before,' he said with an apologetic smile.

'Vero, greetings. No problem. You wouldn't be wearing that shirt in Ynysmant today. Or this week for that matter.'

'I've heard your weather's been poor. No, Aftarena is very nice. I travelled around a lot after I left you, just looking around. And I've ended up here. I like it, it's my sort of climate.'

Merral noticed that his Farholmen dialect was now almost perfect.

'I'm glad for you. What we have at the moment would make you miserable. You have to be born here to put up with it. And congratulations on your Farholmen, Vero. It took me a bit to realise that you were speaking in it. You sound like a native.'

'Not quite.'

'It's fine. Anyway, I was calling to ask you about something we talked about. The world where there was the collective disorder and some thought it was evil, but it was just biology after all. Where was it?'

Vero twitched his nose and scratched his tight curly hair. 'Aah, that's just an interpretation. Sentinels have debated ever since it happened. Which was in 12985 — maybe '86 — and it was on The Vellant. But isn't it a rather an unusual topic for a forester?' His face had acquired a look of curiosity.

Merral wondered how much he should tell him. 'Yes,' he replied carefully, 'the thing is I have a Forward Colony where things are getting a bit odd. It could simply be the bad weather. But I thought your case might provide a lead in.'

Vero's brown eyes widened and he opened his mouth to speak. Then he shook his head as if trying to dislodge a thought. 'Look, I'll send you the best reviews I can find.'

'Thanks. Anyway, how is the visit going?'

'Interesting. I'm enjoying it.'

'So you haven't found anything anomalous yet.'

Vero blinked.

'Well. . . . Just maybe.'

'Can you tell me?'

The brown face on the screen stared at him.

'Er, yes. In fact, I was thinking of calling you about it anyway. It's an odd thing. I've been uncertain how to proceed on it. Can I ask you some questions first? Questions that may seem irrelevant?'

'Go ahead.'

Vero shifted in his chair and then leaned forward towards the screen. 'The Technology Protocols: you would rate them as important?'

A strange question indeed, Merral thought. 'More than important, *vital*. You know the quote: "Outside Scripture, history has known no document of more influence than the Technology Protocols." They make us masters of technology rather than the other way about. It is generally believed that the Assembly would have self destructed without them.'

Vero nodded slightly, 'Now can you remember how the Preamble goes?'

'Testing my memory eh? Well the final AD 2130 version has "The Assembly of Worlds believes that, in his providence, God has provided technology so that, in some measure, the effects of the Fall may be lessened in this life. However, the Assembly also believes that, precisely because of our fallenness, technology can be abused to the detriment of an individual and his or her God-given personality. The Assembly therefore solemnly covenants that the only technology that will be accepted is that which it can be shown will not lead to the loss or damage of individuality or personality." How was that?'

Vero gave another nod. 'Flawless. Now Protocol Six?'

'Six? Oh that one. The shortest. "The rights of an individual to be protected from direct or indirect technological abuse are not extinguished by death."'

There was a further nod. 'And Merral, you understand that to mean – what?'

'Well, I have to think back to college. It's mainly that there is to be no rewriting of history. Because it's banned, it's hard to think of an example. Yes, I know, to alter a visual file to make your partner in a Team-Ball game look like a famous player of the past. I must admit I've never understood why it was in the Protocols. It's never seemed a big thing to me.'

'You are fortunate. Sentinels have to spend time studying the times before the Great Intervention and I can tell you there were many serious instances of this problem. But that's the end of my questions.'

Vero paused, flexed his long fingers and sighed quietly. When he spoke it was in hushed and solemn tones. 'I ask you these things, Merral, about Protocol Six because there is some evidence that it may have been breached. . . .'

It took some time for the significance of the last word to sink in. 'Not here? Surely not? . . . I mean breach of the Protocols is –' Merral ran out of words as the import of the statement sank in. Does he mean here on Farholme? he asked himself in bewilderment.

Vero leaned back in his chair and Merral was aware of the palm trees behind him. 'Was *serious* the word you were looking for?' he suggested quietly.

'I suppose so. I was actually trying to find a more major word.'

'You would be right to do so.' The face on the other side of the world was grim.

'You'd better tell me about it.'

Vero rubbed his flattened nose between his hands and then stared at the screen.

'Sorry, Merral. You won't like this. A voice has told me that there is a problem. Do you know whose?'

Merral, now feeling too perplexed to even try to answer, just shook his head.

'It was the voice of Miranda Cline.' Vero paused to let the name sink in and then repeated it, as if listening to it himself,

'*Miranda Cline*. Although dead these three thousand years she still speaks.'

'*The* Miranda Cline? The alto? The one my Uncle Barrand used on his Nativity piece?'

Vero nodded, unhappiness imprinted on his expression. 'The same, Merral, the very same. In fact, the problem is precisely the audio file you gave me. The one of Rechereg's *Choral Variations on an Old Carol*. The one with Miranda Cline as alto.'

Merral heard himself gasp. If it was barely believable that anyone could breach the Protocols, how much more unbelievable was it that such a breach was linked to his uncle? It made no sense at all. But then, nothing at Herrandown did any more.

Vero was speaking quietly and apologetically, almost as if he was confessing something himself. 'See Merral, I got round to listening to that recording again recently. I liked it, especially Miranda Cline. I'd never heard her sing as well. And one evening here, with nothing much to do, I called up the background to it from the Library and found that there was an interview with Rechereg himself. There he mentioned that the alto part was very hard and very high. And as I heard that, something clicked: something that I should have known. Because I knew about Miranda Cline, and while she was

unparalleled in the lower and mid range, she kept out of the topmost ranges. She was the classic, low second alto. Yet in the file you gave me she sings right up to top G and holds it firmly without break-up for two seconds.'

There was a silence. Outside his room, Merral could hear his father and mother talking softly as they went up to bed. Their world seemed a long way away. Merral heard himself speaking slowly. 'So you are saying that there is no way that her natural voice could have reached that high. But perhaps it was someone else?'

Vero nodded. 'Excellent, Merral, that is quite the line I am taking. The file says it is Miranda Cline and it sounds like her. But there could be a mistake, there are a thousand recreated voices.'

Merral closed his eyes. 'No, he said he was thinking of using her. And when he transmitted it to me the covering note said that he had used Miranda Cline after all.' A faint voice seemed to cry out within him that he was condemning his uncle.

Vero stirred on his chair. 'Well, it could still be a mistake. An error of the machinery. I'm going to have the file checked.' He stared at his fingers, as if seeing them for the first time. 'I suppose it is just possible that there was some sort of coding error. I'd prefer any alternative to what I'm afraid I think is the case.'

'Which is,' Merral stated dully, scarcely able to phrase the words, 'that Barrand altered her voice. In complete defiance of the Sixth Protocol.'

Vero looked away, as if unable to face him, but signifying his agreement by the tiniest nod of his head. 'You see,' he said slowly, after a moment, 'recreateds are at the limits of what we allow. They willingly give their vocal skills to be copied so that their voices can be reused later. But there is a commitment that we do not abuse that gift. Some recreated voices come with specific restrictions of the donors; Falancia Wollan, for instance, felt that her voice was unsuited to dramatic works like opera. But this is something else.' Then he fell into a somber silence.

'Vero, what are you going to do?'

Vero turned slowly back to face the diary. 'I shall transmit the file to my office on Ancient Earth. They have the ability there to take the waveforms to pieces. To definitely say whether it was hers and whether or not it was altered. I will do it in the next few days. I needed to talk to you first.'

'If it is an alteration?'

Vero shook his head. 'Merral, I have no idea. There are no precedents on file. We can hope that it is some sort of psychological problem and treatable. . . .' He looked profoundly miserable and after a moment he went on slowly. 'It all seems so . . . well, disproportionate. A few seconds worth of a single

note on a file from a singer who is long dead. I'm sorry, Merral.'

There was a long silence and Merral felt caught between his own unhappiness and that of his friend. But the issue was plain and he felt it right that he restate it. 'It is not a light thing, Vero. And you as a Sentinel know it, even if we use recreated voices more here than you do. To be one is an honour, to give your voice for things like the Forward Colonies and the Ships. Voices are special. That's why no machine, no diary even, is ever given a human voice, although we could easily do it. The Sovereign Lord made Miranda Cline unable to reach those top notes. To have altered her voice so it did – if that's what happened – is a lie. A twisting of truth.'

Vero nodded his head gently and seemed to stare for long moments into infinity. 'You know, they always say to Sentinels at graduation, "Always pray that you spend your entire life without being needed." I always thought it funny. . . .'

Then his focus shifted back to Merral. 'But what do you think? Tell me that your uncle's hardware is set wrong, that he's deaf . . . that in the transfer one note got changed by some distortion of the electromagnetic field. *Anything*. Tell me, Merral. *Tell me!*'

'I need to think Vero. Wait a minute. Please.'

With his mind reeling, Merral tapped off the video and sound and sat back in his chair. This was too much. He had been worried before Nativity at the possibility that his uncle had lied, he had been made uneasier by this morning's news, and now there was this. Three things. He was aware that his

options were very limited indeed.

He reached for the diary and the image of the dark-skinned man in a pale shirt with the brilliant sunlight behind him returned.

'Right Vero, let me be open with you. I think there is something up at Herrandown that is wrong. I have some other evidence. . . .'

Vero raised a finger, 'A question which you may, of course, refuse to answer. The Forward Colony with the collective instability you mentioned?'

'The same.'

Vero shook his head slowly. 'Oh dear. *Oh dear.*'

There was silence for what seemed like a long time, and then Vero spoke in distracted tones. 'On the positive side Merral, it's fairly isolated. And, at least it's localised. So far. But what to do?'

'Well I'm going up there tomorrow for the day. I think though, your fears are probably right, I think it highly probable that he has wilfully modified the voice parameters.'

Vero rubbed his face with his hands. 'I do not know what to advise. This is surprising. I had assumed that there was nothing here. But now. . . . No, we need more information. I will wait to hear from you before I do anything. Look Merral, can you meet me in Isterrane two days from now? No wait – that will be the Lord's Day. The day after then?'

Merral hesitated, then spoke, 'Yes, if you like. If you think that it's that important?'

'My friend, my reading of the data is that we have either a psychological crisis infecting one individual and probably others. Which is what I hope it is. Or –' He shook his head.

'Or *what?*'

There was a long silence, in which Merral became strangely aware of the perfect stillness in the room, a stillness so deep that he felt he could hear his heart beat.

Vero's voice, when it spoke out of the diary, almost surprised him. 'Or I do not like to say. But I cannot rule out that we are seeing the start of something so significant that . . . ' He tailed off into silence and then shook his head. It was only after another long pause that he spoke again. 'No, I will not speculate. Keep this to yourself, Merral, for the moment.'

'I see. I will abide by that.'

'Oh, and be careful when you go to Herrandown. Look out.'

'Look out for *what*?' Merral asked.

'I only wish I knew.'

They stared at each other, a tension somehow transmitted around the globe. Finally, Merral forced himself to say the words. 'Vero, I need to know. Finish what you said earlier. "Or –" *Or what*?'

Finally, as if being dragged out of the depths, the answer came back, syllable by painful syllable.

'Merral, if what I fear is the case, then the rules we have lived by for over eleven thousand years may be on the point of changing.'

Watchers

Sheila Jacobs

Mike Merrick works for a government agency responsible for removing 'unclean' people from his city. With his partner Jay, he enjoys ridding the city of the old, the sick and the 'illegal' – the renegades who refuse to take the Code. But when he comes across Sunny Cain, the rich daughter of his boss, and she starts talking about a man helping 'illegal' people to escape, he doesn't know what to think.

Watchers is a science fiction thriller which develops into a powerful allegory of the Christian faith.

ISBN 1 8602 4289 8
PB

Price: £7.99
£5.99 Special Offer
Special offer ends 31/08/03

Publication Date: June 2003
Copyright: Sheila Jacobs

Published by Authentic Lifestyle

I
RESCUE

The old city. Half demolished buildings with exposed rooms; rubbish and rubble-strewn roads ending abruptly in gaping holes. Derelict, dead, and filthy – so filthy.

The driving rain, washing the streets, would never cleanse it of its dirt. Not if it rained for a year. Not if it rained for a lifetime.

'There.'

The blip on the car scanner indicated that this was the place.

'He's in that doorway.'

The armoured vehicle slowed down, and its searching beacons threw a shocking beam into the darkness. There was no electricity anywhere in the city. No light. No life. At least, no life worth living. It was darker than the pit of hell – if Mike believed in hell. He didn't. He grabbed his rifle and sprang out of the car.

Chain-link fence, once ten metres high, lay ripped up and pulled down, but nothing stopped Mike. The looming half-burnt out building seemed to rise up in front of him like some half-dead enemy, protecting the Unclean.

'Watchers!'

Who said that?

The pathetic baggage, clutching a carrier bag, scrambled to its feet in the doorway. It put up a hand, shielding eyes from the searchlight's intensity.

'Mercy!'

'No mercy, old man.' Mike raised the rifle, admiring its silent efficiency as the victim slumped to the ground.

He walked up to the body and, in the brilliance, he could see that this Unclean wasn't really very old at all. He was hardly more than a youth.

'Check, Jay.'

Jay was out of breath. 'He's dead, isn't he?'

'You know the rules. Just check him!'

'OK, OK.' Jay bent down, the flat-line on his Laserscan rifle corresponding with Mike's own.

'What's happening with you tonight, Jay?'

'Not feeling so good, I guess.' Jay stood up. 'Unclean terminated. Check.' He stared down at the body. 'Man, what's worse, bringing them here or culling them? I don't know.'

'That's our job.'

Jay shuddered. 'How old are you, Mike? Older than me – much older. You ever wonder why you've lasted this long? I look in the mirror and wonder how come I'm still out here, and I'm only twenty.'

Mike wasn't sure how to reply to that. He was still thinking about what to say when there was a sound of shouting some way off.

'Five minutes west. Come on.'

Jay didn't move. 'Our shift's nearly over.'

'What?'

'Look, why do more than we have to? Why risk it? By the time we get back to the Gate, our shift will be over.'

'I can't believe I'm hearing this.'

'OK, whatever. Can we just go?'

Mike grabbed his partner's arm.

'If you've got a problem, deal with it. I need to know I can trust you.'

'We've been partners for a year now. You know you can trust me, but you enjoy this and I don't.'

'You better hope I didn't hear that.'

'Why?' But Jay knew why.

The shouting was getting louder. Jay was heading back to the car. Mike watched him. He had to be able to rely on his partner. His life depended on it. He couldn't afford to have a partner whose nerve had left him. He should report Jay's less than enthusiastic commitment to the job.

'No one gets out, Jay. No one stops being a Watcher.'

'Yeah, well maybe some do,' Jay called back over his shoulder. 'I've put in for a transfer of duties.'

And no Watcher was transferred anywhere, ever, thought Mike.

Jay's question repeated itself in his mind. 'How old are you?' A feeling Mike was accustomed to having only in the middle of a sleep period rose up inside him. He remembered his age. Why hadn't some Debtor killed him by now, some kid who should never have been born, some old man who couldn't afford to live any more, someone who couldn't get the Code, and had been banished to this living death?

They'd get him one day. Or maybe the Watchers themselves would do it, as soon as he stepped out of line, said the wrong thing – lost his nerve. Mike took his helmet off and ran a hand through his hair. Thinking of age made him made him nervous: not that he would ever admit it to a living soul. Maybe that was why he was especially glad to execute the elderly. He replaced his helmet, looking with distaste at the lifeless form in the rain. He hated all the dross in this forsaken place.

Yet for all his loathing of the old city, Mike felt part of it. Right now, he liked the feeling. Cleanse the city. A feeling of power washed away any temporary fear. It was only when he was back in the New Towns that he really felt uneasy. Somehow, Mike belonged here.

Then the Watcher of all Watchers realised that he himself was being watched. A noise in an alleyway brought a deft movement as he levelled his Laserscan and yelled a warning.

'Stand still for scan check!'

'You can lower than thing. I check out. I've got the Code. I'm not an Illegal.'

'Stand still!'

The figure stood still. The small screen on the Laserscan converted her identification code into a name. By now, Jay had driven the car up close, the searchlight fixed on his partner and the girl.

'See, I never let you down.'

Mike glanced at him. 'Look who we've got.'

Jay looked at the identification. 'That can't be right.'

'What's up?' asked the girl. 'Don't you like my name or something?'

'Shut up,' said Mike. 'Double check it, Jay.'

The girl didn't seem afraid. It was unusual. Everyone feared Watchers.

'It's unreal Mike, but this is Sunny Cain.'

Mike lowered his weapon. The girl was slight and thin, wearing only a shirt and pair of jeans. Her long hair hung in wet strands.

'What are you doing here?'

There was an explosion – it wasn't far away. A wall of flame lit up an old church tower. Mike's priority suddenly became to protect the girl. 'All right, Sunny Cain, let's get you out of this place. Let's move.'

Once in the car, they roared through the pitted streets, jolting through loose rubble that was once a fine main road.

'Are you injured?' Jay asked. 'Miss Cain? Are you injured?'

'No, I'm just great.'

'You're just lucky,' said Mike. He turned to the girl, who was sitting on the hard ledge behind his seat. 'What were you doing in the old city?'

Sunny leaned forward. 'You're Mike, aren't you? Mike Merrick.'

'You haven't answered my question.'

'I often see Jay – it is Jay, isn't it? – at the Relaxation Centre. Do you remember me, Jay?'

'Er – yeah,' admitted Jay. 'I think – yeah.'

'You'd have recognised me if I hadn't been so wet, wouldn't you, Jay? Once seen, never forgotten. I'm afraid you haven't caught me looking my best, Mike. I never see *you* at the Relaxation Centre. Why's that?'

'What were you doing in the city?'

'What are *you* doing here? Targeting anyone who hasn't got the Code? Keeping down the Unclean population? Doesn't that give you a kick? You know, it's funny we've never actually met before. I mean, my father is your boss.'

Something clicked into Mike's brain and he turned away from her in disgust.

'She's playing a game – get into the old city, see a little danger. Some of your privileged friends never get out, you know, Sunny Cain.'

'But I did. You've rescued me, Mike.'

'Jay, maybe we should stop the car right here and let her live out her little fantasy.'

'You won't do that,' said the girl, confidently.

'No, we can't do that,' agreed Jay, ramming his foot onto the accelerator, not at all sure his partner wouldn't order him to stop.

'I've met some people.' Mike heard Sunny's voice low in his ear. 'If you only knew what I know!'

'Who've you met? Names?'

'Oh, I've got a name.' She sat back, smiling. 'A name you'd die for.'

'What name?'

Sunny Cain just smiled. Mike wasn't in the mood to play games. He looked away.

'You're wasting my time.'

'I wouldn't waste your time, Mike.'

Jay was amused now. Mike didn't feel amused or flattered.

'Sunny, if you've got a name, let's have it. If you haven't, OK. If you want to pretend you know something and you don't, all right. But remember it's the law – you must give full details of all meetings with Illegals to Watchers.'

Jay expected him to add 'or else', but he didn't. The coldness of his voice wasn't lost on Sunny. She didn't like being rejected.

'Oh I've got a name, all right. Trouble is, I can't seem to remember it now.'

Jay cursed and manoeuvred the car around several burnt out wrecks of old trucks as they headed towards the regular lights of the highway ahead. Another explosion lit up the sky and, for a moment, it seemed like a new and violent day had suddenly arrived.

'Gate,' Jay spoke into the vehicle's intercom, 'Gate. Request Gate open.' He gave identification details. 'And we picked up a passenger. Sunny Cain. Yes, as in Stirling Cain's daughter. Yep. You heard right.'

The city wall loomed nearer, that great greyness that kept the Unclean from the Clean. Guards were visible now, as the Gate slowly opened.

'I've seen you around, Mike,' said Sunny.

Mike didn't reply.

'You're attractive, you know.'

Still no response.

'My father's afraid of you. Why's that?'

'You tell me.'

She was quiet for a moment. 'Ever been across the water?'

'Across the water? The sea? No. Why?'

Now it was Sunny's turn not to reply.

The car slowed down as they reached the Gate. Jay leaned out and spoke to the Gate guards, and they gazed in at the passenger. Sunny folded her arms across her body and complained that she was cold.

The Gate heaved shut behind them, and Jay breathed a sigh of relief as they pulled onto the wide, broad, well-lit highway. In the distance, the tall buildings of the New Townships became visible.

'Light!' said Jay.

'Glad to be home?' Sunny asked him.

'What about giving us that name?'

'That's if she's got a name,' said Mike.

'I've got a name.'

Mike laughed his sudden, disarming laugh. 'Is there anything in your head that isn't made up? Got to go to the city to get a buzz.'

'Don't judge me, Mike Merrick. You're just the same.'

'No, Sunny Cain. Not the same at all.'

A large black limousine was gliding silently towards them, looking as if it were part of the real night, the night which had been pushed back by the artificial lighting; night which had escaped its boundaries and had slunk back onto the highway.

Jay stopped their vehicle.

'OK, game over.' Mike stepped out of the car and called to the driver of the limousine. 'Here she is. Take her away. Go home, little girl.'

'I remember the name.'

'There's no name.' Mike turned back to the armoured car.

'David Drum. That's a name, isn't it?'

Mike spun round. 'David Drum? What David Drum?'

'Just David Drum.'

'David Drum is dead.'

'Maybe it isn't the same one.'

'You're lying.'

'I'm not. They talk about David Drum in the city. And they don't talk about him as if he's dead. They talk about him as if he's alive and helping people to escape!'

'You're wrong. You're wrong, Sunny.'

She leant against the limousine. 'You wanted a name, and now you've got it, you don't want it after all. Is there no pleasing you?'

'You've got to be wrong.'

'David Drum is alive and well and helping people escape, I tell you. They call it going over the water.'

Mike slung his hands onto his hips. David Drum! One of the leaders of that renegade sect . . . what were they called? That sect that refused to take the Code, the sect that were banned years ago when all religions were herded together under one banner . . . what was that group that wouldn't conform?

'No. John Woodley, Stephen Lewis, Kurt Dane . . . ' Kurt Dane. That was a name he hadn't thought of in a long time. 'And David Drum. All dead.'

'Maybe not as dead as you think.' Sunny moved closer and whispered, 'I'm going to be at the Relaxation Centre tomorrow around four. Perhaps I'll remember even more when I'm relaxed. Think so, Mike?

And with that, she smiled again, and walked to her father's limousine.

'David Drum! That's not possible.' Not possible.

Was it?

The Bloodstone Chronicles

Bill Myers

Through the power of the mysterious Bloodstone, three children are whisked into strange and wondrous worlds. Soon they are visiting places like the Sea of Mirrors, where they are nearly crushed by the weight of their sins, and Biiq, where one doubting child is allowed to experience the deep and unfathomable love that Jesus Christ has for us.

The Bloodstone Chronicles' intriguing and lovable characters help the children learn the powers and secrets of living as citizens in the Kingdom of God.

ISBN 0 3102 4684 9
PB

Price: £12.99
£9.99 Special Offer
Special offer ends 31/08/03

Published by Zondervan
PO Box 749, Harrow, HA1 1DP

Chapter One

It wasn't Denise's fault. It was just some weird rock she'd found in her uncle's attic. And what better gift to give a weird kid than a weird rock. How'd she know it would start to glow in her coat pocket? How'd she know by exposing it to the light of the full moon it would send out a distress call to some sort of "alternate dimension"? What'd she know about glowing rocks? Come to think of it, what did she know about alternate dimensions?

Now it's true, a rock for Nathan's birthday probably wasn't the best of gifts. Then again, Denise and Nathan weren't the best of friends. To say that she hated him might be an exaggeration. To say that at least once a week she had this deep desire to punch him in the gut, well, that at least would be the truth.

The problem was that Nathan was spoiled – big time. But it wasn't all his doing. Ever since the last operation – ever since the doctors said his hip would never be normal, that he'd always limp and have those sharp, jagged pains whenever he walked – Nathan was treated differently. And, being a fairly bright kid, Nathan did what any fairly bright kid would do . . .

He milked it for all it was worth.

He milked it when he didn't want to go to school. He milked it when he didn't want to take out the trash. And he especially milked it to get whatever he wanted from his grandfather.

Yes, sir, Nathan knew all the tricks.

Denise rounded the corner and headed up the street toward Grandpa O'Brien's Secondhand Shop. That's where Nathan hung out when his folks were away on business. With any luck, his older brother, Joshua, might be there, too.

Good ol' Josh. A couple years older than Denise, he was always there for her. He was there to pull her off kids before she pulverized them in fist fights. He was there to help her with the math she could never quite master. He was even there when her father ran off. Denise was only four at the time and could barely remember what the man looked like. But she remembered Joshua. She remembered him playing with her and trying to make her laugh. And she'd never forget the time he held her when she couldn't stop crying. It made no difference how much the other kids teased him. He went right on holding her until she finally stopped.

Good ol' Joshua. Now if only his little brother could learn some of those traits.

As she moved up the sidewalk, Denise listened to the snow creaking and squeaking under her feet. She loved December nights – the way the stars were so close you could almost touch them, the way the store windows glowed with twinkling Christmas lights. She even loved the obnoxious ringing bell of the Salvation Army Santa Claus across the street.

Reaching the Secondhand Shop, she pushed open the door only to be knocked aside by two little kids racing out for all they were worth. Their reason was simple. Nathan and his grandfather were going at it again. . .

"Grandpa, that's the third toy you've given away this week!"

"To be sure, lad, and don't you think I'd be knowing that?" The stout old man had come from Ireland almost forty years ago but still insisted on keeping his accent – and his temper.

Even at that he was no match for Nathan's selfishness. The boy was a pro. Denise stood near the door watching the redheaded kid go after his grandfather with everything he had.

"Grandpa, how do you expect to make a profit?"

"Son, there's more to this life than making a – "

"You've seen the bank statements."

"Yes, lad, but – "

"You know what Mother's accountant said."

"Yes, but – "

"It's all there in black and white."

"I under – "

"If you don't start making a profit you'll lose the store."

"Yes . . . but . . . I . . ." The old man was running out of steam. Denise could see him trying to change gears, searching for a new target. Unfortunately the one he chose happened to be Nathan's heart – an impossibly small mark for anyone to hit.

"It's the Johnson children," Grandpa sighed. "You know how they've always wanted a puppy. And since we got them little wooden pop-up ones last week, and since times have been so hard for . . ."

The old man slowed to a stop. The boy wasn't even listening. Denise watched as Nathan hopped up on the stool behind the antique cash register. He spotted her and grinned, making it clear that this was all a game to him. A game she'd seen him play more times than she could count. And, if she guessed correctly, he was about to enter phase two of the game – the woe-is-me-self-pity phase.

"Times are hard for all of us, Grandpa." He glanced over at the stuffed toy on the counter beside him. It was an English bulldog complete with sagging wrinkles and floppy jowls. By the way it was left half unwrapped, it was obvious that it hadn't exactly met up to his high standards for birthday gifts.

Slowly he turned to his grandfather. One aspect of the self-pity phase was to make sure you either had a catch in your voice or a tear in your eye. Nathan had both. He was good. Very good.

"Oh, Grandpa, I don't mean to complain" – he threw in a couple sniffs for good measure – "but the Johnsons aren't the only ones who want a real dog."

"I know, son, but – "

"And if you're always giving stuff away so you don't have enough money . . . well . . ." He let his voice trail off into silent sorrow.

The old man bit his lip. It was obvious he loved the boy with all of his heart. "I'm sorry, lad. Maybe in a few months I'll be able to afford a nice puppy."

Nathan looked up and gave a brave nod.

Denise could see Grandpa's heart melting.

"But for now, this ol' bulldog here, he ain't a bad substitute, is he?"

Nathan managed to smile and get his bottom lip to tremble at the same time. Yes, sir, he knew all the moves.

Denise wasn't sure what was next, but she'd definitely seen enough. She stepped from the door and started toward the counter.

"Hi, guys!"

"Oh, hi, Denny," Grandpa exclaimed. "So how are you this fine winter evenin'?"

"Pretty good," she said. "So, where's Joshua? Still at basketball practice?"

"I believe so."

She turned to Nathan, who was giving her his famous death glare. She tried not to smile. Here he had gone to all this trouble getting Grandpa right where he wanted him and now she barged in completely ruining the mood. "Happy birthday, Nathan."

"Thanks," he grumbled.

"I brought you a gift." She dug into her coat pocket.

"You did?" Suddenly he didn't sound quite so depressed.

"Yeah. It isn't much, but I think you'll like it." She pulled out the crimson-colored stone and plopped it down on the worn wooden counter.

Nathan stared at it blankly. "A rock?"

"Yeah, but not just any rock. I found it in my uncle's attic. Look at the cool red sparkles in it."

"Great," Nathan groaned as he picked it up. Obviously he didn't share her excitement. "A stupid stuffed dog . . . and now a rock. Some birthday." He tossed the stone back onto the counter where it rolled into a patch of moonlight that streamed in through the window.

"Nathan," Grandpa chided, "where are your manners?"

"Well, it's the truth, isn't it? Mom and Dad are off on some vacation – "

"Business," Grandpa corrected. "They're on a business trip."

"Whatever. And all you do is look out for everybody but me."

"Now, that's not true."

"Isn't it?" Nathan spun around and nailed Grandpa with another woe-is-me look. "What do you call it when you give away so much stuff that you can't afford to buy your own grandson the only present he's ever really wanted in his whole, entire life!"

Nathan scored a direct hit. Denise saw the guilt wash over Grandpa – guilt over giving the toy to the Johnson kids, guilt over not buying Nathan a real puppy, guilt over the boy's parents always being away. You name it, Grandpa was feeling guilty about it.

"All right, all right!" he exploded. He turned and headed for the cash register.

"What are you doing?" Nathan asked innocently.

Grandpa punched the buttons on the old machine and the money drawer rolled out. "You want a puppy, I'll be gettin' you a puppy!"

Nathan slipped Denise another smile as Grandpa grabbed the bills from the drawer, then turned to face him. "I'm takin' whatever money we got here and buyin' you your puppy!"

"But Grandpa," Nathan protested.

"No," the old man said as he stormed toward the coatrack and threw on his cap and scarf. "You've been whinin' and complainin' all week and I'll be havin' no more of it."

"But not *all* the money."

"I've made up my mind, lad." Grandpa slipped into his wool coat, hiked it up onto his shoulders, and headed for the door.

"Grandpa, please, not all your hard-earned – "

"No, sir," he said, yanking open the door and causing the little bell above it to jingle. "I'm goin' to Smalley's Pet Shop to buy you a puppy, and that's final!"

Just before Grandpa shut the door Nathan was able to squeeze in one last protest. Well, it really wasn't much of a protest. "Make sure it's the black one with the white spots!"

The door slammed, once again jingling the bell, and the room fell silent.

Denise could only stare as Nathan broke into a grin. Finally, she was able to speak. "You — you had that all planned, didn't you?"

"Not the part about the rock," Nathan shrugged. "But that worked out pretty good, too, don't you think?"

Denise was stunned.

Nathan laughed. "Come on, lighten up. You'd do it too if you thought you could get away with it."

"No way." Denise could feel the tops of her ears starting to burn like they always did when she got angry.

"Gimme a break," Nathan said. "Of course you would — we all would. That's the only way to get ahead in this ol' world — figure out what you want and go for it."

Sounding like some sort of professor with all the answers, he plopped his feet up on the counter and continued his lecture. Denise watched, both awed and repulsed.

"The way I see it, there are only two types of people" — he leaned back and clasped his hands behind his head — "the haves and the have-nots."

Once again she had this overwhelming urge to punch him in the gut. But this time something other than self-control stopped her. It was the rock. It had started to glow! It was filling with red, sparkling light. And the more Nathan talked, the brighter it grew — as if his words somehow gave it energy.

"You think billionaires get that way by looking out for the other guy?" he asked. "No, sir. They get there by looking out for number one."

By now the glow was bright enough to light up the entire counter. Denise tried to shout, but she was too frightened to speak. She tried to back away, but she was too scared to move. So instead of shouting or backing away she just stood there pointing.

But it didn't matter to Nathan. He wasn't looking. He was too busy giving his speech. Eyes closed and leaning back, he went on and on . . . and just when you thought he had finished, he went on some more.

All this as the red stone behind him continued to grow brighter and brighter, lighting up more and more of the room . . .

Out of the Shadows

Steve Dixon

A dragon, a human sacrifice, a mysterious stranger and a maiden in distress are just some of the elements of this extraordinary fantasy tale, loosely based on the Gospel of Mark. Look deeper into the story and you'll find a whole new perspective on Jesus and the challenge of being a disciple.

Out of the Shadows is the first instalment of *Rumours of the King*, a new three-part fantasy trilogy for children. The book is packed with excitement and adventure, but uses language and style simple enough to draw in even reluctant readers, and keep them hooked right to the end.

ISBN 1 8599 9671 X
PB

Price: £3.99
£2.99 Special Offer
Special offer ends 31/08/03

Published by Scripture Union
207-209 Queensway, Bletchley
Milton Keynes MK2 2EB

CHAPTER ONE

'No! And when I say no, I mean no!'

Ruel's father upended the wooden bowl he was eating from, and tipped the last bit of vegetable stew into his mouth in a way that meant he had said all there was to say. There was a pause – just long enough for his father to start thinking he might have won – then Ruel spoke again.

'But she'll be expecting me,' he said, quietly.

His father, Maaz, lowered the rim of the bowl a fraction and stared at his son. The boy was only twelve but he held onto his father's eyes and did not look away.

Although they seemed rock steady on the outside, both of them had thumping hearts and blood drumming in their ears. The womenfolk- Ruel's mother and sister- held their breath. Little Ezer turned away into the darkest corner of their cramped cottage. He meant to pretend not to notice whatwas going on and play swords with a stick from the fire kindling. Then he changed his mind. He knew from painful experience that if he made a noise at a time like this he was likely to catch what was meant for Ruel.

There was a thud and Ezer jerked round. He was just in time to see his father's food bowl bounce off the hard earth floor and roll away into the shadows. Ruel jumped a fraction, but stayed where he was, sitting rigid on a length of log by the gently crackling fire. He didn't take his eyes off his father. He tried not to blink, and the smoke that always filled their single room made his eyes burn. On the other side of the flames, his father rose — seeming huge in the tiny space. This was the crisis point and they all knew it. How many times over the years Maaz had chased his son round that fire like some kind of game. Often it had ended in laughter. But not this past year. Something was changing. They lived deep in the forest amongst the creatures of the wild, and they all knew what it meant when males locked horns.

All of a sudden Maaz gave a roar. He took a stride and kicked out — but he had kicked at the wooden bowl where it had come to rest. It crashed into the mud wall, taking a chunk out, and came ricocheting back. Ezer ducked as it flew over his head.

'You talk to him!' Maaz shouted at his wife and kicked again.

This time it was the door. It flew open, and before it had time to swing back shut again the big man had ducked through the frame and was out into the fading light of the evening.

There was a moment's silence whilst everyone tried to take in what had happened, then Ezer piped up from the shadows.

'That nearly hit me! It's always me that gets it!'

He lobbed the bowl at Ruel with a pretend growl, and everyone laughed.

'Give it to me,' said his mother, Naama. 'It needs cleaning.'

'Come and get it!' said Ruel, waving it over his head like a prize.

'If you're keeping it — you can wash it,' his sister, Saf ir, told him.

'And everyone else's,' said Naama.

He admitted defeat and tossed it gently back to his mother.

Ruel felt relieved. They all did. Actually, he felt a bit like crying. Safir came to squat down beside him and put her arm round his shoulder. She confused him these days, just like he confused himself. She'd always been his playmate, but now, at sixteen, she sometimes felt more like another mother. His eyes were pricking and he wiped them on his rough woollen sleeve.

'Stupid smoke,' he said. 'I don't think any of it goes out of that at all.' He pointed to the hole in the roof that was standard in the cottages of Hazar.

'If you want a proper chimney, that means living in a town – like Kiriath,' his sister reminded him.

'And that means money,' Naama went on, 'which we haven't got.'

'And leaving here,' said Ezer, 'and all our friends.'

Ezer had got them back to what had started the argument with Maaz, and they all went quiet. Naama gathered the eating things into the basket ready to take down to the river for washing. Maaz had told her to talk to Ruel and she knew she'd have to. She wasn't furious about the situation like Maaz, but she *did* agree with him – Ruel shouldn't go. She must speak.

But it was Ruel himself who kicked the discussion off again.

'What harm can it do?' he asked. He was staring into the fire and sounded as if he was talking to himself. 'She's just an old woman.'

'Then why are you bothered about going to see her?' Ezer put in.

'She's not just an old woman,' Naama reminded Ruel, 'she's Zilla.'

'She's a witch,' Ezer muttered.

'She's just strange,' Naama said. 'She upsets people.'

Ezer asked Ruel what he *did* when he went to see Zilla, and his brother told him they just talked, mostly. Ezer thought that sounded boring.

'It's not,' Ruel explained, 'that's the point. She tells the most amazing stories.'

'That's what your father's worried about,' Naama butted in. 'He's worried she'll give you ideas.'

'Is it bad to have ideas?' Safir asked, quietly.

'It depends what they are,' her mother replied.

'Anyway – why all the fuss all of a sudden?' Ruel asked. 'I've been going to see her for years – ever since the time she pulled me out of the river.'

'I know,' said Naama. 'We owe your life to Zilla – we know that, but – times change, you're getting older, you'll be a man soon…'

Ezer burst out laughing and Ruel would have punched him if Safir hadn't got in between them.

'Your father doesn't want her to give you the wrong ideas – that's all,' Naama went on.

'What kind of ideas are those?' Ruel asked.

'You know very well. You've got to face it, Ruel, she's an outcast – she's lucky she hasn't been driven right away into the forest. And anyone who spends time with an outcast gets to be – well – an outcast themselves. Your father's worried. He's been worried for a long time. He blames himself for not having done something about it before. I blame myself. We've not been good parents to you, Ruel

'Because you've let me talk to an old woman that nobody else will talk to? That's stupid!'

His mother just stared at him. She didn't shout and throw things like his father, but he could see she was upset.

'We just want what's best for you,' Naama said, after a while.

'How do you know what's best for me?' Ruel muttered.

'We don't want you to turn out like her.'

Ruel looked his mother straight in the face.

'I can't think of any better way to turn out,' he said.

His face was set hard and Naama thought how very like Maaz he looked. She knew that as far as Ruel was concerned, *he* had now said all there was to say.

The boy turned away and went to sit in the corner with his little brother. He picked up a stick and started fencing with Ezer, but neither of them put much enthusiasm into it. After a while Safir started things off again. 'Why is Zilla expecting you tonight?' she said.

Ruel answered without turning. 'It's a special day – an anniversary.'

'What anniversary?' Safir asked him.

'It's the day that Hanan was taken away,' Naama said, quietly.

Ruel looked at her, surprised.

'Zilla isn't the only one who remembers,' she said.

'Who's Hanan?' Ezer asked.

Ruel looked as if he was going to say something, but his mother cut in quickly.

'No one,' she said. 'No one important. It was a long time ago. That's another thing that worries your father–' speaking to Ruel now '–he doesn't want you carrying this on.' She gave a glance at Ezer. 'The man *should* be forgotten.'

Another silence. Ruel and Ezer tried drawing something on the mud floor with their sticks, but it was hopeless – there were no windows, and the only light came from the fire – they couldn't see a thing. Naama putsomewood on the fire, but it didn't help much. Safir hooked the strap of the basket on her shoulder and lifted it as if she was going to the river to wash the food things, but then she didn't move.

'Mum,' Safir said, putting down the basket, 'if you don't want Ruel to visit Zilla any more – he ought to go and *tell* her, shouldn't he? It's not fair otherwise – if he doesn't turn up now and then doesn't ever go near her again, she might think he doesn't like her any more. If youre stopping him, he ought to tell her it's your fault he's not coming any more – then it's all straight and honest and she knows what's what. At the very least, he ought to say goodbye.'

She turned to Ruel. 'If you go and see her now, will you make it the last time, and say goodbye?' she asked.

He nodded.

'Mum?' she asked, 'what do you think?'

Naama swept the ash and the mess from their meal out of the door before she replied. She was proud of her daughter. Actually, she was proud of Ruel. She wasn't very proud of Maaz and herself, or anyone else in the village.

'I suppose you're right,' she said.

Safir heaved the basket on her shoulder again and made for the door.

'I'll go and see what Dad thinks,' she said. 'I know where he'll be.'

When Safir came back with the food things, freshly scrubbed from the river, she brought her father back too. Her father brought their two cows. Maaz settled the animals at the far end of the room, behind their bit of fencing, then he sank onto his straw bed by the wall. He didn't look at Ruel when he spoke to him.

'Go,' he said. 'Don't stay long. Don't go again.' Ruel left without a word.

He took a few steps and stopped, breathing deeply. The fresh air always felt great when he came out of the smoky stink of his home – like drinking cool, fresh water – but there was something else good about those deep breaths this evening. He seemed to swell inside himself – to get bigger and bigger without any chance of ever bursting. He knew that he hadn't really won – he'd had to say he wouldn't see Zilla again – and even if he'd got his own way about this evening, it was Safir who'd sorted it out, not him – but at least he'd stood up for himself, he'd spoken up for what he thought was right, and that felt good – that felt like Hanan.

The village of Hazar had only one street and Ruel set off down it with big strides. It was an earth track and in summer it was baked hard; but it was only early spring now, and the mud was up to Ruel's ankles. The street ran east to west – out of the forest, through the village and back into the forest again. To the east, a day's journey by cart, was the town of Kiriath and Baron Azal's castle. To the west was the sea: but no one knew how far, or what was in between. Going west, the villagers kept the path clear as far as they needed into the forest, but beyond that it probably faded out to nothing. Hazar might even be the end of the road. That's how it felt anyway – no one ever came in from the west. To the north were the fields, hacked out of the forest so long ago no one could remember; to the south were the rocks and the river. Everything else was trees.

Up and down the street, the villagers were driving their animals home – mostly cattle, some pigs. Ruel nodded to them or said goodnight as they passed. They nodded back or said a word or two in reply. All that was normal, but there seemed to be something different about it this evening. Suddenly Ruel realised what it was – he was looking at his neighbours in a different way now – looking at their eyes – trying to read their thoughts. Did they really think the same way about him as they thought about Zilla? Were they starting to? Would they start to? Because his mother was right – Zilla was an outcast.

It wasn't just what she said. She didn't help herself by the way she looked. Being old, she couldn't help having white hair – but did she have to make it into something that looked like a bush grown wild? And did she have to tie all those little strips of coloured cloth all over it? And did she have to wear such colourful clothes? Everyone else wore dull colours – browns, dirty looking blues and greens. But somehow, Zilla had learned the art of dyeing. No one knew what she used – berries or special roots that only she knew about – but she could make the most incredible *bright* colours. And she could never seem to stick to one colour for the rough gowns she wore: they were always sewn together from bits of every colour you could think of. She looked like a rainbow that had fallen out of the sky and landed in a tangled, mixed-up heap. Then there was the jewellery – not that any of it was real jewels, or gold, or even metal – all bits of stone or wood that she'd painted and strung round herself. You could hear her coming a mile off – she rattled.

Everyone thought she was mad – even wicked, although they never came out and said just how or why exactly. People were always making comments – not just the children, the grown-ups too. Whenever they wanted to make a mean joke about someone, it was always Zilla they picked on. Ruel realised he didn't want to be treated that way. He realised something else too – he might have stood up for himself at home just now, but he had never stood up for Zilla in the village. He might not have laughed at the jokes, but he'd never said they were wrong. He wasn't breathing quite so deeply, or feeling quite so good about himself by the time Zilia's cottage came in sight.

Only the miller and the blacksmith lived in a different style of house to Ruel's cottage. The rest lived in exactly the same kind of house – thatched, one room, straw beds round the walls, animals fenced off at the far end, everything else you owned hanging in bags from the beams where even someone Safir's height could bang their heads on them. Most of the places were the same size as Ruel's, some were smaller. Zilia's was the smallest of them all; and it was right on the western edge, where the track disappeared into the trees. In this twilight, you could easily miss it if you didn't know it was there. It was so small that the roof came down to the ground – like a tent. And the thatch was so old that it was green with all the things growing on it. It could have been a mound, Ruel thought – which made Zilia's home feel a bit like a burrow.

Ruel opened the door without knocking or calling, as he'd done hundreds of times before. Zilla knew it was him and didn't even look up. Her little fire was burning in its square stone enclosure in the middle of the tiny room, and she sat on her bit of log, staring deep into the flames.

'Come in, dearie,' she said, in her soft, dreamy voice. 'Come and sit down.'

Ruel sat beside her and kissed her dry old cheek. He'd no idea how old she was – just about the oldest in the village, that was for sure. She ruffled his hair and squeezed his hand for a moment. It was only then that she managed to tear her eyes away from the fire and look at him. She had big eyes, dark grey like a winter sky before it snows, and they always looked serious – even when she was making a joke. But Ruel knew there wouldn't be any jokes tonight.

'Now, have you eaten?' she said, starting to heave herself up off the log. 'if you just hang on a minute, I'll get you a nice–'

'No, Zilla – I've had something–'

'I've got some fruit pie, I could–'

'No really.'

Zilia's food – where she got it and how she cooked it – was as much of a mystery as the things she did with coloured cloth. Ruel didn't often get out of her cottage without some of it inside him. She seemed to have a need to feed people – and he supposed he was the only one who ever came near her these days to be fed. It was usually quite good food too – but different. He never asked what was in it.

It was rare for anyone not to feel hungry in Hazar, but tonight Ruel really didn't have any appetite.

'I can't stay long,' he said. Better to get it over with.

'Never mind, dear.' She patted his hand. 'Maybe another time.'

'There won't be another time.'

'Why's that, then, dearie? Are you going away somewhere?'

Ruel took a deep breath. 'There's been some trouble at home,' he said. And he told her about it all in a rush so she couldn't interrupt him.

She didn't say anything for a while when he'd finished. She sniffed a bit, and he knew she was crying. Those big grey eyes seemed to be made for staring or crying – she did each of them a lot, and Ruel found them both disturbing. Zilla was not an easy friend to have. Ruel could well have felt relieved that he wouldn't be seeing her again, but he didn't.

'They're right, dearie,' she said at last. 'You mustn't be cross with them. They're only doing what's best for you. I should have said it myself – I'm just a selfish old woman that should know better. Off you go now – it's good of them to let you come and tell me – off you go quickly now,' and she started prising herself off her log again as if she was going to see him out.

'No!' he said. 'Not yet.'

'You must do as your parents tell you, Ruel.'

'But what about Hanan? We haven't talked about Hanan.'

Zilla's eyes went suddenly soft and deep, as if the real Zilla wasn't on the bright surface of them any more but had fallen miles inside herself – as if the greyness of her eyes was made up of thick mist or cloud that you could fall through for ever. She sank back onto the log.

'I thought you'd want to talk,' Ruel said, softly. 'That's why I came.'

And so they went through it again – the story they'd shared since Ruel had first got to know her -since the day she'd dragged him out of the river. It had been a freezing winter's day, four years ago, and he'd been playing by the water. He had slipped on an icy stone and pitched straight in. The river was swollen and carried him off before anyone had seen what had happened – away downstream to the lonely spot where Zilla was pounding her washing. She had dragged him out and desperately tried to keep him alive. He was frozen stiff and she'd known that if he passed out he'd be dead. She'd hugged him and shook him and talked to him endlessly about everything she could think of. She'd held onto him with everything she'd got, and he'd lived. He remembered hardly any of it afterwards – apart from one story she had told –

a story that had seemed to clutch onto him as Zilla had clutched him and dragged him out of the icy depths – the story of Hanan.

Zilla had got half way through telling it now when a furious banging at her door cut her short. Ruel opened it and found himself staring at Safir, standing in the moonlight.

'It's my sister,' he called to Zilla.

'Bring her in, dearie, bring her in – maybe *she'll* have some of my pie.'

'No, no,' said Safir. She was breathless from running and her eyes looked wild. 'You must come home quickly.'

'What is it?' Ruel asked.

'The Reaper – he's been seen in the forest – it's not safe to be out.'

Zilla's dreaminess went in an instant. 'Go on, dear,' she said, 'you must go straight away.'

Ruel went back to Zilla and hugged her tight.

'I'll miss you,' he said. 'I won't forget.'

Then Ruel and Safir were out in the night. It was quite dark now – the full moon making weird shadows everywhere. Ruel was furious at the danger his sister had been in.

'It's not safe for you to be out alone, if The Reaper's been seen,' he said – the darkness and danger turning his voice into a whisper. 'Why did Dad send you?'

'He didn't,' she hissed back. 'I was getting wood from the stack when I heard some men talking – they reckoned they'd just seen him in the forest – so I came for you straight away.'

'You idiot – what if he'd got you?'

'What if he'd got you? I wasn't going to let you walk home alone with him out there!'

'What if he gets both of us?'

'Come on then, let's run!'

Safir grabbed his hand and they pelted for the safety of home.

From Dust and Ashes

Tricia Goyer

In the aftermath of war, as Nazis flee newly-liberated Austria and Allied troops are discovering the horrific truth of the concentration camps, a story begins to unfold between an American GI, the wife of an SS guard and a survivor of the camps.

From Dust and Ashes is a historical thriller inspired by actual events surrounding the liberation of a concentration camp at the end of the Second World War. It demonstrates how the power of forgiveness can overcome even the most horrific tragedy.

ISBN 0 8024 1554 7
PB

Price: £9.99
£6.99 Special Offer
Special offer ends 31/08/03

Published by Zondervan
PO Box 749, Harrow, HA1 1DP

Twenty-Five

The sky had just begun to lighten when the train chugged in. Like a dragon with smoke puffing from its nostrils. it roared closer, heaving to a stop with a drawnout sigh.

Tickets had been issued for three to Hamburg, Germany. From there Michaela, Marek, and Kasia would receive new papers before moving on to Poland.

The Red Cross had provided traveling clothes, but they were much too large for the thin frames. Helene straightened the collar on Michaela's dress, thinking that the travelers resembled children playing dress-up.

Anika clung to Helene's skirt. Kasia rocked Petar in her arms as Helene pulled Michaela into her embrace, wrapping her arms around the woman's sharp shoulder blades. The train whistle blew, and a cry caught in Helene's throat. As they tearfully rocked in each other's arms, the sky seemed to open up and a misty rainfall filled the air.

"Heaven is crying with us," Michaela said.

Helene didn't even attempt to answer.

Michaela finally pulled back, and the two examined each other at arm's length. Helene stood tall over Michaela. Her shoulder-length blonde curls couldn't be more different than Michaela's cropped dark hair. Still, Helene knew Michaela was the beautiful one where it mattered most.

Helene gazed into Michaela's face, trying to imprint the memory of it into her mind. Her eyes were redrimmed and weary. Still, Helene never wanted to forget the love she saw there. The love that had made such a difference.

A man stepped from the train and hurried past them. Then a couple with a small child. Soon it would be time for Michaela to board.

Helene bit her lip. Kasia handed her the baby and said a word of thanks. Then, as if sensing the two women needed to be alone, the brother and sister boarded.

"Thank you for the shoes." Michaela studied the sturdy brown boots on her feet.

"I told you I would find some," Helene said with a tilt of her chin. "I'm sorry my father couldn't come," she added, refusing to believe this was really good-bye.

"We said our farewells at the house. I will miss him greatly." Michaela squeezed Helene's hand. "Even more, I'll miss you. You saved my life. I can never repay you."

Helene tried to speak, but the words wouldn't come. She tried again. "I thought I was the one helping you. But I was the one saved. I only offered bread. But what you gave me—" Helene placed her hand over her chest. "What you gave me, I can never repay. The life you showed me lives here. I have found a new life. Your work here is complete."

Michaela stood on her tiptoes and kissed Helene's cheek. "That is the only reason I can let you go," Helene continued. "God has called you to share this good news with others as you did with me."

The train whistle blew again, and Helene took a step back. Michaela crouched before Anika. The young girl released her mother's skirt and flew into Michaela's arms. Helene glanced at those on the platform around her. After years of knowing her every move was being watched, she couldn't help but wonder who at the station was observing this scene. What did they think of an SS child in the arms of a former prisoner?

Michaela's lips moved, and Helene knew her friend was saying a prayer over Anika. Michaela stood and placed a hand upon Petar's head and did the same for him.

"As soon as I arrive, I will write," Michaela promised.

Helene nodded, pulling Anika toward her. "Go now. Before you miss your train."

Michaela stepped through the train doors. Helene waved to Marek and Kasia in the window and caught a glimpse of Michaela's face before the train rolled forward and disappeared down the tracks.

The platform still buzzed with the motion of dozens of bodies – serviceman, displaced persons, and villagers. Yet Helene felt more alone than ever.

She took Anika's hand and hurried toward the house. The rain continued to fall, and by the time they reached the front door they were soaked.

She would bathe the children, dress them, feed them, and play with them. Perhaps she'd prepare a tea party with Anika and bounce her son upon her knee.

Still. Helene knew that her heart would not be there. Through the rest of the day and into the night, her thoughts would be with the train as it increased the distance between them.

That night, after her children were tucked into their beds, Helene lay awake, unable to sleep. She heard a train's whistle and wished it signaled her friend's return. She imagined the Red Army's heavy-booted footsteps and willed them to stay away.

Austria had been carved like a side of beef, with the four Allied powers choosing their own cuts. St. Georgen rested north of the Danube – the border of the Russian zone. Only a river crossing away, Helene knew, dwelt the symbols of those carefree months after the war. Peter, Coca-Cola, bubble gum, and jazz music had receded to the opposite bank.

But God is with me, whichever side of the river I'm on, she reminded herself. *And in Him I will trust.*

Later, during the darkest point of the night, a clamoring outside stirred Helene from her bed. She heard a woman's scream, then men's laughter.

Wrapping a blanket around her shaking frame, Helene approached the front window. On the small street that ran alongside their house, a Russian jeep was parked with its headlights off. The men's shouts were directed at a helpless young woman. They pulled her into the jeep, then sped away.

Where are they taking her? What will they do? Helene stepped back from the window. She jumped when a hand touched her shoulder.

"It's just me," her father said. He tucked her under his left arm. A rifle rested in his right hand. "This is a gift from Peter," he said. "Liberated from the Germans."

Helene understood. "You warned me they were coming."

Her father stepped to the window. "Thirty thousand of their comrades were killed in that compound on the hill. They're here for revenge."

"But the guards are gone. All those involved have left." Even as the words spilled from Helene's mouth, she knew it wasn't true. She remained. And her father, who'd kept supplies for the Nazis, had stayed. Even the priest who once housed a dozen men was still there. Although most of these people had no choice at the time, they could still be considered sympathetic toward the Nazis.

A new oppression had come to their town. Helene snuggled deeper into her father's arms.

The next morning, Helene's father was gone when she awoke. She peered at the spot where the woman had been taken the previous night. The memory of her screams caused Helene to jump at the slightest noise. The streets were quiet now. But she knew, out there somewhere, the Russians lurked.

She fed her children and then gave Anika paper and scissors. As the girl played, Helene stood at the window, watching for her father. Finally she saw him, moving toward the house in quick steps, his brow lined with worry.

"It's as we thought." He quickly entered the room and latched the door behind him. "A group of prisoners has already been taken to Siberia."

Helene gasped. "Prisoners?"

"Ja, those considered enemies of the Russian state. Nazi sympathizers. They're accusing many of cooperating with the enemy. Those already taken are being sentenced. Only those who are 'of service' to the occupational forces will remain. Even now Russian tents are being set up where American ones recently stood."

"How many of them are here?"

"The men you saw are only the tip of the sword. They have come to protect the borders. The full occupational forces have yet to arrive."

Helene glanced at Anika, who was cutting a piece of red paper into the shape of a heart. She lowered her voice. "Are the borders closed?"

"Ja. "

"All of them?"

"All of them."

Helene collapsed onto the chair. *I deserve this. I am an enemy*. But as soon as the words filled her head, others took their place. She could hear Michaela's voice. *No, you are forgiven. Your slate has been wiped clean.*

In God's eyes, perhaps, but not to the rest of the world. To the Russians she was simply the wife of a former guard.

"There is a way out." Her father sat in the chair beside her. " It is risky, but it is our only chance."

Helene stared into his gray eyes. He seemed so old. So tired.

"There are many who want to get out. Even Jewish survivors who are still weak. Farmers are rowing them across the river." He placed his hands over hers. "I want you to go tonight. With the children."

"In a rowboat? Across the Danube? But it is so wide and strong. Nein, it's too dangerous." She stood, then leaned against the table. "I can't. If anything happened to them–"

Her father stood and placed his hands on her shoulders. "There is no other way. You know you will be found. Too many know. And even those most loyal can be bought … or threatened."

"What about you?"

"I have already been sought out. First by the Nazis for storage, then by the Russians for men. They want to use our home for boarding." He kissed her head. "As long as I provide a room and *schnitzel, I* will be taken care of. I am an old man. I pose no threat."

"I can't leave you again. I couldn't bear it."

"Be strong, my daughter. Think of the children. When things settle down, then perhaps I can join you."

"Either you come too, or I'm not going."

His eyes flashed vulnerability for a moment, and then the willful expression returned. "You don't understand. There are dynamics I cannot begin to tell you about." He held her face in his hands. "The Lord knows I'd do anything for you and for the children. But I cannot leave. Not yet. You have to trust me in this."

The determination in his eyes told Helene he wasn't going to change his mind. "But cross the river? Isn't there another way?" Her thoughts went again to the man she had depended on so many times over the previous months. "What about Peter? Can we get word to him? Can he come to help?"

"Nein. From the moment of surrender, no U.S. soldier has been allowed into the Soviet zone. You must go. They are already collecting names. Names of former Nazis."

"But even if I get across, where will I go?"

Her father took a knife from a kitchen drawer and carefully sliced the stitching on the lining of his jacket. He pulled out a paper from inside, neatly folded, and handed it to Helene.

She unfolded the sheet and saw the seal of an American eagle. The date on the paper was two weeks old.

Dear Captain Standart,
By my own witness, and by others of the Eleventh Armored Division, the

*bearer of this paper, Helene Völkner, compassionately helped the troops of our
division in their efforts to save the lives of the victims of Nazi atrocities.*

*In return for protection for herself and her children, Mrs. Völkner has agreed
to cooperate with the U.S. Department of Investigation in their efforts to
secure the names and ranks of SS officers and guards at Camp Gusen.*

If you have any questions about Mrs. Völkner, please feel free to contact me.
Sincerely,
Sergeant Peter Scott

Helene held the paper to her chest. "You want me to disclose the
names of the guards?" A knot formed in her stomach. "You've had
this planned all along. You and Peter. You knew, when faced with
danger, I'd have to comply."

"We were hoping it would not come to this. We knew no
American serviceman would be allowed in, but we had no idea the
Russians would shut down the border to locals so quickly."

Helene considered the danger of giving out such vital information. She thought of Arno Schroeder. His face, his taunts, his threats.
He was just one man. There were hundreds like him who had disappeared, never wishing to be found. Many who would do anything to
keep her silent.

Then again … maybe she'd have a chance to work for the side of
good rather than evil.

"Could you give the names?" he asked.

"Of course. I know them all. Their positions. Their wives. Their
families. After all, I attended their parties. I visited their homes. I was
one of them."

Helene refolded the letter and set it on the table. She thought of
Peter's care, his interest in her and her friends. Had it been real? She
thought of the American actors in the movies set up for the GIs'
amusement. They played their parts well. Had Peter's interest been
just an act? Had he played the part of an honorable hero only to win
her confidence? Maybe he'd known who she was from the
beginning. After all, who else but an SS wife could give the U.S.

Army all the information they could ever need?

Helene tried to control her shaky voice. "When did he approach you with this idea?"

"He did not approach me, but I him … just in case it came to this."

"So, this was your plan?"

"Our second plan. Our first was to have you leave with Michaela if she had chosen to move to Germany." He lowered his gaze. "You could not leave with Peter alone. Nonfraternization, you know. But you could safely travel with her, especially if she were employed by the U.S. Army. After all, she had no laws about who she could befriend."

Helene dropped her head. The more she heard, the more she realized she didn't want to know. "But Michaela went one way, and Peter the other."

"So here you are."

"Still, that doesn't answer my question. What will I do when I get to the other side?"

"Someone will be waiting to take you to Linz. Once there, find an American serviceman. Give him the letter and ask to be taken to Captain Standart. He will know how to contact Peter, and Peter will connect you with the right people."

"Peter is expecting me?"

Her father rubbed his mustache. "He knows it's a possibility."

"I have to think about it."

"Of course." He paused. "But remember what you saw last night. Leaving will be dangerous, especially with two little ones. But staying could be even worse."

Helene didn't need to hear any more. She picked up the letter and shuffled to her room. Anika still slept on the bed, Petar in his cradle. Her heart swelled with love for them. They were so helpless. They didn't realize who they were in the minds of the Russians. They didn't know their father had been an accomplice to the murder of thousands as their mother stood by and watched.

Oh, God, it is so difficult. She dropped onto the bed and curled into a ball. The foolish decisions she'd made long ago mattered so much now.

Helene knew what she had to do. It was the only way. Her father knew it. Peter did too.

Helene gazed about the room, taking it all in. She would leave everything behind again. Her father. This place. The memories, both good and bad.

Helene noticed something glimmering on the floor in the corner, half covered with dust. She rose from the bed and reached for it.

My wedding band. How many weeks ago had she pulled it from her finger and thrown it across the room? Yet even so, she had not been able to escape its hold. She would forever be Friedrich's bride.

Helene slid the ring onto her finger. She would go. She would give the names. And as she kissed her sleeping baby, Helene hoped more than anything God would go with her.

Angels Watching Over Me

Michael Phillips

Mayme and Katie are two teenagers from very different worlds – one is the daughter of a slave, the other the daughter of a Shenandoah plantation owner. Orphaned by murderous gangs of Confederate outlaws in the aftermath of the American Civil War, they must stick together to survive, while facing up to their own pain and sorrow.

Angels Watching Over Me is the touching and inspirational story of these two young women as they learn to live through their ordeal, with only each other and God to depend on.

ISBN 0 7642 2700 9

PB

Price: £9.99
£6.99 Special Offer
Special offer ends 31/08/03

Published by Bethany House Publishers
11400 Hampshire Avenue South
Bloomington, Minnesota 55438

Winds of Change

A hot sun rose that spring day over the peaceful landscape.

That's how Katie always began to tell it. I reckon the same sun came up and shone down over us both that day, though we were in a different part of the county and all my family were slaves on another plantation six or eight miles away.

The slaves in their quarters, Katie said, looked outside early, saw the heat rising in waves from the damp ground, and sighed.

The fields would be hot, the work hard. The winter had been a mild one, and slave work during those months was more mild too. Today they would feel the beginning of the intense labor that always came at this time of the year. Rolling hills and valleys in that region stretched for hundreds of miles in every direction. Its soil was rich and fertile. In it grew lots of things that brought prosperity to those who owned it.

But it wasn't a very good place or a happy time to be alive if your skin was black. My people knew that as well as the slaves of Katie's father.

He came out from his early breakfast to announce they would complete the ploughing of the eastern fifteen acres today. If the warm weather held after last week's rain, they would move straight to the northern twenty-eight which bordered the river, the master told them. He wanted it ready to plant by next week. The wheat was already in. Now it was time for the cotton. He returned to the plantation house to finish his breakfast. The male Negroes hitched up the teams, loaded the tools and themselves in three wagons, and set out for the fields. Their women would follow with water and food once the domestic chores were done.

By noon the sun had climbed high, and the damp heat felt more like June than April. No breeze offered relief. Even spring days could get downright uncomfortable in North Carolina, but it was a lot hotter than usual for this early in the season.

A white girl slipped along a wide dirt pathway between two partially cultivated fields. Out of that same dirt her father's cotton crop would be sprouting in white puffy balls four months from now. A golden retriever bounced along at her heels. Rusty had been her constant companion since her father brought him home for her as a pup a year before.

The girl was Kathleen Clairborne. She always told this part of her story as if it were somebody else. She sometimes described it as the time before the person inside her woke up. I reckon everybody's got to comeawake sometime. This happens at different times and different ages. Sometimes it's circumstances that wake people up, sometimes pain or hardship. It's an odd thing I've noticed as I've seen more of life – happiness alone doesn't usually do much to help folks wake up on the inside. What wakes people up the quickest is some kind of tragedy or grief. Most of the time, I suppose, it's just getting older and starting to *think*.

It's sad, though, that some people never do seem to come all the way awake no matter how long they live.

But as Katie looked back later on the little girl walking in the fields, she said it felt like she was a different person then. She hadn't come awake yet.

She had as few worries in the world as a girl can have. Her carefree gait suited this kind of a Saturday. She understood as little about cotton, which the black people were digging the earth to make ready to grow, as she did about the growing season. Neither was she aware of the great amount of slave labor required to make a plantation owner such as her father a wealthy man. Katie wore nice frocks decorated with ribbon and lace and played with expensive dolls that came from places like England or France. But she had never given any thought to why she had them. Her life was full of music and books and pretty things.

Nothing particular had driven her outside that Saturday morning. Her actions, Katie said later, were guided by impulse, not decision. She had tired of playing inside and now simply found herself moving along the road eastward away from the house with one of those dolls under her arm. She had not *decided* to go for a walk. She just found herself doing so. Katie did what came into her head and took what happened in life, without wondering where it came from or why.

Flies buzzed about, and bees busily conducted their springtime business, and they had plenty to do because there were wild flowers blooming all across the moist, green, humid countryside. In the heat, Katie had slowed her movements to a lazy stroll. Even Rusty had decided to save his energy and simply sniffed at the grass on each side of the path.

I can still smell the land on a day like that. There's nothing like the moist earth in the South after a spring rain. Now and then the distant low of a cow could be heard as Katie walked along, though in the heat, even their moos sounded weary. A thin haze lay over the hills in the distance, as it usually did. The earth and its inhabitants were alive with growth and activity. Yet at the same time a sleepy tranquility hung over the land, subdued under the smokelike mist clinging to the mountains in the west.

More changes were in the air, however, than Katie or her father, or than I or my family where we lived, or than *anybody* realized. New breezes were blowing – that's how Katie used to describe it. But the slaves with sweat pouring off their black foreheads in Shenandoah County northeast of Charlotte, between the Piedmont Plateau and the Blue Ridge Mountains, they couldn't yet feel them either.

They would feel them soon enough. So would Katie. So would I. Four years later, destiny would bring us together. When that time came, cruelty and terror would be carried on those winds of change. For many in both races, the storm would bring heartache and destruction. Lots of good folks would die for the cause that both North and South called freedom. Others would learn to grow strong, though it wouldn't be easy, and that kind of inner strength would cost them many tears.

But most people alive in 1861 knew nothing of the significance of the times, or realized that history was about to be made. Or that they would be part of it.

Kathleen O'Bannon Clairborne didn't know it. Neither did Mary Ann Jukes.

We were both oblivious to the fact that we were living in a newly created nation calling itself the Confederate States of America. We had not heard of Fort Sumter, almost two hundred miles southeast on the South Carolina coast, where troops were already gathering to defend the right of those Southern states to maintain their independence.

And so Katie went on with her life as she always had. The slaves did their work and she played with her dolls.

But winds of change were in the air. Folks would have no choice but to come awake eventually.

Even two little girls.

Desert Rose

Linda Chaikin

When Jack Halliday strikes it rich in a silver bonanza, his wife and daughter Annalee hurry to join him in Nevada. But when lawman Brett Wilder arrives in town looking for the gun-slinger who crippled his father – and he suspects Jack of the crime – things change drastically.

In the middle of this, Annalee and Brett meet and fall in love. Unsure of the truth, they're forced to face up to what they believe about God, justice, and mercy. *Desert Rose* is a love story set in the Wild West for all fans of histori-cal romantic fiction.

ISDN 0 7369 1234 7
PB

Price: £8.50
£6.50 Special Offer
Special offer ends 31/08/03

Published by Harvest House Publishers
Eugene, Oregon 97402

One

San Francisco, 1858

Annalee hurried down the narrow dark alleyways of San Francisco's notorious Barbary Coast district with the hem of her black cloak floating behind her.

Several times she ducked out of sight between tall wooden shops and narrowly constructed houses near the wharves and warehouses. Although most of the gambling dens, saloons, and theaters were a few streets fiu-ther north, even here she could hear boisterous male voices and the thrill foolish laughter of women.

In another hour, with nightfall, the rowdiness would increase. Her mother had spoken about gangs called the "Sydney Ducks or "Hounds." These merciless ruffians would set fires in order to steal and murder. Large areas of San Francisco had several times before been burned amid looting and loss of life.

A clammy mist dung to her face and throat as though it were drizzling. Odors, from barrels of fish destined for the wharf markets satiated the briny air.

Footsteps staggered toward her, echoing on the wooden walkway. Annalee quickly ducked into a small alcove by one of the shops. She hid in the shadows beside steps leading to a door, her breathing loud in her ears. She drew the hood of her damp cloak snuggly around her cheeks, making certain her auburn curls were tucked well out of view.

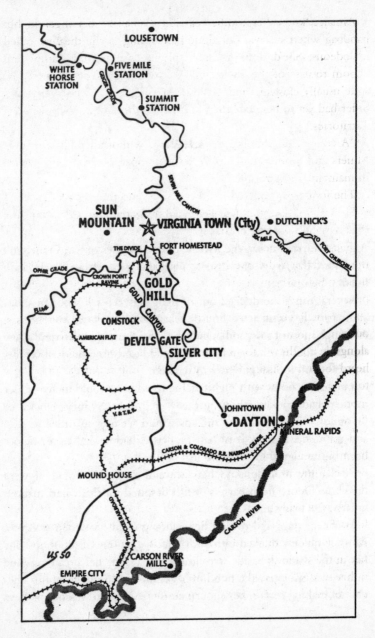

Annalee knew her mother carried a small.44 derringer in her handbag when she was out alone performing in the theaters, called melodeons. She'd done so since playing the mining camps and "boom towns" of the 1840s and '50s, where gunfights and trouble were usually close at hand. Little had changed in a decade. Law and order had yet to be established in many of the camps of the western Territories.

"A savage land," her mother often said, "without deputy marshals." Miners and businessmen alike often participated in vigilante justice to maintain a level of order.

The footsteps stumbled past her, fading into the fog.

She waited a moment longer before stepping out from the shadows and hurrying on her way.

The fog was thickening with the onset of darkness as she neared the theater where her mother was performing in a melodrama. Piano music rang out from taverns across the street, and someone shot off a pistol.

Vigilant, Annalee kept close to fog-bound buildings. The boisterous voices grew louder. With her heart beating in her throat, she ran alongside the theater toward the entrance. For a horrible moment she heard footsteps chasing her. Whirling, she waited, but the only thing to emerge from the mist was an echo. *Don't be such a coward. If Mother comes here twice a week to play the theater, so can you. It's only right to bring her this good news from Pa!*

"Never take foolish risks, expecting God to deliver you," her mother often warned. "He expects us to be prudent. But when we do find ourselves in danger, we should always call upon Him to rescue us."

It was her mother's custom to gather them all together and pray for their safety before she left the Sacramento farm where they were living with an aunt, Weda. Annalee breathed a prayer of dunks for her safe anivd at the theater.

Inside, the lamps were few and dim. If she was disappointed at its shabbiness, she tried to deny it She reminded herself that this was not typical of the theaters her mother had performed in during her heyday. The crowds here would shout to one another across the room, even interrupting the actors as they delivered their lines or sang popular songs. Female customers were not permitted in most of these local theaters. But when someone like the rising child star, Lotta Crabtree, came to sing, dance, and mimic, the town firemen, known as the Knickerbocker Hook and Ladder Company, would show up to keep things orderly and respectable.

Would any of the firemen be here tonight when her mother acted in the drama? It was unlikely. It saddened Annalee that her mother had to work in such a place. Her voice and acting ability had once been acclaimed in the Sacramento newspapers. Well, matters would soon change. She smiled, thinking of the letter in her handbag.

At this hour the theater was empty. Annalee stood still for a moment, catching her breath in the cold, silent shadows. The big room reeked of damp wood, stale tobacco, and, of course, liquor. There were always noises in empty buildings, and this one creaked with old timber.

She glanced about. In the dimness she didn't see anyone who might challenge her presence, so she sped down the shadowy aisle to steps that led up to the stage. Her mother, the once-popular Lillian O'Day, would have a room backstage where she could dress and study her lines. It wasn't likely to be much, but Annalee could remember a dressing room with plush red velvet and a chandelier when she was a child. That, however, had been in a theater in one of the gold boom towns around Sacramento.

Annalee climbed the wooden steps onto the stage, but she paused a moment before the musty curtain. She turned slowly and faced the dark rows of empty chairs.

What would it be like to perform here? What if she were singing? Would she have enough poise to step out before a crowd this size and sing her heart and soul?

Her mother had told her, "The Lord has given you an angel's voice, my sweet, but one to be dedicated to the choir at church:."

With some effort, Annalee reined in the words that were echoing through her mind and focused her attention on the matter that had brought her to San Francisco.

Her hand shook a little as she removed the envelope from her handbag. She felt the same surge of excitement as when she'd first received the letter from Jack Dawson who was actually Jack Halliday, her father.

The emotional fog they'd been wandering in for months was now lifting at last Annalee was convinced there was good news in the letter. She smiled down at the envelope. On the back flap her father had humorously sketched a cartoon of an old prospector with a bag of gold slung over his shoulder. It would bring her mother a smile too – and perhaps a great deal of money!

He had struck it rich!

Energized earlier by that expectation, Annalee had rushed into the farmhouse and shown the drawing to her aunt

"I'd not set too much store on that cartoon, child. Your pa could always draw mighty good. When he was a boy, he wanted to be an artist, but gamblin' and liquor done ruined Jack. He's just showing the flavor of the times in Washoe."

"Maybe, but I'm taking this to Mama anyway. I'm going to San Francisco by stage first thing tomorrow morning."

Weda's forehead had wrinkled. "Do you think you should, child? Are you up to it?"

"I'm well enough now. Don't worry, Aunt Weda. This letter is important. I just know it."

"Well … maybe, but you be mighty careful on the Barbary Coast?'

The musty old curtain rubbing against Annalees arm brought her back to the moment. She imagined the thrill her mother would receive when Annalee produced this long-awaited and much-prayed-for letter. Her pa had been gone for nearly two years.

Jack Halliday was somewhat of a mysterious person to Annalee. He was often away, and when he came home to Saaamento, he had nothing whatever to do with farming. He dressed in black broadcloth and frilled white shirts, and he owned a pair of pistols he kept in well-oiled leather holsters. He wore his guns "tied down." which for some reason caused a few whispers. When Annalee grew older she knew why. Gunslingers tied down their guns for fast and ready use.

The lapses of time between his visits had grown longer the older Annalee became. It was especially hard on her small brother, Jimmy.

Her pa's winsome smile and green eyes won just about everyone to his side, though, and when he did show up at the farmhouse, it was a happy time. He always brought candy, and presents, and a fancy new hat or dress for Lillian. She pretended to be shocked by the gift and asked him where he'd gotten the money to buy such lavish things. And the answer was always the same: He would laugh and say he'd hit "pay dirt."

Annalee had learned that what he really meant was that he'd been lucky at cards.

She believed this because even when he was home he'd go over to the Sacramento River to one of the gambling riverboats and be gone a few days. On one occasion he never came home. She'd heard her uncle tell her aunt that there'd been big trouble and that Jack had to run."

Behind the theater curtain, Annalee stood in the dimness before a narrow wooden hall that served as a passage to several rooms. At the far end, a door stood half open. Low, urgent voices, one of them belonging to her mother, drifted toward her.

Annalee couldn't say why, but she felt her muscles tensing as she quietly approached. She stopped by the door, peering through the narrow opening between the door and doorjamb.

The room appeared to be a lounge for the entertainers. There was a worn horsehair sofa, a low table, and some chairs.

Lillian O'Day was wearing the one remaining gown she still possessed worthy of the stage. It was a familiar blue taffeta with a princess lace collar and puffed sleeves. The lace was rather limp. Annalee had helped mend the lace just last week after her mother had caught a sleeve on a door frame nail. The crinolines, too, were patched and losing some of their pomp. Even so, it remained a fine dress, and Annalee's younger sister, Callie had asked to wear it to a church picnic on Saturday.

"You're too young to wear it," Annalee had protested.

"Annalee's right, dear. And it's not the sort of dress to wear to a church picnic."

"I don't know why not," Callie had pouted. "Sally wore a dress off the shoulders to the last barbecue."

"And was brought home early by her grandmother," Annalee had reminded her.

Callie had looked at her crossly. "You're just mean-spirited because you can't wear it."

Memory of the sisterly spat vanished as Annalee watched her mother pace the hardwood floor and shake her head. She looked distraught.

It can't be true!'

Confused, Annalee wondered, *Is she practicing her lines?* Her mother would be playing opposite Harper Browne tonight, an actor who'd also written the play. Her mother had said he was an unknown, but he had talent for creating short melodramas. One day he would work for John Maguire, the power man behind San Francisco theater.

Lillian clasped her hands together, fingers intertwined, and brought them to her chin. "How will I explain this to my children? Oh, tell me it isn't true!"

Annalee was mesmerized. This was the first time she'd actually seen her mother performing. *If Callie could see her now, there'd be no stopping her wish to follow in Mama's footsteps.*

Although Annalee knew "Lillian O'Day," had been a famous stage name a decade ago, it surprised her to see her mother in action. Why, she was a good actress. No, she was better than good. Her mother should have been able to perform in New York, not just the theaters of the West's boom towns.

But Annalee's thoughts stumbled when a man came up behind Lillian and spoke gently. One glimpse of the tall broadshouldered man told her he was not Harper Browne. She had seen Harper in Sacramento when hed briefly called on her mother about doing the play with him. Harper was a young man with hair redder than her own, a slim man of medium height with a ready smile.

This man was entirely different, yet vaguely familiar…

"I'm sorry, Lillian" came a Louisiana drawl. "I'll do everything I can to help you."

In a flash, Annalee was shaken awake. Why, this man was Macklin Villiers. She'd seen him for the first time in the spring when he'd come by the farmhouse. Her mother had introduced him to her and Callie as their father's cousin from New Orleans.

He was a stalwart man in his thirties with smooth golden ash hair and a carefully trimmed ribbon mustache. A deep cleft in the middle of his chin added to his handsome appearance. Cousin Macklin looked as though hed come into prosperity recently. He wore a well-tailored chestnut-colored jacket, and his amber-yellow vest was of watered silk. A gold watch chain looped stylishly from his vest pocket and flashed in the light from the lamps.

When Macklin came to the farmhouse, hed been dressed as a miner in rugged clothing. He'd spent the evening around the supper table filling her little brother's ears with tales about the gold mines. Macklin had gone with their father and Uncle Charlie, their Aunt Weda's husband, to the Fraser River in 1858, when there'd been the huge cry of "gold on the Fraser."

Annalee had heard it said that over eighteen thousand men had sold or abandoned their farms and possessions to make that long, hard trip to British Columbia by sea or by land. Some gold had been found on the sandbars, but for most Californians like her father, cousin, and uncle, there'd been little.

Those forty-niners had straggled back to California broken in health and in spirit to find San Francisco in the throes of a financial depression.

Then new hope revived old broken dreams. A promising new "bonanza" was discovered in the Carson River Valley across the

Sierra Mountains down in Nevada at some diggings called Washoe. Her father and all other seekers of gold and silver had answered the siren call once again. All, that is, except Macklin. He'd informed them over supper on that spring night that he was through prospecting. He was going into banking.

Macklin Villiers now stood touching his gold watch chain. "It's natural you'd feel this way, Lilly, but I'm here to tell you it is true. It brings me no pleasure. The law is looking for him now, and if he tried to cross the badlands into Utah, it's likely the Indians got him."

Annalee stood silent, stunned.

"There's some mistake, Macklin. There has to be. Jack had his faults, theres no denying them, but he wouldn't go as far as killing."

Annalee's fingers gripped the envelope containing her fathers letter.

"I wish I could tell you otherwise, Lilly, but … there's a witness. A respectable man, a Sacramento lawyer. He swears he saw the whole thing. Jack didn't know he was at the diggings when he shot Frank Harkin in the back."

Annalee nearly gasped aloud.

Her mother walked away to the table, her back toward him, her head lowered.

"I'm sorry," he said again. "I didn't fancy telling you this, but I thought it was better I do it than the law."

"I … I don't want my children to know. If … Jack was killed by Indians, let them think it was for another cause than running from a gunfight."

"Well, they won't learn it from me, but the news is out. Eventually they'll hear about it."

"They'll be older then. More able to handle it. Especially Jimmy."

Annalee's heart was beating like a drum. She stepped back farther into the shadows, aware of sudden weakness.

Her mother was saying, "I can't believe it of him – to shoot a man in the back – " her voice caught on a painful sob.

"It's the way of greed. In this case, for silver. There was a hot argument over who owned the claim. They fought. Harkin won the fight. Jack had had too much liquor. And hed been gambling. When Harkin mocked him and turned to walk away, jack picked up his gun and shot him in the back."

Annalee's moan mingled with her mother's.

"No one knows for sure where he is. Until the trouble started, he and Harkin were placer. mining near Johntown. Someone saw Jack ride off toward the Forty Mile Desert soon after he killed Harkin. By now he could be in Salt Lake looking for Samuel. Trouble is, Piutes are out that way too. Plenty of 'em. A family coming toward the Humboldt River from Utah in a wagon were butchered this summer by Piutes."

Annalee wanted to run to her mother, to burst into the room and throw her arms around her, but love held her back. It would hurt her mother even more if she knew she'd heard what Macklin had just said.

Annalee's eyes filled with scalding tears. Her shaking fingers latched onto the letter. Whatever good news it had held was now useless, written before Frank Harkin's death.

Macklin's strained voice continued, "I'll be in San Francisco for a few days. I'll do what I can to help you get Jack's financial affairs sorted out He must have sent you some legal papers."

Her mother was weeping now, unashamedly.

Annalee wept with her in the dimness of the hall. She listened to Macklin's bootsteps walking in her mother's direction. Annalee imagined his solacing hand on her shoulder.

"I'll handle this, Lilly. You don't need to worry about a thing. There's no reason for your son and daughters to know what really happened."

Tears continued to splash down Annalee's cheeks. As she backed away slowly, softly on the wooden planks, Macklin's voice became muffled by the sound of her own heartbeat

She turned, and in a few more steps was pushing her way back through the curtain onto the stage and then tiptoeing down the stairs into the shadowed theater.

Perhaps her father was dead – would that be for the better?

Fear turned her mouth dry. No. Her pa was not a Christian, and now he'd killed a man. What hope was there for him? The law would have him hanged if he was caught.

Outside the dismal theater, she found the heavy fog settling like a smothering mask. With shaking fingers she pulled the hood of her cloak over her hair as cold wisps of dampness encircled her. The stark, ugly words she had just heard repeated themselves in her mind.

Her pa had shot a man named Harkin – a man working with him on a claim in Washoe-in the back.

Annalee had intended to stay the night in San Francisco with her mother. She had imagined a gala evening after the show; they would celebrate Jack's silver strike. But now the gloom of death and misery wrapped about her like the fog, bringing her down.

Was there even a coach home to Sacramento tonight? Suddenly she realized what a fool she'd been. She rebuked herself for not planning more carefully.

Gilmore School, of course! Callie was attending the girls' school and could take her in –

No, she couldn't do that, either. If Callie saw her now, she'd know something dreadful had happened. And what reason could she give her sister for being in San Francisco without their mother knowing? Callie was not one to take excuses for an answer. She'd force the truth from her some way.

Then I'll just have to get home tonight

Now feeling weak and fatigued, she paused on the street to catch her breath. There should be a stage. There had to be.

A rig came by, and she stepped out and lifted her hand, hailing it.

She climbed into the back and found her voice weak. "The Overland Stage depot."

As the old horse plodded its way down the bawdy street, she closed her eyes and shivered inside her damp cloak. "Father, strengthen me … please … and my mother. Comfort us and give us both wisdom."

The words of Psalm 34:18 came to her mind and brought light into the dark confusion of disappointment and despair. "The LORD is nigh unto them that are of a broken heart; and saveth such as be of a contrite spirit."

The Proposal

Lori Wick

The year is 1810, the place London, England. A wealthy aristocrat thinks he's found true contentment without the love of a woman in marriage. But when a relative dies, leaving behind three children which he is forced to look after, his life changes dramatically.

With echoes of Jane Austen, *The Proposal* is period fiction for readers who love a romantic yarn with carefully-drawn historical detail. It's a moving story of how sometimes God can break in and change our hearts – and our lives – forever.

ISBN 0 7369 0558 8
PB

Price: £8.99
£6.99 Special Offer
Special offer ends 31/08/03

Published by Harvest House Publishers
Eugene, Oregon 97402

Chapter One

Aydon
London, England
May 1810

"And where did you say this was?" Mr Collins asked as he frowned fiercely at the new help, a young man who was now sweating from every pore of his body.

"It was on the floor in the back hall, Mr Collin's."

"The postmark on this letter is five days past. How could it have been missed in the hall all these days?"

"I don't know, sir. Betsy just gave it to me."

"Who is Betsy?"

"We were hired at the same time, sir. I believe she works upstairs."

Mr Collins' eyes narrowed with even more danger

"Mr Jennings will hear of this. You may be discharged."

"Yes, sir."

The crushed but humble face of the young man before him softened Mr Collins' heart a bit. He continued more kindly, "As you know, Mr Jennings is out for the evening. He probably won't receive this until morning. If I can put a word in for you, I will, but know this, young Geoffrey, it will not happen again."

"Yes, sir. Thank you, sir."

"You are dismissed."

As Geoffrey walked away, Mr Collins, long in the employ of Mr

William Jennings, stood thinking about his next move. He had several options and after just a moment's deliberation, took the second one and turned to locate Bates, Mr Jennings' man. It didn't take long. He ran him to earth in the servants' dining area, where he sat with a cup of tea and the day's post.

"This just surfaced," Mr Collins informed him, setting the letter on the table.

"It's five days old," Bates responded with a frown.

"Precisely. Do I tell him tonight?"

Bates looked up at his old friend and smiled wryly.

"You forget, Collins, that when he returns from Lady Wendt's dinner, we won't be doing anything tonight but keeping the house quiet."

Mr Collins had a smile to match his friend's before leaving to secure the letter on his desk, knowing he would have to face his employer come morning.

"Jennings?" Knightly called out as he entered the veranda. "What are you doing out, here?"

Mr William Jennings, the man he sought, glanced over his shoulder, not at all sorry to be out of Lady Vendt's stifling ballroom and in the fresh air.

"It was a bit warm in there," Jennings said briefly as Knightly joined him at the railing.

"Yes, and getting warmer. Did you see Louisa Dent tonight? Her husband leaves for France, and she throws off every inhibition."

Jennings shook his head in disgust and said, "I've known for many years what Dent has yet to find out: Most women cannot be trusted."

"I'll say," Knightly agreed fervently, draining the glass he'd brought out with him

"Knightly?" a female voice called from behind the men just as they were beginning to enjoy the silence. "Are you out here?"

"Yes, Augusta, I'm here." Knightly turned from the railing. 'Are you coming back in, Jennings?"

"I think not," that man replied. He was tired and wished to go home.

"We'll see you later," Knightly said and moved toward his wife.

Jennings did not reply. He was in need of solitude and knew that home was the only place he could be guaranteed of that.

The carriage delivered Jennings to the front of his London home precisely on time, but that man barely took notice. Though footmen in attendance and his man, Bates, didn't often see him elated, at times they sensed a lighter mood. Not tonight. Tonight he seemed far away, his mind in deep thought.

In the eyes of Jennings, Lady Wendt's dinner party had been dreadful, full of women who had nothing more on their minds than catching a rich husband or gossiping about a woman who had. His dinner companion had been a vain, blonde creature so occupied with herself she had never stopped speaking. It had given him a headache.

Now in his dressing room, having stated that he wished to be alone, Jennings slowly loosened the cravat at his throat, telling himself that tonight's dinner party would be the last. In truth, he didn't know why he'd gone in the first place.

His mood growing more pensive by the second, he waited only until his throat was free to retire to his study to sit by the fire. No other lights burned, and for long moments he stared into the flames.

Jennings had not been reared to distrust women, but his own good mother was dead, and his sister, a woman he'd admired for many years, had changed since she'd founcl God, cementing Jennings' belief that women were not all that trustworthy.

Jennings hated to even think about the change. It made him angry. That anyone with half a brain would embrace the teachings of an ancient book and say they were lifechanging, was incomprehensible to him.

Prior to her religious experience, his sister had been a brilliant woman. Articulate and keen – why, that's what had drawn Frank Palmer to the altar thirteen years ago. They'd been a promising couple. But Jennings couldn't stand to be around either of them any longer. For him, the relationship was over.

Warm from the fire, Jennings felt fatigue creep over him. The blaze lulled him as his irritation drained away. At moments like this, when his sister and her family came to mind, and only if he was very tired, he asked himself if he'd made the best choices. Maybe he should have looked into a family for himself. Maybe having sons to carry his name would have been worth taking a chance on a wife, but he would be thirty-four on his next birthday, and though not old by many standards, Jennings felt he was now too set in his ways to accommodate a family.

Sleep began to crowd in, and Jennings fought it. Just when he thought he could nod off in the chair, Jennings, a man of discipline, made himself rise and find his bed. The cool touch of the linens against his skin was enough to rouse him for a time, but the day's activities and the busyness of his mind were catching up. Asleep before the clock struck one, he never heard a sound.

"How did he take the lost letter?" Bates asked.

"I can't tell you. He didn't want the post with breakfast."

The two men looked at each other before going on about their duties.

The staff was accustomed to a life of order and discipline, so this was a surprise to them. Jennings was not an unreasonable man, but he liked his routine. And since he rarely stepped from the routine himself, it left his servants in something of a quandary. They carried on as best they could.

Bates went soundlessly into the room to see to his master's needs, but clearly Mr Jennings' mind was elsewhere. He seemed to be eating the breakfast in front of him without notice or even taste. All over the house, people were moving about quietly and for his comfort, and faint sounds of this activity drifted even to the small dining room where he sat, but there was no outward recognition of anything.

This went on for an hour before Jennings reached for the day's newspaper. He had only just immersed himself in an article on finance when Bates came to the dining room, this time to interrupt.

"I'm sorry to disturb you, sir, but a situation has arisen."

Jennings, wanting his solitude at the moment, still put the paper aside.

"Yes, Bates, what is it?"

"Some children have been delivered to our door, sir. The coachman insists that they are to come here to Mr William Jennings." Bates paused a moment but then went right on. "And if I may be so bold, sir, I have also brought you the post. On top is a letter that was given to Mr Collins yesterday. It was misplaced for a few days."

As keen as the sister he admired, Jennings was lifting the letter and opening it to read just moments later. The news that a cousin he barely knew existed had died was surprising enough. Learning that the man was leaving his three children to him was staggering. Jennings sat utterly still for a full three minutes before standing to face Bates.

"Where are these children right now?"

"In the foyer, sir. The coachman would not be swayed."

Jennings consulted the letter again.

"Three children?"

"Yes, sir. Two boys and a small girl."

"'And their father's just died," he said almost absently.

Bates remained quiet.

"Ready a room they can all sleep in tonight."

Jennings made his way toward the foyer. It didn't take long to identify his guests. Standing in a sober mass were three children. The boys stood side by side, but the girl tried to stand behind her older brother. Upon seeing Jennings approach, the older boy gently pulled his sister out to stand next to him.

Jennings went directly to the oldest child.

"I'm William, Jennings, your father's cousin," he said, putting his hand out to shake the boy's. "I'm sorry for your loss."

"Thank you, sir. My name is Thomas Jennings. This is my brother,

James, and my sister, Penelope. We call her Penny."

"Hello, James," Jennings greeted him, shaking his hand as well. But when he turned back to the little girl, she was already trying to hide behind her brother.

"May I ask you a question, sir?" Thomas, pale from the events of the last weeks, took the courage to ask.

"Yes, you may, Thomas."

"Were you expecting us, sir? Is this where we are to stay?"

As though a present had been dropped from heaven, William Jennings saw what had been given to him. The answer to the boy's question came from Jennings' mouth just heartbeats before it entered his mind.

"Yes, Thomas. This is where you're to stay."

The young man, near his thirteenth birthday, bowed slightly in acknowledgment. His ten-year-old brother and six-year-old sister made no comment or movement at all.

"How are they?" Jennings asked, hovering near the base of the main stairway and waiting for Mr Collins to descend.

"Settling in, sir."

"Did they need anything?"

"No, sir. Young Master Thomas assured me that he would see to things and make us aware of their needs."

"Are they coming down?"

"I don't believe so right now, sir. I heard Master James say that the little girl needed to sleep."

"What's her name again?"

"Penny, sir."

"That's right. "

"Is there anything else, sir?"

"No, Collins. Thank you."

Mr Collins had all he could do not to shake his head. He'd never seen his employer so anxious or animated. He couldn't wait to learn Bates' opinion on the matter.

Left alone at the bottom of the stairs, Jennings debated his next move. The children needed time to settle in to their new surroundings – they'd been through quite an ordeal but at the same time he wanted to get to know those boys. Many times in his life he had yearned for this very thing: sons to share his life with, and now he had two of them! It was almost too fantastic to be real. Last night he'd been mourning his choices, and now he had two sons without the trouble of a wife.

His mind ran with the things he wanted to tell them and show them. Not sure when they would be ready to come down, Jennings retired to his study to prepare for such a time.

"It's all right," Thomas said to his sister as he stroked her hair and tried to believe his own words. 'Just go to sleep."

"I'm cold," she sobbed.

Thomas shifted the covers up closer to her face.

"The fire is high; you'll be warm soon. Just close your eyes, Penny."

The little girl did as she was told, but not before whispering, "I need Papa."

Thomas didn't reply. He wanted their father too. From his place at the edge of the bed, Thomas looked over to where James sat by the fire. Normally rather bookish, James hadn't read a word since their father's death. Even now he looked into the flames, seemingly unaware of much else.

A glance down at Penny told Thomas she was asleep. She'd traveled in wide-eyed terror all the way to London, and he knew she was exhausted. Moving quietly to the fire with James, Thomas took a moment and looked at the room they were in. It was a large room with two wide beds. They would be very comfortable in here, but something in his young heart told him not to get too relaxed.

"Is she asleep?" James asked quietly.

"Yes."

"I'm hungry," James admitted.

"I am too."

James looked at his brother. "Do you want me to ask for something?"

"I thought I'd wait until Penny woke."

James looked surprised. "She could sleep for hours."

Thomas nodded, knowing how true that was. He could see they had little choice.

"I'll go, but we might need to take turns so one of us can sit with Penny."

"All right. You go first."

"Well, we'll see," Thomas said as he made for the door.

Jennings had tried very hard to find more to do in the study, but a sudden need to move about found him in the large entryway. For this reason he spotted Thomas' descent almost as soon as the lad was on the stairs.

"Is everything well, Thomas?" Jennings asked as soon as Thomas finished the last step.

"Our room is very nice. Thank you, sir."

"Is there something you need?"

"My brother and I find we're a little hungry."

"Of course you are," Jennings said immediately. "Why don't you go and get James, and the two of you can join me for tea."

"Actually, sir, I feel that one of us needs to sit with Penny, so if we could eat separately, that might be best."

"Very well," Jennings said, his face giving nothing away. In all his plans for the boys, he'd forgotten their sister again. "I'll just have something sent up, shall I?"

Thomas paused but still managed to say what was on his mind.

"At the risk of sounding ungrateful, sir, I don't wish to have Penny disturbed."

For the first time Jennings actually looked at this boy. His eyes were red while the flesh around them looked bruised from lack of sleep. He was pale, even to his lips, and he looked as though the world had been set on his shoulders. Jennings knew a compassion he'd not felt in years.

"Of course you don't want her disturbed, Thomas. Come with me and eat something, and then James can take your place."

Knowing nothing but relief that he'd been understood, Thomas went gratefully, planning to eat swiftly so that James would not have to sit hungry much longer.

He wouldn't have hurried so much had he realized the day was going to be spent in their room watching Penny sleep.

Thomas Jennings woke slowly the next morning. He could feel James' warmth beside him and realized that he'd slept hard all night. Shifting his neck a bit after feeling its stiffness, he pushed up against the headboard before looking at his sister's bed.

Penelope Jennings, dark hair a mass around her face, sat looking across at him.

"Are you awake, Thomas?"

"I'm awake."

"Do they have food in this house, Thomas?" she asked.

"Come here," he said, motioning to her with his hand.

Not a very large six-year-old, Penny slipped off her bed and climbed up onto the one her brothers shared. Thomas had curled his legs in, and Penny sat on the counterpane in front of him.

"You slept all night," Thomas said when she looked at him, reaching to push some of the hair from her face.

"Do we go home today?"

"No, Penny, we're staying here."

"Will they let us have food?"

"Yes. Are you hungry?"

Penny nodded and Thomas looked at her face. If the portraits didn't lie, she was a picture of their mother as a child, the mother who had died having her.

"Is Papa happy with Jesus, or does he miss us, Thomas?" Penny suddenly asked.

Rested as he was, the oldest Jennings child still felt tears sting at the back of his throat.

"He is happy with the Lord Jesus, Penny, and he trusts the Lord Jesus to watch over us, but I think if Papa had had a choice, he would have wanted to stay and take care of us."

James rolled over then to face his siblings.

"I was thinking about that too. I think if Papa knew he was going to die, he would have told us about William Jennings, so it wouldn't have been such a surprise."

"Did he know William Jennings?" Penny asked.

"He knew of him," Thomas said. "I'm sure of that, but I don't know if they had much contact."

A noise in the hall just then gave the children hope. It was hard to tell if it was too early for breakfast, but they wouldn't know until they dressed and ventured forth. And that plan went well until they got to Penny's hair. Mrs Murch had seen to things before they left Morehouse, the children's home, so this was the first time Thomas had been left with the task. He found in a hurry that the tresses had a mind of their own – just curly enough to be difficult and just thick enough to make it a challenge. Thomas ended up brushing Penny's hair out and leaving it to fall down the little girl's back. It was never left that way at home, but they were all growing more hungry by the moment, and it would do for now.

Hungry as Penny was, leaving the room was hard. The house was large and strange, and she didn't want to see William Jennings again. He didn't look at all like her papa, who had been a man who smiled most of the time, and she was a little bit afraid of him. Nevertheless, her stomach was quite empty. She kept glancing toward her brothers, who seemed to know their way around, and was startled when they suddenly spoke to someone.

"Good morning, Mr Collins," Thomas ventured. "Are we too early for breakfast?"

"Not at all, Master Thomas. Please come this way."

"Thank you."

Penny brought up the rear of this foursome, her eyes taking in statues and paintings that were far above her head.

"Here you are," Mr Collins offered once they were in a room with a large table. Thomas directed Penny to a seat. James sat next to her, and Thomas sat across the table.

"Breakfast will be served momentarily," Mr Collins informed them before leaving.

Penny waited only until he exited the room to fix her dress. She had sat on it awkwardly, and the neck was choking her. Putting a small glass figurine on the table, she shifted until she was comfortable

"Oh, Penny," James chided, sounding aggrieved. "You didn't bring Mr Pat with you."

The little girl looked upset as she took it back in her hand.

"Will Mr Jennings be angry?"

"No, but there's no place for it at the breakfast table. You should have left it in the room."

"Put it in your pocket," Thomas suggested, not wanting James and Penny to argue.

Penny did so, her eyes large and sober. James looked her way and felt bad.

"It's all right, Penny. I just don't want us to make a mistake and get booted out of here. I don't know where we would go."

"Is that going to happen, Thomas?" Penny asked.

"No, Penny, I don't think so, but Father would want us to be on our best behavior."

Penny nodded, looking as lost and little as she felt.

Relief, however, was on the way. Not aware that they were up already, Jennings did not join them, but platters of food began to arrive, and in little time all hunger was forgotten.

The report back to Cook that the three children were good eaters made that woman's day. She started baking cookies, four different varieties, with plans to get word to the children that they were to visit her in the kitchen and have samples as often as they liked.

"I think this is the door," Thomas said as he led his siblings toward the back of the house and outside a short time after breakfast. Once the door was shut behind them, they stood and took in a high-walled garden, quite large and overflowing with flowers. It was nothing like the rolling hillsides at home, but the fresh air was nice, and the flowers in William Jennings' yard were beautiful.

"Stay on the path," Thomas directed when Penny started forward.

That little girl was careful to obey, and when she came to a stone bench, she sat down, noticing that it was just her size. Thomas and James moved to look at the lattice work on a trellis, and that was where Jennings found them.

"Good morning, Thomas. Good morning, James. How was your night's rest?"

"Very good, sir. Thank you."

"And breakfast? Did you have enough to eat?"

"Plenty, sir. Should we know the times for meals, Mr Jennings? Were we too early this morning?"

"Not at all. Why don't you tell me when you like to eat, and I'll see to it that Mr Collins alerts the staff." Remembering again that he was going to have to give the boys time, he mentioned tactfully, "I'm often out in the evenings, but maybe we could breakfast or lunch together."

"Thank you, sir. We would enjoy that."

"Is this a sundial?" James asked, having been distracted by the instrument high on the stone wall. He'd never seen one that didn't sit on a pedestal or base on the ground.

"Yes, it is. I found that at an auction a few years ago and thought I had a good spot for it. What do you think, James?"

"I think it's a perfect spot. I've read about these but have never seen one. Our father had a sundial in the yard, but the base broke which tipped it slightly. After that it was never correct."

"I bought this trellis at the same time," Jennings went on to add, walking over to put his hand on it. "Did you happen to notice it?"

"Yes. It looks heavy."

"It's very heavy. It was too large to come through the house, and they had quite the time getting it over the wall."

"Is there no door in the wall?" Thomas asked, wishing all of this was as normal as it must have looked.

"There is, but it's too small." The gentleman went on speaking about various things in the garden, but Penny did not join the other three. When she had heard the door open, she scooted off the bench and behind a bush. She could see her brothers from where she was, but at the moment they didn't look for her. Penny listened to their conversation and relaxed a little when she realized their host had not come to boot them out. Even though she heard the calm, quiet sound of Mr Jennings' voice and did not find him as scary as she remembered, Penny hoped her brothers would not miss her until he had gone back inside.

The Screwtape Letters

C. S. Lewis

One of Lewis' most famous works, The Screwtape Letters is the satirical correspondence of an experienced devil to his young nephew, Wormwood. With short letters giving advice on tempting and confusing human beings away from God, the book develops into a sly take on human life, by turns hilarious and painfully honest about our pride and sin.

This special edition, published to mark the book's sixtieth anniversary, includes for the first time a final 'Screwtape Letter' written by Lewis for a British newspaper shortly before died.

ISBN 0 0062 8060 9
PB

Price: £7.99
£5.99 Special Offer
Special offer ends 31/08/03

Published by Harper Collins
77-85 Fulham Palace Road
Hammersmith, London W6 8JB

Preface

I have no intention of explaining how the correspondence which I now offer to the public fell into my hands.

There are two equal and opposite errors into which our race can fall about the devils. One is to disbelieve in their existence. The other is to believe, and to feel an excessive and unhealthy interest in them. They themselves are equally pleased by both errors and hail a materialist or a magician with the same delight. The sort of script which is used in this book can be very easily obtained by anyone who has once learned the knack; but ill-disposed or excitable people who might make a bad use of it shall not learn it from me.

Readers are advised to remember that the devil is a liar. Not everything that Screwtape says should be assumed to be true even from his own angle. I have made no attempt to identify any of the human beings mentioned in the letters; but I think it very unlikely that the portraits, say, of Fr Spike or the patient's mother, are wholly just. There is wishful thinking in Hell as well as on Earth.

In conclusion, I ought to add that no effort has been made to clear up the chronology of the letters. Number XVII appears to have been composed before rationing became serious; but in general the diabolical method of dating seems to bear no relation to terrestrial time and I have not attempted to reproduce it. The history of the European War, except in so far as it happens now and then to impinge upon the spiritual condition of one human being, was obviously of no interest to Screwtape.

C. S. LEWIS
MAGDALEN COLLEGE,
5 JULY 1941

The Screwtape Letters
1

My dear Wormwood,

I note what you say about guiding your patient's reading and taking care that he sees a good deal of his materialist friend. But are you not being a trifle *naive*? It sounds as if you supposed that *argument* was the way to keep him out of the Enemy's clutches. That might have been so if he had lived a few centuries earlier. At that time the humans still knew pretty well when a thing was proved and when it was not; and if it was proved they really believed it. They still connected thinking with doing and were prepared to alter their way of life as the result of a chain of reasoning. But what with the weekly press and other such weapons we have largely altered that. Your man has been accustomed, ever since he was a boy, to have a dozen incompatible philosophies dancing about together inside his head. He doesn't think of doctrines as primarily 'true' or 'false', but as, 'academic' or 'practical', 'outworn' or 'contemporary', 'conventional' or 'ruthless'. Jargon, not argument, is your best ally in keeping him from the Church. Don't waste time trying to make him think that materialism is *true*! Make him think it is strong, or stark, or courageous – that it is the philosophy of the future. That's the sort of thing he cares about.

The trouble about argument is that it moves the whole struggle on to the Enemy's own ground. He can argue too; whereas in really practical propaganda of the kind I am suggesting He has been shown for centuries to be greatly the inferior of Our Father Below. By the very act of arguing, you awake the patient's reason; and once it is awake. who can foresee the result? Even if a particular train of thought can be twisted so as to end in our favour, you will find that you have been strengthening in your patient the fatal habit of attending to universal issues and withdrawing his attention from the stream of immediate sense experiences. Your business is to fix his attention on the stream. Teach him to call it 'real life' and don't let him ask what he means by 'real'.

Remember, he is not, like you, a pure spirit. Never having been a human (Oh that abominable advantage of the Enemy's!) you don't realise how enslaved they are to the pressure of the ordinary. I once had a patient, a sound atheist, who used to read in the British Museum. One day, as he sat reading, I saw a train of thought in his mind beginning to go the wrong way. The Enemy, of course, was at his elbow in a moment. Before I knew where I was I saw my twenty years work beginning to totter. If I had lost my head and begun to attempt a defence by argument I should have been undone. But I was not such a fool. I struck instantly at the part of the man which I had best under my control and suggested that it was just about time he had some lunch. The Enemy presumably made the counter-suggestion (you know how one can never *quite* overhear what He says to them?) that this was more important than lunch. At least I think that must have been His line for when I said 'Quite. In fact much *too* important to tackle at the end of a morning,' the patient brightened up considerably; and by the time I had added 'Much better come back after lunch and go into it with a fresh mind,' he was already half way to the door. Once he was in the street the battle was won. I showed him a newsboy shouting the midday paper, and a No. 73 bus going past, and before he reached the bottom of the steps I had got into him an unalterable conviction that, whatever odd ideas might come into a man's head when he was shut up alone with his books, a healthy dose of 'real life' (by which he meant the bus and the newsboy) was enough to show him that all 'that sort of thing' just couldn't be true. He knew he'd had a narrow escape and in later years was fond of talking about 'that inarticulate sense for actuality which is our ultimate safeguard against the aberrations of mere logic'. He is now safe in Our Father's house.

You begin to see the point? Thanks to processes which we set at work in them centuries ago, they find it all but impossible to believe in the unfamiliar while the familiar is before their eyes. Keep pressing home on him the *ordinariness* of things. Above all, do not attempt to use science (I mean, the real sciences) as a defence against Christianity. They will positively encourage him to think about realities he can't touch and see. There have been sad cases among the modern physicists. If he must dabble in science, keep him on economics and sociology; don't let him get away from that invaluable 'real life'. But the best of all is to let him read no science but to give him a grand general idea that he knows it all and that everything he happens to have picked up in casual talk and reading is 'the results of modern investigation'. Do remember YOU are there to fuddle him. From the way some of you young fiends talk, anyone would suppose it was our job to *teach*!

Your affectionate uncle
SCREWTAPE

2

My dear Wormwood,

I note with grave displeasure that your patient has become a Christian. Do not indulge the hope that you will escape the usual penalties; indeed, in your better moments, I trust you would hardly even wish to do so. In the meantime we must make the best of the situation. There is no need to despair; hundreds of these adult converts have been reclaimed after a brief sojourn in the Enemy's camp and are now with us. All the *habits* of the patient, both mental and bodily, are still in our favour.

One of our great allies at present is the Church itself. Do not misunderstand me. I do not mean the Church as we see her spread out through all time and space and rooted in eternity, terrible as an army with banners. That, I confess, is a spectacle which makes our boldest tempters uneasy. But fortunately it is quite invisible to these humans. All your patient sees is the half-finished, sham Gothic erection on the new building estate. When he goes inside, he sees the local grocer with rather an oily expression on his face bustling up to offer him one shiny little book containing a liturgy which neither of them understands, and one shabby little book. containing corrupt texts of a number of religious lyrics, mostly bad, and in very small print. When he gets to his pew and looks round him he sees just that selection of his neighbours whom he has hitherto avoided. You want to lean pretty heavily on those neighbours. Make his mind flit to and fro between an expression like 'the body of Christ' and the actual faces in the next pew. It matters very little, of course, what kind of people that next pew really contains. You may know one of them to be a great warrior on the Enemy's side. No matter. Your patient, thanks to Our Father Below, is a fool. Provided that any of those neighbours sing out of tune, or have boots that squeak, or double chins, or odd clothes, the patient will quite easily believe that their religion must therefore be somehow ridiculous. At his present stage, you see, he has an idea of 'Christians' in his mind which he supposes to be spiritual but which, in fact, is largely pictorial. His mind is full of togas and sandals and armour and bare legs and the mere fact that the other people in church wear modern clothes is a real – though of course an unconscious – difficulty to him. Never let it come to the surface; never let him ask what he expected them to look like. Keep everything hazy in his mind now, and you will have all eternity wherein to amuse yourself by producing in him the peculiar kind of clarity which Hell affords.

Work hard, then, on the disappointment or anticlimax which is certainly coming to the patient during his first few weeks as a churchman. The Enemy allows this disappointment to occur on the threshold of every human endeavour. It occurs when the boy who has been enchanted in the nursery by *Stories from the Odyssey* buckles down to really learning Greek. It occurs when lovers have got married and begin the real task of learning to live together. In every department of life it marks the transition from dreaming aspiration to laborious doing. The Enemy takes this risk because He has a curious fantasy of making all these disgusting little human vermin into what He calls His 'free' lovers and servants – 'sons' is the word He uses, with His inveterate love of degrading the whole spiritual world by unnatural liaisons with the two-legged animals. Desiring their freedom, He therefore refuses to carry them, by their mere affections and habits, to any of the goals which He sets before them: He leaves them to 'do it on their own'. And there lies our opportunity. But also, remember, there lies our danger. If once they get through this initial dryness successfully, they become much less dependent on emotion and therefore much harder to tempt.

I have been writing hitherto on the assumption that the people in the next pew afford no *rational* ground for disappointment. Of course if they do – if the patient knows that the woman with the absurd hat is a fanatical bridgeplayer or the man with squeaky boots a miser and an extortioner – then your task is so much the easier. All you then have to do is to keep out of his mind the question 'If I, being what I am, can consider that I am in some sense a Christian, why should the different vices of those people in the next pew prove that their religion is mere hypocrisy and convention?' You may ask whether it is possible to keep such an obvious thought from occurring even to a human mind. It is, Wormwood, it is! Handle him properly and it simply won't come into his head. He has not been anything like long enough with the Enemy to have any real humility yet. What he says, even on his knees, about his own sinfulness is all parrot talk. At bottom, he still believes he has run up a very favourable credit-balance in the Enemy's ledger by allowing himself to be converted, and thinks that he is showing great humility and conde-scension in going to church with these 'smug', commonplace neigh-bours at all. Keep him in that state of mind as long as you can,

Your affectionate uncle
SCREWTAPE

The Great Divorce

C. S. Lewis

In his classic novel *The Great Divorce*, Lewis ponders in prose the timeless question of the existence of Heaven and Hell – is it possible that one could exist without the other?

With unrivalled skill and literary panache, Lewis constructs a compelling fantasy story of how ghosts occupy the real world with us, demonstrating the consequences of all of our everyday actions. It is a thoughtful and provocative story – pure fantasy, but packed with truth.

ISBN 0 0062 8056 0
PB

Price: £6.99
£4.99 Special Offer
Special offer ends 31/08/03

1

I seemed to be standing in a busy queue by the side of a long, mean street. Evening was just closing in and it was raining. I had been wandering for hours in similar mean streets, always in the rain and always in evening twilight. Tuime seemed to have paused on that dismal moment when only a few shops have lit up and it. is not yet dark enough for their windows to look cheering. And just as the evening never advanced to night, so my walking had never brought me to the better parts of the town. However far I went I found only dingy lodging houses, small tobacconists, hoardings from which posters hung in rags, windowless warehouses, goods stations without trains, and bookshops of the sort that sell *The Works of Aristotle*. I never met anyone. But for the little crowd at the bus stop, the whole town seemed to be empty. I think that was why I attached myself to the queue.

I had a stroke of luck right away, for just as I took my stand a little waspish woman who would have been ahead of me snapped out at a man who seemed to be with her, 'Very well then. I won't go at all. So there,' and left the queue. 'Pray don't imagine,' said the man, in a very dignified voice, 'that I care about going in the least. I have only been trying to please *you*, for peace sake. My own feelings are of course a matter of no importance, I quite understand *that*' – and suiting the action to the word he also walked away. 'Come,' thought I, 'that's two places gained.' I was now next to a very short man with a scowl who glanced at me with an expression of extreme disfavour and observed, rather unnecessarily loudly, to the man beyond him, 'This sort of thing really makes one think twice about going at all.' 'What sort of thing?' growled the other, a big beefy person. 'Well,' said the Short Man, 'this is hardly the sort of society I'm used to as a matter of fact.' 'Huh!' said the Big Man: and then added with a glance at me, 'Don't you stand any sauce from *him*, Mister. You're not *afraid* of him are you?' Then, seeing I made no move, he rounded suddenly on the Short Man and said, 'Not good enough for you, aren't we? Like your lip.' Next moment he had fetched the Short Man one on the side of the face that sent him sprawling into the gutter. 'Let him lay, let him lay,' said the Big Man to no one in particular. 'I'm a plain man that's what I am and I got to have my rights same as anyone else, see?' As the Short Man showed no disposition to rejoin the queue and soon began limping away, I closed up, rather cautiously, behind the Big Man and congratulated myself on having gained yet another step. A moment later two young people in front of him also left us arm in arm They were both so trousered, slender, giggly and falsetto that I could be sure of the sex of neither, but it was clear that each for the moment preferred the other to the chance of a place in the bus. 'We shall never all get in,' said a female voice with a whine in it from some four places ahead of me. 'Change places with you for five bob, lady,' said someone else. I heard the clink of money and then a scream in the female voice, mixed with roars of laughter from the rest of the crowd. The cheated woman leaped out of her place to fly at the man who had bilked her, but the others immediately closed up and flung her out . . . So what with one thing and another the queue had reduced itself to manageable proportions long before the bus appeared.

It was a wonderful vehicle, blazing with golden light, heraldically coloured. The Driver himself seemed full of light and he used only one hand to drive with. The other he waved before his face as if to fan away the greasy steam of the rain. A growl went up from the queue as he came in sight. 'Looks as if *he* had a good time of it, eh?

… Bloody pleased with himself, I bet … My dear, why can't he behave naturally? – Thinks himself too good to look at us …Who does he imagine he is? … All that gilding and purple, I call it a wicked waste. Why don't they spend some of the money on their house property down here? – God! Id like to give him one in the ear-'ole.' I could see nothing in the countenance of the Driver to justify all this, unless it were that he had a look of authority and seemed intent on carrying out his job.

My fellow passengers fought like hens to get on board the bus though there was plenty of room for us all. I was the last to get in. The bus was only half full and I selected a seat at the back, well away from the others. But a touslehaired youth at once came and sat down beside me. As he did so we moved off.

'I thought you wouldn't mind my tacking on to you,' he said, 'for I've noticed that you feel just as I do about the present company. Why on earth they insist on coming I can't imagine. They won't like it at all when we get there, and they'd really be much more comfortable at home. It's different for you and me.'

'Do they *like* this place?' I asked.

'As much as they'd like anything,' he answered.

'They've got cinemas and fish and chip shops and advertisements and all the sorts of things they want. The appalling lack of any intellectual life doesn't worry *them*. I realised as soon as I got here that there'd been some mistake. I ought to have taken the first bus but I've fooled about trying to wake people up here. I found a few fellows I'd known before and tried to form a little circle, but they all seem to have sunk to the level of their surroundings. Even before we came here I'd had some doubts about a man like Cyril Blellow. I always thought he was working in a false idiom. But he was at least intelligent: one could get some criticism worth hearing from him, even if he was a failure on the creative side. But now he seems to have nothing left but his self-conceit. The last time I tried to read him some of my own stuff … but wait a minute, I'd just like you to look at it.'

Realising with a shudder that what he was producing from his pocket was a thick wad of type-written paper, I muttered something about not having my spectacles and exclaimed, 'Hullo! We've left the ground.'

It was true. Several hundred feet below us, already half hidden in the rain and mist, the wet roofs of the town appeared, spreading without a break as far as the eye could reach.

2

I was not left very long at the mercy of the Tousle-Headed Poet, because another passenger interrupted our conversation: but before that happened I had learned a good deal about him. He appeared to be a singularly ill used man. His parents had never appreciated him and none of the five schools at which he had been educated seemed to have made any provision for a talent and temperament such as his. To make matters worse he had been exactly the sort of boy in whose case then system works out with the unfairness and absurdity. It was not until he reached the university that he began to recognise that all these injustices did not come by chance but were the inevitable results of our economic system. Capitalism did not merely enslave the workers, it also vitiated taste and vulgarised intellect: hence our educational system and hence the lack of 'Recognition' for new genius. This discovery had made him a Communist. But when the war came along and he saw Russia in alliance with the capitalist governments, he had found himself once more isolated and had to become a conscientious objector. The indignities he suffered at this stage of his career had, he confessed, embittered him. He decided he could serve the cause best by going to America: but then America came into the war too. It was at this point that he suddenly saw Sweden as the home of a really new and radical art, but the various oppressors had given him no facilities for going to Sweden. There were money troubles. His father, who had never progressed beyond the most atrocious mental complacency and smugness of the Victorian epoch, was giving him a ludicrously inadequate allowance. And he had been very badly treated by a girl too. He had thought her a really civilised and adult personality, and then she had unexpectedly revealed that she was a mass of bourgeois prejudices and monogamic instincts. Jealousy, possessiveness, was a quality he particularly disliked. She had even shown herself, at the end, to be mean about money. That was the last straw. He had jumped under a train …

I gave a start, but he took no notice.

Even then, he continued, ill luck had continued to dog him. He'd been sent to the grey town. But of course it was a mistake. I would find, he assured me, that all the other passengers would be with me on the return journey. But he would not. He was going to stay 'there'. He felt quite certain that he was going where, at last, his finely critical spirit would no longer be outraged by an uncongenial environment – where he would find 'Recognition' and 'Appreciation'. Meanwhile, since I hadn't got my glasses, he would read me the passage about which Cyril Blellow had been so insensitive …

It was just then that we were interrupted. One of the quarrels which were perpetually simmering in the bus had boiled over and for a moment there was a stampede. Knives were drawn: pistols were fired: but it all seemed strangely innocuous and when it was over I found myself unharmed, though in a different seat and with a new companion. He was an intelligent-looking man with a rather bulbous nose and a bowler hat. I looked out of the windows. We were now so high that all below us had become featureless. But fields, rivers, or mountains I did not see, and I got the impression that the grey town still filled the whole field of vision.

'It seems the deuce of a town,' I volunteered, 'and that's what I can't understand. The parts of it that I saw were so empty. Was there once a much larger population?'

'Not at all,' said my neighbour. 'The trouble is that they're so quarrelsome. As soon as anyone arrives he settles in some street. Before he's been there twenty-four hours he quarrels with his neighbour. Before the week is over he's quarrelled so badly that he decides to move. Very likely he finds the next street empty because all the people there have quarrelled with *their* neighbours – and moved. If so he settles in. If by any chance the street is full, he goes further. But even if he stays, it makes no odds. He's sure to have another quarrel pretty soon and then he'll move on again. Finally he'll move right out to the edge of the town and build a new house. You see, it's easy here. You've only got to *think* a house and there it is. That's how the town keeps on growing.'

'Leaving more and more empty streets?'

'That's right. And time's sort of odd here. That place where we caught the bus is thousands of miles from the Civic Centre where all the newcomers arrive from earth. All the people you've met were living near the bus stop: but they'd taken centuries – of our time – to get there, by gradual removals.'

'And what about the earlier arrivals? I mean – there must be people who came from Earth to your town even longer ago.'

'That's right. There are. They've been moving on and on. Getting further apart. They're so far off by now that they could never think of coming to the bus stop at all. Astronomical distances. There's a bit of rising ground near where I live and a chap has a telescope. You can see the lights of the inhabited houses, where those old ones live, millions of miles away. Millions of miles from us and from one another. Every now and then they move further still. That's one of the disappointments. I thought you'd meet interesting historical characters. But you don't: they're too far away.'

'Would they get to the bus stop in time, if they ever set out?'

'Well – theoretically. But it'd be a distance of light-years. And they wouldn't want to by now: not those old chaps like Tamberlaine and Genghiz Khan, or Julius Caesar, or Henry the Fifth.'

'Wouldn't want to?'

'That's right. The nearest of those old ones is Napoleon. We know that because two chaps made the journey to see him. They'd started long before I came, of course, but I was there when they came back. About fifteen thousand years of our time it took them. We've picked out the house by now. Just a little pin prick of light and nothing else near it for millions of miles.'

'But they got there?'

'That's right. He'd built himself a huge house all in the Empire style – rows of windows flaming with light, though it only shows as a pin prick from where I live.'

'Did they see Napoleon?'

'That's right. They went up and looked through one of the windows. Napoleon was there all right.'

'What was he doing?'

'Walking up and down – up and down all the time – left-right, left-right – never stopping for a moment. The two chaps watched him for about a year and he never rested. And muttering to himself all the time. "It was Soult's fault. It was Ney's fault. It was Josephine's fault. It was the fault of the Russians. It was the fault of the English." Like that all the time. Never stopped for a moment. A little, fat man and he looked kind of tired. But he didn't seem able to stop it.'

From the vibrations I gathered that the bus was still moving, but there was now nothing to be seen from the windows which confirmed this – nothing but grey void above and below.

'Then the town will go on spreading indefinitely?' I said.

'That's right,' said the Intelligent Man. 'Unless someone can do something about it.'

'How do you mean?'

'Well, as a matter of fact, between you and me and the wall, that's my job at the moment. What's the trouble about this place? Not that people are quarrelsome – that's only human nature and was always the same even on Earth. The trouble is they have no Needs. You get everything you want (not very good quality, of course) by just imagining it. That's why it never costs any trouble to move to another street or build another house. In other words, there's no proper economic basis for any community life. If they needed real shops, chaps would have to stay near where the real shops were. If they needed real houses they'd have to stay near where builders were. It's scarcity that enables a society to exist. Well, that's where I come in. I'm not going on this trip for my health. As far as that goes I don't think it would suit me up there. But if I can come back with some *real* commodities – anything at all that you could really bite or drink or sit on – why, at once you'd get a demand down in our town. I'd start a little business. I'd have something to sell. You'd soon get people coming to live near – centralisation. Two fully-inhabited streets would accommodate the people that are now spread over a million square miles of empty streets. I'd make a nice little profit and be a public benefactor as well.'

'You mean, if they *had* to live together they'd gradually learn to quarrel less?'

'Well, I don't know about that. I daresay they could be kept a bit quieter. You'd have a chance to build up a police force. Knock some kind of discipline into them. Anyway' (here he dropped his voice) 'it'd be *better,* you know. Everyone admits that. Safety in numbers.'

'Safety from what?,' I began, but my companion nudged me to be silent. I changed my question.

'But look here,' said I, 'if they can get everything just by imagining it, why would they want any real things, as you call them?'

'Eh? Oh well, they'd like houses that really kept out the rain.'

'Their present houses don't?'

'Well, of course not. How could they?'

'What the devil is the use of building them, then?' The Intelligent Man put his head closer to mine. 'Safety again,' he muttered. 'At least, the feeling of safety. It's all right *now:* but later on … you understand.'

'What?,' said I, almost involuntarily sinking my own voice to a whisper.

He articulated noiselessly as if expecting that I understood lipreading. I put my ear up close to his mouth. 'Speak up,' I said. 'It will be dark presently,' he mouthed.

'You mean the evening *is* really going to turn into a night in the end?'

He nodded.

'What's that got to do with it?' said I.

'Well … no one wants to be out of doors when that happens.'

'Why?'

His reply was so furtive that I had to ask him several times to repeat it. When he had done so, being a little annoyed (as one so often is with whisperers), I replied without remembering to lower my voice.

'Who are "They"?' I asked. 'And what are you afraid they'll do to you? And why should they come out when it's dark? And what protection could an imaginary house give if there was any danger?'

'Here!' shouted the Big Man. 'Who's talking all that stuff? You stop your whispering, you two, if you don't want a hiding, see? Spreading rumours, that's what I call it. You shut your face, Ikey, see?'

'Quite right. Scandalous. Ought to be prosecuted. How did they get on the bus?' growled the passengers.

A fat clean-shaven man who sat on the seat in front of me leaned back and addressed me in a cultured voice.

'Excuse me,' he said, 'but I couldn't help overhearing parts of your conversation. It is astonishing how these primitive superstitions linger on. I beg your pardon? Oh, God bless my soul, that's all it is. There is not a shred of evidence that this twilight is ever going to turn into a night. There has been a revolution of opinion on that in educated circles. I am surprised that you haven't heard of it. All the nightmare fantasies of our ancestors are being swept away. What we now see in this subdued and delicate half-light is the promise of the dawn: the slow turning of a whole nation towards the light. Slow and imperceptible, of course. "And not through Eastern windows only, When daylight comes, comes in the light." And that passion for "real" commodities which our friend speaks of is only materialism, you know. It's retrogressive. Earth-bound! A hankering for matter. But *we* look on this spiritual city – for with all its faults it *is* spiritual – as a nursery in which the creative functions of man, now freed from the clogs of matter, begin to try their wings. A sublime thought.'

Hours later there came a change. It began to grow light in the bus. The greyness outside the windows turned from mud-colour to mother of pearl, then to faintest blue, then to a bright blueness that stung the eyes. We seemed to be floating in a pure vacancy. There were no lands, no sun, no stars in sight: only the radiant abyss. I let down the window beside me. Delicious freshness came in for a second, and then–

'What the hell are you doing?' shouted the Intelligent Man, leaning roughly across me and pulling the window sharply up. 'Want us all to catch our death of cold?'

'Hit him a biff,' said the Big Man.

I glanced round the bus. Though the windows were closed, and soon muffed, the bus was full of light. It was cruel light. I shrank from the faces and forms by which I was surrounded. They were all fixed faces, full not of possibilities but impossibilities, some gaunt, some bloated, some glaring with idiotic ferocity, some drowned beyond recovery in dreams; but all, in one way or another, distorted and faded. One had a feeling that they might fall to pieces at any moment if the light grew much stronger. Then there was a mirror on the end wall of the bus – I caught sight of my own.

And still the light grew.

Ghosts

Adrian Plass

In Adrian Plass's latest novel, a group of old friends who last met up as twenty-somethings get together for a weekend in a country manor house. There, they begin to face up to disappointment, regret and pain, realising that life hadn't quite been all they'd hoped for. But is it possible that their 'ghosts' might be the key to their healing?

Ghosts is a mature and moving novel, as Plass deals with serious issues of life and death with his trademark light touch.

ISBN 0 5510 3109 3
HB

Price: £9.99
£6.99 Special Offer
Special offer ends 31/08/03

Part One
Loss

I seem to wake.

My bedroom is in darkness, the rectangle of my curtainless window less black only by a margin of the deepest shade of grey. I am lying on my back, and remain in that position as if paralysed, my eyes wide open, flicking from side to side as I listen intently. My anxiety is to establish urgently the absence of sounds that would be out of place in a safe, secure house at night. In fact, the loudest sound is my own panic-stricken breathing. I fancy, in addition, that I can hear my heart throbbing and hammering against the wall of my chest. It is as though, in that crucial instant before waking, I have received an overwhelming, crushing shock.

I remember! Of course I remember.

The noise that destroyed my sleep was a thunderous knocking and crashing on the top and bottom of my bedroom door, a veritable rain of blows, catapulting me into consciousness with brutal, wrenching abruptness.

But — and here is the crucial question — this wild knocking, did it happen in my sleep? Was it the final instant or climax of a dream? That is possible. I have known such things before.

Or not?

Could there actually be, at this very moment, a person or persons standing outside my door, waiting for me to climb from the shelter of my bed to discover the cause of such inexplicable urgency?

No, that idea is foolish and illogical. If there is a man or men who have

*somehow forced the locks of a door in my house and made their way up my
stairs, why should they take the time and trouble to hammer on my unlocked
bedroom door with such grotesque violence?*

*If their intention was originally robbery or murder, am I seriously to believe
that, in the course of a short journey from the top of the stairs to this side of
the landing, they have, by some obscure process, been so infected with courtesy
that they now feel obliged to warn me of their presence?*

*On the other hand, if, unfathomably, their motive is an innocent one, why
do they not simply come into my room and disclose the nature of the
emergency that has made it necessary for them to break into my home and
disturb my sleep?*

*No, no, the outrageous knocking was a dream. It was the end of a
nightmare. I know it was. In the past I have safely woken from so many
nightmares. Actually, I have woken from every single nightmare that I have
ever endured. For all my life.*

Not all.

All but one.

*But I have certainly woken from this nightmare of meaningless knocking,
and now I shall go back to sleep. In fact, that is my plan for dealing with the
situation. I shall go back to sleep. I shall close my eyes and simply drift back
into sleep. Suddenly it will be morning.*

I close my eyes and wait for sleep to come.

I wait.

*I cannot sleep until I have opened that door. The mindless battering and
kicking on the wooden panels that woke me just now was certainly nothing
more than a nightmare. However, the fact remains that I cannot sleep until I
have opened that door. There will be no one there, of course. There is never
anyone there. But it is necessary for the sake of my peace that I should pull
that door open, look carefully round it and see with my own two eyes that the
landing is empty and clear of intruders. After that sleep will come. Yes, after
that sleep will come easily.*

*I push back my bedclothes. I swing my feet to the floor I stand and begin
to feel my way carefully through the pitch darkness towards the door I am
halfway there when a cold shiver of realization passes through me. What can*

I have been thinking of? My bedroom at night is never this dark. The world outside my window is never as opaque as it appears now. The window is, in any case, in the wrong place. I was mistaken. This is not my bedroom. I am not awake. I never did wake. I dreamed that I slept. I dreamed that I woke. Dear God! I thought that I was awake, but I am in a nightmare. And now I am to be driven onward by that nightmare. There is no longer a choice between continuing across this alien room and returning to the bed that I naively believed to be mine. Opening that door and confronting whatever may lie behind it is my inescapable assignment. I am close to tears at the prospect of some shrieking abyss of insanity on the other side, and I am right to be petrified. The logic of nightmare interlocks as tightly as the logic of the waking world, but the one is as far removed from the other as hope is removed from despair

I am at the door There will be nothing. I place my hand on the handle. There will be nothing. I push the handle down. There will be nothing. I pull open the door Oh! A scream rises in my throat like vomit, but does not emerge. It is like choking on terror. There is something. Two figures are silhouetted within the frame of the door, nearly filling the space. One is large and shambling, slightly bent over, the other smaller. I peer at them but cannot make out the features of either. They do not speak. They do not move. Why, in God's name, do they say and do nothing? It is as if they know that by remaining silent and motionless they will bring me to the sharpest, uppermost pinnacle of this shrieking spiral of fear

I say, my voice contained within a thin, parchment-like skin of self- control, 'Yes, can I help you? Did you want something?'

I cannot see their mouths, but I know that they are grinning horribly in the darkness now. They are amused by the grovelling terror that makes me say stupid, polite things to people who have callously broken into my house and smashed their fists and feet against my door. They have won. Again. Yet again I perceive that I am what I am. I am so full of trembling hysteria that I fear my spirit will unravel or disintegrate.

My sole advantage is the certain knowledge that this is a dream. I may have learned the truth in time. I am not awake. This is a dream. I can escape. There is a way of escape. Surely nightmare is not permitted to break its own rules.

As the larger figure makes a sudden slight movement in my direction, I close my eyes and allow everything that I am to fall back on to the smooth, yielding darkness behind me. Releasing body and mind, I slide at ever-increasing speed down the long, steep slopes of a strangely exhilarating descent into abandonment.

In a final rush of excitement and dread I collide soundlessly with the real world, perspiring and trembling, awake in my own bed, my heart filled with a dark emotion that is much less and much more than the fear of nightmare.

There is an old schoolboy joke that goes, 'How do you know when an elephant's been in your fridge?' The answer is, 'You can tell by the footprints in the butter.'

Losing someone you have loved and lived with carries echoes of that silly joke. The one who was half of your existence is gone, but, between them, the vastness of her life, and the elephantine, Jurassic creature called death, leave paradoxically tiny marks or footprints all over your house, your heart and your life. For a long time these marks of passing are to be found everywhere, every day. Each new discovery is likely to trigger a fresh outburst of grief.

Some of them really are in the fridge. On the bottom shelf stands a carton of skimmed milk, a small aspect of the scheme that she devised to make sure of losing a few pounds before going on our planned sunshine holiday in late summer. She bought it on the morning of the day before she was taken ill. The carton should have been thrown out a long time ago, but the dustbin outside my back door is somehow not large or appropriate enough to contain the implications of such an action.

Upstairs, on the table next to her side of the bed sprawls an untidy pile of books that she has been devouring, dipping into, hoping to read. One of them was about pregnancy and childbirth. This was to have been the year …

Beside the books stands a tumbler, nearly filled with water.

The books should be returned to the bookcase, but the exact order and positioning of them on the bedside table, the sheer disarray of them, is a unique product of her hands, of her attention and her inattention, and will be lost for ever as soon as they are moved or removed.

Her lips were still warm when they touched the cold, hard smoothness of that glass as she sipped from it. The amount of water that remains was precisely determined by the extent of her thirst.

She has no choice now but to give up exactness and inexactness.

These tiny museums of personal randomness are all that is left to me.

How many times and in how many ways is it expected that one should have to say goodbye? I assent and assent and assent and assent to the death of the person I love, yet still she phantoms to life and fades once more to her death in the sad ordinariness of an unfinished packet of cereal, a tube of the wrong-coloured shoe polish, a spare pair of one-armed reading glasses in a drawer, CDs I never would have learned to enjoy, the Bible that is not mine, its thousand pages thickly cropped with markers that were sown over a decade, but have yielded their harvest in another place, her sewing-box filled with 'bits and bobs that might be useful one day', familiar doodles on a pad beside the phone, and, buried behind coats hanging in the hall, a wide, dark-blue woollen scarf that, when I bury my face in it, still smells of her.

I disposed of such items as the milk carton eventually. Of course I did. There was never any serious danger that I would descend into some kind of Dickensian preservation mania. The books were returned to their correct position on the shelves. I tipped away the water and washed the invisible prints of Jessica's lips and fingers from the tumbler. It took about half a minute and meant nothing immediately afterwards. I noted how the glass shone and sparkled as I replaced it with its fellows on the top shelf of the cupboard above the draining board. It was, after all, only a glass. Tomorrow I would be unable to identify which one of that set of six had contained the last drink that my wife had enjoyed in her own home.

In fact, after the very early and most intensely anguished days I became reasonably good at clearing and sorting and dealing with things of this kind as soon as they appeared, albeit sometimes by gritting my teeth or through little bursts of sobbing, conduits carrying away the overflow of continual grief.

The problem was that it never seemed quite to end. Months after Jessica's death I was still having to cope with less frequent but no less unexpected reminders of her life and her death. Some of them came from outside the house, brought by the regular postman, a young man with shiny spiked hair and a brick-red complexion who continued to whistle his way up our front path every morning as if, in some strange way, the world had not stopped turning. He brought letters addressed to Jessica that had important things to say about her mobile phone, or her library books, or which bulbs she might like to order for planting in the autumn, or the amount of credit she had on her British Home Stores card, or the fact that she had come so close to winning eighty thousand pounds in some magazine draw that the act of returning the enclosed slip and ordering a year's subscription to the magazine in question was little more than a tedious formality I answered the ones I needed to and binned the rest.

One or two were innocently cheerful communications from friends or acquaintances from the past who knew nothing of what had happened to Jessica. I replied with as much brevity as politeness would allow, and tried to spend as little time as possible looking at the letters of condolence that followed.

One summer morning, six months to the day after I had leaned down to kiss my wife's cold lips for the last time, a letter with a Gloucester postmark dropped on to the front mat. It turned out to be from one of Jessica's oldest friends, but it was not for her. It was addressed to me.

Dear David,

I do hope you remember who I am, now that so many people in the church know who you are, and I hope you won't mind ploughing through what is probably going to be quite a long letter. My married name (I'm separated from my husband now) is Angela Steadman, but when we knew each other it was Angela Brook. That's what I've gone back to calling myself now that I'm on my own again.

I was in the same youth group as you many years ago when we were all going to St Mark's, so I'm in my latish thirties now, as I suppose you must be. I used to go around with your Jessica, who was my closest friend all through school, and a biggish girl with frizzy hair called Laura Pavey, I was sort of blonde with high cheekbones and a goofy smile and enjoyed wearing bright jumpers in the winter and was a bit bossy and talked too much. Is that enough for you to identify me by? It's enough for most people. The bossy bit usually rings a bell!

We only knew each other for a relatively short time after you started going out with Jessica, but we actually did quite a few things together. Decent coffee at Laura's parents' lovely house round the corner in Clifton Road after the group to get rid of the taste of that thin, rank church coffee, quite a lot of Saturday mornings at Wilson's, the cafe at the top of the steps opposite the station where everyone got together to find out if there were going to be any parties they could crash. Two coffees between five or six of us – if we were lucky! It's just come to me that we all went on a church weekend together once as well, some school or something down in the south I think it was. Coming back now? All very happy memories for me.

Anyway, as you know, apart from Christmas cards Jessica and I pretty well lost touch with each other over the years, but I was very fond of my friend and I never forgot her. I always told myself that one day I'd make the effort to meet up with her again, and with you, of course, so that we could chew over old times. Yes, well, we should just go ahead and do these things and not talk about them, shouldn't we? I know it's nothing compared to how you must be feeling, but I am filled with a terrible, desolate sadness when I think that it's too late now. Having said that, there is one last thing I can do for Jessica, and that's why I'm writing to you.

David, I think you might be very surprised to hear what I'm going to tell you now. You see, Jessica wrote me quite a long letter only a day or two before she died. In it she talked about what had happened to her, how sudden it had been and how serious it was. She obviously knew perfectly well that she had a very short time left to live. People usually do, in my experience. Of course, as soon as I read this I was on the point of jumping in the car and driving for however long it took to get to her bedside, and that's exactly what I would have done, except that she specifically asked me not to. She wanted me to wait until a few months had gone by and then write to you. I'm doing what she asked.

Jessica sent me something to give to you, David, and when I managed to talk to her for a very short time on the phone at the hospital she was very insistent that I must take responsibility for deciding how and when that should happen. I was a bit taken aback, as you can imagine. Nothing like this has ever happened to me before or to anyone else I know. But one thing's for sure. I'm not going to let anyone or anything stop me from getting it right – for Jessica's sake.

Before I tell you what I've decided to do I think I'd better just fill you in briefly on what's been happening to me over the years since we last met. We all know what's been going on in your life, of course. I've never actually been to one of your meetings, but I gather they're pretty powerful and helpful and that sort of thing. I, on the other hand, have remained happily obscure – well, obscure, anyway.

As I think you probably know, or knew, but I don't blame you in the slightest for forgetting, I went off and did Art and History at Bristol – absolutely loved it, then I poodled around for a bit before getting a really nice, really badly paid job at a gallery in Cambridge. That's where I first met my husband, Alan. He was up in Cambridge on business one day and he'd ducked into our gallery to get out of the rain. Blinking rain! Bringing the good news and the bad news all in one package. To cut a long story short, this Alan being a nice-looking, independent-minded, charming sort of chap, we got on very well, exchanged phone numbers, kept in touch after that first encounter and began meeting on a regular basis. And, to cap it all, he was a Christian! Amazing! I couldn't believe my luck. About six months later we got engaged, and the autumn after that we were married in York, which is where my dad had moved to after my mum's death. It all felt so perfect. We prayed together, we laughed together about the same things, we shared dreams about what we might do in the future.

One of our commonest dreams was to find some kind of big old ramshackle property in the country, do it up and somehow make money out of it. A few years later, after both our parents had gone, there was enough money to think seriously about doing it. Well, to cut an even longer story short, after a lot of very enjoyable searching all over the country – marvellous times – we found somewhere. It was an ancient place, and when I say ancient I mean it. There were stones in the cellar dating from Roman times, and in just about every century since then someone seemed to have added something to the building. And just to add a little spice to the whole thing, the place had a well-documented reputation for being one of the most haunted houses in England! And is it haunted, I hear you ask? I'll tell you more about that when/if I see you.

We bought it. It was a mess, but we bought it. We figured that once it was cleaned up and we'd gone round the sales and bought some authentic stuff to put in the rooms, we'd be able to charge the public to come in and look round the place. It was so exciting and such fun. We had this dynamic girl called Karen who came in every day from the village to help, and within two or three months the thing was up and running. Seeing the very first paying customers walk through the door was an amazing experience. There was still an enormous amount to be done to the house, but we reckoned we could do that as we went along and according to how the money was going. It was marvellous having Karen to help. She was practical, versatile, quick, and all the other things you need someone to be when you've taken on a venture that every now and then seems just too big to handle. And I got on really well with her. We were great buddies, Karen and I, we really were. Like sisters. And all that good stuff lasted right up to the point when she and my husband stood side by side like discontented servants at the kitchen table one cold morning when I was bleary-eyed and barely awake, and announced that they'd fallen in love and were going to go away together. Alan was good enough to explain that he needed someone 'more feminine and adaptive', someone who didn't feel the need to dominate him all the time.

I don't want to say any more about that now. It puts my whole being out of joint. I can hardly write the words down without smashing something.

I'm still at the house, and still trying to run it as a business.

Right! That's me in a rather crushed nutshell, and here's my suggestion. Id like to have a bit of a weekend reunion down here at the house, and I really want you to be part of it. It would probably run from Friday evening to Sunday morning or afternoon. I've still got some addresses and numbers from the old days, but you know how it is. People selfishly get married and move and emigrate and things, without any regard for people who are trying to organize reunions. I'm going to try for seven or eight of the folks you and I might remember best, and we'll see how we go. I gather that these things can turn out pretty dire if they're handled badly, so I want to plan at least a rough agenda that gives the weekend half a chance of being useful in some way, or at the very least enjoyable, for everyone who comes. I hope the idea of the ghosts won't put them off. I suspect the fact that we'll have to share expenses a bit will probably put them off a lot more!

There you are, then. I've enclosed a list of some possible dates. I assume your diary gets filled up pretty quickly – I suppose you're back on the speaking trail by now – so the sooner you reply the sooner I can fix it with the others. If you can't or won't come on any of those dates, and you don't come up with any alternatives either, then I won't do it at all. In which case you won't be getting what I was given to pass on to you. That would not be good, because we are both going to have to face Jessica again some day. She was very sweet, but what a temper! Seriously, this may be the last thing you want to do, but please do it. Ring, write, ask any questions you like, but just do it!

More details when you reply

Love and blessings (if there are some about)

Angela (Brook)

Safely Home

Randy Alcorn

Ben Fielding thinks he's got the perfect plan. By shifting production of his electronic components to China, he'll save his company millions of dollars. But on a visit to China, where he meets his former college roommate Li Quan, Ben is faced with the shocking reality of the persecution of Christians as his old friend is taken to jail, forcing him to rediscover Jesus through Li's faith.

Illuminating the harsh truth of life in the modern persecuted church, *Safely Home* challenges the reader to live and die for a faith that will last for eternity.

ISBN 0 8423 5991 5
PB

Price: £10.50
£7.50 Special Offer
Special offer ends 31/08/03

Published by Tyndale House Publishers, Inc.
351 Executive Drive
Carol Stream IL 60188

1

THREE MEN watched intently as peculiar events occurred, one right after the other, on opposite sides of the globe.

"What's happening?" asked the first, tall and dark skinned.

"I don't know," replied the man with long black hair. "But wheels are turning, aren't they?"

"Things appear synchronized," said the third man, compact and broad shouldered. "A pattern is emerging. Something great seems poised to happen. Something else lurks in the shadows. It seeks to devour the greatness before it is born."

"Two destinies are converging. But neither suspects it."

The tall one pointed toward a great palace in the distance. "He searches to find the right man for the right hour. Is this the hour? Is this the man?"'

"And if so, *which* man? Or both? We see far more clearly than they do. But still our minds are too small to figure it all out."

"The soil was tilled and the seeds planted twenty years ago," the broad-shouldered man said. "No. A hundred years, at least. Now we will see what fruit the vine produces, or whether it will wither and die."

"Hanging in the balance are not just two men," said the longhaired man, "but two families, perhaps two nations."

"Indeed, two worlds."

"The loss could be immense. Or the gain immeasurable." His voice trembled.

"We must watch closely as the tapestry is woven ... or as it unravels."

"We must do more than watch." The tall man reached out one hand to the other two, who grasped it firmly, the muscles of their forearms taut. They now looked like warriors.

"The stakes are high."

"Higher than they can possibly imagine. Higher than we ever dreamed when we walked that world."

'Somebody's got to make the tough calls," Ben Fielding muttered. "And I don't see anyone else volunteering."

He picked up the phone from his oversized mahogany desk at the far side of his window office on the thirty-ninth floor of the U.S. Bancorp Tower. It was a bright September morning, and Oregon was the best place in the world to live in the fall, but he had more important things to do than admire the view.

"Doug? We need to talk."

"Sure," said Doug Roberts from his desk in the sales department. "What's up?"

"I have a management team meeting right now. Might take an hour. I'll call you in when it's over. Be sure you're available. I've got a conference call before lunch, and I won't have much time."

"Okay, Ben. But what do you want to talk about?"

"I'll call you when I'm ready." Ben still gripped the phone tightly three seconds after he'd finished talking. Finally he put it down.

Doug was his cousin, his mom's sister's son. They'd grown up on the East Coast, a few hundred miles apart. They'd spent most holidays together, wrestling in the snow or exploring the beach or playing Parcheesi in front of the fire. Those were the days ... when life was simple, and loyalties easily maintained.

Now they both worked in Portland, Oregon, on the opposite seaboard, for Getz International, a leading-edge multinational corporation. As a department head fifteen years ago, Ben had offered Doug a sales job, and he'd jumped at it. They were both young and hungry back then.

Doug had so much potential. Why had he forced his hand? Once he'd been an asset to Ben. Now he'd become a liability.

That Doug was family made it messy. Ben would probably have to skip the holiday gatherings this year. Doug had backed him into a corner. He had to send a clear message to all the employees – Ben Fielding doesn't tolerate insubordination, and he doesn't play favorites.

"Martin's in the boardroom." His secretary's voice over the intercom yanked Ben back to the moment. "They're ready for you."

"On my way."

Ben stopped in front of the mirror on the back side of his office door, ran a comb through his hair, then straightened his Shanghai silk tie. He went to the door of the conference room, took a deep breath, and calculated his entrance, He walked in briskly but not too hurried. He stood tall and smiled pleasantly without grinning, a smile he'd practiced in the mirror. Dressed in a black Armani with a boxy Italian fit, Ben Fielding was a self-made picture of style, poise, and competence. There were eight men in the room, and every eye was on him.

"Hey, Ben," Martin said, "we're talking about that dream you spelled out for us ten years ago – selling one of everything to a country of 1.2 billion people!" Suddenly Martin's broad smile evaporated. "Travis here and a couple of the team have voiced some concerns."

Ben raised his eyebrows and stared at Travis.

"The situation's not stable," Travis said, looking at his Palm Pilot instead of Ben. "I don't trust that government."

"China won't be bullied by anyone," Ben said. "That's what Hong Kong was all about. And Macao. They won't let 'foreign devils' control their destiny. What's theirs is theirs."

"And what isn't theirs eventually will be," Travis said.

Ben shrugged. "I'll say it again. If one nation dictates everybody's future, it won't be America. It'll be China. The sooner everybody comes to terms with that, the better we can position ourselves."

"One thing's for sure," Martin said; "there's not another semi-conductor or microchip company with our access to Beijing and Shanghai. Between Ben and Jeffrey, we've established one major beachhead."

Martin Getz, showing straight white teeth in a smile so big it drew in everyone, was CEO of Getz International. His father had started the company in 1979, just before the computer revolution changed the world.

"Okay, okay, guys. What's the report on the Shanghai factory?"

"All indicators are positive," Jeffrey said. "Production's still going up. With socialism loosening its grip and workers getting more for their labor, there's a new Chinese work ethic. Without all those paranoid safety and antipollution regulations, they get done in a week what takes us a month – and their Q.A. tallies are better."

"I don't want to hear this," Johnny said, his suit lapels flaring as he leaned back, playfully covering his ears. "There are certain things lawyers shouldn't know."

"We can't impose American standards on them," Ben said. It was a mantra he'd repeated at many team meetings. "And even if we could, we don't have the right. But we can demand the highest product standards. And we're getting great results. These people are bright, smart, eager to work. They don't know about unions; they're just grateful to make a living and be able to buy a refrigerator, a TV, maybe even a computer."

Ben's confident voice commanded attention. There was a presence about him. Martin was the boss, but Ben was the brains and energy. Everyone knew it.

"China's still our fastest growing market?" Martin asked.

"In another few years they'll be our biggest customer – period," Ben said. "China has a skyrocketing economy with hundreds of millions of residences that'll add computers and a dozen other electronic devices in the next ten years. Dayton's assembling the network cards in Mexico. They'll ship direct from there to our joint-venture partnerships in-country and bypass China's trade restrictions. It brings the end product cost down and gets it into more hands. Getz benefits inside China; then we score again when it's shipped back here at a fraction of the cost, and we sell it through traditional distribution channels. Our competitors' heads will be spinning. In the next few years they'll be eating our dust."

"They'll never catch up," Martin said, all teeth again.

"I wish I shared your confidence," Travis said. "Seems to me we're walking on a minefield. It's a shaky economy. Human rights issues, overbuilding in Shanghai ... not to mention Beijing's ability to pull the plug on anyone for any reason."

It's capitalists and communists scratching each other's backs," Ben said. "Sure, they've got problems. They know the state-owned enterprises are inefficient, banks are folding, and pollution's terrible. There's still a lot of trial and error, but they're learning fast. I've been saying it since my first trip to Beijing – China's our future, guys. It offers us the most cost-effective partnerships on the planet. And it's a dream market come true."

"Just make sure they keep needing us, Ben," Martin said. "You too, Jeffrey. We don't want them to get any ideas of doing it on their own."

"Oh, they've got the ideas, alright," Ben said. "They're swimming in U. S. and Japanese technology, and they can imitate it like nobody else. Give them a decade, and they'll be improving it. Eventually, they'll be our strongest competitors. We'll be racing to keep up. But meanwhile, we've got the edge. Russia couldn't handle free enterprise, but these people can. Their work ethic gets stronger every day, while ours gets weaker. Another six to eight years, and they'll be putting America to shame."

Martin looked at Ben with undisguised admiration. "Ten years ago when you told us you could bring in millions of dollars if you studied Mandarin on company time, I thought you'd gone crazy. But it worked. Boy, did it work! They trust us – you and Jeffrey, especially. You speak their language, know their culture. That's our edge." Martin stood up. 'And I want to shore up that edge. I've been chewing on an idea since that Fortune 500 CEO think tank I attended in Chicago a couple of months ago."

Martin looked around the room the way he always did before announcing an idea he was particularly proud of. Several of the men, including Ben, braced themselves. Nobody ever quite knew what Martin would come up with next.

"I'd like to send Ben or Jeffrey to spend maybe six weeks living among and talking with typical Chinese citizens, the type that might work in our factories and eventually buy our products. Ben, what about that old roommate of yours from college? He lives in China, right? A teacher, isn't he?"

Ben nodded. Li Quan's youthful face invaded his mind and infused it with bittersweet memories. It was just like Martin to spring this on him with everybody watching. As it began to register, it didn't seem a good idea at all. It had been twenty years since he …

"Getting inside the mind of the typical consumer would help our sales strategy and deepen our reservoir for those Chinese advertising campaigns that marketing's been talking about. And it would be great PR on both sides of the ocean. We'd be the company that sent a Mandarin-speaking VP to live with Chinese nationals to see what they're like, to learn what they need. It's the 'we care about the common man' angle. It would impress the Chinese, our board, stock-holders — everybody. A big image-booster for Getz. The advertising potential is enormous. Ben or Jeffrey could end up in a prime-time commercial sitting next to some Chinese guy grinning at his computer!"

The other members of the management team looked at each other to see which way the wind would blow. Then they all stared at Ben. He hesitated. But when Martin felt this strongly about an idea, it nearly always happened. You might as well go with him and look brilliant and loyal. Everyone nodded.

"Anyway, more on that later," Martin said. "Let's hit the agenda. Our third-quarter profits are going to blow them away. When this hits Wall Street, things are going to fly. Hold on to your hats, boys.

Your profit shares could increase ten percent overnight."

An hour later Ben walked out of the conference room, glad-handing his associates and feeling the warm rush of competitive adrenaline. As he came out the door, he saw Doug Roberts standing by a photocopy machine. His stomach churned. He looked at his watch.

Conference call in six minutes. "Doug," he called, "meeting'll have to wait until Monday morning. My office, 7:30."

"Sure. But what are we going to —"

"7:30 Monday. My office. I've got a conference call."

Ben strode past his secretary, Jen, and into his office. He shut the door behind him and flopped down on the plush visitors' couch.

Until their lives took different turns, Doug had been not only family, but a close friend. Ben knew he couldn't afford to think of him that way anymore. And if Doug still considered Ben a friend, well … he wouldn't much longer.

2

IS THIS the day I die?

Li Quan asked himself the familiar question as he wiped sleep from his eyes. Why couldn't he be courageous, like his father and great-grandfather?

He lit a candle and watched Chan Minghua sleeping, slight and vulnerable. *Minghua* meant "bright flower." She was that and more to Li Quan.

Pulling himself off the thin pad he used for a bed, Quan walked barefoot on the frigid cement floor to the cot four feet away. He knelt down beside eight-year-old Li Shen, resting his forehead against the crown of his only son's head. He reached out to the child's pudgy hands, then touched a finger to his pouty lips. How could this thick, round boy have come from birdlike Ming?

Is this the day I die?

He'd asked himself the question every day since he was Shen's age. Every day the answer had been no. But his father had taught him, "One day the answer will be yes, and on that day you must be ready."

It was on a Sunday his great-grandfather Li Manchu had been beheaded. And it was also on a Sunday his father, Li Tong, lying in a beaten lump, had died in prison. Here in the cold predawn outside Pushan, it was another Sunday.

"It is time?" Minghua whispered, her voice a feather falling upon silk. Candle flame dancing in her brown eyes, she looked as she had ten years ago, at their wedding in Shanghai.

Quan kissed her delicate forehead, ashamed that he, a poor and lowly man, was so unworthy of her. Already in this short night he'd dreamed again that he held her wounded body – Ming's life running red through his fingers in a dark rain.

They moved swiftly, silently, performing their 2:00 A.M. Sunday ritual. Ming awoke Li Shen and gave him a little bowl of sticky rice, holding up his yawning head.

Quan wrapped a gray blanket around his neck, then squeezed into his dark green parka. Stuffing one hundred and forty yuan into his trouser pocket, he stepped outside and strapped a bundle to the back of his bicycle. He knotted the bundle, double-tying and double-checking the knots. Ming and sleepy-eyed Shen followed, coats bulging like overstuffed cushions.

Quan positioned Shen on the seat in front of him. The boy put his hands on the bars and closed his eyes, head nodding. Ming pedaled beside them, a silent shadow. Face stinging, Quan watched the quarter moon cast shadows on the dormant rice fields. He wished there were no moon – its light made the ride easier but more dangerous. He preferred safety over ease.

The road of frozen mud cut between buttresses of naked hills.

Even here, ten kilometers outside Pushan, an unnatural silvery dust floated on the wind. He felt the grit on his tongue and spit it out. For a moment the air was God's air, fresh and clean, but then the burning smell of factories assaulted him again.

Quan bounced over hard ruts, pressing tightly against Li Shen. Seeing shadows ahead, he instinctively began the rehearsal. "Our son is sick," he said to the wind. "We are taking him to a friend's for medicine."

Was that a glint of light behind the tangle of boughs and dead leaves? A policeman holding a lantern? He held his breath, the corners of his eyes freezing shut.

No. The shadows were fence posts. Li Quan hung his head, wishing he were a brave man who did not whisper lies into the wind.

The three spoke nothing lest the silence, once pierced, would bleed on them, as it had before.

After four kilometers dark clouds rolled in, as if an artist were suddenly changing his mood on a canvas. The moon hid from the coming storm. They'd have to face a squall on the ride home, Quan thought. That might be better – storms kept curious eyes indoors.

"Slow," Quan said to Ming, as they wobbled blindly onward, the ruts herding them, sky so low now it brushed his face.

At seven kilometers, he saw white wisps of smoke rising from a chimney. A welcome sight. But if he could see it, so could others. He pushed down his fear to that hollow place inside.

They got off their bicycles and quickly walked them behind Ho Lin's house, making no sound. They leaned them against the dark side, hidden in the shadows, by the chicken coop. Quan brushed his hand over other bicycles, counting them. Fourteen.

He walked to the back door, knowing they'd crossed the line of no return. From this moment all excuses for being out in the night were futile.

The door opened. "Ni hao," Quan said. "How are you?"

"Ping an – peace to you," old Ling Ho replied, a childlike smile stretching his tight, dull skin in the candlelight. He gestured toward

two large pots of tea, hovered over by his wife, Aunt Mei, whom Quan's mother always called "Fifth Sister." Mei smiled sweetly, reminding him of his mother. She bowed her head. Quan wanted the tea, but since he and his family seemed to be the last to arrive, he ushered Ming and Shen forward.

Quan nodded and returned smiles to the twenty others, especially the three at the rear. He regretted his smiles were forced and nervous. The Li family sat on a backless bench, coats on, leaning into each other's warmth.

The dull luminescence cast an eerie hue over the Spartan one-room house, bare but for a bench, some chairs, a bed, and one hearty bonsai, a dwarfed juniper Mei managed to keep alive. When the church had been smaller, with ten of them, they'd sat in a circle, but now they had four small rows, the last being the bed's edge.

Zhou Jin stood up, eyelids heavy but eyes sharp. His upper teeth protruded in a yellow smile, distinguishing him from most of the wary prune-faced men of Mao's generation. The draft was a wind upon Zhou Jin's wispy hair, a wind that stirred the room, then came out of the old man's lips.

"Zhu, wo men gan xie ni feng fu de zhu fu. Lord, we give you thanks for your abundant blessing."

"Xiexie, thank you," someone murmured.

"Xiexie," Ming said. Whispers of thanks erupted around the room.

Yin Chun, Jin's wife, carefully handed him a treasure wrapped in linen. He unwrapped it gently. He turned pages with a light touch, then read:

It was by faith that Abraham obeyed when God called him to leave home and go to another land that God would give him as his inheritance. He went without knowing where he was going. And even when he reached the land God promised him, he lived there by faith–for he was like a foreigner, living in a tent. And so did Isaac and jacob, to whom God gave the same promise. Abraham did this because he was confidently looking forward to a city with eternal foundations, a city designed and built by God.

This had been one of the favorite passages of Quan's father, Li Tong. He remembered the old man's face, the look of longing in his eyes as he would recite the verses. Quan also remembered how embarrassed he'd been that his parents were so ignorant, so uneducated and naive. He squirmed in his seat, the joy of the words eclipsed by the memory of his transgressions.

All these came to their end in faith, not having had the heritage; but having seen it with delight far away, they gave witness they were wanderers and strangers, not of this earth. For those who say such things make it clear they are searching for a country of their own. If they had been thinking of the country from which they went out, they would have had chances of turning back. But instead, they were longing for a better country — a heavenly country. And so it is no shame to God to be named as their God; for he has prepared a city for them.

Hearing the ancient words of Shengjing filled Quan's heart with sweetness and sadness.

"This world is not our home," Zhou Jin whispered to his flock. Everyone leaned forward to hear, as thirsty men lean forward to put their lips in a mountain stream. "Yesu says, 'There are many rooms in my Father's home, and I am going to prepare a place for you. If this were not so, I would tell you plainly. When everything is ready, I will come and get you, so you will always be with me where I am.'"

Groans and yearnings, arising from soulish depths, filled the room.

When Jin finished reading, he handed the Bible back to his wife. She covered it in the linen cloth, as if wrapping a body for burial or a treasure for safekeeping.

It was bold to have Shengjing here, Quan thought, and bold that he and three others had brought their Bibles too. He'd been at house churches where people wrote out Scripture portions for the meetings; then the pastor would collect the handwritten copies and put them together to read the complete text. This way, if police interrupted the meeting, no Bible would be lost.

Pastor Zhou Jin gazed at the church, his children. "Remembering where our true home is will help us today as we speak of light and momentary troubles, which achieve in us an eternal weight of glory."

As he said the word glory, lightning flashed in the eastern sky. Moments later God's voice shook the earth; then his tears fell from heaven.

Quan felt a hand on his shoulder, chilling him. He turned to see Wu Le, who'd been coming only six weeks. Quan didn't know him. He smiled nervously as Le's palsied fingers, covered with thin white hairs, passed forward a worn hymnal, paper so thin Quan could read the words two pages back. The church sang – too loudly, Quan thought – "Yesu, we praise your name forever...."

Is this the day?

Quan's great-grandfather had been murdered as a young pastor. Quan's grandfather, Li Wen, then eight years old – Shen's age – had witnessed the execution. A vivid image of his decapitation had haunted Quan's dreams all his life. Wen's son, Li Tong, was Quan's father – also a pastor, sentenced to prison during the cultural revolution. One day, after a beating, he didn't get up. Quan's smiling mother became a pastor's weeping widow, and shy, bookish Quan became the object of cruel taunts.

The pastor's voice drew him back. "Sister Wu Xia has tuberculosis. Brother Wang An is in the hospital. They do not know what is wrong. Zhou Jin has many aches and pains," he said of himself, "I know what is wrong with me. I am an old man!" They laughed.

"Some of our people suffer not from illness or age," Zhou Jin said, "but from persecution. Yesu said he was hated for being who he was, and his servants will be too. He said, 'Unless a kernel of wheat falls to the ground and dies, it remains only a single seed. But if it dies, it produces many seeds.'"

After thirty minutes of prayer, craggy-faced Zhou Jin sat down in an old wicker chair, reading verses slowly, leaning forward. Specters from the flickering candles cut across his ancient brow. He spoke each word with the gentle obstinacy of a long obedience. "Whoever serves me must follow me…. My Father will honor the one who serves me.'"

Quan could never look at Zhou Jin without thinking of his own father. The old man raised his arms, exposing red, callous wrists. The sight stabbed Quan. Teachers and students in the communist school had ridiculed him because his father's faith made him a "public enemy." Quan's Baba had been capped a counterrevolutionary, in contrast to the heroic "revolutionaries," who practiced strict conformity to the Chairman's social order. Quan vividly remembered the posters put on their front door. One read "Lover of Foreigners," another "Reeducate these Poisonous Snakes!" In his mind's eye he could still see them clearly, the precise colors and flourishes of the characters.

As a young man Quan had tried to disbelieve in God. He never wanted to stand out or be noticed. He'd tried to embrace the ideals of the Party. He'd longed to blend into the dark green background of modern China. To this day, he wouldn't wear reds and yellows and bright colors. Quan had even joined the student Red Guards to deflect the shame of his parents' stubborn refusal to comply with the demands of the new China. While all the other boys' fathers took them fishing, Quan's father was in jail. His father had said many times, "One day I will take you to the Great Wall." He hadn't. He died. Li Quan had never shaken off the disappointment of his father's unfulfilled promise.

Quan had tried hard not to be a Christian. He had succeeded too, until he went to college in America. But one day his big American roommate, Ben Fielding, had invited him to a meeting of Christians on the Harvard campus. His questions and doubts and resentments fell in the face of truth. The faith that had been his mother's and father's became, for the first time, his own, far away in that foreign land where he had studied to become a college professor. Though they had long since lost touch with one another, Quan thought of Ben often and prayed for him daily.

"Zhu Yesu says, 'No one who puts his hand to the plow and looks back is fit for service in the kingdom of God."

It was still coal-black outside, 3:30 A.M. Curtains were drawn. Quan rubbed his earlobe and the rough, spidery five-inch scar on his neck. Church must end before the prying eyes of sunrise.

Old Zhou Jin began singing a hymn Quan had heard and reluctantly sung many times since childhood: "One day I'll die for the Lord."

Is this the day?

As the church sang, Zhou Jin raised his hands again. Li Quan rehearsed every scar on his father's back and arms, the scars he used to run his fingers over, before Father went to prison the last time. His father would be Zhou Jin's age. If only ...

"Bie dong!"

Li Quan stiffened at the shouted command not to move. The voice behind him rang with the authority of the Gong An Ju, the Public Security Bureau.

Quan swept his left arm over Shen, pulling him close against him and Ming.

With a quick glance Quan said to them both, "Look down. Be still." Quan had learned the drill long ago, hiding in house church under his mother's skirt. Pushing his eyes sideways and glancing through narrow lids, to his left he saw two green uniforms. To his right, two more.

"Do not move," commanded a harsh baritone voice from behind.

At the front right a young policeman held a Type 54 pistol. Quan had seen one close up. It had been waved in his face, then struck against his skull. Mao had said it – government by the barrel of a gun.

Suddenly, Quan's right elbow was banged by the heavy butt of a Type 56 assault rifle, the PSB's version of the Russian AK-47. Not only China's antiforeign politics, but its weapons had come from a foreign power. But police seldom carried weapons, at least not like this.

Quan's head remained bowed, but he peeked up so he could barely see the PSB captain standing three feet in front of him.

Narrow-waisted, with oarsman's shoulders, he reminded Quan of a giant wasp. The man stared at the twenty-four believers with the pinched eyes of cold assessment. A three-inch scar, much more prominent than Quan's, rough sewn in his burlap skin, hung over his right eyebrow. Quan didn't recognize him – too many police were transferred in and out. Besides, he never took a close look at PSB, for fear they would look back.

The captain was dressed sharply in a green uniform, straight black necktie, pants neatly creased, cap exactly positioned. The only imperfection was the slight tilt of his shoulder badge. This minor flaw comforted Quan, a reminder the government machinery was not perfect.

Scarbrow raised his hand, fingers pointing inward like gray claws. He grabbed Zhou Jin's shoulder, then pushed him back against Quan. He stood in front of the hushed assembly. His smoked-glass eyes raked the room.

"This is an illegal *jiaotang!*"

His accent reminded Quan of the villages over the mountains.

"This gathering is not registered with the Religious Affairs Bureau," the PSB man said, making this appear the ultimate offense. "You are not part of the Three-Self Patriotic Movement!"

Narrowing his gaze, the captain's mouth fell into a short-fused frown. "You meet in the night like the criminals you are."

He strode across the front of the room, as if making it his own. His gait was arrogant and sure, every movement calculated to intimidate. He looked like he'd walked on the necks of a thousand peasants and enjoyed every step. He was giving a virtuoso performance.

"You have been distributing illegal foreign propaganda."

With dramatic flourish, he waved a thin brown object, gripped tightly by the ends of his gray fingers. Though unmarked, Quan knew what it was – a case containing a compact disc. The movie about Jesus. Last month he and Ming had brought eighteen neighbors into their little house to watch it. "Yesu speaks Mandarin!" the amazed neighbors had said. Five became Christians. Three of those were here this morning. Quan had seen them in the back. Already he'd gotten them into trouble. He longed to turn his head to see them but dared not.

"You are cultists, devious and immoral, no better than the Falun Gong," Scarbrow said. "Do you think you are above the law? If you must worship foreign gods, there is a registered church!"

The nearest registered church was fourteen kilometers, away. Just two legal meeting places for a city of a half million. The Li family had only their bicycles. But even if they could get there, they would find infiltrators in the church, people who watched everyone and reported everything. Spies and informants were well rewarded. Even some of the house churches had them.

"Criminals!"

Quan quietly stared down at his twenty-year-old dress shoes. His thoughts turned again to the one who'd given them to him, to the last time they'd seen each other. Ben Fielding, his college roommate. Once, Ben had overheard another Chinese call him *Dabizi*. Ben liked the name and insisted Quan call him that. But Quan was too polite to tell him what it meant – "Big Nose," the slang term for Westerners. When he finally found out, Ben laughed and told Quan he wanted it for his permanent nickname. So Ben became Dabizi, and he always called Quan "Professor." Quan prayed for Ben as he stared at his shoes. They had promised to pray for each other every day. He hoped Ben was praying for him now.

Scarbrow waved his rifle. "We must crack down on all lawbreaking activities to safeguard social stability."

Shen's pudgy face scrunched. The dour-mouthed captain lowered his gaze and stared at the boy. Shen's upper lip quivered. He started to cry. Quan looked at Shen, silently pleading for him.

We never should have come back to China. I was at the top of my class. I was asked to teach at Harvard. We could have immigrated. Ming could have become a U.S. citizen with me. Why did I return to this? Why did I put Ming at risk? And now… my son. What kind of a father endangers his only son?

Doubts assailed Li Quan, as they often did.

"Illegal churches are enemies of the state. We must kill the baby while it is still in the manger. You do not deserve to live!"

The giant wasp pointed at Li Shen, who trembled under his gaze.

Slowly, Ming took off her silk scarf, bloodred, and gently pressed it against Li Shen's quivering lips. Quan peered down at his only son's eyes, begging him to be silent, making unspoken promises, knowing he could not keep them.

Protect my son, Yesu. Please.

"It is illegal to teach religion to children under eighteen! How dare you defy the law?" He lifted his hand, poising it in midair two feet away from Li Quan's face.

The father set his jaw in preparation for the impact, grateful it was he who would take the blow, and not his only son.

And the Shofar Blew

Francine Rivers

Dynamic young preacher Paul Hudson is committed to building his church – but what price is he willing to pay? As Paul's zeal and ambition build, he begins to lose sight of the one who called him. As Paul and those around him struggle to discern what it truly means to live out their faith, they must ultimately choose between their own will or God's plan.

This relevant and timely contemporary novel from one of Christian fiction's most popular authors, is a searching portrayal of God at work in his community of believers, the church.

ISBN 0 8423 6582 6
HB

Price: £17.50
£9.99 Special Offer
Special offer ends 31/08/03

Published by Tyndale House Publishers, Inc.
351 Executive Drive
Carol Stream IL 60188

Chapter One

1987

SAMUEL MASON sat parked in his white DeSoto across the street from Centerville Christian Church. The old place was like him; it had seen better days. Half a dozen shingles were still missing from the steeple, blown off in the windstorm of '84. The paint was chipped, revealing aging gray clapboards. One of the high, arched windows was cracked. The lawn was dying, the roses overgrown, and the birch tree in the courtyard between the church, fellowship hall, and small parsonage had some kind of beetle killing it.

If a decision wasn't made soon, Samuel was afraid he would live long enough to see a For Sale sign posted on the church property and a Realtor's lockbox on the front door. Reaching over, he picked up the worn black leather Bible lying on the passenger seat. *I'm trying to keep the faith, Lord. I'm trying to trust.*

"Samuel!" Hollis Sawyer limped along the sidewalk of First Street. They met at the front steps. Hollis gripped the rusted iron railing with his left hand, planted his cane, and hitched his hip, lifting his prosthetic leg to the second step. "Otis called. He said he'd be late."

"Trouble?"

"Didn't say, but I heard Mabel talking at him in the background. He sounded pretty frustrated." Samuel unlocked the front door of the church and looked in at the once mauve now sun-bleached gray carpet in the narthex. Hollis winced as he limped across the threshold. Samuel left the door ajar for Otis.

Nothing had changed inside the foyer in years. Faded tracts remained stacked in perfect piles. The frayed edge of the carpet was still pulled back from the door to the small ministerial office. The dusty leaves of the silk ficus tree in the corner continued to host a spider. Another web was in the corner of a high window; someone would have to get the ladder out and swipe it down. But who would be willing to climb a ladder when a fall might land their old bones in a convalescent hospital? And calling in a professional to clean was out of the question. There was no money.

Hollis hobbled down the aisle. "It's as cold in here as a Minnesota winter."

The sanctuary smelled as musty as a house closed up all season. "I can turn on the heat."

"Don't bother. By the time the place warms up, our meeting will be over." Hollis stepped into the second pew, and hung his cane on the back of the one in front of him, as he eased himself down. "So who's preaching this Sunday?"

Samuel took the pew across from him and set his Bible beside him. "Sunday is the least of our problems, Hollis." Resting his wrists on the back of the front pew, he clasped his hands and looked up. At least the brass cross and two candlesticks on the altar were polished. They seemed the only things to have received any attention. The carpet needed to be cleaned, the pulpit painted, the pipe organ repaired. Unfortunately, the workers were fewer each year and the financial gifts dwindled despite the generous spirits of the parishioners, all of whom were living on fixed incomes, some only on Social Security.

Lord . . . Samuel's mind went blank as he fought tears. Swallowing the lump in his throat, he looked at the empty choir loft. He remembered a time when it had been full of singers, all robed in red and gold. Now there was only his wife, Abby, who sang every few Sundays, accompanied by Susanna Porter on the piano. As much as he loved the old gal, Samuel had to admit Abby's voice just wasn't what it used to be.

One by one, the programs of the church had dried up and blown away like dust. Children grew up and moved away. The middle-aged became elderly, and the elderly died. The pastor's voice echoed with no live bodies to absorb his sage words.

Oh, Lord, don't let me live long enough to see the doors of this church locked on Sunday morning.

For forty years, he and Abby had been part of this church. Their children had gone through Sunday school and been baptized here. Pastor Hank had performed their daughter Alice's wedding ceremony, and then conducted the memorial service when the body of their son, Donny, had been brought home from Vietnam. He couldn't remember the last baptism, but memorial services were coming all too often. For all he knew, the baptismal had dried up.

Samuel felt dried up, too. Old, dry bones. He was tired, depressed, defeated. And now, a new tragedy had befallen them. He didn't know what they were going to do to keep the church functioning. If they couldn't find a way, what would happen to the small body of believers who still came every Sunday to worship together? Most were too old to drive, and others too shy to travel the twenty miles down the road to worship with strangers.

Are we all going to be relegated to watching TV evangelists who spend threequarters of their time asking for money? God, help us.

The front door of the church banged shut, and the floorboards creaked under approaching footsteps. "Sorry I'm late!" Otis Harrison came down the aisle and sat in a front pew.

Samuel unclenched his hands and rose to greet him. "How's Mabel feeling?"

"Poorly. Doctor put her back on oxygen. She gets downright crabby dragging that tank around the house. You'd think she could sit a while. But no. I have to keep a sharp eye on her. Caught her yesterday in the kitchen. We had a shouting match. I told her one of these days she's going to turn on that gas burner, light a match, and blow us both to kingdom come. She said she couldn't stand eating any more frozen dinners."

"Why don't you call Meals on Wheels?" Hollis said.

"I did. That's why I'm late."

"They didn't show up?"

"Came right on time, or you'd still be waiting for me. Problem is, I have to be there to open the door because Mabel flatly refuses to do it." The front pew creaked as Otis settled his weight.

Over the years, Samuel and Abby had spent numerous pleasant evenings at the Harrison house. Mabel had always prepared a feast: stuffed game hens, homemade angel food cakes, and roasted or steamed vegetables from Mabel's backyard garden. Otis's wife loved to cook. It wasn't a hobby; it was a calling. Mabel and Otis had welcomed new families to the church with a dinner invitation. Italian, German, French, even Chinese cuisine – she was game to try anything, to the delight of everyone who sat at their table. People used to stampede to whatever casserole or pie Mabel set on the long, vinyl-covered potluck tables. She'd sent cookies to Donny when he was stationed in Hue, Vietnam. Otis used to complain that he never knew what to expect for dinner, but no one ever felt sorry for him.

"She's still watching those cooking shows and writing out recipes. Drives herself crazy with frustration! Drives me crazy right along with her. I suggested she take up needlepoint. Or tole painting. Or crossword puzzles. Something. *Anything!* I won't repeat what she said."

"What about an electric stove?" Hollis said. "Or a microwave?"

"Mabel will have nothing to do with an electric stove. And as for a microwave, our son gave us one a couple of Christmases ago. Neither one of us can figure out how it works, except to set it for one minute and warm coffee." Otis shook his head. "I miss the good old days when I never knew what she'd have on the table when I came home from work. She can't stand long enough to make salad these days. I've tried to do the cooking, but that's been a complete disaster." Grimacing, he waved his hand impatiently. "But enough of my troubles. We've got other things to talk about, I hear. What's the news on Hank?"

"Not good," Samuel said. "Abby and I were at the hospital last night with Susanna. She wants Hank to retire."

Hollis stretched out his bad leg. "We should wait and see what Hank says."

Samuel knew they didn't want to face facts. "He's had a heart attack, Hollis. He can't say anything with a tube down his throat." Did they really think Henry Porter could go on forever? Poor Hank was way past pretending to be the Energizer Bunny.

Otis frowned. "That bad?"

"He was doing visitation at the hospital yesterday afternoon, and collapsed in the corridor just down the hall from the emergency room. Otherwise, we'd be sitting here planning his memorial service."

"God was looking out for him," Hollis said. "Always has."

"It's time *we* looked out for his best interests, too."

Otis stiffened. "What's that supposed to mean?"

"Samuel's just had a long night." Hollis sounded hopeful.

"That's part of it," Samuel conceded. A long night, indeed, of facing the future. "The truth is this is just one more crisis in a long series of crises we've faced. And I don't want to see this one put us under. We have to make some decisions."

Hollis shifted uneasily. "What time did you and Abby get to the hospital?"

Anytime the discussion turned toward unpleasant things, Hollis leapfrogged to another subject. "Half an hour after Susanna called us. Hank hasn't been feeling well for a long time."

Otis frowned. "He's never said anything."

"His hair has gone completely white in the last two years. Didn't you notice?"

"So's mine," Hollis said.

"And he's lost weight."

"Wish I could," Otis said with a chuckle.

Samuel strove for patience. If he weren't careful, this meeting would turn into another gab session on the miserable state of the world and the country. "About a week ago, Hank told me about a friend from his college days who's dean at a Christian university in the Midwest. He spoke very highly of him and of the school." Samuel looked between his two oldest friends. "I think he was trying to tell me where we should start looking for his successor."

"Now, wait a minute!" Hollis said. "This isn't the time to retire him, Samuel. What kind of blow would that be for a man flat on his back?" He snorted. "How would you like it if someone came into your hospital room, stood over you, and said, 'Sorry you had a heart attack, old friend, but your useful days are over'?"

Otis's face was red and tight. "Hank's been the driving force of this church for the past forty years. He's been the steadying hand at the helm. We can't do without him."

Samuel had known it wouldn't be easy. There was a time to be gentle, and a time to be direct. "I'm telling you, Hank isn't coming back. And if we want this church to survive, we'd better do something about finding someone else to stand at the helm. We're about to drift onto the rocks." Hollis waved his hand. "Hank was in the hospital five years ago having bypass surgery. He came back. We'll just invite some guest speakers until Hank's back on his feet. Like we did the last time. The Gideons, Salvation Army, someone from that soup kitchen on the other side of town. Ask them to come and talk about their ministries. They'll fill the pulpit for a few Sundays." He gave a nervous laugh. "If push comes to shove, we can always have Otis show his Holy Land slides again."

Samuel's heel came off the floor, moving up and down silently as it always did when he was tense. What would it take to get through to his old friends? Did the Lord Himself have to blast the ram's horn in order to get them to move on? "Susanna said their oldest granddaughter is expecting a baby this spring. She said it would be nice to see Hank with a great-grandchild on his knee. They'd like to be part of their children's lives again, to sit together in the same church, in the same pew. Which one of you wants to tell Hank he hasn't earned the right to do those things? Which one of you wants to tell him we expect him to stand in that pulpit until he drops dead?" His voice broke.

Hollis frowned and then looked away, but not before Samuel saw the moisture in his eyes.

Samuel leaned his arm on the pew. "Hank needs to know we understand. He needs our thanks for all his years of faithful service to this congregation. He needs our blessing. And he needs the pension fund we set up years ago so he and Susanna have something more to live on than a monthly check from the government and the charity of their children!" He could barely see their faces through the blur of tears.

Otis stood and paced the aisle, one hand shoved in his pocket, while he scratched his brow with the other. "The market's been down, Samuel. That fund is worth about half what it was a year ago."

"Half is better than nothing."

"Maybe if I'd pulled out of tech stock earlier . . . as it is, he's going to receive about two hundred and fifty a month for forty years of service." Samuel shut his eyes. "At least we've been able to keep up their longterm health-care policy."

"Good thing he applied in his midthirties, or we wouldn't have enough for premiums." Otis sank heavily onto the end of a pew. He looked straight at Samuel, who nodded, knowing he and Abby would have to come up with the money, as they had whenever there wasn't enough in the offering plate to meet expenses.

Hollis sighed. "Five years ago, we had six elders. First we lost Frank Bunker to prostate cancer, and then Jim Popoff goes to sleep in his recliner and doesn't wake up. Last year, Ed Frost has a stroke. His children arrive, rent a U-Haul, stick a For Sale sign in their front lawn, and move them to some residential-care facility down south. And now Hank . . . " Hollis's voice hitched. He shifted his hip again.

"So," Otis drawled. "What do we do without a pastor?"

"Give up!" Hollis said.

"Or start over."

Both men stared at Samuel. Otis snorted. "You're a dreamer,

Samuel. You've always been a dreamer. This church has been dying for the past ten years. When Hank heads north, it'll be dead."

"Do you really want to close the doors, lock them, and walk away?"

"It's not what we want! It's what has to be!"

"I don't agree," Samuel said, determined. "Why don't we pray about it?"

Otis looked dismal. "What good is praying going to do at this point?"

Hollis stood up. "My leg's seizing up on me. Got to move." He took his cane from the back of the pew and limped to the front of the church. "I don't know what's happening in our country these days." He pounded his cane on the floor. "I brought up all four of my children to be Christians, and not one of them attends church anymore. Only time they ever go is on Christmas and Easter."

"Probably commuting to work all week," Otis said. "It takes two people working to pay for a house these days, and then they have to replace the car every few years because they're driving so much. My son puts 140 miles on his car every day, five days a week, and his wife about half that. And then it costs them $1,800 a month for child care. Plus insurance, and . . . "

Yada, yada, yada. Samuel had heard it all before. The world stinks. The new generation has no respect for the older. The environmentalists are all hippies from the sixties and the politicians are all crooks, adulterers, and worse. "We know the problems. Let's work on solutions."

"Solutions!" Otis shook his head. "What solutions? Look, Samuel. It's over. We have a congregation of what?"

"Fifty-nine," Hollis said dismally. "On the membership roster. Thirtythree made it to church last Sunday."

Otis looked at Samuel. "There. You see how it is. We haven't got the money to pay the bills. We haven't got a pastor to preach. The only child we have in the congregation is Brady and Frieda's grandson, and he's only visiting. Unless you want to take over,

Samuel, I say we walk away gracefully."

"Gracefully? How do you shut down a church *gracefully?"*

Otis reddened. "It's finished. When are you going to get it through your thick head, my friend? The party was fun while it lasted, but it's over. It's time to go home."

Samuel felt the heat well up from deep inside him as though someone were blowing softly over the dying embers inside his heart. "What happened to the fire we all felt when we came to Christ?"

"We got old," Hollis said.

"We got tired," Otis said. "It's always the same people working while the rest sit in the pews and expect everything to run smoothly."

Samuel stood up. "Abraham was a hundred when he fathered Isaac! Moses was eighty when God called him out of the desert! Caleb was eightyfive when he took the hill country surrounding Hebron!"

Otis harrumphed. "Eighty must've been a whole lot younger back in Bible times than it is now."

"We came together in this place because we believe in Jesus Christ, didn't we?" Samuel clung stubbornly to his faith. "Has that changed?"

"Not one iota," Hollis said.

"We're talking about closing down the church, not giving up our faith," Otis said hotly.

Samuel looked at him. "Can you do one without the other?"

Otis puffed up his cheeks and scratched his brow. His face was getting red again. Always a bad sign.

"We're still here," Samuel said. "This church isn't dead yet." He wasn't backing down, no matter how much Otis huffed and puffed.

"There was $102.65 in the offering plate this past week." Otis scowled. "Not even enough to pay the utility bill. It's past due, by the way."

"The Lord will provide," Samuel said.

"The Lord, my foot. We're the ones paying all the time. Are you going to pay the property taxes again, Samuel?" Otis said. "How long can this go on? There's no way we can keep this church going now, especially without a pastor!"

"Precisely."

"And where are you going to get one?" Otis glowered. "Last I heard, they didn't grow on trees."

"Even with a new pastor, we haven't got the money to pay the bills. We'd need more people." Hollis sat down and stretched out his leg, kneading his thigh with arthritic fingers. "I can't drive a bus anymore, and I'm not up to going door-to-door like we did in the old days."

Otis skewered him with a look. "We haven't got a bus, Hollis. And now that we haven't got a pastor, we haven't got a service to invite them to." He waved his arm. "All we've got now is this building. And an earthquake would probably bring it down on our heads."

Hollis laughed bleakly. "At least then we'd have insurance money to send Hank off in style."

"I've got an idea." Otis's tone dripped sarcasm. "Why don't we turn this old place into a haunted house on Halloween? Charge ten bucks a head. We could pay off all our bills and have enough to give Hank a love offering."

"Very funny," Samuel said dryly.

Otis scowled. "I'm only half kidding."

Samuel looked back and forth between the two men solemnly. "We still have thirty-three people who need fellowship."

Hollis's shoulders dropped. "All of us with one foot in the grave and another on a banana peel."

Samuel stood his ground. "I vote we call that dean."

"Okay." Otis raised his hands. *"Okay!* If that's what you're after, you've got my vote. Call that dean. See what he can do for us. Nothing, I'm betting. Call whomever you want. Call God, if He's bothering to listen anymore. Call the president of the United States for all I care. I'm going home and make sure my wife hasn't set the kitchen or herself on fire." Shoulders slumped, Otis walked up the aisle.

For all Otis's bluster and protestations, Samuel knew his old friend didn't want to give up any more than he did. "Thanks, Otis."

"Just don't go getting some hotshot who'll bring drums and an electric guitar!" Otis called back over his shoulder.

Samuel laughed. "That might be just what we need, old buddy."

"Over my dead body!" The front door of the church banged shut.

Hollis hauled himself to his feet, took his cane from the back of the pew, and sighed deeply. He looked around for a long moment. "You know . . ." His eyes went shiny. His mouth worked. Pressing his trembling lips together, he shook his head. Raising his cane in a faint salute, he limped up the aisle.

"Keep the faith, brother."

"Night," Hollis said hoarsely. The door opened again and closed firmly.

Silence filled the church.

Samuel put his hand on his Bible, but didn't pick it up. He prayed, tears running down his cheeks.

Samuel drove up the narrow driveway, passed under the carport, and pulled into his garage. The back door of his small American bungalow opened, and Abby stood in the light waiting for him. She kissed him as he crossed the threshold. "How did the meeting go?"

He touched her cheek tenderly. "I'm going to call Hank's friend tomorrow."

"Thank God." She crossed the kitchen. "Sit down, honey. I'll have your supper warmed up in a few minutes."

Samuel put his Bible on the white Formica table, pulled back a chrome chair, and sat on the red vinyl seat. "We've got our work cut out for us."

"At least they'll listen to you."

"Only because they're getting too tired to argue anymore."

Abby smiled over her shoulder. "Don't get cynical this late in the game. Something like this can make us feel young again." She punched in numbers on the microwave.

"Otis says I'm a dreamer." He watched Abby put silverware and a napkin on the table in front of him. She was as beautiful to him now at seventy-four as she had been at eighteen when he married her. He took her hand. "I still love you, you know."

"You'd better. You're stuck with me." The microwave pinged. "Your supper's ready."

"Otis was fit to be tied when he got to the church. Mabel is having a hard time of it again. Back on oxygen."

"So I heard." She set the plate before him. Meat loaf, mashed potatoes, green beans. "I called her this evening. We had a long chat." She took the chair opposite him.

He picked up his fork. "Was she behaving herself?"

Abby laughed. "I could hear someone talking about layered salads in the background; then Mabel turned the television down."

"Poor old soul."

"Oh, stuff and nonsense. Half her fun is frustrating Otis. She knows exactly which buttons to push to make him jump."

"She doesn't miss cooking?"

"Not as much as he wishes she did."

"Women. You can't live with them and you can't live without them."

She left her chair and opened the old refrigerator. She poured a tall glass of milk, set it down in front of him, and sat again. She could never sit for long. It was against her nature. She tented her fingers and watched him. Despite his lack of appetite, he ate, slowly, so she wouldn't worry. "Susanna will be relieved, Samuel. She's wanted Hank to retire since he had bypass surgery."

"They won't have much to live on. It's not as though they have a place to sell."

"I think Susanna will miss that old parsonage. She told me they have about ten thousand in savings. Thank God we have a retirement fund to give them. Otherwise, they'd be depending on their children to help support them."

Samuel told her the bad news. Abby bowed her head, saying

nothing. He set his fork down and waited, knowing she was sending up one of her desperate prayers again. When she raised her head, her face was pale, her eyes moist. He shared her shame. "I wish I'd been born rich instead of handsome." The old joke fell flat. Abby reached over and put her hand on his. He shook his head, unable to speak.

"I wonder what the Lord is doing this time," she said wistfully.

"You're not the only one."

Blessed Child

Ted Dekker and Bill Bright

A young orphan boy raised in an African monastery must be rescued and brought to the US. But Jason Marker, the embittered Peace Corps representative given the mission, soon finds that this is no ordinary boy. Just ten years old, Caleb has extraordinary miracle-working powers.

Back in the US, Caleb finds himself at the centre of a story of greed and political intrigue and with a price on his head. Soon Jason finds himself fighting for Caleb's survival.

Blessed Child is a novel that pushes the boundaries of Christian fiction, and a reminder of the awesome power of the Holy Spirit.

ISBN 0 8499 4312 4
PB

Price: £9.99
£6.99 Special Offer
Special offer ends 31/08/03

Published by Zondervan
PO Box 749, Harrow, HA1 1DP

1

Three Months Later
Minus 3 Days

Jason brought the open-topped Peace Corps Jeep to a stop and turned off its ignition. The engine coughed once and died. He hauled himself up by the roll bar and studied the browned valley ahead. The Ethiopian Orthodox monastery known to locals as Debra Damarro, loomed against the rolling hills, a square fortress hewn from solid rock. Why the ancients had built here, in such a remote corner of Tigre in northern Ethiopia, so far from the beaten track of worshipers, was beyond him, but then so was the tenor of Orthodoxy in general. And Christianity, for that matter.

Acacia trees swayed in the courtyard, serene in the afternoon heat. Jason kept his eyes fixed on the iron gate where Daal insisted he would be met and speedily serviced. The Eritrean invasion was only three days old, but already the Eritrean Peoples Liberation Front (EPLF) had brought the border dispute as far south as Axurn to the west; it was a wonder they had not overtaken these hills yet. But then Ethiopia wasn't taking the sudden invasion along its northern border lying down. They were obviously keeping the enemy forces occupied elsewhere, where more than a single remote monastery was at stake.

It was not the first time Eritrea had made this absurd claim to the land beyond its drawn borders. Absurd because even the pagans knew that Orthodox Ethiopians would defend their northern holy sites to the death. The queen of Sheba had first brought Solomon's wisdom and, according to many, his child, here to her castle near Axumn, fifty miles to the southwest. The Jewish religion had swept through the hills, and several hundred years later, the Ark of the Covenant had followed–also to Axurn, the priests insisted. A growing contingent of scholars at least agreed with the Ethiopian Orthodox community that the Arles last known resting place was indeed somewhere in northern Ethiopia.

Christianity had first come to Africa here, along this northern border. And now for the second time in ten years, Eritrea was openly disputing that border. It was like trying to argue that Florida really belonged to Cuba.

Absurd.

Most of the relief workers in the surrounding towns had already fled south to the country's capital, Addis Ababa, with the first evacuation order.

Most. But not Jason Marker. Daal, his Irob interpreter, had begged him for this one favor. To deliver this one orphan stranded at this remote monastery to safety. And why would he risk his life to save a single child in a land where a hundred thousand would die in the next famine? Why would he head north, closer to the EPLF forces, instead of blazing a trail south as demanded by the Corps?

Perhaps because he *was* in the Corps: the kind of man who at least on occasion threw caution to the wind for a sense of greater purpose. Or maybe to appease the guilt he felt at having decided to leave Ethiopia for good.

But most likely because he wasn't really risking his life at all. The Eritreans would probably not harm an American. Daal had sworn nothing less before running off to see to his own family. So Jason would engage in this one last humanitarian mission and close this chapter in his life. And just as well – working in Ethiopia had been like trying to extract water from a bag of flour.

Jason wiped the rolling sweat from his forehead, rubbed his hand on his khakis, and dropped back into the seat. The monastery seemed quiet enough. He reached for the key, and the faint rumble of an engine drifted through the air.

His hand froze. It wasn't the Jeep's engine, of course. He hadn't turned the key. Jason scanned the horizon quickly. The road ran past the monastery and climbed the hills to the right, disappearing into valleys and reappearing on the distant hills beyond like a tan snake.

He saw the trucks then, tiny dots slinking into a valley several miles off. A small grunt escaped his throat, and for a terrible moment he couldn't think. He snatched up his binoculars and peered at the trucks. EPLF! It was an EPLF column, headed toward the monastery, no more than ten minutes off. Which meant what?

That Daal had been wrong?

Jason's doctorate was in agriculture, not military maneuvers, but he hardly needed an education to tell him that this was not good. His heart was doing the job splendidly.

He spun around in a panic and grabbed for the old bolt action .30-06 he used for the occasional hunt. His sweaty palm slapped at the worn wood stalk and managed to claw it off the back seat before sending it clattering to the floorboards behind.

What was he thinking? Take on the Eritrean army with a thirty-ought-six?

Jason fired the Jeep's engine, shoved the stick forward, and dropped the clutch. The old World War II vehicle jerked forward. He tore for the gate, blinking against the simple thought that he was headed the wrong way. He should be *leaving*.

It wasn't terribly clear why he did continue for that closed iron gate. At any moment his arms would yank the steering wheel and whip the Jeep through a one-eighty. But they did not.

A figure in robes suddenly ran for the gate and threw it open. Jason roared through and braked the Jeep into a skidding stop, three meters from the monastery's foundation. Wide, sweeping steps cut from sandstone rose to an arching entry. Heavy wooden doors gaped open to a dark interior. Behind him the gatekeeper was yelling in Amharic.

Blessed Child

Jason slid from the seat and bounded up the steps two at a time. He ran through an internal circuit and into the cavernous sanctuary. He slid to a stop on the polished stone floor. To say that the room was empty would have misstated the matter. Although Jason was indeed alone in the huge domed sanctum, an imposing silence filled the space, heavy enough to resonate through his skull with a distant ring. His blood pounded through his ears.

High above him a yellow face covering half the dome peered down unblinking, engaging his eyes.

"Sire!"

Jason spun.

The voice echoed across the sanctuary. "Sire, you are not permitted in this room. It is for priests–"

"Where's Father Matthew? Do you have a Father Matthew here? I have to see him!"

The white-draped priest stared at Jason as if he'd just swallowed a small boulder. He held an ancient text in his arms, a huge book browned by time.

Jason lowered his voice. "Please, man. Forgive me, but I have to see Father Matthew immediately. Do you know that there are soldiers –"

"It's quite all right, Phillip."

"You knew they'd be coming? That's not what Daal told me. He said this would be a simple in-and-out trip to collect the orphan and take him to safety. Somehow it isn't feeling quite so simple."

"Ah, Daal. He was always a bit smooth with the tongue. Rather like a lot of priests I know. It's a case of humanity, I suspect; insisting on some brand of the truth altogether unclear, but made clearer with insistence." He shuffled on and held up a finger, half turning. "What you cannot establish with wit you can always further with a little volume, don't you think?"

Ordinarily Jason would have chuckled at the old man's own wit, but the image of those trucks plowing over the hills outside tempered his humor. The priest was muttering now, and his echoes sounded like a chuckle through the tunnel. They hurried deeper into the earth.

"Maybe you could just bring the child out to the Jeep," Jason said. He was having a hard time communicating his urgency to the old senile goat. "Maybe I should go back and—"

"Do you believe in God?"

They broke into a torch-lit room furnished with a single wooden table and two chairs. The priest turned to face him. His long eyes sagged in the surreal orange light.

"Do I … yes, of course —"

"Or do you just say that you believe in God to appease me? I see doubt in your eyes, young man."

Jason blinked, stunned. Father Matthew was dearly out of touch. Outside a war was looming and he wasted time philosophizing about God in the bowels of some lost monastery. The old man spoke hurriedly now.

"Do you believe that Jesus Christ was a madman?"

"What?"

"Do you believe that when he announced that his disciples would do greater things than he had, he was delusional?"

'What does this have to do with anything? We have to get out, man!"

"I thought not," the priest said. "You do not believe. And yes, we are short on time. But our lives are in God's hands."

"That's fine, but if you wouldn't mind I would like to get out of here before the bullets start flying. I'm not sure your God is quite so attentive to my interests."

"Yes, I can see that you're unsure."

"And why did you call me here in the first place, if you're so confident that God will save you?"

"You are here, aren't you? I will assume that he sent you. So then he is saving us. Or at least the child. Unless we are too late, of course."

Jason shoved the logic from his mind and tried to control his frustration. "Then please help your God along and get me the kid."

The priest studied Jason's face. "I want your word. You will die before allowing Caleb to come to harm."

Jason balked at the man's audacity.

"Swear it."

It was an insane moment and he spoke quickly, to appease the man. "Of course, I promise you. Now get him please."

"We found him at the gate when he was a baby, you know. Abandoned here by a retreating Eritrean commander who had just killed his mother during the last war. She was a European nurse. The soldier left a scrawled note with the boy seeking absolution for his sins."

Father Matthew stared unblinking, as if the revelation should explain some things. But the tale sounded rather par for the course in this mad place.

"The boy is no ordinary child. I think you will see that soon enough. Did you know that he has never seen beyond the gate? You will only be the fourth man he has ever laid eyes on in his ten years of life. He has never seen a woman.

"He's been in this monastery his whole life?"

"I raised him as a son. Where I go he goes. Or in this case where I stay, he has stayed. Except now. Now God has sent you to deliver the boy and I am bound by a vow to remain here."

He reached inside his tunic and withdrew an envelope. He handed the brown packet out to Jason, who looked unsure. "These are his papers, granting him refugee status outside of Ethiopia."

"Outside? I was under the impression that I was taking him to Addis Ababa."

"As long as he is in this country; his life is in danger. You must deliver him to safety beyond our borders."

Jason was about to tell the old man that he was losing true north when a door suddenly burst open to their right. A boy ran into the room, grinning from ear to ear.

"Dadda!" He spoke in Amharic, but he didn't look Ethiopian. His skin was a creamy tan and his dark hair hung in loose curls to, his shoulders – he was clearly of mixed race. A simple cotton tunic similar to the priest's covered his small frame.

The boy ran up and threw his arms around the priest's waist, burying his face in the man's tunic. Father Matthew palmed the envelope, smiled, and dropped to his knees to hug the child. "Hello, Caleb." He kissed him on his forehead and looked into the boy's eyes – eyes as brilliant blue-green as Jason had ever seen.

"Caleb, your time has come, my son." He smoothed the boy's hair lovingly.

Caleb faced Jason with those large, round eyes. The priest had prepared the boy already, and Jason wondered what the boy knew.

A tremor shook the ground and Jason instinctively glanced up. It was a shell! A shell had detonated outside!

Father Matthew's hand grabbed Jason's and pressed the envelope into his palm. The old man's eyes were misted by the flame's light. "Promise me, my friend, I beg you! Take him beyond our borders."

"I will. I will. Get us out of here!"

The priest's eyes lingered for a brief moment, searching for truth. He whirled for the boy, who stared at the ceiling as another rumble shook the room. He snatched Caleb's hand. "Follow me! Run!"

The small shuffle steps Father Matthew had employed to lead Jason down gave way to long strides, and Jason raced to keep Father and son in sight. The priest was an enigma but certainly no idiot. His voice called back as they ran.

"They are firing on the village behind the monastery. We still have time. I have asked the others to distract them if necessary."

"Distract?"

"We have a moat behind for water. It will be burning with oil."

The child ran silently, on the heels of his father. They burst into the same sanctuary Jason had been scolded for entering earlier. Now another figure stood at its center, spinning around to face them as they rushed in.

She wore a navy blue tunic not unlike you might see on any street corner throughout Ethiopia, but the woman was clearly not Ethiopian. A hood shrouded a deeply tanned face. She seemed to arrest even the old priest's attention for a moment.,

"Oh yes, I'd nearly forgotten about you, dear," Father Matthew said. He turned to Jason. "This is the nurse Leiah. She came to us a few hours ago from a French Canadian Red Cross camp in Eritrea that was overrun."

"A woman," Jason said, not because the discovery was notable, but because everyone knew women were strictly prohibited past the gates of any Ethiopian Orthodox monastery. Yet here was most definitely a woman. A Frenchwoman.

The woman glanced at the door leading to the courtyard and then back to Jason. She approached him quickly. "Take me with you!" she said in perfect English. She turned to Father Matthew. "Father, tell him he must take me with him!"

Her blue eyes begged. She grabbed his shirt and tugged gently toward the door. "Hurry! We have to leave."

A loud detonation shook the sanctuary and Jason ducked with the sound.

"Take her," the priest said. He knelt and took Caleb in his arms again. He drew the boy close and whispered in his ear. When he pulled back, tears snaked from his eyes, wetting each cheek. "Remember what I have taught you, my son. Remember it well. Listen to your heart; the eyes will deceive. Remember." He spoke in Amharic.

"Let's go! Hurry," Jason urged them. For all the talk of delivering these to safety, they wouldn't make it past the front gate if they didn't leave now. Assuming the gate was not already overtaken.

"Dadda. . ." the boy said.

"Go with God, Caleb. His love is better than life."

"Dadda . . ."

Jason grabbed the boy's arm and tugged him toward the arching entry. Leiah, the woman, was already at the door craning for a view on either side. She spun to them.

"Hurry, hurry!"

"Jason," the priest said. "What's soft and round and says more than it should?"

Jason spun back. "Wha–?"

"The hem of a tunic." Father Matthew smiled. "An old Ethiopian riddle about modesty that will make sense to you one day. Remember it."

They ran from the monastery together, Leiah in the lead, with Jason and the boy following behind. The midday sun blinded Jason for an instant. He released the boy's hand and took the steps more by feel than by sight.

Behind him Father Matthew's voice urged a faltering boy. "Go! Run. Run to the truck and climb in. It will be all right. Remember my riddle, Jason."

There was no sign of soldiers on this side of the monastery, but the detonations of what Jason assumed to be mortar fire shook the ground behind them. Black smoke boiled into the sky. Father Matthew's burning moat. Oil.

Jason spun to see the boy picking his way down the broad steps on his tiptoes. His round eyes glanced around, petrified. Jason bounded up the steps, grabbed the boy around the waist, and ran for the Jeep.

"Give him to me!" the nurse demanded, her arms outstretched from the back seat. He shoved the boy toward her. She gathered Caleb and set him on the seat beside her. The boy immediately covered his eyes with his hands and buried his head in her lap.

"Get us out of here! Hurry, man!" Leiah said.

"I am. I am! Hold on!"

The engine roared to life with the first turn of the ignition. Jason rammed the shift stick forward and floored the accelerator. The Jeep spun in a circle, raising dust on all sides. He angled the vehicle for the gate and grabbed another gear.

Behind them an explosion shook the courtyard. They were lobbing the explosives to the front! Ahead the gate was dosed. The gatekeeper ran out, pointing frantically to Jason's rear. He glanced back and saw the first truck emerging from a cloud of smoke beside the monastery – a Land Rover painted in desert camouflage.

Jason didn't let up on the gas pedal. He had the engine wound out in third gear, screaming for the closed gate.

"Open it! Open the gate!" he screamed, motioning furiously with his hand.

The gatekeeper flew for the latch, like a ghost in his flowing white robes. He shoved the gates open and ran for the monastery, uttering sharp cries barely heard above the thumping explosions behind them.

The Jeep struck one of the gates with a clang and shot out onto the driveway. Jason shoved the gearbox into high gear, veered off the road in his haste, corrected with a jerk of the wheel, and centered the vehicle on the road leading from the valley.

"Stay on the road! Watch the potholes!"

Her warning came too late and their right wheel pounded through a hole the size of a Volkswagen. Jason cleared the seat a good foot before crashing back down. He glanced back to see Leiah's white face. The boy was still buried in her lap, oblivious to the world.

"Watch for the holes!" Leiah yelled.

"I am!"

Behind them a huge explosion ripped through the air, like a thunderclap rumbling across the sky. Jason's heart slammed against the walls of his chest, loud in his ears, spurred by a mixture of terror and euphoria. Machine guns stuttered in long bursts. This was no abstract attack on a village. They were destroying the monastery wholesale, an unspoken taboo, even during an invasion. The monasteries had survived a thousand years precisely because of the reverence they commanded. Slaughter of women and children was far more common in this land than the destruction of a shrine.

They had nearly reached the crest of the first hill when Jason looked back again. What he saw ran through his chest like a spike on the end of a sledgehammer. He caught his breath. The monastery was without ambiguity history, crumbled and smoking, a remnant of its former structure. No soul could possibly have lived through such a pounding. And if one or two did manage to find the sunlight alive, a ring of trucks with mounted machine guns awaited to make certain they did not savor it too long.

Jason saw the destruction in a glance. But he forgot it almost immediately in favor of another sight that nearly drove him from the road. It was the sight of a lone truck barreling down the road behind them.

Leiah must have seen the look on his face, because she spun to face the valley. Machine-gun fire cut through the air, a small popping sound, like popcorn in a microwave.

"Move it! They're catching us!" she screamed.

Something snapped in Jason's mind. The euphoria of their escape was smothered by horror. They were being pursued.

"Faster! Drive faster!"

"Shut up! I'm driving as fast as I can! Just shut up and let me drive!"

They crested the hill and roared into the next valley. For a few seconds, maybe ten, they were alone with the growling of their own engine. And then the larger Land Rover broke over the hill and screamed after them.

Jason felt panic wash over his spine. They were going to die. He knew that with dread certainty. His life would end this day.

The Note

Angela Hunt

Peyton MacGruder is a journalist with a problem: she's just been told that the column which supports her as a single woman in Florida will be cut unless it attracts more readers.

But Peyton's own problems soon pale into insignificance. When an airliner crashes into Tampa Bay killing everyone on board, she is given the story. And her discovery of a scrap of paper in the wreckage that simply reads 'T – I love you. All is forgiven. Dad', changes her world forever.

The Note is an inspiring novel and a powerful story of God's love and forgiveness.

ISBN 0 8499 4284 5

PB

Price: £9.99
£6.99 Special Offer
Special offer ends 31/08/03

Published by Tyndale House
Wheaton, Illinois 60189

One

WEDNESDAY, JUNE 13

The sultry breeze carried not a single hint that the summer afternoon would give birth to the worst aviation disaster in American history. At New York's bustling LaGuardia Airport, thousands of passengers clutched belongings, flashed driver's licenses, and gripped boarding passes before departing for farflung destinations across the globe.

Every one of them had made plans for the evening.

At gate B-13, 237 passengers waited for a jet that would carry them to Tampa International Airport. Their reasons for traveling were as varied as their faces: some hoped for a few days of fun, others looked forward to work, others yearned to see family. A pleasant mood reigned in the lounge area despite the jet's late arrival. Chuck O'Neil, one of the PanWorld gate attendants, told jokes to pass the time. Four standby passengers smiled in relief when they were told seats were available.

PanWorld Flight 848, which had originated at TIA, touched down at LaGuardia at 2:38 P.M.., almost an hour late. Two hundred fifty passengers and crew disembarked from the Boeing 767, which had developed problems with a pressure switch in the No. 1 engine. The trouble was nothing unusual, considering the age of the twenty-two-year-old plane, and Tampa mechanics had corrected the problem while others performed routine maintenance.

In the gate area, families kissed their loved ones good-bye while other travelers placed last-minute calls on their cell phones. Five passengers were PanWorld employees utilizing one of their employment perks: free travel on any flight with available seating. Debbie Walsh, a ticket agent with PanWorld, was taking her nine-year-old son to visit his father in Florida.

Forty-nine-year-old Captain Joey Sergeant of Tampa stepped out for a cup of fresh coffee before returning to the cockpit. With him were flight engineer Ira Nipps, sixty-two, of Bradenton, Florida, and first officer Roy Murphy of Clearwater. Together the three men had logged more than forty-six thousand hours of flight experience.

On the tarmac, PanWorld employees loaded the belly of the plane with golf bags, suitcases, backpacks, and two kennels—one occupied by a basset hound belonging to the Cotter family from Brooklyn, another by a ten-week-old Siberian Husky, a present for passenger Noland Thompson's grandchildren in Clearwater. While baggage handlers sweated in the afternoon sun, mechanics poured twenty-four thousand gallons of fuel into the jet.

The flight attendants boarded the waiting travelers with little fuss. Among the 237 passengers were Mr. and Mrs. Thomas Wilt, who planned to cruise the Caribbean from the port of Tampa; Dr. and Mrs. Merrill Storey, who hoped to buy a condo in St. Petersburg; and the Darrell Nance family – two parents and four children, all bound for Disney World after a day at Busch Gardens. First-class passenger Tom Harold, defensive coach for the Tampa Bay Buccaneers, boarded with his wife, Adrienne. To celebrate their fortieth wedding anniversary, the couple had taken a quick trip to New York to catch her favorite play, *Les Misirables,* on Broadway.

Forty-eight of the PanWorld passengers were students from Largo Christian School – recent graduates whose senior class trip had been postponed until mid-June to avoid conflicting with final exams. The students and their nine chaperones had missed an earlier flight, and many were openly thanking God that the airline could accommodate the entire group on Flight 848.

Shortly before 4:00 P.M.., flight attendants sealed the doors, then airline workers pushed the 767 back ftom the gate. On the flight deck, Captain Sergeant started the four Pratt & Whitney engines. After checking with air traffic controllers in the tower, the plane taxied to its assigned runway.

At 4:05, controllers cleared the jet for takeoff. By 4:15, Flight 848 was airborne, her wheels tucked back into the well, her nose lifted toward the stratosphere. After a short circling climb over New York Harbor, Captain Sergeant began a graceful turn to the south, toward Florida and sunny skies.

The pilots couldn't have asked for better weather. Temperatures in Tampa were in the high eighties, the humidity a sultry 70 percent. No clouds marred the horizon for as far as the pilots could see. The captain took the jet to 35,000 feet, typical cruising altitude for the 767, and held it at 530 miles per hour. Once the plane was safely settled into her flight path, he checked the passenger list and noticed that he flew with two empty seats. Florida flights often sold out at this time of year.

The passengers set about the business of making time pass as quickly as possible. They dosed their eyes to nap, clamped on head-phones, browsed through magazines, or peered at dusty paperbacks they'd picked up from the airport bookstore. The high school graduates in the back of the plane laughed and shouted across the aisles as they shared stories of their Manhattan adventure.

The flight attendants unfastened their seat belts and whisked out the drink carts, murmuring "Watch your elbows" with every step they took down the aisle.

One of those flight attendants was Natalie Moore. She had joined the flight in New York at the last moment, filling in for a steward who had taken ill. Before leaving New York she told a roommate she was looking forward to her first visit to Tampa. A rookie with the airline, she had graduated from flight school in Atlanta and moved into Kew Gardens, a New York neighborhood primarily populated by young flight attendants who worked out of LaGuardia and Kennedy Airports.

As the hands of her watch moved toward five o'clock, Natalie and her coworkers began to serve dinner. Passengers had a choice of entrées: baked chicken breast or sirloin steak, both accompanied by green beans and salad. As soon as the flight attendants served the last of the dinner trays, they cleared their cart and pushed it aft to begin cleanup. The flight from New York to Tampa did not allow much time for lingering over dinner, and only because Flight 848 flew during the dinner hour was a meal offered at all.

At 6:06, after nearly two hours of uneventful flight, Captain Sergeant began his descent. At 6:18, air traffic controllers at Tampa International cleared the incoming flight to drop from 15,000 to 13,000 feet. As usual, the pilot responded by repeating his instructions: "PW 848, out of one-five for one-three."

On board, passengers on the right side of the plane caught a dazzling view of Florida's Sun Coast – white beaches, pool-studded backyards, and green treetops, all bordered by the wide, blue expanse of the Gulf of Mexico.

In the galleys, flight attendants locked the drink carts into their stowed positions, getting ready to make a final pass down the aisle. Natalie Moore moved through the cabin reminding passengers to be sure their seatbacks and tray tables were in their upright and locked positions. As she waited for a rambunctious teenager to comply, she bent to glance at the horizon. The sun, slipping toward the ocean, had painted the sky in a riot of pinks and yellows.

At 13,389 feet, while Natalie and the other crew members went about their work, the torrent of air rushing past a loose screw on the fuselage outside the fuel tank created a spark. The electrical fuses tripped, and at 6:29 the plane's radio and transponders fell silent. Captain Sergeant sent a distress call, but no one heard it.

The loose screw continued to spark.

A few moments later, a man sitting in row 24, seat C, noticed three of the attendants huddled in the galley, their arms around each other. One wiped away a tear, while another bowed her head as if to pray.

"Isn't that nice." He nudged the woman sitting next to him. "Look

– they've had a tiff, and now they're making up."

Their disagreement must not have been serious, for the flight attendants immediately separated. "Ladies and gentlemen," a male voice called over the intercom, "this is the captain. Please give attention to the flight attendant in your section of the plane. We have experienced a loss of power due to an electrical disruption, but we can still land safely. In order to prepare for this event, however, we ask that you remove all eyeglasses, then give your attention to the flight attendants as they demonstrate the crash position."

Leaning forward, the man in 24-C looked out the window and saw that they were descending in a curving path, moving over water toward land. Though the atmosphere in the cabin hummed with tension, he remained hopeful. The jet was coming down in a relatively smooth spiral above the choppy waters between the Howard Frankland and Causeway Campbell Bridges. The airport lay just beyond.

As the people around him fumbled to obey the flight attendants, he pulled a sheet of paper from his coat pocket and scribbled a message. Glancing out the window again, he saw the blue of the water and felt a flash of inspiration. Digging in another pocket, he produced a plastic bag, then tucked the note inside and secured the seal.

Smiling, he looked up at the pale stewardess standing in the aisle, her mouth a small, tight hyphen. "Sorry," he said, noticing that everyone around him had already bent forward to prepare for an emergency landing. I wanted to take care of something. I'm sure we'll be all right, so tonight I'll laugh and give this to my –"

He never finished his sentence. A spark from the fuselage ignited the fuel vapors, and Flight 848 exploded. At 6:33 P.M., pieces of the plane began to rain down into the waters of Tampa Bay.

Among the shards and debris was a note.

Two

TWO HOURS EARLIER

Across town, at the *Tampa Times* office, Peyton MacGruder received a note. The summons came in the form of an e-mail, and, as usual, Nora Chilton minced no words:

Need to see you at once.

Peyton sighed at the imperial command from the lifestyles editor, then checked her watch. Four-forty-five, which meant she couldn't slip away and later claim she hadn't seen the message. E-mail at the *Tampa Times* flew through the office at the speed of electricity, and Nora didn't miss a trick.

Peyton made a face at the computer monitor. If Nora kept her more than fifteen minutes, she could kiss her tennis game goodbye. Karen Dolen, a news writer and Peyton's tennis partner, had a husband and three hungry kids to feed by six-thirty, so tennis couldn't be postponed.

After checking her computer's "in" basket to be sure nothing more appealing had arrived, Peyton stood, picked up her backpack, then glanced at the blonde head hovering over a keyboard at the desk across the aisle. "I'll see you tomorrow, Mandi, but probably after lunch. If anyone asks, I've got a morning appointment in St. Pete."

Mandi Sorenson, a college intern who had filled Peyton's morning with insistent and irritating offers to help, looked up and blinked. "What was that, Ms. MacCruder?"

"It's Peyton, and I said I'll see you tomorrow."

"Okay." As Mandi lowered her wide gaze back to the obituary forms some soul from local news had contributed to the cause of Keeping Mandi Quiet, Peyton shouldered her backpack and tried to remember if she had ever been that bug-eyed with wonder. Probably not. One of her college profs claimed she'd been hardwired for skepticism, and even as a student reporter for the *Independent Florida*

Alligator she'd not been easily impressed. What was a newspaper office, after all, but a collection of computers and a motley assortment of writers?

"And the older I get," Peyton mumbled, moving through the maze of desks, chairs, and rolling file cabinets, "the more motley the writers."

Nora Chilton's office was situated in a row of offices at the back of the building. As Peyton moved toward the expanse of wide-windowed rooms, she nodded to two men in navy suits — out of towners, from the look of them. No Floridian wore dark colors in June. She watched the strangers disappear through the senior news editor's doorway, then leaned against the doorframe of Nora's office and rapped on the open door with her knuckles.

From behind her desk, Nora glanced up over the rim of her tortoiseshell reading glasses. The petite editor was sitting erect in her chair, her head capped by a curled mass in a uniform shade of brown, the surest sign of home hair coloring.

"Come on in, Pat," she said, lowering her gaze to the papers in her hand.

Stepping into the office, Peyton resisted the urge to correct the woman. Her name was *Peyton,* not Pat, Pate, Patty, or Mac, but Nora Chilton insisted on giving everyone in her department a nickname. Peyton wasn't sure why, but she suspected Nora wanted to cultivate friendlier relations between writers and editors.

Fat chance.

"Pat," Nora said, dropping the papers as Peyton slid into the guest chair, "thanks for coming in. This will only take a moment."

Peyton waited, one brow lifted, as Nora glanced out at the newsroom beyond her door. After a moment of silence, she spoke again, her voice lower. "Did you happen to see the bean counters out there?"

The corner of Peyton's mouth lifted in a wry smile. "The two guys in suits?"

Nora leaned forward, the grim line of her mouth thinning.

"Accountants from New York. They're after us to tighten up."

Folding her hands, Peyton waited while Nora shuffled the pages on her desk. "We've been asked to give special attention to the figures ftom our latest readers' survey.

Readers'survey? Like malevolent genies released ftom a bottle, the words loomed up and shadowed the office, killing Peyton's hope of a pleasant meeting. Her column, "The Heart Healer," had never scored high in the *Times'* reader polls. Peyton liked to think she had lots of readers, people who were too busily productive to bother with questionnaires.

"Here are the figures." Nora slid one of the pages across the desk. "According to the latest focus group, your column ranked lowest of our five regular features. I'm sorry, Pat, but the numbers don't lie. And if a column isn't pulling its weight, something's got to change."

Peyton's lips parted as she stared at the paper. "The DriveThrough Gourinet" occupied the top position, followed by "The Pet Yet," "The Quick Cook," and "The Car Caretaker." Like a lead weight, "The Heart Healer" sat heavily at the bottom of the list.

For a moment her head buzzed with rationalizations. Plucking the most obvious defense from the top of the swarm, she said, "It's not entirely my fault, you know. I inherited this column. If it were up to me—"

"It's not up to you, and, if it's any comfort, the column does rank high with one particular audience." Nora's thin mouth curved in a barely discernible smile. "'The Heart Healer' came out on top with women over eighty-five. I suppose that's because nursing-home residents don't drive, cook, have pets, or eat often at McDonald's."

Peyton narrowed her gaze. Nora's sense of humor – if that's what it was – left something to be desired. I don't know if I'd put much stock in those polls, Nora. They're only collections of random opinion."

"But opinion is important in the lifestyles section. We're not producing hard news – we're what people read for pleasure." She leaned forward, the set of her chin telegraphing her infamous stubborn streak. "Emma Duncan had *great* numbers when she was writing 'The Heart Healer.' At one point, this department was receiving over a thousand letters a week, all for Ernma-"

"Yeah?" Peyton's voice went hoarse with frustration. "Well, Nora, let's not lose sight of one important fact – Emma Duncan is deceased. And because you didn't want to lose her readers, you gave her column to me. I'm doing my best to keep the thing going, but did you ever think that maybe the entire *concept is* dead?" She leaned back, scrubbing her hand through her short hair. I mean – 'The Heart Healer.' How sentimental is that? No professional writer would volunteer to write that sappy stuff today. It may have been timely twenty years ago when Emma began to write, but now–"

"The concept will still reach readers." Nora's voice held a note of irritation. "But perhaps it's time we had another writer take a crack at it. We can always move you to something else."

Peyton's inner alarm bell began to clang. Move her? To what? She'd left the frenzy of the sports department to write "The Heart Healer." While the homespun column wasn't much of a creative challenge, the regular schedule had been good for her peace of mind. Sports writing required too many late nights, too many encounters with testosterone-fueled men, and too many squabbles with Kingston Bernard, the senior sports editor.

She couldn't deny that "The Heart Healer" had done better in years past, but she'd made considerable progress in the ten months since Duncan's death. The readers had rebelled at first, probably resenting Peyton's professional approach, and for a few weeks reader mail virtually disappeared. But over the last six months Peyton had received an average of twenty-five letters or e-mails per week. Not huge by Dear Abby standards, but respectable. Peyton liked to think that while her version of the column may not have appealed to Emma Duncan's readers, she was appealing to *someone*.

"Nora," she firmed her voice, "the problem is a difference in approach. I came out of journalism school; I learned to write from a properly detached perspective. Emma got plucked from the neighborhood; she wrote about her kids and dogs. My work may not resonate with Emma's crowd, but the column is accurate and useful. A lot of local people are looking for practical, simple information–"

"I can't afford to reserve front-page space for a useful column appealing to only a limited number of people." Nora's brown eyes snapped behind her glasses. I hate to be the one to tell you, but few of our readers are interested in step-by-step procedures for conducting a title search. Nor do busy families want the recipe for modeling clay. And what was that piece you wrote last month? How to seal seasonal clothing in plastic by reversing the hose on a vacuum cleaner? Honestly, Pat, no one's interested in those things." Her brows rose, twin wings of disdain. I have a hunch those topics don't even interest you."

The words stung, but Peyton knew she held the upper hand. As an over-forty female, if they let her go she could sue them for both age and gender discrimination … and they knew she wouldn't hesitate to call a lawyer.

Peyton pulled her shoulders back. "I'm a good writer. You can't say I haven't met my responsibilities and deadlines."

"No one's saying you don't write well." Nora leaned back in her chair, some of the frostiness bleeding out of her expression. "Your speed amazes me, and you have a great eye for detail. But there's more to doing a column than putting all the words in the proper place. A good columnist writes with passion, and I just don't feel that in your work. Emma Duncan, God rest her soul, had it. If she wrote a piece about tomatoes, by the time you finished reading you not only knew how to plant them, you wanted to run out and plant an *acre.*"

"You want me to get excited about tomatoes?" Peyton threw up her hands. "I'm sorry, Nora, but I'm not what you'd call *passionate* about gardening. But I can write a competent column about anything you'd want to name. I've come up through the ranks; I've paid my dues. I can't help it if 'The Heart Healer' attracts readers who want to know about title searches and clothing storage. They write letters, I answer them. It's that simple."

Nora leaned back in her chair, then pulled off her glasses and set them on the desk in a deliberate gesture. "Honestly, Pat" — she inclined her head in what seemed a condescending posture — "I don't think you're a bad writer. You're good, and you've got the awards to prove it. But 'The Heart Healer' isn't pulling its weight. Let me put one of the other girls on it, someone who's married and has a kid or two. And we'll move you back into the sports pool or maybe give you a shot at local news."

Not trusting herself to speak, Peyton shook her head. No matter how Nora presented Peyton's transfer, her move from columnist to reporter would be seen as a demotion, especially if she got tossed back into the reporters' pool. The thought of once again covering dull city council meetings made her head ache. After fifteen years of newspaper writing, she should have been promoted to editor. She might have been, if she wasn't continually butting heads with anal-retentive types who clung to outmoded rules and regulations like children who refused to be weaned from the breast.

"My column is fine," she insisted, lifting her gaze. "It's working." "The numbers don't lie." Nora tapped the report with her glasses. "Only little old ladies are reading your stuff, Pat, and I think those numbers came from nursing homes where the residents read everything out of sheer boredom." She lowered her gaze, stubby lashes shuttering her eyes. I think it's time you let me give 'The Heart Healer' to someone who cares less about writing to her peers than to her readers."

Again, the words stung. What was wrong with writing to a certain standard of excellence? Did the *Tampa Times* want writers to dumb down their work and appeal to the lowest common emotion? Emma Duncan, not exactly the most brilliant bulb in the chandelier, had written maudlin stories about her poodle and Chihuahua, for heaven's sake. The lady had never won an award, while Peyton's résumé was liberally peppered with honors. Yet Nora seemed to be saying that "The Heart Healer" needed someone who had kids and pets in order to make the column work.

Odd that, in a day when women were empowered, emancipated, and responsible for their own fulfillment, the old prejudice against unmarried females could rear its head and nip at an exposed ankle. In the office Peyton made no secret of how much she enjoyed her freewheeling singleness. Few people knew that she had once reveled in a husband's love and the scent of a man on a freshly slept-in bed. Yet a rain-slick road brought that life to an end, erasing a wonderful man and the family that might have been …

Abruptly, Peyton closed the door on memories she'd locked away a thousand times before. Raking a hand through her hair, she struggled to find a weapon against the editor's relentless logic. "Nora, I'm receiving twenty-five letters a week. And you know what they say for every letter we get, at least a hundred people intend to write but never do."

"Even twenty-five hundred readers are not enough to convince the bean counters." Nora's voice scraped like sandpaper against Peyton's ears. "We live in a major metropolitan area with a substantial population of retirees. 'The Heart Healer' is intended to appeal to the upper-age demographic, so it should be reaching at least seventy-five thousand people. You should be receiving over seven hundred letters a week." She paused, then added: "Emma Duncan did."

Peyton swallowed hard, realizing how little her twenty-five letters meant to the number-crunchers in the executive offices. The newspaper's daily circulation was 250,000, so her reader mail represented only 1I percent of the total daily subscribers.

"The Heart Healer" *wasn't* working.

But how could she surrender it? She'd worked so hard to make certain her column differed from Dear Abby and Ann Landers and all the other advice columnists. In each "Heart Healer" column she answered only *one* letter from a reader, going far beyond the usual pithy answers to give specific, detailed guidance. Along with the admittedly dry topics of title searches and insurance, she had given advice to mothers who needed to comfort daughters who'd suffered miscarriages, fathers who feared losing angry teenage sons, and mothers who worried about teenage daughters. Quoting whatever psychology expert's book she happened to have within reach, she'd given practical, expert, useful advice.

Her readers didn't need passion – they needed understandable answers.

"Please" – she scarcely recognized her voice – "don't take me off 'The Heart Healer.' Give me some time to adjust it; let me rethink my focus."

Nora's eyes glinted behind her glasses. "I was hoping to give Janet Boyles a shot at that column. I think she's ready for it."

Peyton forced a smile even as Nora's words spread ripples of pain and betrayal. Peyton had thought she and Janet were friends, but if the television writer had been jockeying for her spot …

"I'm ready for anything." Peyton forced herself to hold the other woman's flinty gaze. "Give me three months. If the numbers haven't improved by then, let's retire 'The Heart Healer' and institute a new column with a different concept."

"'I'll give you three weeks," the editor said, crossing her arms. "That's when we'll take our next readers' poll. If 'The Heart Healer' hasn't shown marked improvement, I'm giving Boyles a shot." She glanced toward the sea of desks beyond the door. "In the meantime, you might want to think about where you'd like to go next-back to sports or regional news."

Peyton clenched her fist, well aware that she was occupying sacred ground. Emma Duncan's untimely death from a heart attack, at her desk, no less, had elevated the woman to virtual newsroom sainthood. "The Heart Healer" could tank with *ten* different writers, yet Nora and the top brass would still want to keep Emma Duncan's column on life support.

So Peyton had to do something … and her approach had to work. She needed something incredible and novel – and she'd need breathing space to pull it together.

"I have vacation time coming," she said, exhaling slowly. "Why don't I take next week off and give this some serious thought? That will give me two weeks to try out a new approach."

Nora's gaze rested on her, as remote as the ocean floor, then the editor nodded. "Sounds like a good plan. Sure. File your Friday column by deadline tomorrow, and we'll run the 'on vacation' notice beginning Monday."

"My Friday column's done. I'll file it now."

Nora lifted a brow. "Topic?"

"How to select a good laptop computer. One of my readers has to buy one for her grandson." Rising from the chair, Peyton slung her backpack over her shoulder. "Thanks," she called as she left the office, though she felt anything but grateful.

And as she wandered through the newsroom, she pressed her hand to the back of her neck and wondered how in the world she was supposed to produce passion in a how-to column that had outlived its usefulness. Clearly, Nora Chilton didn't think she could do it.

Peyton would have to prove her wrong.

Covenant Child

Terri Blackstock

The victims of the tragic loss of all their close family, twins Kara and Lizzie Holbrooke are cut off from a large inheritance and forced to live with uncaring relatives. While the billion-dollar estate is managed by their stepmother, the twins grow into hard-drinking, shoplifting, promiscuous teenagers.

On their eighteenth birthday, the girls must decide if they will accept an offer that could change the course of their lives. But can children who've only known poverty and deprivation ever believe in a free gift of love and grace?

Covenant Child is an engrossing, dramatic read with a powerful message at its heart.

ISBN 0 8499 4301 9
PB

Price: £7.99
£5.99 Special Offer
Special offer ends 31/08/03

Published by W Publishing Group
A division of Thomas Nelson
PO Box 141000, Nashville, Tennessee

One

There's a question that haunts me in the blackest hours of night, when wasted moments crowd my dreams and mock the life I know. The question is this: How could a child born of privilege and promise grow up with nothing?

I was Somebody when I was born. Lizzie, my twin, says we were heiresses all along. "Our grandfather was a billionaire," she says. "Just *think* of it, Kara!" There were newspaper articles about us when we were three. They called us the "Billion Dollar Babies."

But these Billion Dollar Babies wore Goodwill hand-medowns. We ate dry cereal most nights for supper, right out of the box, picking out the raisins to save for our school lunches the next day. In my memory, we never formally observed a birthday, because no one around us considered that day worthy of celebration. We were worthless no accounts to most of the people in town.

But all along we had an inheritance that no one told us was ours.

I sometimes try to remember back to the days before we were three, but my memories are tainted with the lies I've been taught and the pictures I've seen. I can't quite sift out real recollections from my faulty assumptions, but I do know that the things I've laid out here are true. Not because I remember them, but because I've studied all the sides, heard all the tales, read all the reports … and a few things have emerged with absolute clarity.

The first thing is that my father, Jack Holbrooke, was the son of *the*

Paul Holbrooke, who did something with microchips and processors, things I can't begin to understand, and amassed a fortune before he was thirty. My father, Jack, got religion in his teens and decided he didn't want to play the part of the rich son. He became a pilot instead, bought a plane, and began flying charter flights and giving lessons. He disowned himself from the Holbrooke money and told his father that, instead of leaving any of it to him in his will, he preferred that he donate it to several evangelical organizations who provided relief and shared the gospel to people all over the world.

My grandfather tolerated his zeal and noted his requests, then promptly ignored them.

My mother, Sherry, was a teen runaway, who left Barton, Mississippi, at fifteen to strike out on her own. She wound up living with a kind family in Jackson, and she got religion, too.

She met my father in Jackson, when he put an ad in the paper for some office help at his hangar, and they fell in love around the time she was nineteen or so. They got married and had Lizzie and me less than a year later.

She was killed in a car wreck when we were just weeks old. Our father raised us himself for the next three years. I've seen pictures of him, and he looks like a kind, gentle man who laughed a lot. There are snapshots of him kissing us, dunking us like basketballs in his father's pool, chasing us across the lawn of the little house we lived in, reading us books, tucking us in. There are three birthday photos of our father lying on the floor with two cake-smeared redheads tearing into boxes of Barbies and Cabbage Patch dolls.

Sometimes I close my eyes and think hard, trying to bring back those moments, and for a while I convince myself that they are not just images frozen on paper, but they're live events in my head somewhere. I even think I can smell that cake and feel my father's stubbled face against mine. I can hear his laughter shaking through me and feel his arms holding me close.

But in truth, my memories don't reach that far back.

I don't even think I remember Amanda. Lizzie says she has more impressions of her than memories, that the snapshots just bring those *impressions* into clearer focus. I guess that's true with me, too.

But I wish I could remember when she met our father and us, how she wound up being his wife, how she was widowed and robbed of her children, and how she spent her life trying to keep a promise she had made to him … and to us.

But, according to Lizzie, truth is truth, whether it lies in your memory banks or not. So I'll start with Amanda's story, the way it was told to me, because it is very much the beginning of mine.

Two

My father was playing guitar the first time Amanda saw him. He sat on a metal folding chair at the corner of the crowded rec room, watching the animated faces and soaking in the laughter around them as he strummed some tune that she didn't know. She would later tell that her eyes were drawn to the red hair that was in dire need of a cut; the open flannel shirt, its tails draping down along the sides of the chair, a plain white T-shirt beneath it; jeans that looked as if they'd been washed a dozen times too many; and torn, dirty tennis shoes that spoke of age and overuse.

Her best friend, Joan, who'd attended the Bible study for single professionals for several months, told her he was a pilot. But Amanda knew little else about him.

When the group had been called to order, people found places to sit along couches and rocking chairs in the big, rustic room. Amanda chose a spot near the guitar player and sat on the floor with her arms hugging her knees. He smiled at her and kept strumming.

The leader turned the meeting over to him, and he began to lead the group in praise songs and rock-revved hymns, and she finally heard the voice, deep and gentle, unadorned, as it brought them all into worship. When he'd finished singing and playing, he put the guitar down and took a place beside her on the floor. His presence birthed a sweet homesickness inside her for something she couldn't name. She had known right then that he held some treasure that belonged to her, one she longed to unearth and possess.

When the meeting was over, he held out a hand. "Name's Jack."

"Nice to meet you, Jack." She shook his hand, feeling the guitar calluses on his fingertips against the bottom of her hand. "I'm—"

"Don't tell me. Let me guess." He held tight to her hand. I once worked at a fair and did this for a living."

"What? Played guitar?"

"No," he said, "guessed names. Now don't tell me. I can do this. I'm psychotic, you know."

She laughed. "You mean psychic?"

"Yeah, that, too." He winked as he gazed into her eyes. "Let's see. I'm getting an *A*.

Her eyes widened.

"An *M* "

She snatched her hand from his.

"Amanda!" he blurted.

"How did you know that?"

"I told you."

"I know. You're psychotic. But really. How?"

Grinning, he picked his guitar back up. "I asked somebody when you came in."

Her face grew warm as he rose, took her hand, and pulled her to her feet. He was a good seven inches taller than she.

"So how do you feel about chocolate milkshakes?" he asked.

"Tell you the truth, I haven't given it a whole lot of thought."

'Well, you should. Now aren't you grateful I came along to get you thinking about it?"

"Are you asking me to go have a milkshake with you?"

"I was trying to be a little more suave than to ask straight out, but yes," he said, "I was asking you for a date."

Though he'd charmed her quickly and thoroughly, he grew more serious over their shakes as he showed her pictures of Lizzie and me. Her heart sank that a man so young already had the baggage of divorce to drag around. "So how did you get custody?"

"Custody?" He frowned, then his eyebrows arched. "Oh, no, you don't understand. I'm not divorced. My wife died."

The smile on her face collapsed. "I'm so sorry."

"It's okay." His voice was soft, and he swallowed as if the memories still went down hard. "It happened three years ago, when they were just babies. Car accident. I've gone through all the textbook stages of grief. I'm in the acceptance stage now." Though his words sounded flip, she could see in his eyes that they didn't come easily.

"So you've been raising the twins alone ever since?"

"That's right. But they're doing great."

Quiet beat out the seconds between them, and finally, he said, "So how's the shake?"

"Everything I hoped." Her face grew warm, and she had to look away.

He took her back to the retreat center and held her hand as he walked her to her car. "If you'd agree to let me buy you dinner this weekend, I could introduce you to Stapley's Steak-on-a-Stick. It's the favorite of all your best amateur guitar players."

She was twenty-five years old, but felt as giddy as a fourteen-year-old with a crush. "I'd love to have dinner with you, Jack. And as good as the Steak-on-a-Stick sounds, I'd rather be introduced to your girls."

He laughed then. "No kidding?"

"Why would I be kidding?"

"Because they don't exactly make for a quiet, peaceful meal, if you know what I mean."

"I love children," she said.

"Okay, but you asked for it. Tell you what. You can come to my house, and the girls and I will cook dinner for you. How's that sound? We make a mean spaghetti."

She fished through her purse for something to write on. "Just give me an address and a time, and I'll be there. Only let me bring something."

"The girls would be downright insulted if you did. Besides, how can we impress you if we let you help?"

She started the car, still laughing under her breath. "All right. I'll see you then."

He wrote down the address and gave it to her through the door, then took her hand from the steering wheel and kissed it with Rhett Butler finesse.

She wore a silly smile as she drove away.

That night, she lay awake in bed thinking about this man with two little girls whom she hadn't expected to enter her life. He wasn't the kind of man she was looking for. Her checklist of "Mate Traits" did not include a previous marriage or three-year-old girls. But here she was, her mind and heart lingering on him, keeping her from a moment's sleep.

She couldn't wait to thank Joan for taking her to the Bible study.

"It'll be a good boost for you, Amanda," Joan had said. "It's kept me grounded for a long time now, and it's fun. You need to get out and meet some people, get your mind off of your problems."

Amanda's problems were'nt that easy to put behind her, however. They were significant, and lingering, and there were times when she found herself sinking into a mire of depression. Her lifeline had been the Scripture passages she had committed to memory.

"When you pass through the waters, I will be with you; And through the rivers, they will not overflow you. When you walk through the fire, you will not be scorched, Nor will the flame burn you."

Isaiah 43:2 had proven true in her life, just as Deuteronomy 31:6 had: *"Be strong and courageous, do not be afraid or tremble at them, for the LORD your God is the one who goes with you. He will not fail you or forsake you."*

When she'd found herself going under, she had grabbed hold of those words, and they had slowly pulled her out until she could breathe and look up with gratitude, instead of down with self-pity.

The uterine cancer was behind her now. Surgery and six months of chemo had taken care of that. Her hair had grown back in just as thick and blonde as it was before the cancer, and it had finally reached a length that didn't advertise her condition. The color had returned to her face, and she no longer looked emaciated and sick.

But the effects of the disease remained. She would never have children, at least not of her womb. It was the one thing she'd wanted in her life-a real family of her own, one that could erase all the longings of her past and make her feel safe and part of things.

She was reconciled to adopting children when she was ready ... but her fears remained. After all, what man would want to marry a woman who couldn't bear him children?

Her father tried to turn her plight into a positive. "Honey, this is a great filter for the men who don't deserve you. Either they love you the way you ought to be loved, or they hit the road. The Lord knows what He's doing."

Could it be that the Lord had a guitar-playing pilot with twin daughters in mind for her?

That question stayed with her for the next several days as she waited for Saturday to come.

My father prepared us for her visit the way one would prepare a classroom for a visit from a queen. He told us that a "very nice, very pretty lady" wanted to meet us, and that she was especially fond of little girls with curly red hair.

By the time Saturday night came, we were ready and waiting, decked out in our best garb and all atwitter with anticipation.

She rang the bell fifteen minutes early.

My father opened the door, that trademark grin on his face. We stood just behind him, peeking through his legs at the woman who was everything he'd described. "Thank goodness," he said. I forgot to ask for your phone number, so I couldn't confirm that you were coming. I figured you would have come to your senses by now and backed out, but I was praying you'd show up anyway."

Amanda pegged us right then as Anne Geddes material, with our big blue eyes and red mops of Shirley Temple curls.

Lizzie wore a Cinderella dress and a tiara on her head. My tastes were more eclectic: a straw fedora, a hot pink feather boa, a brown sweater, and cobalt blue leggings.

"They dressed up for you." My father had a laugh on the edge of his voice. "Lizzie's Cinderella, and Kara's some cross between Crocodile Dundee and Zsa Zsa Gabor."

She stooped down and got eye level with us. "Look at you," she said. "You look exactly alike. I'm glad you dressed up so I could tell you apart."

'We made ba-sketti." Lizzie grabbed Amanda's hand and pulled her inside. "Wanna see?"

"And we're off." My father laughed as he closed the door and followed our lead.

Amanda would remember for years how the bubble of delight floated up in her chest as she followed us into the kitchen. She saw one chair pulled up to the sink, and another to the counter. Lizzie climbed onto the chair in front of the sink full of suds.

"Lizzie likes to wash dishes," my father said with a wink, "so I have her washing these jars of spaghetti sauce. Not that we used them, you understand."

"No, of course not."

"'And Kara likes to stir. They're both very helpful." He smiled a little too brightly and crossed his eyes.

I leaned a little too far, and the chair began to scoot away. My father dove to rescue me as I fell. I didn't miss a beat, but went back to stirring my salad.

"I'm impressed," she said. "How many rescues like that do you handle at each meal?"

"Oh, four or five … dozen." He winked at her and popped a piece of French bread into his mouth. "That's the beauty of a tiny kitchen. I can reach either of them without too much effort."

I've driven by that little house we lived in and watched the children who live there now run and tumble in the yard behind it. The neighborhood still looks safe and sweet, though age has tattered the homes. I'm told it was new when we were small, though. With only two bedrooms, I suspect the house was adequate for our needs. In the pictures I've seen of us in that house, the place was always clean and neat, though unimpressive. One snapshot tells the story of our brief art careers. Finger paintings and silhouettes and little construction paper butterflies covered the refrigerator, and two pairs of tiny little tennis shoes sat beside the door.

I study those pictures with sadness, because it truly looked like a home.

That night, we fought over the plates in our special twin language that no one else understood, and our father called out, "Talk English, girls."

Amanda gave him a curious look.

"They have this unique language they use to talk to each other," he said. "Lots of twins do it, but I try to stop them when I hear it."

"It must be amazing having twins."

"It's interesting; that's for sure."

Amanda — the nice lady who looked like the princess we'd expected — gave us each two plates to settle our argument. She watched as we arranged them in a three-year-old style that would have chafed Amy Vanderbilt.

As we shoved the silverware around, my dad turned back to Amanda.

"So, how are we doing? Are you ready to run away screaming just yet?"

"No," she said, a giggle bursting out of her, "they're absolutely precious. And you're doing such a good job with them."

We beamed and worked harder to get the table set just right.

"Well, I understand rebellion kicks in in another few years, so I have a long way to go."

We had set three plates so close together that they were touching, and one was alone across the table. "Daddy, that's yours," I announced.

"They want to sit by you," he said. "You don't know how lucky you are. Shame you wore white pants. I'd better get you a towel."

He insisted she put the towel over her lap to protect her from our soiled little hands and sauce splashing from carelessly slurped noodles. We always slurped with great gusto.

But Amanda didn't worry about spaghetti sauce on her clothes. She was flattered that we liked her enough to want to be close to her.

Amanda recalls that we went to bed early that night. My father hosed us down in the bathtub while she cleaned up the dishes, and then we ran in to say good night in our bare feet and flannel pajamas, dragging battle-weary blankets behind us. She followed him into our little room to kiss us good night and watched as we debated over which bed to sleep in – Lizzie's or mine – because we always slept together. We curled up together, legs entangled and arms flung over one another. We had that uncanny twin closeness that scientists find fascinating. Sometimes we dreamed the same dreams as we lay together, like two halves of the same body. Neither of us could ever sleep alone.

When Amanda speaks of that night, she gets a catch in her throat. According to her, my father wore a soft, vulnerable expression when they returned to the living room. He dropped down next to her on the couch. "Bet you never thought you'd have a date like this."

"It's been fun. I love being around the girls."

"That's good, because I kind of hate being away from them." He leaned back, resting his head on the back of the couch. Looking over at her, he said, "So tell me about you."

"What about me?"

"Everything. Starting with how your parents met."

She laughed too loudly. "You're kidding, right?"

He shifted to face her. "What? You don't think a man could be fascinated with you?"

His eyes were serious, like they'd been when she'd first seen him strumming that guitar. "My parents met in the emergency room after a Fourth of July picnic that went bad."

"Fireworks accident?"

"No. Potato salad accident. My mother's cooking, actually. She almost killed half the town."

"So your father had a thing for dangerous women?"

"Actually, no. Not right then. But she felt so guilty that she took phenomenal care of him until he was better. *Then* he fell in love with her. Her cooking did improve, eventually."

"Great story." He shifted his body to face her and set his elbow on the back of the couch. "So … then you were born and grew up into a beautiful woman who would catch my eye at a Bible study."

The grace in that statement made her heart swell, and by the time the evening was over, she was head over heels in love with my father, and counting the blessings that seemed enough to last for the rest of her life. And ours, too.

Sit back and relax

THE NEGOTIATOR
Dee Henderson
1 5767.3819 1

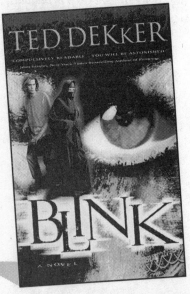

BLINK
Ted Dekker
0 8499.4371 X

25 appetisers of **summer fiction** to change your life...

Sit back and relax

THE
RESURRECTION
FILE
Craig Parshall
0 7369.0847 1

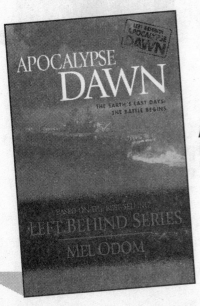

APOCALYPSE DAWN
Mel Odom
0 8423.8418 9

25 appetisers of **summer fiction** to change your life…

Sit back and relax

THE SECOND THIEF
Travis Thrasher
0 8024.1707 8

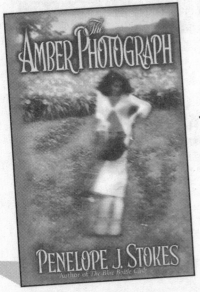

THE AMBER PHOTOGRAPH
Penelope Stokes
0 8499.3722 1

25 appetisers of **summer fiction** to change your life...

Sit back and relax

THEODORA'S DIARY
Penny Cola Culliford
0 0071.1001 4

FLABBERGASTED
Ray Blackston
0 8007.1837 2

25 appetisers of **summer fiction** to change your life…

Sit back and relax

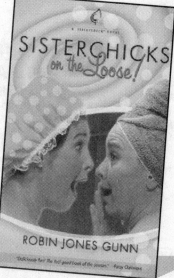

SISTERCHICKS ON THE LOOSE
Robin Jones Gunn
1 5905.2198 6

THE SHADOW AT EVENING
Chris Walley
1 8602.4269 3

25 appetisers of **summer fiction** to change your life...

Sit back and relax

WATCHERS
Sheila Jacobs
1 8602.4269 3

THE BLOODSTONE CHRONICLES
Bill Myers
0 3102.4684 9

25 appetisers of **summer fiction** to change your life…

Sit back and relax

OUT OF THE SHADOWS
Steve Dixon
1 8599.9671 X

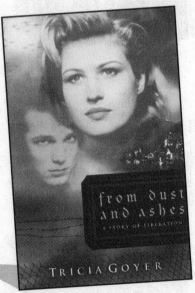

FROM DUST TO ASHES
Tricia Goyer
0 8024.1554 7

25 appetisers of **summer fiction** to change your life...

Sit back and relax

ANGELS WATCHING OVER ME
Michael Phillips
0 7642.2700 9

DESERT ROSE
Linda Chaikin
0 7369.1234 7

25 appetisers of **summer fiction** to change your life...

Sit back and relax

THE PROPOSAL
Lori Wick
0 7369.0558 8

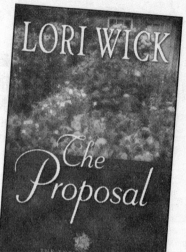

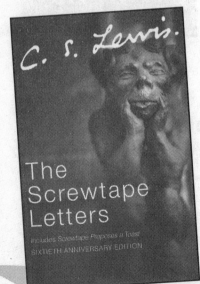

THE SCREWTAPE LETTERS
C S Lewis
0 0062.8060 9

25 appetisers of **summer fiction** to change your life...

Sit back and relax

GREAT DIVORCE REISSUE
C S Lewis
0 0062.8056 0

C. S. Lewis.

The Great Divorce

GHOSTS
Adrian Plass
0 5510.3109 3

25 appetisers of **summer fiction** to change your life…

Sit back and relax

SAFELY HOME
Randy Alcorn
0 8423.5991 5

AND THE SHOFAR BLEW
Francine Rivers
0 8423.6582 6

25 appetisers of **summer fiction** to change your life..